A Teacher's Life for me

(The Probation Year)

by

Peter Nicholson

*To Doreen + Ron
Best wishes
Nicholson*

COPYRIGHT

Every effort has been
made to contact copyright holders of
any material reproduced in this book. If any have
been inadvertently overlooked, that will be rectified
at the earliest opportunity.

This book is a work of fiction.
Names, characters, businesses, organisations,
places and events are either the product of the
author's imagination or are used fictitiously.
Any resemblance to actual persons, living or
dead, or events or locales is entirely coincidental.

No part of this publication may be reproduced, stored
in or introduced into a retrieval system, or
transmitted, in any form or by any means, without the
prior permission in writing of the author, nor be
otherwise circulated in any form of binding or cover
other than that which it is published and without a
similar condition including this condition being
imposed on the subsequent purchaser.

Copyright © 2021 Peter Nicholson
(The moral right of the author has been asserted)
All rights reserved.

Dedicated to:

My mother Bernadine who was always there for me and also to Kath whose encouragement kept me writing

Chapter One

The life-changing letter had fallen through my letter box two weeks earlier. It'd said that I had a job at Cromwell Street Primary School as a 'Probationary Teacher' for the Fourth Years. This was the time when jobs in teaching were two a penny. I'd spent the past three years at the Teacher Training College learning all about the way in which children learn, being given lectures by ex-teachers who'd had the foresight to get out of main line teaching and pass on their experiences to people like me who thought that teaching was a vocation and that all you needed was the will to teach. I'd made the decision to go into teaching after spending three years in mundane jobs, doing this and that to earn an honest crust.

My years at the college had not been wasted altogether, I did find out the best drinking houses in town and how to evade paying for a round when it counted most. Now the time had come to actually enter into the real world of teaching. True, I had been into a few schools as a student, much to the enjoyment of the children I had been let loose on. The fun the children had had with their student teacher because they were not a 'real' teacher and they knew full well that they could get away with murder, particularly as the student teacher didn't know what to do when things started to get hot in the class room. The children did have the sense to be on their best behaviour when 'The Examiner' came in to see the student teach. It was due to this that I may have got through my teaching practices, that and the bribes that the children were paid to be on their best behaviour when these Examiners came in. Eventually, after three years I had earned my teaching certificate to say that I was now a qualified teacher.

Cromwell Street Primary School was not my first choice of school. It wasn't even my last choice. It wasn't even on my list of schools! This was the school that was mentioned in hushed whispers. This was the place where Teachers went and were never heard of again. It had a reputation that made people quake in their shoes. When that letter came through the letter box I opened it with anticipation, knowing that it was from the Education Office by the logo on the envelope. I was hoping that it was my first choice of school, St Ninians, the poshest school in town. One where all the children were taken there in chauffeur driven cars, where parents were involved in all school activities and where a school trip meant a trip abroad skiing.

Well, this was it. I had my briefcase packed with a dictionary, an aid to my bad spelling, a supply of pens and pencils of all different colours, depending on the situation they might be needed for, and my packed lunch for the day. The briefcase had been a present from my late Father who had worked in a lost property office.

The motif on the briefcase looked very impressive and it reminded me of the reverse side of a three penny bit, although I never found out what it meant. I thought that it would complement my three piece suit very well. I meant to give the right impression on my first day, with both the staff and the pupils. A final look in the mirror, a quick wipe to get rid of the jam on my chin from breakfast, a comb through my hair and I was then ready to face anything the day might throw at me. One final check - hanky, clean for the occasion, bus fare, spare change and one more visit to the toilet just in case, then I was off into the wild blue yonder.

Waiting at the bus stop I began thinking. Had I locked the front door, did I turn the grill off, did I pull the chain in the toilet? There were so many things to think of. It was my intention to get to the school early so that I could get the feel of the place, the building, and the staff, see the pupils arriving in the playground, and make myself known to the Caretaker. Yes, the Caretaker. I had been told very early on in my teaching practice that the one person to get on well with was the Caretaker. That was the one person who could make or break you. Too many Teachers in the past had made enemies of Caretakers and had paid dearly for it later on. Not enough emphasis had been put on the Caretakers of schools at teachers training college. In fact at college we had never been told anything about the Caretaker. It was purely by good luck that I had been told of the value of getting to know the Caretaker, by an old, experienced Teacher I got to know well during my teaching practice. Well, that would be my goal for the day, get to know the Caretaker. I looked at my watch, (another good find by Dad), although the hour hand did have a habit of sticking to the minute hand and I had turned up to lectures at four o'clock instead of two o'clock, but never mind it looked impressive. Seven forty five a.m. and the journey would take me about half an hour. That would give me plenty of time to have a look round before school starting at nine o'clock.

The bus was on time; well - according to my timetable it was on time. I boarded the bus and sat down near the front. I could have sat anywhere on the bus as I was the only passenger. The Conductor sauntered up to me and said in those dulcet tones that only bus conductors can adopt, "Any fares please?" Stupid really as I had only just got on and he knew full well that I hadn't paid yet. I could not believe my answer, "One to Cromwell Street School, please." One, yes one. I was the only one. The conductor stared at me in disbelief for a moment and then said, "Are you sure?" "Yes, I'm only paying for one," I replied. "No, are you sure that you want to go to Cromwell Street School?" he stammered. Alarm bells started to ring in my head. I looked at him and could see the fear in his eyes when he mentioned Cromwell Street School. "Er, yes, one to Cromwell Street School please," I repeated again but looked him in the face. His cheek started to twitch as he said, "That'll be one and three pence please, and good luck." He ripped off a ticket and gave it to me as I gave him a shilling and a three penny bit. He walked to the front of the bus and shouted to the Driver, "Another silly bugger for the madhouse, Harry." The driver turned round and viewed me with a sort of look that one might get from an Undertaker who had come to visit the very ill at a hospital, wearing a look of expectancy and remorse. I felt a shiver go down my spine. The conductor walked to the platform at the back of the bus. He put his hand on my shoulder as he went past and said, "Never mind son, but they should have told you." I daren't look round or ask him what he meant.

Maybe this was some sort of joke he and the driver, Harry, had when there was no other passenger on the bus. Yes that was it, a joke. Put it behind you, I told myself, after all I had played some wicked jokes on people at college over the past three years (jokes that people were still trying to get their own back on me). I sat there thinking of them and started to chuckle out loud. I then felt a hand on my shoulder again which startled me. I turned and saw it was the

Conductor. "Are you all right sir, still time to get off you know?" "Yes, I'm fine thanks," I replied rather embarrassed. For the rest of the journey my thoughts were of the day and what it might bring. I knew that it was quite common for new Teachers to be allocated a school. There was a pool of new Teachers at the end of July each year who were allocated jobs in schools throughout the county. In a way I was lucky that Cromwell Street was in the town I was living in. Some of my friends were allocated jobs at the far end of the county and were having to move nearer their school. It was good to have a job I told myself, rather unconvincingly, as I thought of the bus conductor's earlier remarks to his driver.

I looked out of the bus window. The scenery started to change. Gone were the prim colour coded houses with gardens to match. Gone were the tidy paths and gutters. The bus was now moving through an estate that thought the Second World War was still raging. Houses with windows broken and boarded up, shells of once fine cars with their guts ripped out, rusting in what were supposed to be gardens, although they looked more like refuse tips. The paths were littered with rubbish, tin cans, bric-a-brac and I'm sure I saw some kind of unsavoury rubber-ware lying in the gutter. As the bus turned down Cromwell Street it stopped at the first bus stop and waited. I looked out of the window and saw a high brick wall. Someone had chalked on the wall, 'Abandon hope all ye that enter here.' "Changed your mind have you sir?" came the stentorian tone of the bus conductor. The driver was looking round at me again. I turned to the Conductor and said, "Sorry?" "This is it mate. Cromwell Street Primary School, and may God have mercy on your soul," he replied, then started to laugh. He shouted to the driver, "He's still got time, hasn't he Harry?" The driver just gave the thumbs up sign, agreeing with the conductor. I muttered something, got up out of my seat and proceeded to get off the bus. The conductor was still laughing as the bus pulled away. I was left to compose myself before entering this new experience.

Tuesday the 3rd of September 1968 was going to be a day to remember, I told myself as I walked through the gateway into the school yard. The yard was completely empty, silent and peaceful. The school loomed up before me. A three storey Victorian school, purpose built for the time. Over the main doorway were the words 'Board School 1880 ' - the other two entrances had over their doorways 'Infants ' and ' Juniors.' Across the yard was a brick building from which emerged a man in overalls, who, on seeing me, came marching across. I looked around me and seeing no other person in the yard realised that he was heading for me. When he reached me he looked me up and down, took off his cap, gave a half bow and put out his hand to shake mine.

"I'm Mr Johnson, the Caretaker here. Pleased to meet you. We've been expecting you, but before you go to see Mr Yardley the Headmaster can you come and have a look at my toilets?" Before I could give any reply he about turned and started to stomp his way towards the brick building at the far side of the yard, the same building I'd seen him come out of minutes earlier. "Come on, sir," he called to me. I had no alternative but to follow him.

We walked into the toilet block together. "Take a look sir," he said, "Look over there near the urinals! The kids pee there, it seeps through the wall and onto the floor. Makes a right mess it does. In summer it stinks horrible and in winter it's like a bloody skating rink, begging your pardon sir. We've reported it many times but nothing gets done." At first I didn't know what to say. I could see from Mr Johnson's face that he expected some kind of comment from me. "Er, do all the children use these toilets?" I asked in an official sort of way. "They all used to, but the older kids told the younger ones this place was haunted. They'd wait until a younger kid wanted to have a shi.., er, a 'Number Two,' then one of the older kids would blow down the cistern overflow pipe from the outside. It made a hideous noise inside the cistern, frightening the shit out of the kid. It certainly cured constipation in the younger ones, but after a while they refused to use these toilets believing they were haunted. After the kids started messing themselves in the class rooms we had to have special inside toilets built for the younger kids. Take a look at those bowls, very clean but look at the cracks. I don't know how long they'll last," he told me pointing at various cubicles. I looked in, just in case if I didn't then I might hurt his feelings. "Yes, very impressive Mr Johnson, and very clean," I said trying to bull him up.

"You won't forget will you," he said, "about my toilets." "No," I said, not quite knowing what he was on about, but I felt that it would be better to humour him. If I were to be working here then he was going to be one of my allies, and trusted friend whom I could rely on in the future. "Good," he said, "Now I'll take you to Mr Yardley's room. He should be in now. He's expecting you."

I followed Mr Johnson back across the empty yard, through the main entrance, walking down a long corridor on a floor that had such a shine that it seemed a shame to walk on it. Halfway down the corridor was a turning to the left then a flight of stairs. "This way, please, sir," said Mr Johnson sounding almost apologetic that we had to go up these stairs. "Mr Yardley's room is at the top of the building, so we have to go up two flights of stairs," he said. The stairs on the second flight were quite steep. Each side of the stairs was covered with green Victorian wall tiles, these too, like the corridor floor, were shiny and polished. There was a certain smell to the building that all schools seem to have, a bit like the smell hospitals have when you first walk in there. The smell soon wore off because you got used to it and tended not to notice it after a while. We turned left at the top of the stairs and were faced with a Victorian oak panelled door on which a shiny brass plate proudly displayed the words 'Mr Yardley, Headmaster.'

Mr Johnson rapped on the door and waited for an answer. We didn't have to wait long, as a voice yelled out, "Enter!" Mr Johnson opened the door wide, revealing me holding my briefcase in front of me, knuckles white and clutching the carrying handle with a vice like grip, trying to project my best introductory smile. Mr Yardley was sat behind his desk opposite the door, this so that he could face anyone entering his domain. The instant he saw me standing there he jumped up from his seat, grabbed his mortar board, placing it on his head, unfortunately the wrong way round, muttered some profanity, replaced the mortar board the right way round and made his way around his desk, for all the world looking like 'Mr Pastry.' In his eagerness to greet me he got his black gown caught on an open drawer in his desk. One moment the esteemed Mr Yardley was making his way round his desk like a stately galleon, the next his head jerked back, followed by a ripping sound. He disappeared backwards behind his majestic desk with a thunderous crash, followed by a few seconds of deathly silence. There was another muttered profanity from behind the desk then Mr Yardley re-appearing looking rather dishevelled. Was this some kind of test, I wondered? I stood there trying not to snigger and to put these incidents out of my mind, although it was very difficult. By this time Mr Yardley was round at the front of his desk and ushering me to a chair to the left of his desk. "Thank you Mr Johnson, you can go now," he said. Mr Johnson looked at me and silently mouthed the word "TOILETS," bowing slightly and closing the door behind him as he left.

I was still standing by the chair, holding my briefcase. "Please, do sit down. How was your journey to the school, fine I hope? Now, you must have coffee and biscuits before I take you around the school," said Mr Yardley. I couldn't get a word in, so I just sat there and let him continue. He pressed the intercom and ordered coffee and the biscuits, emphasising the word 'biscuits' as though they were something rather special. He looked across at me and smiled. I then remembered my letter from the education department telling me of my appointment here. "I have my letter here," I started to say, searching my inside pockets. Blast, it wasn't there. I tried to think quickly. I'd had it this morning when I was eating breakfast just to make sure that I had all the details. Yes I remember, I dropped jam on it and took it to the bathroom to wipe it off, then placed it on the radiator to dry off. That's where the letter still was, on the bathroom radiator. "Er, the letter, it seems that I...." I began. "Not to worry, old man," said Mr Yardley, "I know about the letter. Look, I have to meet the staff in a moment. You stay here and have your coffee and biscuits then when I'm finished with the staff I'll show you round the school and see what you think."

Mr Yardley got up walked to the door, opened it gave me a smile and disappeared, closing it theatrically behind him. I was left alone in this old decrepit room. Shelves full of books that looked as though they had never been removed since first being put there. I turned and looked at the wall behind the door. There on the wall I couldn't believe what I saw – a moose's head, complete with antlers and I'm sure a smile on its face. Mr Yardley's desk was awash with letters and papers. In the middle of the desk was a blotter, immaculate and white. As I sat there, alone, a song started going through my head, 'I'm into something good,' by Herman and the Hermits. My thoughts were disturbed by a slight knock on the door and before I could say anything it opened and in walked a woman in her mid-fifties carrying a tray with silverware on it. There were also some bone china cups, saucers and side plates. In the middle of the tray was a gold rimmed plate, and on a paper doyley, delicately arranged, were my favourite biscuits, chocolate digestive. The woman said, "I'm Mrs Grant, the School Secretary. Please help yourself to coffee and biscuits." She placed the tray onto the desk, stood back, and looked down at my briefcase then back at me.

"If you don't mind me saying so, you seem to be quite young to have your job," she said with some amazement in her voice. I was flattered, although I was actually twenty six years old, people said I had a young face. "I'm older than I look," I said with some pride. She then said something to me that didn't quite make sense, "Let's hope you get Mr Yardley sorted out soon. He's been looking forward to meeting you today. Well, I've got a lot to do, first day back and all that you know. Nice meeting you, enjoy your coffee and biscuits, oh, I see that you already are." I felt guilty, for by that time I was demolishing my third biscuit. I did say that they were my favourite and who can resist seeing a full plate and being told to help one's self? I poured a coffee, sat back in the chair and thought to myself that this teaching lark wasn't too bad after all.

It's hard to describe my thoughts for the next ten minutes or so, all kinds of things went through my mind. These thoughts were disturbed when Mr Yardley returned. "Sorry to have kept you, but we have to get things sorted out, first day back and all that." He looked at his watch, "Almost time for the school bell," he said looking at me and smiling. Just then there was a knock at the door and it was opened by a small, portly looking man with a balding head who was obviously out of breath. "Headmaster, we have a big problem, it's about the fourth years. We seem to be short of...... I'm sorry. I do beg your pardon, I didn't realise you were here," he stammered when he saw me sitting there with my briefcase at the side of my chair. "Please excuse me," said Mr Yardley, and taking the gentleman to one side started to whisper something to him. I managed to catch a few words. "He's not here yet..... no word from him....... split the class.....yes, split them," there was a definite look of trepidation from the balding man when the words 'split them' were mentioned. After that voices returned to a normal pitch, "Yes, thank you Mr Percy, and if you can sort out that little problem please. I shall be taking up most of the morning with our esteemed friend here," stated Mr Yardley waving his hand in my direction. I enjoyed the moment and smiled at Mr Percy. He half smiled in my direction, gave a sort of bow and went out of the door muttering to himself. "That's Mr Percy, my Deputy Head. He's with Class 1, our five year olds. Very good with our younger children, but with the......., no, no, never mind, you don't want to know about that," stated Mr Yardley. "Now, if you're ready, we'll start our tour of the school. I'd like you to take particular note of the roof and the number of cracked and missing tiles. They've been reported but nothing seems to get done." I replied, "Mmmm, yes right, I'll take note of them." This seemed to make Mr Yardley very happy and a big smile appeared on his face. "Right, off we go then. You can leave your briefcase here if you like. It should be quite safe," he said, oozing confidence and leadership.

We walked out of his room, "Down here we have the Secretary's office, our stock rooms, and stops quite a few break-ins being so high and stock being heavy, and at the end - our art room and we've just managed to get a television for our new television room," said Mr Yardley. We looked into the Secretary's office, "You've met our Mrs Grant I believe. She's my right hand man, so to speak. Now, let's go to the next floor, mainly class rooms for the upper school. On the lower floor are the younger classes. The small children are not allowed up the stairs unless they have a note from their Teacher. As you can see the window frames here are original, most can't be opened now," said Mr Yardley.

The tour round the school was very impressive. Mr Yardley went to great lengths to tell me about various architectural oddities with the building and how he was having trouble with them. On being introduced to members of his staff I noticed that my name was never mentioned, but each member of staff I met was extremely courteous and, unusually, I though, rather subservient. All they said was "Pleased to meet you," or "Glad you could come." Now, I'm not a person of many words so I just smiled at all these people and shook their hands. What surprised me was the look on their faces when we shook hands. It was as if they were shaking hands with royalty. Mr Yardley seemed rather proud as he conducted me around his kingdom, taking great pleasure in introducing me to his co-workers in this institution of learning. I surreptitiously glanced at my watch, ten past two, curse that hour hand. I wasn't sure when I was to meet my class or when I was to be given my timetable. I wasn't even sure that I should say anything to Mr Yardley as he was like a pig in muck showing me round. He must have spotted me looking at my watch. "Ah yes, time is getting on, isn't it. Well, we'll return to my office to get some things finalised, unless or course there is anything else you want to see while we were walking round?" he enquired. "No, no thanks, I think we've seem most of the school now, and anything I haven't seen I can see later. Perhaps I can walk round when school has finished and get myself acquainted with the building?" I replied. Mr Yardley glanced at me, a puzzled look on his face and then said, "Well yes, if you can afford the time, but you'll be busy with other things surely?" he said. "No, I'm sure I will be able to find time to look round the building after school. It's the least I can do. It will be a pleasure," I said, smiling at him. Mr Yardley was very pleased at this and was beaming from ear to ear. "Excellent," he remarked, "Excellent."

As we walked back to the Headmaster's office we could hear the incantations of 'Times Tables' being chanted by children in various class rooms. With one class that we went past we could hear children's voices singing, mostly rather flat and out of tune, the hymn 'All things bright and beautiful." Yes, things were turning out to be 'All things bright and beautiful' on my first day. By the time we arrived back at Mr Yardley's office he was whistling a tune to himself and seemed a man at one with the world. However, this was not to last, for as we walked past the Secretary's office she came running out. "Mr Yardley, I must have a word with you, it's very urgent. We've had a telephone call from ...." went on Mrs Grant. "Not now, Mrs Grant." said Mr Yardley, "If it's important then Mr Percy can handle it. I have some important details to get sorted out in my room with our esteemed visitor," he said. "No, you don't understand, Mr

Yardley, the telephone call was about the......" stammered Mrs Grant. The headmaster was not to be phased, "Look, please not now! See Mr Percy and that's my final word on the matter. I don't want to be interrupted for any reason. I repeat, not for any reason. Now return to your work," snapped Mr Yardley. He looked at me, smiled then ushered me through the door into his office. He gestured at me to sit down and walked round to his side of his desk and sat down. "We'll have coffee a bit later on, after we have started to make some notes," said Mr Yardley. 'Well, what do you think of our school?" he asked me. A strange sort of question I thought. Could this be some sort of test and he was trying me out to ascertain my suitability for the job. How do I answer such a question? I know, I thought, I'll stall for time. "Well," I said," It's very, er, its very big and er, tidy, yes tidy." "Tidy? "exclaimed Mr Yardley, with an extremely puzzled look on his face. I could tell at once that this had not been the right answer, or at least not the answer he'd been expecting. "Tidy!" he repeated, "But don't you think the whole place is a shambles, that we shouldn't be teaching in a place like this? We should be teaching in a modern purpose-built school." Mr Yardley put on his spectacles, half bi-focal, which he perched on the end of his nose, picked up a newspaper and passed it over to me, "Look at this, a new school that's just been opened on the city's new estate. Why can't they build something like that here?" "You mean demolish this place?" I said, with feeling. "Why yes, yes that's right. And with your help we can do it," said Mr Yardley. "We could get rid of the outside toilets, make a space for a school sports field with enough room for a football pitch, a purpose build nursery," I was starting to get carried away. Mr Yardley's face was, by this time, beaming and he started to rub his hands together like Fagin after he had successfully taught a new pickpocket his trade.

"Well, aren't you going to take some notes?" enquired Mr Yardley. I bent over and, without looking, opened up my briefcase but it fell over. Unfortunately, my sandwiches and an apple fell out onto the floor. Mr Yardley looked surprised as I sank to my knees to recover my lunch. The sandwiches were easy, the apple, alas, wasn't. It had rolled under Mr Yardley's desk. I crawled under the desk just as there was a loud knock on the door and Mr Percy burst in. "I'm sorry Headmaster, but I must see you at once, Mrs Grant told me she has tried to tell you," blurted out Mr Percy. "Mr Percy!" snapped Mr Yardley, "I gave strict instructions that I was not to be disturbed for any reason, and I meant for any reason!" "I'm sorry, Headmaster, but it's about your guest. He's not who you think he is. Mrs Grant received a telephone call to say that the Member of Parliament who was coming to see us this morning has had a traffic accident and was knocked down. He's in hospital!" said Mr Percy.

I was cowering under Mr Yardley's desk listening to all this. Things started to fall in place. The coffee, the 'special' biscuits, followed by the guided tour round the school, suddenly it all made sense. What was I to do now? Should I stay put under the desk or arise and face the music? I didn't have to wait long. Two sets of legs approached, the legs owners waiting for me to resurface from under the desk. "Could we have a word, please?" proclaimed a sarcastic voice from Mr Yardley. I arose from under the desk, minus my apple and looking sheepishly at Mr Yardley and Mr Percy. "If you're not who we thought you were, just who the hell are you?" snapped Mr Yardley. The tone of his voice had changed, he was certainly not the congenial jolly chap that he'd been five minutes earlier, more like the Grand Inquisitor from the Spanish Inquisition.

"But, you were expecting me," I stammered, "I was sent a letter from the Education Department to say that I have a job here, starting today. It stated that I was to take Year Four." "Oh my God," yelled Mr Yardley, "Do you mean to say that you are our new Probationary Teacher?" "Yes, that's me," I said, trying to sound efficient. Mr Yardley was, by this time, bordering on the apoplectic, "I don't believe it, I really don't. How could this have happened? I mean, it's just not on. Tear this school down you said, demolish it. Go on - get out! Mr Percy, show him to his class. Give me time to cool down. The humiliation of it all. If this gets out I'll be a laughing stock," went on Mr Yardley. He slumped into his chair muttering to himself. Mr Percy pointed to the door. I picked up my briefcase walked to the door then turned to Mr Yardley. "Excuse me sir," I started, "do you think I could have my apple back, it's just there under your...." "What," yelled Mr Yardley, "an apple, you want an apple. Get out, and get rid of that damned briefcase. Pretending you're someone you're not!" "Yes of course sir. Er, you can have the apple if you want, I just thought that ...'" Mr Percy grabbed my arm and led me out of the door, "Don't push your luck, old chap," he whispered, "just get out while you can. He might have calmed down by home time."

I followed Mr Percy down the stairs, past those green Victorian wall tiles and along the corridor. I felt like a condemned man taking his final journey to the execution chamber. To make matters worse, Mr Percy said but not one word. He occasionally turned to look my way and indicate the direction we were to walk. The sound of children was getting louder and more confused. Every now and again there was the commanding shout of an adult voice, bellowing some instruction whereupon an immediate cessation of children's voices took place. We reached our destination. The plaque on the door said, "Stiff Room," (the 'a' had been changed for an 'i'). The change looked fairly recent and I wondered if anyone besides me had noticed it. Mr Percy spoke only one word to me, "In!"

I opened the door and walked in. "Sit," stated Mr Percy. I sat. Well that was not quite the case. I tried to sit but the chair I chose to sit in must have had a wonky leg. Alas, for the second time that day I found myself rolling around the floor. "Oh no, haven't they thrown that bloody chair away yet?" moaned Mr Percy. No - "Are you all right, old chap?" or "Have you hurt yourself?" No, I thought, just be concerned about the bloody chair why don't you. "Get up boy," he said to me rather condescendingly, and started to walk towards a large table. I got up and sat in the wonky chair. Mr Percy would have made it to the table without further ado if he hadn't have tripped over my carelessly placed briefcase. I must admit, he went down rather hard, catching the side of his face on the wooden arm of a chair on the way down. The air was explicitly blue for the next few minutes. Multifarious curses, profanities, swear words and words I hadn't even heard of before. Mostly they were about my briefcase and the remainder about his doubting regarding my parentage. I rushed to help him but in doing so, missed my own balance. Missed is the wrong word, I did a spectacular exit, followed by a fall from my wonky chair, joining Mr Percy on the floor, fortunately my fall was cushioned as I landed squarely on him. This set Mr Percy off on a further burst of curses and profanities. When we finally sorted ourselves out, I suggested to him that he put a cold compress on his face to bring out the bruise and reduce what by now was quite a severe swelling. I thought that I should try to pacify him; after all I didn't want to be in the bad books of both the Head and the Deputy Head before I had even met my class. What a momentous day this was turning out to be.

Yes, my class, what had happened to 'my class?' Class Four I knew would be waiting for me and here I was in the stiff room, sorry, staff room with the Deputy Head who was currently at the well chipped Belfast sink splashing cold water on his face. I looked at my watch, mainly out of habit I suppose, twenty past eight. Blast that hour hand; well it was twenty past something. Mr Percy must have seen me looking at my watch. "You'd better stay here until after break then you can round up your class and start to get to know them before dinner. I'll go and see the Headmaster and try to get things sorted. God knows when we last had a start to the term anything like this." He left the staff room, being careful to see where my brief case was and then made a detour to the door.

Well, this was it, I told myself. I was a proper teacher at last. I tried to picture myself in a class room, my hands clasped behind me, and started to pace up and down the staff room, imagining being in a class room. There was a knock at the door and before I could say anything two pupils came in. "Oh sorry sir," said one. "Kettles," said the other, as if I knew what they were one about. They both walked across the staff room to the sink where they started to fill some electric kettles and a small boiler. After that they went to a cupboard and started to get mugs and cups of all sizes out. "Oh bugger, what's happened to Parrots cup this time? I bet the silly old fart's had a coffee with Yard-brush and left his cup there. Go and see if it's in Yard-brushes office will yer," said a ginger haired girl to her friend. The friend turned to leave and saw me. She dug the ginger haired girl in the ribs and whispered, "That bloke's still in here, he might have heard you saying about Parrot." "Just go and get his cup will yer," replied the ginger haired girl. Her friend left with saying another word. The ginger haired girl sorted the cups and mugs out on a table near the sink and then departed, giving me a wry smile as she did so.

I looked around the staff room. The walls were littered with union posters telling of long past meetings, adverts for theatrical events, newspaper cuttings of various events and oddities and in the corner of one wall was a very large timetable. I was drawn to this impressive document to see if I received a mention. I looked down one side then across the top. I wasn't mentioned. I searched for the class. Year Four, yes there it was. Where the name for the teacher should have been there was a blank. So I was the blank. I looked at the other names and classes and tried to imagine what the teachers might look like. Under 'Games' was a Mr B. Thomas, I imagined him as a Welsh rugby full back, built like a brick outhouse. 'Domestic Science' was a Mrs E. Peterson. I tried to imagine a Peterson person, small, plump and always laughing.

Before I could imagine anyone else there was a sound of a buzzer and a few seconds later, what sounded like pandemonium? I automatically looked at my watch, twenty to nine. Well whatever the time was, it must be playtime by the sound of it. I decided to sit down and wait for the action to start. Action in a staff room at playtime is organised chaos; people breeze in and usually make their way to the coffee or tea after selecting the correct mug, then sit down for an update on current happenings. True to form that started happening. People entered and made their way to the sink. There was a shout from someone near the sink, "They're not on, they've not been switched on! Who's been in the staff room before playtime and not switched them on. The first day back and no hot water for the tea!" People started to sit down after someone had taken the initiative and switched the kettles on.

"Why are you sitting there?" someone said to me. I looked up and saw a man with a large beard and an impressively bald head. He must have been in his fifties, dressed in a three piece suit and wearing a bow tie. You could easily have mistaken him for a lawyer. "Sorry," I said, not quite understanding what he meant. "I asked why you were sitting there?" he said, but this time in a louder voice as though I were a little simple. The staff room started to go quiet and people were looking over in my direction. "He wouldn't know it's your chair, Ivan. Sit somewhere else for a change, after all it's a new term in a new school year," a voice from the other side of the room called out.

"I've sat in that chair for the past twenty three years after coming back from the War! I'm not going to change now," replied Ivan in stentorian tones. Rather sheepishly I apologised and got out of Ivan's chair. I looked round for another chair. "Come and sit over here with us," said a rather prim looking female. I gratefully took up her offer.

"I'm Miss Stark and this is Mrs Cook, we're both with the First Year infants. Are you going to be working here?" Before I could answer, Mr Percy walked into the room. "That's a bit of a black eye you've got there Mr Percy," cried out a Welsh voice, "Have you been fighting with the wife?" - "Or someone else's wife," called out a second voice. There was laughter from different parts of the staff room.

Mr Percy looked a tad uneasy about the taunts, but before he could say anything else another teacher started to complain to him. "Why did you send that Farthingale boy to my class? You know what he's like. His flatulence is worse than ever. We started to get the cooking ingredients together for our fairy buns and he started farting as we were breaking the eggs. We wasted nearly two dozen eggs before I realised he was in the class room. The children were all complaining about the smell. In the end I had to send him with a message to Mike over in the chemistry lab." Mr. Percy seemed to be at a loss for words. The thin, skinny complainant, a woman who had a pair of bottle-bottomed glasses perched on the end of her nose continued going at him ten to the dozen. "So you're the one who sent me Farthingale. He didn't have a clue why he'd been sent. It explains the smell. I thought it was the kids experiment gone wrong again. I gave them all detention for mixing the wrong chemicals," said someone, who I presumed, was the aforementioned Mike. Mr. Percy grasped the bull by the horns, as it were, and introduced me to the staff. One member of staff, whom I had been introduced to earlier that morning, interrupted Mr Percy saying that wasn't I was the important guest that Mr Yardley had been expecting. "No, there was a bit of a mix up there, Mr Telford, and I think that we should let things rest about that," stated Mr Percy. He continued, "Class Four will be back with their new form teacher after playtime, so if you have any Class Four children in your classes, send them back to their own class room."

Miss. Stark and Mrs. Cook looked at me apologetically and said that there were both sorry. Before I could ask them what they meant, Mr Percy came over and said he would show me where my class room was and where my class might be at the end of playtime. He also gathered up some papers and a folder and passed them to me. "These are yours," he said," timetables for you and the children, school rules, holiday dates and important dates throughout the year that you will need to know about. Come along." As we walked down corridors, stairs and round corners I was getting quite lost. At last we made it to the playground. "That's your class room," said Mr. Percy, pointing to a prefabricated building at the end of the playground. "It was thought better to keep Class Four away from the main school just at the moment. Anyway, your class will be here at the end of playtime. Have fun, and we'll see you at dinner time, (he also said something which I didn't quite hear but sounded vaguely like 'God willing')." As he walked away and left me standing there like a little boy whistling in the dark, I thought, this is it then, a Teacher at last! I then began to think about the reactions of Miss. Stark and Mrs Cook in the staff room and wondered what they could have meant.

Chapter Two

The children were at play and the sounds of them shouting, laughing and talking filled the air. I walked into 'my' prefab, a cast off from the war years by the look of it. Inside I was greeted by rows of desks all facing a blackboard. There were display boards at the back of the room with signs which said, "Our art pictures," and "Our best work," under which were empty spaces. It was apparent that because it was the beginning of a new term the children hadn't time to have anything put up yet. I walked over to the teacher's desk at the front of the class, under the blackboard, from where I could view the children in my charge. I had fixed ideas in my mind about how I was going to run the class and how the children would respond to my requests. I had read all the books at college and had attended all the lectures on child psychology and child development. The main thing I wanted to be to the children was a teacher and a friend, someone they could rely on.

I was starting to get lost in a whirlpool of educational wonderment when I heard a whistle and a male voice booming out, "Keep still, that boy over there, put him down and you boy, stop crying, the blood will stop if you hold it tight. On the next whistle go to your lines." There was a whistle and the sound of children running, then the noise of chattering outside my class room. I nervously went outside to be greeted by a line of children waiting for me. "Are you our new teacher," "What's your name," "Dun't look very happy does he!" "Is this Class Four?" I asked with a smile on my face. "Course it is - that's why we are lined up here. Are you our new teacher or just someone who's going to babysit 'till dinner time?" said a small ginger haired boy who had an angelic face but a strange smile. "Yes," I reassured him, "I am your new teacher and not a babysitter 'till dinner time. Will you all go into the class room and sit down please - and no noise."

Now that I'm more experienced, I would have realised something. These children hadn't been in the class room before, so those first in through the door picked the "best" seats in the class and wanted their friends to be next to them. I think the best word to describe the next ten minutes would be pandemonium. I tried my best to keep order over the confusion by being diplomatic and using charm, neither of which worked. In the end it was just up to me shouting "Stop!" Those children who did not have seats were told to sit in vacant positions in the class. Comments came from seated pupils such as "Not having her next to me, she stinks, she's always peeing herself," or" "He's got dicks, my mam says I haven't to play with him cause he's got dicks," and " He's got the dreaded disease and I don't want to catch it." My reply to all these comments were "They'll sit there for this lesson and I might move them later."

At last, the children were seated and quiet. "Now children, I am your new teacher and I hope we are going to get along fine this coming year. For our first lesson I want you to write a story about what you did during the holidays. I'll put the title and the date on the board and you'll copy it out and write your story." As soon as I turned to the board pandemonium broke out. This time, the once seated children were out of their desks over at the cupboard fighting with one another. Once again my voice came to rescue as I yelled that magic word, "Stop!" Miraculously the children stopped. I asked one child what was going on. "We're getting the pencils and paper sir," she replied. "Everyone sit! You, you, and you, give out the pencils. You and you give out the paper. The rest of you stay in your seats and as soon as you get your pencil and paper start the exercise." I turned back to the board to finish off the title, feeling a little proud of myself that I'd managed to bring order to the class without too much bother and in doing so had exerted my authority over the children.

The next hour was spent going round the class looking at the children's work and helping some of the children with spellings and grammar. However, it was while I was helping one child that I noticed a strange smell. "Do you want to go somewhere, boy," I said, trying to be tactful. "Yes sir," replied the boy," I would like to go to prison." "Where???" I replied, somewhat mystified. "Prison, I would like to go to prison, and then I could see my Dad and Uncle Charlie. They got nicked during the holiday, that's what I'm writing about. Have you got a bike sir?" said the boy. "No, I haven't got a bike, but when I said do you want to go somewhere I meant did you want to go to the toilet," I said. "No, I don't need the toilet, I went at playtime, though there was no paper," replied the boy. "Are you going home at dinner time?" I inquired. "Yes sir," he said." "Well can you change your trousers before you come back to school this afternoon please," I said before moving back to the fresher air around my desk.

As the children continued working at their desks I decided that I would find out their names. I had a copy of the register and started calling out the children's names. Each child was told to raise their arm when his or her name was called. I tried to put faces to names and names to faces. I wrote out a plan of the room and put names on the plan for later use. In no time at all it was dinner time. I dismissed the children row by row and was left with a contented feeling that I had completed my first morning as a fully-fledged teacher. I went round the class and collected the papers in. Some papers were full, others not so full. Oh well, time for lunch.

Yes, lunch, now what did I do with my briefcase? Yes, there it is next to my desk. I went over to my desk, opened my briefcase and got out my sandwiches. I started looking for my apple and remembered where it was, with Mr Yardley! Taking my sandwiches I decided to go to the staff room to eat my lunch and find out more about the school from the staff. I went out of my class room across the yard and into the main building. Now, down a corridor and up some stairs I seemed to remember, but as I got to the top of the stairs nothing seem familiar. I was lost. Never mind, keep going, I must get somewhere in the end. I went up another set of stairs and was faced with a class room door. I went in and found myself in a room that must have been the school library. The room was very long with bookcases filled with books on either side of the room. At the far end of the room was another door. I decided to try that door to see if there was another way down or to somewhere that seemed familiar to me.

I reached the far door and found that it was locked and while I was there I heard a strange clinking of keys on the other door. I shouted out and turned and ran across the room to the closed door. Disaster - the door had been locked. I began shouting for help and banging on the door. Nothing! I waited a few minutes and began shouting for help and banging on the door. Still nothing. Well, there was nothing for it but to eat my sandwiches here in the library. In a way I suppose it was a good job that I had my sandwiches with me.

At least I was not going to go hungry over dinner time. After my meagre lunch I tried again banging on the door and shouting for help. Surely someone would come and help me. I went over to the windows - the windows that were meant to open but had been painted so many times that they wouldn't. I looked out and could see the street below. No-one was about, so even if the windows could open no one could help me.

I looked at my watch, twenty to whatever. Although my watch looked very flash and expensive it was absolutely no use for telling the time with. One of the first things I must do with my first wage packet, if I ever got one, was to buy a new watch that told the time correctly. I was getting side tracked, I must think about the problem in hand. How to get out a locked room? I looked around the room and found some paper and pencils. I know, write a message on the paper and make paper 'planes with them and send them out of the window. If I sent enough then someone would surely find one and get help. I must work quickly. Now, make the message simple so that then I can write more of them. "Locked in top room of school. Need help quick!" Yes, that would do, straight to the point.

I worked quickly and soon had a dozen paper planes made. On a quick search of the windows I found one that would open slightly, giving me enough space to launch a paper plane into the street below. Very soon there were several paper planes floating out of the window. I felt very proud as some flew quite a distance, unfortunately others just seem to collapse and fall out of sight. Due to the wall around the school I was unable to see if any of the planes that made it over had been recovered by anyone. It was now just a case of sitting and waiting and see what would happen.

It must have been ten minutes later when I heard a bell ringing and the sound of a fast car. I rushed to the window and just caught the sight of a black car speeding past and the sound of a bell coming from it. Strange, I thought, must be something going on down the street. I went back to where I was sitting and carried on reading a book I had found on one of the shelves. The title of the book was a bit ironic, 'Great Escapes.' There was a noise at the door and the sound of a key turning. I stood up, book in hand and went towards the door to be faced with two policemen, Mr Yardley, Mr Percy and Mr Johnson. "Oh no, not you again," wailed Mr Yardley. "This doesn't look like a kidnapped child to me, Fred," said Policeman Number One, "Still, better to be safe than sorry." "What's your game?" he asked me, "Why pretend that you're a kidnapped child trapped in our library?" "Kidnapped child!!?" I stammered, "I don't know what you mean. All what happened was that I got locked in here and couldn't get out so I wrote out a message on paper aeroplanes and threw them out of the window." "It's that nutty Mrs Braithwaite again! I told the Sergeant that there wouldn't be a kidnapped child in the school. No one would want to kidnap a kid from round here, no one in their right mind that is. Still we've got to check these things out," said Policeman Number One. "Before we go, sir, can I confirm that you haven't got a kidnapped child up here with you?" I looked at Policeman Number One and his accompanying Sergeant in amazement and blurted out, "No, there was just me here, locked in until a few minutes ago when you came in." "Pity," said Policeman Number One, "If there had been a child in here, me and the Sarge would have won five pounds from the lads at the station. It's always the same when Mrs Braithwaite rings - a false alarm. We're running a book on her. The first time we get a score from one of her tip offs then we collect the kitty. Well, we can't stay here with you lot, we have work to do, unlike some around here. Bye all." With that the two Policemen left, leaving the remaining four of us to sort things out.

"It's not been a good day for you, has it lad. And there's still the afternoon to go," said Mr Yardley. "Look if you are...... no if you could just.. what I mean to say is... that, er. Bloody hell, words fail me with you. Mr Percy take over, Mr Johnson lock up again - when everyone is out of the room this time please, " said Mr Yardley. He went off shaking his head and muttering strange words again, I think that he definitely doubted my parentage. Mr Percy looked at me and waved his hand in such an imperious way that I knew he wanted me to follow him. Out we went, down the stairs and made a turning through some double doors. That's where I'd gone wrong, I'd forgotten the double doors. As soon as I had got through them I remembered where I was. Mr Percy went into his room and I followed. "Sit!" he bellowed.

I sat facing a desk that was spotless. In the very centre was a blotter which had pink blotting paper in it. Above it was an inkwell set complete with fountain pen. Mr Percy positioned himself behind his desk then sat down; placing his hands together on the desk then took a long look at me. There was then an even longer pause during which I was unsure precisely what it was I should do during this time. I nervously crossed my legs, and then thought better of that, uncrossing them. I was very conscious of my hands so I put them on my knees, which didn't seem right, so I folded them, which also didn't seem right. I scratched my head, hoping for inspiration.

"When you have finished behaving like a chimp on heat, fidgeting around on the chair, we'd better get down to business," boomed Mr Percy. "You've only been here a matter of hours and already Mr Yardley looks as though he's been through a full term, thanks to you. May I remind you that you are a Probationer and that you better keep out of his way for the rest of this term, never mind the week. I could talk at great length, but it's time for afternoon lessons. I don't want any further trouble or disruption from you or your class this afternoon," warned Mr Percy. "Er, yes sir. There won't be any bother again," I said. I rose and went to the door, turned and looked at Mr Percy, "I turn left here and down the stairs and through the door on the right." "On the left, on the left, then through the door marked exit. That's the way out, and once you are outside, your class room is across the yard. If you're lucky your class may be lining up in a few minutes for this afternoon's lessons. O.K.?" said Mr Percy in a manner that denoted he thought he was addressing the village idiot. I muttered a quick thank you and left. On my way down the stairs I thought that I'd got off quite lightly. Now, just the afternoon to get through and that would be my first day over. Surely, nothing much to go wrong with that.

As I walked across the yard I had the afternoon's lessons running through my mind. A drawing lesson, possibly a drawing to go with the writing the children had done this morning. At least I might get to know who could draw in my class. Children were hustling and bustling in the yard, running here and there, shouting, laughing, talking - all the noises one hears from a busy school yard. There was a shrill whistle and the noises stopped, so did the movements of everyone, including me. At the sound of a second whistle the children ran to their lines, pushing and shoving to be first in their line.

My class were already in line waiting for me, their Teacher. I felt proud, children waiting for me to usher them into class. As I got closer, expectant faces all waiting for me to say those words, "Yes, in you go." After saying that I realised I'd said the wrong words because they all went in, in one untidy clump. What I should have said was, "In one line, in you go," now I had to try to sort out the outbreak of World War Three." "Everybody stop and line up again outside!" I yelled. Gone was the once proud teacher of a few minutes ago, now replaced by a shrieking banshee who was hoping that this incident was not being watched either by Mr Percy or Mr Yardley. With the children back outside, I addressed them with the right words this time, "Yes, in one line, in you go." " Wish he'd make up his mind, in or out," came a voice from the line. I pretended not to hear it.

The children filed into the room in one line. Once there I told them to sit in the same places they'd been in prior to lunch. The all went to their relevant places, all except one. The boy with the ginger hair and angelic face, he stood at my desk holding a cardboard shoe box. "This is for you, sir," he said, with a self-satisfied smile on his face. At first I was lost for words, I mean - a present for the teacher on the first day! This was amazing, a record maybe. I must have made an impression with this angelic child. "Well thank you, er, and tell me, what's your name, I seem to have forgotten it?" I said, smiling to show to the rest of the class that I was well pleased with this offering. "It's Billy, sir. Billy Preston. I'll just give them a shake for you before you open them," once again, that self-satisfied smile from this angelic boy.

I wasn't sure what he meant by the words "I'll just give them a shake!" Give what a shake, and why would 'they' want a shake? I also noticed that the rest of the class were sat spellbound, watching every move Billy or myself made. Billy shook the box rigorously. The box made a sound of things being moved about, little wonder considering the enthusiastic shake he gave it. Then, smiling, he handed the box over to me, keeping hold of the string that was tied round the lid. As I took hold of the box, I didn't notice he was holding the string and as I moved, I caused the string to tighten and undo. This in turn led to the box lid to fall from the box. The next thing that happened was absolute pandemonium. Green things, being exposed to the light and also rather annoyed at being shaken, saw their chance of freedom and decided to leg it. Frogs! I'm not sure how many Billy had managed to pack into the shoe box but it seemed like hundreds. Frogs shot everywhere, so too, did the children. Some thought it was their job to catch the escaping frogs others thought the best place was as far away as possible from the jumping and by now irate frogs. Some girls sat at their desks crying, others joined in trying to catch them. I was stood at the front of the class holding an empty shoe box, trying to weigh up the situation.

    I remembered at college being told that some days, things in the class room might get hectic. What were we told to do about it - go with the flow, that's what! I was never told about a situation similar to that which I now found myself in. I think that it was something like, "Go with the flow!" How the hell was I supposed to go with the flow, with kids chasing frogs around the class room whilst the others were scared shitless? There was only one thing for it. "STOP!" I yelled at the top of my voice, "STOP whatever you are doing. STOP!" The chaos subsided and calm was returning to the room once more. Apart from the odd frog jumping and the 'sniff, sniff,' of children crying I seemed to have established order once more. "Leave the frogs and sit in your places. Billy, I shall see you at playtime. You four boys near the window; it will be your job to catch the frogs and put them in that large jar with the lid on it." I pointed to a large jar that was standing on a table near the back of the class. "Children, those frogs won't hurt you. If you've caught one, give it to the boys, who'll put it in the jar. Now, I want you to draw me a picture to go with the writing you did this morning." The paper was handed out and the children started to settle down to some work at last. Whilst they were working I called the register, desperately trying to learn the children's names as I did so. A short time later, the four boys informed me they had caught all of the frogs. "Find a suitable place for them at play-time, will you please," I instructed them, not giving much thought to the word 'suitable.'

It was while we were having this calm and industrious work going on that Mrs Grant, the School Secretary, came into the room. She was carrying an assortment of files. "I've just come in for you to check this form about your payslip and get your bank details, so that you'll be paid at the end of the month," explained Mrs Grant. Now the word, pay, made me very attentive. I looked through the form and signed it; I also entered my bank's name and address. As this was going on, we were both unaware of an un-captured frog looking for refuge somewhere dark and out of the way. Such a place was available in an open lever arch file that it spotted on my desk. Quick as a flash it was in, and settling down for some rest, peace and quiet. I handed the form back to Mrs Grant, who put it in the lever arch file and closed it. "I better get these files to Mr Yardley before the Chairman of the Governers sees him. Yours was the last to be done. You seem to be winning here," she said with a smile, turned and left the room. Well, if she reported back to Mr Yardley that I was in full control here in my class room it could make up for the day's previous bad luck.

I was by now bordering on a euphoric high and also gaining more and more confidence. In no time at all it was playtime. I ordered the children out, row by row and in single file. Yes, I was getting the hang of it now. Billy was waiting for me to have my word with him, also the four frog catchers were there to put the frogs, "in a suitable place." "Just wait outside boys, while I have a chat with Billy, then you can put the frogs away," I said with a fair bit of confidence.

Billy looked at me with his angelic face which crumpled as he began to cry. "They were my best frogs," he said, "I thought you'd be pleased with them." His line of defence caught me on the hop. I was going to give this child a good talking to, telling him how naughty he'd had been for letting the frogs escape, causing chaos in my class room and frightening some of the children. What could I do, tears were now rolling down the poor chaps face. I was beginning to feel rather upset myself. Had I jumped to the wrong conclusion that this child was a demon from hell whose main purpose in life was to cause total devastation? "Now don't cry, Billy. Accidents do happen and I'm sure this was an accident. Thank you very much for your kind gesture of giving me your best frogs. I think you should go to the toilets and get your face washed and then have your playtime. Tell those boys to put your frogs in a suitable place as you go out, please," I said to him in my most friendly, 'hope everything is all right now,' voice.

As I walked across the school yard to the main buildings to find the staff room I saw Billy talking to the four frog catchers, who then disappeared into the class room. As I was going into the main building I was met by Mr Percy coming out. "I'm looking for someone to do this play-time's yard duty," he said to me. I had no choice but to volunteer my services. "Good man," he said, "All you have to do is walk round and make sure that there are no fights or that things aren't getting out of control." With that he retreated back into the building before I could ask any further questions.

As I walked around the school yard I saw that Miss Stark was also on duty. She came across to have a word with me. "Caught you out did he?" she asked. "Sorry?"
I replied, "I'm not sure what you mean." "Parrot, he caught you out to do the yard duty. The old sod doesn't like doing it himself so he asks for volunteers," she said. Now I was puzzled. "Who is Parrot," I asked. "That's the name the kids call Mr Percy, Percy Parrot. Haven't you noticed the way he repeats himself. Some of the kids in the top year are very good at mimicking him, but don't say that I said so. You keep to this side of the yard and I'll go over to the other side," she explained. As she walked away she was greeted by four little girls who all wanted to hold her hand, after a quick word from her the girls were holding each other's hand either side of Miss Stark. Very soon playtime was over, with no untoward events or happenings taking place. The children lined up, teachers collecting them from their lines. My class members were all waiting outside the class room waiting for me.

I herded my children into class, instructing them to sit down. I noticed that the frogs were gone. I asked the frog catchers if they had found a suitable place for them and they told me they had done so. I collected the drawings and along with the pieces of writing from the morning started to put them into my briefcase. As I did so Billy started coughing rather loudly, startling me and causing me to drop the papers into my briefcase. I looked up at Billy and automatically closed the briefcase. I asked him if he was alright and he assured me that he was fine. I nearly asked if he had a frog in his throat, but resisted. I explained to the class that I would start to read them a classic story, mainly because I couldn't think of anything else to do for the last twenty five minutes. "I shall begin with Robinson Crusoe," I said. "That's for boys," said one of the girls. "Can't we have Little Women, or Black Beauty," asked another girl. "That's soppy stuff. We want adventure stories with lots of fighting and killing," said a small passive looking boy on the front row. "We'll have Robinson Crusoe first," I explained, only because it was the only book I could get my hands on at that precise moment., "After we've listened to the story, we could have a class vote on which book I should read next," I said, hoping to get the support of all the class. There were a few grunts and O.K.'s and then they all seem to settle down to listen to the story.

Before long it was home time. The children bade me good night and I was left alone in my class room. My first day as a teacher was over. The day had been quite eventful in one way or another but the time had passed quickly. Roll on the next day, I thought, what will tomorrow bring I wondered? I collected my briefcase, and, as I did so, made a mental note not to bring it into school again. I looked at my watch, ten past seven. I really must get myself a new watch I thought. I wasn't sure at what time the buses stopped outside the school, so there was no telling how long I was going to wait for a bus at the bus stop.

I approached the bus stop with an air of unabashed nonchalance and without a care in the world. I then remembered that I needed one and three pence for the bus fare. I searched my pocket for some change, nothing in my left pocket. As I started to lower my briefcase to the ground so that I could check my right hand side pocket, a small voice started to talk. " Yorr, yorr yorr, your nn,nnn ,nnnot ggg,ggg gg gggoing, tt,tttt,to pp, ppp," it went on. I put my briefcase down and looked at a small boy from whence the voice had emanated. "Sorry, son, what are you trying to say," I asked in a polite and understanding voice. "Ttt,tttt too lll,.late," came the reply and he ran off. How strange, I thought, and wondered what he was on about. Still checking my right hand side pocket I couldn't find any change. All I had was a ten shilling note in my wallet. Oh well, that would just have to do, I hoped that the bus conductor would be understanding.

Five minutes later as the bus arrived, I picked up my briefcase and got on board, making my way inside the lower deck and sitting behind a rather large woman and a small boy. I put my briefcase between my legs. The conductor came to collect his fare. "Fares please," he yelled as he approached. I pulled out my wallet and offered him the ten shilling note for my fare. "A one and three penny, please," I said. "Who do we have here then, bloody Rothschild? A ten shilling note indeed," said the conductor sarcastically. "I'm sorry, I don't seem to have any smaller change," I said apologetically. "Oh that's alright sir, you soon will have," he said and after giving me my ticket started counting out my change - all in pennies, all 105 of them! My pockets were bulging with pennies. As the conductor was rather big I didn't like to say too much to him, anyway he might be the regular conductor for this run and it was more than likely that we'd meet again. No point in making enemies.

As I settled into the seat looking out of the window at a rather desolate estate, the large woman in front of me turned to her child and said in a loud voice, "God, have you bloody shit yourself again!" She then gave the little boy a smack with her hand. The little boy started to cry, looked over his shoulder and said to his mum, "It's not me mum, honest. I haven't, not today." Then looking at me he said, "Maybe it's the mister, maybe he's farted." Another crack from mum and more tears. I noticed a rather pungent smell, getting stronger all the time. Bad eggs, no, not that, the boy was right, someone had definitely farted, or worse. I tried to put it out of my mind, although the little boy crying and sniffily saying, "I haven't mum, honest," between heaving sobs, which didn't help. I know, I thought, read the children's papers from this morning that will take my mind off things. As I leant forward to open my briefcase the smell became almost overpowering. Maybe this kid's mum was right. The little sod had shat himself because the noxious odour was more apparent under the seat.

I opened my briefcase to get the papers out, but what happened next was a complete shock to me and the rest of the passengers on the bus. Frogs! My four frog catchers had found a 'suitable' place for the frogs - my briefcase. Now at their second opportunity to be free for that day, they all decided to make a break for it. Do you know how high a frog can jump? I didn't until then. Try catching one frog when six jump up together. It's impossible, I know because I tried. Before you could say 'eggs are eggs' the frogs were free and jumping all over the bus. On the bus floor, on the seats - and worse, even on the passengers. One frog thought the large lady in front of me had a Lilly pad on her head, her hat, and made a jump to land in it. The lady felt it land and reached up to remove the unwanted object off her hat. When she realise what she had in her hand she screamed, her little boy laughing through his tears until his mum cracked him again for laughing at her, then followed even more tears.

The conductor had been up the stairs collecting fares. He must have heard the large lady scream because he came rushing down the stairs ready for trouble. His exact words as he saw this jumping mass of green objects are unprintable but he must have had the same teacher as Mr Percy because he knew the same sort of words Mr Percy had used that very morning when tripping over my briefcase. By this time, the other passengers were up out of their seats trying to catch or stamp on the frogs. "It's that silly sod over there," said one of the passengers pointing to me, "He let these little buggers out for some fresh air." The conductor made no bones about what he wanted next. "You," he said, "Off my bus and take your pets with you." He rang the bell non stop until the driver looked around, realised there was some trouble and stopped the bus. As he started to get out of his cab the bus conductor got off the bus to have a word with him. I decided that it might be a good time for me to make a getaway without my frogs. I grabbed my briefcase, which seem to slide along the floor. Strange, I thought, and then I saw it - a very large and squashed dog turd. So that was the mysterious smell was and that was what the boy at the bus stop was trying to warn me about. I had to move quickly; I was already in the bad books about the frogs; I hated to think what the conductor was going to say when he found the dog shit.

With the conductor off the bus seeking help from the driver, it was my chance for a clean getaway. I say clean, however as I turned to get down the aisle I swung my briefcase which caught an upright bar used for holding when the bus was full. The case stopped in full flight, the dog turd didn't. It shot from the bottom of the briefcase like a new-style weapon from a James Bond spy film, right into the lap of a passenger who was trying not to take any notice of the frogs and mayhem on the bus and was gazing out of the window. He must have thought it was a frog landing on his lap because he picked it up without examining it. He soon looked, though, when he squeezed it through his fingers. I wasn't staying to find out what happened next. "Don't let him get off without his frogs!" shouted one of the other passengers as I made it to the footplate. Another tried to grab me but caught hold of my bulging pockets which tore, spilling pennies all over the foot plate and onto the road and the pavement. A group of kids were walking by and seeing that I was not staying to pick up the loose coins began to scramble around on their hands and knees. The conductor, seeing that I was doing a runner, came sprinting around the side of the bus and not seeing the kids picking up the coins, fell over them. I turned when I heard his outraged yell and saw two legs sticking up out of a privet hedge at the side of the pavement - alas, the conductor's.

I ran down some side streets until I was sure that I wasn't being followed, then started to walk. I hadn't been in this area before so I wasn't too sure where I was and where I was going. Just then I heard "Sir, do you want a lift anywhere," came a shout from a child. They called me sir, so that means they recognised me from school. I turned and saw a boy with a man, standing next to a car. As it was quite a distance into town and not knowing when the next bus would be due, this was an ideal opportunity for me. I walked over the road to where the child and man were standing. "That's very kind of you, if you're going into the town it would be nice if you could drop me off near the bus station," I said smiling at the boy trying to remember if I'd seen him before.

"Just waiting for two of my mates, then we can drop you off in the town. We might have to make a stop before we get there though," said the man, who didn't introduce himself. I was so pleased to have met this 'Good Samaritan' that I just said that it would be fine. "Here they are, Dad," said the boy as he saw two men approach, one who was carrying what I thought was a snooker cue wrapped in brown paper. "I got it Harry," said the man carrying the 'snooker' cue. "Who the 'ells this?" he said when he saw me. "Oh, it's one of the kid's teachers at the school. He just wants dropping off in town. We can do that after we've made our stop," said my Samaritan. I smiled innocently, not wishing to cause a fuss and make things easier.

We all got into the car, except for the small boy. The man he had been with looked under the dashboard and pulled out some wires. He saw me looking from the back seat and said that he had forgotten his keys and usually started his car like this. He bared two wires, joined them together and the car coughed into life. One of the other men, sitting in the front seat, leant over and looked at the dashboard, saying, "That's good, plenty of petrol in this one." His remark sounded strange to me, but never mind, I was getting a lift into the town. We drove down streets that I'd never seen before then turned onto a main road. "This is it," said the man with the snooker cue, "Park the car at the kerb and keep the engine running." The driver obeyed and stopped the car outside a Betting Shop. The other two men got out of the car and looked around before going into the Betting Shop.

I thought that they must have gone in to collect their winnings from some bets. A few minutes they came running out of the shop and jumped into the car. "Go, go, go!'" screamed the man with the snooker cue, although the brown paper was starting to come away and the snooker cue seemed to be made of metal. The other man was carrying a holdall, filled with bundles of something. The car shot away at great speed, then turned off the main road and shot down some side streets. "I don't want you to be late, sir," said the driver who could see me through his driving mirror. I smiled and said that I was in no hurry and that he didn't have to speed to get there. One of the men started to sniff and said to the driver, "There must have been a dog in here because I can smell dog shit." I'd forgotten about my briefcase.

Now, call me old fashioned, but I had more than a vague suspicion that things were not as they seemed to be. Things didn't feel quite right and it was apparent that I was in the wrong place at the wrong time. I started to recognise parts of the town. "Just drop me here, please," I said, "This will do fine. Thanks very much and it's been nice to meet you all." The driver slowed the car down, pulled into the kerb and stopped. I tried the door on the offside but it wouldn't open, "I'm sorry," I said to the burly man next to me, "but the door seems to be stuck. Can I get out on your side please." The man grunted something and opened the door and had to get out in order to let me out. He was holding the holdall in his arms and as I got out the bottom of my briefcase caught him on the leg, depositing some dog shit on his trousers. He didn't seem too happy about it for as he got back into the car he was shaking his leg and not looking what he was doing dropped a bundle from the holdall before closing the car door. Trying to be helpful I picked it up just as two things happened. Firstly, a Policeman appeared from round a corner, second, the driver on seeing the Policeman pulled away from the kerb rather quickly, making the car tyres squeal. I tried to indicate to the man in the back that I'd picked up his dropped bundle but it was too late, the car had already pulled away. The Policeman seeing the car speed away came across to me holding the bundle. "He dropped this out of the car," I said to the Policeman in all innocence. The Policeman was writing something down in his little book looking towards the speeding car. "How many were in the car, sir?" he enquired, "And have you seen them before?" As he was asking the question he was opening up the bundle. It contained banknotes, plenty of them. The policeman snapped an order to me, "Stay here, I must ring the station," and then he ran to a police phone box, which luckily for him was on the street corner. I could see him talking and waving his hand in the direction the car had taken. A wasted gesture I thought as the person on the other end of the phone couldn't see anything. He finished his conversation and walked back over to me with a smile on his face. "I must thank you, sir, for your help. It seems those people who dropped this bundle have just robbed a bookmakers not far from here and would have made a clean getaway had it not been for your observant eye spotting them drop this bundle. I'm not sure why they should stop here, unless they were splitting up, but with your help they should be caught soon. I've given the station the number of their car and the direction it was going. Now, if you can just give me a description of the men I'm sure we'll soon catch them."

It was all starting to fit into place. If I were to say that I'd been in the car when the men had committed the robbery then I was an accessory to the crime. I'd better be economical with the truth here and tell the Policeman what he thought he wanted to know. Before I could start to say anything he helped me. "Now sir, as I walked around the corner there, I saw you walk towards the car and see the bundle on the floor, pick it up and offer it to the people in the car just as it pulled away at great speed," said the Policeman, "Can you give me a description of the people in the car, I know it might be difficult as you may not have seen much of them." "I'm sorry, but it seemed to happen all too fast, I can't add any more to what you've already said," I told him with some relief. The Policeman wrote down my name and address and also where he could contact me during the day. He also told me that the police would probably be in touch with me to help further with their enquiries.

I walked away feeling quite happy with myself, thinking of the newspaper headlines, 'Local teacher helps police capture hardened criminals.' That would be a smack in the eye for Mr Yardley, having a hero on his staff. Another thought hit me. What if the men in the car said I was with them when they'd robbed the Bookmakers? Would the newspaper headlines then say, 'Local teacher involved with criminals in robbery.'

I shuddered; Mr Yardley would certainly get rid of me from his staff. I would never get another teaching job; I'd have a police record and might even go to prison. My happy feeling had gone down the pan and now I was truly worried. What was to happen to me?
Well, there was one thing, I could do nothing to change things now, if it was going to be, then so be it, or whatever it was that those Shakespearean characters would say in situations like this.

Chapter Three

I woke the next morning at 6.30, feeling rather tired as I'd been dreaming all night of two things. Me, - 'the hero,' and me, - 'the villain.' I'd seen myself being interviewed by the media asking me for my story of how I'd helped the police catch the notorious villains. Then I saw Mr Yardley as a High Court Judge and me in the dock waiting for sentence - and just as he was going to pass sentence after finding me guilty of robbery along with my accomplices, a bell started to ring. With great relief I realised that it was only the alarm clock telling me it was time for me to get up.

As I was getting shaved I looked at myself in the bathroom mirror and told myself that things couldn't be as bad as yesterday. My mind went through the events of the previous day and I started to shudder. Things couldn't possibly get any worse than yesterday - could they? My briefcase was in the outhouse where I intended it to stay for I hadn't cleaned the doggy poo off the base of it and secondly, I wouldn't be tempted to take it to school with me. I looked at the clock and realised that I'd have to hurry if I were to catch the same bus as yesterday. The bus! I hoped that I might get the same bus conductor as yesterday morning and not the same conductor as the evening. I grabbed my jacket and saw the ripped pocket. The only other jacket I had was a sports jacket, which was rather bright for school. Still it was a jacket and I needed a jacket. It would have to do for today, or until I got my other jacket was repaired.

I ran to the bus stop with only minutes to spare, the bus arriving at 7.45 prompt. As I was getting on, the conductor was coming down the stairs. "You again is it," said the conductor, "I thought one day would have been enough for you! Going back for more heartache at the madhouse are we?" "Oh, yes," I replied as I made my way to a vacant seat halfway down the bus. The conductor followed me and waited for his fare. "One and three," he said to me, "That is, if you're going to Cromwell Street School again." I put my hand in my pocket and took out a two shilling piece and offered it for my fare. "It's a bloody funny route is this one, I'll tell you," he said as he gave me a ticket and searched in his bag for the change. "According to my mate at the depot he had a lunatic on this run last night. Seems he got on the bus and let all his pet frogs loose, bloody things went everywhere. There were still some of the little buggers jumping around when the bus came into the depot to be cleaned. One of the cleaners stepped on a frog and fell arse over tit down the stairs, luckily she wasn't hurt. So be careful who you sit next to on this run," he said, and then moved off down the bus shouting, "Any more fares, please!" I knew that I'd have to get a bus at a different time when I left school this evening because if the same conductor was on the morning run then the odds were that the conductor from the disastrous run last night might be on the same run tonight. I sat looking at the same scenery that I'd looked at for the first time the previous day.

Half an hour later the bus was turning down Cromwell Street. I got up to get off the bus and as I stood on the foot plate the conductor looked at me and said, "Good luck, you might need it." I smiled and got off the bus after it stopped, then walked through the school gates. Mr Johnson was in the yard sweeping twigs and leaves that had blown from the trees from over the wall around the school yard. I looked in his direction and called out to him, "Good morning, Mr Johnson, nice day again." He turned, looked at me and grunted something that sounded like "Bleeding impostor," and carried on sweeping. I made my way to the main building and the staff room. I was thinking to myself about the day and what I might do with the children. Maybe some P.E. - see what the children were like at ball games. I wondered who might be best at running in the class, who was going to be the weak one who said his mam didn't want him to do P.E. this week 'cos he'd got a cold.

My thoughts were disturbed as the familiar voice of Mr Percy called out to me from the window of his room, "Over to my room at once please." Mr Percy didn't sound too happy, matter of fact the tone of his voice seemed quite angry. Maybe the police had been in contact with the school about the little misunderstanding with my lift into town last night, or could it be something about the way in which I have been teaching the children. Those and a myriad other thoughts went through my head as I walked up the stairs to Mr Parrot's office. I knocked on the door and waited. "Come in," shouted Mr Percy. I went in. "Sit," he snapped," I see that you have left that bloody briefcase at home, thank goodness. What do you think you are playing at?" I thought he was on about the lift; he must have been told. Well here goes, "It was a mistake I...," before I could continue Mr Percy jumped in. "I'll say it was a mistake. I told you yesterday that Mr Yardley looked as though he had been through a whole term, thanks to you, and now you say it was a mistake."

"You see, "I started," I didn't know who they were, I..." "The creature in question is called a frog, and they usually live in ponds, not folders or files that are due to be delivered to Mr Yardley," said Mr Parrot. Files - frogs – oh no, not frogs again. I was confused; he wasn't on about the lift into town but about some frogs and Mr Yardley. My puzzled look must have conveyed a message to Mr Percy for he continued with the story of the frog. "As I understand it, Mrs Grant came to your class room to get your signature on a document for Mr Yardley. The files were 'frog free' at the time. From your class room to Mr Yardley's room the file gained a passenger, namely a frog. It could only be from your class room. Mrs Grant was not responsible for placing the creature in the file. Yours is the only room it could have come from. Were you teaching any frogs in your class yesterday by any chance?" he said in a strange manner. Not thinking I answered, "Er, yes there were some frogs in the room yesterday, but I….."

"So, the frogs came from your room and ended up with Mr Yardley. Unfortunately for Mr Yardley he had a visit from the Chair of Governers, and whilst they were having a cup of tea Mrs Grant placed the file on his desk. It was then the frog decided to make a break for freedom, in the direction of Mr Yardley, just as he had a cup of hot tea in his hand. The sight of a frog leaping towards him made him spill the hot tea over his lap and, again unfortunately for him, caused him to utter words he shouldn't have. The Chair of Governers apparently didn't see the frog and thought the words were directed at him and immediately left the room before Mr Yardley could explain. Now things are very strained between the two, which is very bad for all concerned. So, a word of warning, keep well away from Mr Yardley, don't even let him see you. Keep out of his sight, for this week at least. You can't afford to have any trouble whatsoever. This morning we have an assembly in the hall for the primary children. This will be the first assembly for the Year Threes as they have moved up from the infants, the infants have their own assemblies.

Assembly will be straight after registration, so get your class in the hall on time. You better get to your class, as school will be starting soon. Off you go," he said, waving his hand, his finger pointing to the door. I had no chance of giving an explanation; I'd had my trial and had been found guilty. I left the room in silence, apart from the sound of my footsteps on the highly polished floor.

I walked out of the main building thinking of the tête-à-tête I'd had with Mr Percy and making a mental note not to get into any scrapes that might involve Mr Yardley. The children were starting to fill the yard like a leaking tap fills a bucket. I went into my room and found that the register had already been given out. I sat at my desk and browsed through the names in this carefully written document. I had been told at college that the register is a legal document and had to be regarded as such, keeping a strict record of all children, present or otherwise. I tried to picture each child in my mind's eye. One child that I could not forget was Billy Preston; I became very nervous when I saw his name in the register. I heard a whistle, then children running and shouting very excitedly then quiet. I walked to the window and saw that my class had started to line up outside the room on the yard. A good start to the day I thought, well, better than yesterday. Any start was surely going to be better than yesterday.

The children were lined up outside my class room waiting patiently for me to appear and lead them into the class. I went out and led them inside. I told the children to sit in the same places as they'd sat in the day before. This way I had some chance of remembering the names of the children. I looked round the class and saw that most of the children were present. I decided to call the register and to my relief Billy Preston was absent. I told the children they had to line up for assembly. From the back of the room came the comment, " Oh no, it will be 'Yard Brush' taking the assembly, he's a boring old fart." Before I could identify the culprit, another voice commented, "Bet he starts talking about his boring holidays, he always does at the start of the new term." "Quiet!" I said, trying to gain order with the class. However the next voice got me thinking, "I'll take bets on how long it is before he scratches his nose." This time I'd seen the owner of the mystery voice, "Explain yourself, Jimmy Moses."

"Well, sir," started Jimmy Moses, "I'm willing to take bets on how long it takes before old 'Yard Brush' scratches his nose after he starts his assembly. Are you a betting man sir, I can give you good odds?" His face was all lit up with excitement, thinking he had a new customer in me. "Er, no, I don't make bets very often," I began before remembering that I was talking to one of my pupils, "And you should not be taking bets in school! Anyway what are the odds? No, no, forget that question. Now, in one line, walk out and across the yard to the assembly hall," I said in a commanding voice.

The children walked across the yard, as they had been instructed, and I followed, rather like a shepherd controlling his flock of sheep. Other classes were reaching the assembly hall as well as mine. I told the children to wait at the door which they did. I then went to the front of the line and saw Mr Percy who directed me to a space half way down the hall. I led my children in and lined them up where I had been directed.

Other classes were now also lined up all facing the stage at the front of the hall. The stage had stairs on either side of it giving access from each side. The class directly in front of the stage were very small and mostly dressed in what appeared to be the school uniform. The children seemed very nervous and scared. Mr Thomas, who's class was behind mine, came up to me and saw me looking at the class at the front and said, "Look at those poor little buggers, frightened to death they are. This is their first time in the 'big' assembly and I bet the other kids in here have told them horror stories about the assemblies here." He then looked towards the back of the hall at the top class. These kids were quite tall, some being head and shoulders above others. "God," said Mr Thomas, "That bloody Neil Young is misbehaving in his line and Ivan hasn't seen him. If I pull him out I will have to stay behind with him in detention tonight and I want to be home early. Word of warning; don't pull kids out of their class in assembly or you might have to stay back with them in detention the same night. Let's pretend we haven't seen him. Check watches," as he said this, he looked at his watch, "One minute fifteen seconds to go before we have the Führer giving his rendition of his boring holidays."

Strange, I thought, Mr Yardley seems to have a reputation with both his staff and pupils of being boring in assemblies. I would have to make my own mind up on this matter and judge for myself. I looked at my class, all standing in a straight line, waiting patiently and most important of all, the strange silence, not only from my class but from all of the classes. I glanced at the top class and could see the boy Mr Thomas had seen misbehaving and he was still misbehaving. He should have more sense, as he was the tallest boy in the top class and his strange antics could be seen by all the staff, who all must be wanting to get away early as they were all ignoring him. Nothing could be done now, for the doors swung open at the back of the hall and in walked Mr Yardley. I say walked; it was more of a march. He reminded me of the Emperor Napoleon inspecting his troops as he strode down the hall, his footsteps being the only sound in the room full of about two hundred people. As he walked, sorry, marched along, he looked quite a sight with his mortar board and gown. Under one arm he held a book, possibly a bible or diary, and he held the front of his gown with his other hand. On the way from the back of the hall to the front he eyed each class as he went by making the comment, "Good," or "Well done," as he passed by. The children, on hearing this remark, would try to stand up straighter and smile, which looked quite comical from some children.

Mr Yardley got to the stairs and walked swiftly up them as though he was about to receive an Oscar for his performance for his entrance. He marched to the centre of the stage and looked over the pupils of his school. There was still total silence from everyone. Then it happened, he saw Neil Young, who was still messing about on the back row. Mr Yardley shouted, and I mean shouted, one word which reverberated around the room, "NEIL!!!"

No one quite expected what happened next. All the children in the class at the front of the stage started to get down on their knees after this order. Mr Yardley couldn't believe his eyes and started to stammer and stutter. Kids in other classes started to laugh at this, which only made things worse. The staff around the edges of the hall, I'm sure, were smiling at this sight, but were trying to get order from their classes before Mr Yardley blew up even more. Unfortunately, the piano player was the class teacher of the poor mites who were now on their knees, some in tears, frightened by Mr Yardley's booming voice. He didn't know what was going on, so he stood up and looked over his piano at a sight I'm sure he would never forget - all his class on their knees and upset. He quickly went round to try and restore order and get the children back on their feet, and most importantly stop the crying.

My Yardley couldn't take any more. He turned in a very military manner and marched off the stage, past the confusion, which was Class Three, down the hall and out of the door at the back of the room. He did say something to Mr Percy as he passed by, after which Mr Percy almost ran to the stage to take over the confusion which was the assembly. It was then I noticed that not only did Mr Percy repeat himself, but he also stuttered in moments of stress. This was one of those moments. He stood on the stage, arms outstretched as if to calm things down, "C ccan wwwwe ppp please hhhave the hhhymn 'Aaall th things bbbb bright and b b b beautiful."

That would have been fine if Mr Sharpe, the Class Three teacher, had been at the piano but he was the wrong side of it still sorting out his class. On hearing Mr Percy's words he tried to get to the right side of his piano from halfway down his class's line. He would have reached the piano with no delay had it not been for the wet patch that had been created by a frightened child. However Hush Puppies do not like to change direction quickly, particularly on wet parquet floor. They just skid and slide, which is what Mr Sharpe did. His Hush Puppies stopped sliding as he reached the edges of the wet patch, but Mr Sharpe didn't. He seemed to do a flying tackle on the piano, which brought the decorative vase of flowers crashing down on to his head. Things now went from bad to worse. Now most of the school were crying with laughter, including the teachers. Some of the third year children started to cry when they saw their teacher hurt, others thought it was funny and started laughing out loud - others were just confused by the whole sequence of unfortunate events.

Mr Percy took charge yet again and told the top year staff and children to go back to class; assembly for that day was cancelled. Some members of staff went to Mr Sharpe's aid, who was by now sitting under the piano rubbing his head and muttering things that maybe he shouldn't. I tried to make sure that my class were in line and quiet, which they were. When it came to our turn, we walked out of the hall, across the yard and back to our class room.

As we walked across the yard there was some talking from the back of the line. There was an argument kicking off and Jimmy Moses seemed to be the one others were picking on. I went to see what the trouble was. "Tell 'im, sir, he 'as to pay up. Old Yard Brush didn't scratch 'is nose or tell us about 'is 'oliday so he's lost 'is bet and 'as to pay up," complained one of the smallest boys in the class, Timmy Swallow. "Betting isn't allowed in school, Jimmy, so give all the money back to the people you took it off," I said with confidence. "But sir," went on Timmy," he should pay us ten to one odds 'cos old Yard Brush didn't scratch 'is nose." I looked sternly at the small crowd that had now gathered and said in a commanding voice, "Jimmy will give you your money back, and there will be no more betting in school. Do you hear that Jimmy, no more betting in school, with anyone, otherwise there will be serious trouble for you, understand?"

Jimmy looked at me as if about to argue but instead he shrugged his shoulders and said, "Yes sir, they'll get their money back as you say." I felt a sense of victory as I strode off and led the children into the class room. I'd decided that we should do some basic maths. The children were a mixed ability class so they were soon working at different levels with their work. As I expected Jimmy Moses was very good at maths. The children wanted to talk about the incident in the hall but I felt it better that I should quash any talk of it. Very soon the Milk Monitors were asking if they should get the milk for the class. I looked at my watch only to remember that it didn't work properly, but I wasn't going to let the children know that. "Oh, is that the time already," I exclaimed," Yes, Milk Monitors, go and get the milk please." Out trotted two children who had told me they were the monitors from last year. I had told the children that I would be looking for the 'best' children to take over the job for this year. That, I thought, would be a carrot to hold over the children to get them to behave, should I need one.

The two children left the room and came back about five minutes later carrying the milk crate between them. They then began to distribute bottles of milk, giving one to each child. One of the children gave out the straws that were sitting on the top shelf of the book cupboard. I gave the command to "Stop working and drink your milk." There was a frantic plopping of milk tops being opened then silence for a few minutes, followed by the slurping of the final dregs of milk from the bottom of the bottles. The Milk Monitors went around and collected the empties, filling the crates and taking them back to where they'd got them from in the first place. Another child came forward and asked for the bag for the blind dogs. I said I didn't know what she meant. She explained that all the silver paper and milk tops were collected and sent off to be used to raise money to buy dogs for the blind. "The bags in your cupboard," she explained, "It's usually a big black plastic bag, shall I look for it?" I nodded in agreement and a few minutes later the child appeared and started to collect all the tops from the rest of the class. As she walked past me the smell of sour milk from the bag was too much. "Make sure you fasten the top tight," I said to her, hoping the smell wouldn't leak out at any time. I looked out of the window and saw that children had been released from other classes for playtime so I carefully dismissed by class in a regimental order, sorted some books and equipment out for the next lesson and made my way to the staff room.

By the time I got to the staff room most of the staff were in and either sat down or getting their tea or coffee at the table. Mr Thomas was complaining in a rather loud voice, "That bloody new teacher has told Jimmy Moses that all bets are off this morning, I stood to win at least twelve pounds this week. That should have made up for the packet I lost last term." At this he turned and saw me. "Ah, there you are. It's quite obvious that you don't know about Jimmy Moses and his father and the betting. We all know that Jimmy is taking bets, everyone except old Yardley and Parrot, so don't spill the beans! From time to time we get big wins. This morning would have been one of our biggest takes from him, but you have given him the excuse not to pay out." I looked surprised and shocked, "But, but it's not legal," I started. "Cobblers," said Mr Thomas, "It's a bit of fun and it's teaching Jimmy lessons for when he takes over his dad's betting shop. In future turn a blind eye to Jimmy's betting activities." Mr Thomas went and sat down and I got myself a tea, mulling over what had been said to me. Teaching was starting to be an eye opener, things which they didn't tell us about at college.

I settled down to my cup of coffee as Mr Percy came into the room. He looked at me and said, "Mr Yardley would like to see you as soon as you've dismissed your children at dinner time. Please don't keep him waiting too long. You do remember where his room is don't you? We don't want any of yesterday's capers of kidnapped children in the school again, do we?" Before I could give any answer he walked over to the boiler to get his tea. "Don't look too worried," said a kindly female voice. It was Miss Stark. I turned and smiled. "It can't be too bad, at least he wants to see you a dinner time and not now, so that's a good sign," she said," I expect it will be something to do with your timetable or , err, something." The 'or, err, something ' didn't sound too good, but at least she seemed to be on my side. Again I smiled and we started a conversation about general matters. The weather, pop music, television and newspapers all seemed to come into the conversation somewhere. Very soon it was time for us all to rinse our cups out, pay a quick visit to the loo and then go and collect our children for the second half of the morning.

The time from the end of playtime to dinner time passed by quite quickly. I dismissed the children for dinner and made my way to Mr Yardley's office. Very soon I was outside his door knocking on it. His door had three lights on it, a bit like traffic lights, red, yellow and green. Over the red light were the words 'do not disturb', over the yellow 'wait' and over the green 'come in.' The Yellow light was on so. I had to wait. The light then changed to green and I entered the room. Mr Yardley was sat behind his desk. He looked up at me and told me to take a seat.

"I've had the police on the phone this morning about a robbery that took place at a bookmakers last night. They've told me that thanks to you and your quick thinking a substantial amount of money was recovered. They've told me that the men that committed the robbery can be very dangerous but they have a good idea who they are and are looking for them. They have also mentioned there might be a reward for your actions," as he said this he looked at me and smiled. "After this I think that yesterday's incidents can be forgotten about, although there is a matter of a cleaning bill for my trousers as I understand you were responsible for the frog! I'll let you have the bill in due course. Have a nice lunch. Thank you," and with that he pointed his hand to the door. I rose from the chair and mumbled, "Thank you, yes sir," and left. As I closed the door the light changed from yellow to red.

I walked away from his office in a kind of daze. The words, "the men that committed the robbery can be very dangerous" started to go round my head. However the thought of getting a reward compensated the worry of the dangerous men. My meeting with Mr Yardley wasn't all that bad after all. Anyway, it's lunchtime and I was starting to feel a bit peckish so I made my way back to my class room to pick up my packed lunch that I had made that morning. Cheese and tomato sandwiches, a packet of crisps and some biscuits. I had to make a decision whether or not to have my lunch in the staff room or in my class room. My mind was made up when I got to my class room because when I opened my bag and got my packed lunch out and saw the sandwiches, which had been wrapped in greaseproof paper, they were all soggy and limp. I couldn't sit in the staff room and start eating those in front of the other staff so there was nothing else to do except to eat them there and then. After I was finished I would go over to the staff room and get myself a cup of tea. Also I thought it was a good idea to get the afternoon's lesson prepared.

Chapter Four

Monday morning seemed to come round fast; this was my second week. As usual I grabbed a quick marmalade sandwich and cup of tea, my usual breakfast, got my new briefcase and ran for the bus. I managed to get to school by eight forty, another five minutes and I would have been deemed late by Mr Percy, As I reached the staff room and got my mug for the starter cuppa of the day Mr Yardley walked into the staff room, which was usual for Monday mornings, but this morning he seemed very pleased with himself. He called for quiet and said that he had something very special to tell us all. "We have been chosen," he said," to be one of the few schools in the town to have a colour television set to be used in school for the schools programmes. As we will have only one television set there will have to be a timetable made out as to which classes will be using it on what days. I have the schools television guide which gives the programmes that are going to be shown this term. There are enough guides for one each so can you all take a copy. Will all members of staff please look at it and see if there are any programmes that you think will be useful to your class and hand in your list to Mr Percy and he will make out a timetable. The television will be based in the class room that is being used as the music room. I know that Mr Sharpe uses this room on a dinner time for his music group and other teachers use it through the week but we will have the room timetabled as to when there are no television programmes being shown so it can be used as a music room and when there are schools programmes it will be the television room. I have seen Mr Johnson and he have arranged an aerial point to be fitted in the room for the television. If you are the last person to use the television set please move it into the store room and make sure the door is locked. The key will be handed back to the office where Mrs Grant will keep it in the key cupboard. The Governers have backed the decision for the television to be used and may pop in to see it being used."

This was good news indeed. While the kids were watching the television then I could be doing my marking and then it would free me for the evening. I must get hold of that television guide and see what's on a Thursday or Friday and that would free me for that evening. Even better if it's the last lesson in the afternoon, yes I must get hold of that guide. "Right staff, time to go and get your children in off the yard, it's nearly time for the bell," said Mr Percy, "and if anyone wants the television guide copies they will be sent round the classes today. Please indicate if you wish to use the television and which program you would like to see. If you are not interested please initial the guide to say that you have seen it." There was mixed messages coming from different members of staff, some saying that it was a great idea and others saying a waste of time, kids watch too much television at the moment so why bring it into school. Already, if some of the staff were anti television, then there must be a good chance that I would be able to get my name on the television timetable. So off I went, carrying my mug of tea to collect my class who should by now be starting to line up.

As I was walking across the yard to where my class was lined up it started to spit with rain. No, please, not an indoor playtime. I had been told that when it rained we would have to have an indoor playtime. I had only experienced one before when I was on teaching practice. I was sheer hell as I had been left with the class while their class teacher went for their break. The children were supposed to sit quiet and play games or do some drawing or other work on paper. This paper was recycled from exercise books that had not been filled from the previous year. Experienced class teachers had special boxes that were for wet playtimes only with various board games, cards, paper and coloured pencils. These boxes were added to as when the teacher thought items might be good for wet playtimes. I had no such boxes in my class being a new teacher and not thinking about wet playtimes. I must add this to my "to do" list but that's not going to help me today. Maybe I might be lucky and the rain will stop before playtime. Anyway I better get these kids in before they get too wet and start smelling like wet dogs in the class room.

When I reached the line there was some kind of dispute going on. Before I could say anything I was being shouted at from all directions. "Sir, can I fetch the milk," No sir, let me, I want to do it." "Don't let him, he's a nutter, he'll get lost." "Stop," I shouted," and line up and what all this about?" "Sir, it's Tommy and Freddie, they're both away today, and they fetch our milk," said Nicola Thompson, one of my brighter pupils. "Right, who's standing straight and quiet and will be sensible to bring our milk," I said knowing that this would bring them all to order. Nearly at once all the children fell silent and were standing upright like stair rods, all wanting the job of going for the milk. Without thinking I pointed to two boys and said, "You two, go and get our milk from Mr Johnson." The two boys in question rushed from the line and disappeared round the back of the building to where the milkman would offload crates of milk outside Mr Johnson's lobby. Mr Johnson had to make sure that the crates were marked for each class with the required number of bottles for that class in each crate. Pupils from each class had to go and collect the crates at the start of each school day and they would be responsible to take the empties to where they collected the crate from. The crates were supposed to be collected before the bell went to start the day.

"In you all go," I said to the rest of the disappointed class and in they went. When they reached the class I told them to get their reading books out and read quietly while I was going to call out the register. I strode over to my desk where the register was waiting for me. These are delivered before school starts by various members of the top class to each class room. Not only do I have to take the register but also do a dinner register and record what each child is doing for lunch. It's expected that the staff that have a school lunch, which is a free lunch for the teacher, will have it with the children at their table. However the teacher takes their chance as they don't know in advance which table they will be in charge of in the dining room. One of the better meals is the roast pork dinner which comes with apple sauce and you can usually tell when this meal is on as most of the staff put their names down for dinner.

I go through the register giving both Mark Robinson and Terry Rogers their mark along as they were the ones that have gone for our class milk. I look at my watch, nearly time for assembly, but the boys should be back by now. As we were lining up the boys were still missing. I can't be late with my class and I don't want to be in bad books again with Mr Yardley or Mr Percy as I wanted the use of that television. There was no other way but to go to the assembly and let Mark and Terry catch us up in the hall. With a bit of luck Mr Percy will think they are late for school and it will put me in the clear.

However as our class lined up and went over for assembly Nicola Thompson called out to me saying "Do you think it was a good idea to send Mark and Terry for the milk sir?" "What do you mean, Nicola?" I said nervously. "Well they do have a bit of a reputation, sir. Last year they were sent on an errand by our teacher and she didn't see them for the rest of the day. But I think they like you so they might be back soon."

"Yes, thank you Nicola, I really wanted to know that." I said, I was going to ask where Mark and Terry was but time was pressing and I was sure there must be a good explanation to why they were late with the milk, "Right class, over to assembly, one line now and no talking." The class walked from our class room across the playground and into the main building, down the corridor to the main hall. The rest of the school were almost there. I walked the children into the hall and to our place halfway down. The children knew the routine and went to their place without too much bother. I took my place at the end looking down the row of children, boys in front of the girls. One more class to come and then all the school would be ready for Mr Yardley and his Monday morning assembly. Finally Mike Charlesworth and his class came into the hall. All the school was now present and awaiting our head to appear as usual. Classes standing in silence in straight lines with members of staff at the end of each class looking out for pupils out of line or talking. Then Mr Yardley came down the hall, his footsteps the only sound with the occasional "Good," and "well done," as he looked down each line of pupils. He was dressed as always in his black gown, bible or dairy in one hand and the other hand holding the front of his gown and his mortar board on his head so straight that I'm sure you could put a spirit level on it and find it was perfectly level. I wondered how long he took placing it on his head so that it was so straight. As he passed by me he glanced in my direction with a strange look and passed me by. Strange, I thought, why would he give me such a look, never mind my conscience was clear.

He marched up the stage steps and greeted the school with "Good morning school," and waited for the reply, which soon came. "I have some good news for the school. We have been selected from all the schools in the town to be one of a few to have a colour television to be used in our lessons. Your teacher will be telling you more about it and when your class may have the chance of watching it. I'm sure that it will help in your lessons. The Governers are very pleased that we have been given this opportunity and they will be asking how we have been using it as we progress through the term." However at that point a voice from somewhere near the back of the hall was heard to say, "Can we watch Popeye and Olive Oil," unfortunately Mr Yardley heard this and the colour of his face changed from pink to bright red. "Who was that, I'm waiting, who was that boy then, making silly remarks? Mr Telford, was it a boy from your class. I think the voice came from your class." Tony Telford hadn't been listening as staff usually switched off when Mr Yardley started talking on the stage. "Erm what, yes that's right, Mr Yardley," said Tony not knowing what he was saying yes to. "Then find him Mr Telford and send him to my room and I will sort his out after assembly, I'm waiting," demanded Mr Yardley. Tony had no choice but to walk down his line of boys and pick out the likely candidate. When he got to the end he saw a strange looking boy who was stood by himself at the other end of the line in another class - Farthingale. Tony grabbed the boy who started to complain that it wasn't him and started to do what he did best - farting. That was the reason that he was stood by himself. None of the other kids could stand the smell. "Get to my room at once and no answering back otherwise it will be worse for you boy," hailed Mr Yardley from the stage, "Mr Telford, escort that boy to my room and make him wait with my secretary and I'll deal with him after assembly" Tony did as he was told and left the hall with Farthingale still muttering and complaining that it wasn't him.

Mr Yardley went on with the assembly with the rest of the school listening in silence. He rambled on about something or other and then it was time for the hymn. Mr Sharpe came forward and told the school what hymn we would be singing, sat down at the piano and played the intro, stopped jumped up, looked at the school and said, "Now," sat back down and carried on playing while the school joined in with the singing. I thought to myself how good he had perfected that move over a number of years at the school, quite a feat and he wasn't that small either. One day, I thought, he's going to sit back down too quickly and that chair will give way.

Assembly over, Mr Yardley told Mr Percy to take over and dismiss the children as he walked back down the hall and out back to his office. As he walked out Tony walked in with a smile on his face. I was curious so when Tony got near I whispered, "What's so funny?" "It's that Farthingale boy," he replied," he was farting all the way to the office and when I told Mrs Grant that I had to leave him there with her until Mr Yardley got back from the assembly she gave a look of horror. I'm sure he had followed through with his farting. I left him there with his smell."

"Oh right," I said and tried to imagine what would happen when Mr Yardley got to the office. I turned to my class, who were waiting for me to lead them out of the hall and back our class room. It was then that I realised that my two boys were still missing. I hoped that they would be back at the class room waiting for us. No such luck, no sign of the missing boys. Should I send out search parties for the missing boys or just wait. I decided on the latter and got the class into our class room and started the first lesson which was English. I had just got the introduction of the lesson over when the door open and our missing boys appeared with our missing crate of milk. "Sir, sir, you seen the new television, it's come and we've been helping Mr Johnson set it up, well not helping watching Mr Johnson set the television up in the music room," said Terry. "Ok boys, put the milk on the corner and sit down and get your English books out, we're on page 12 in the comprehension book. Read the passage and answer the questions at the bottom of the page," I said with a sigh of relief that they were back. I just started to go round the class to see how the children were getting on with the exercise when there was a knock on the door. "Come in," I called out. A small boy came into the class room holding a booklet in his hand. "Mr Percy said I had to bring this to you, sir," said the small boy and handed over the leaflet. I recognised it at once as the schools television guide. "He said that you have to look at it and put your name on the front to say that you've seen it then pass it over to Mr Telford when you have finished with it," said the small boy. He then turned and left the room without another word. The children stopped their work and looked up at me as I stood there with the television guide. I had an idea that I could use this to my advantage. "Yes, this is the television guide and I'm going to see if our class will be able to watch some programs over the coming weeks. That is, if you behave yourselves, otherwise I will tell Mr Percy that some other class can have our turn with the television," I said to the class. "Now get on with your work while I look through this guide and see what programs we might be able to see".

So for the next ten minutes I searched the guide to see what programs were suitable for our class. Then I saw it. A program on a Friday afternoon called "Making music," a program for children to make music and their own instruments, and the good thing about it was that it came on at 3-15 and went off at 3-45 which meant it fell just after afternoon playtime and finished just before home time. I would be able to get most of my marking done while the kids watched the program and I would be free for the weekend - perfect. I got a piece of paper out and wrote down the program name, the day it was on and the time. As an added bonus I could send away for the teacher's guide to the program which would give lesson plans and hints of what to get for the program. I put my name on the front of the guide and asked Nicola to take it to the next class, which was Mr Telford. The lesson flew by and in no time at all it was time for the milk to be given out before playtime. Thankfully, it was dry; the rain had stopped so no wet playtime. I must get some wet playtime kit sorted as sooner or later we were going to have a wet playtime and I had better be prepared for it. I looked around the class to see who could give the milk out. Both Mark and Terry were sitting rigid to be picked to give the milk out. I relented and said, "Mark and Terry, as you both did a good job in collecting the milk you can give it out to the class." Both boys sprang from their seats and made their way to the milk crate and started giving it out. I was amazed how quickly they not only gave the milk out but the straws as well. "Sir, there's two spare bottles, can Mark and me have them please sir," said Terry. So that was their ploy, to have an extra bottle of milk. "Yes, OK, you can have one each," I said, "but only after you have collected the empty bottles and tops." Within minutes all the milk had been drunk and the two boys were going round collecting the empties. After this was done the two boys were standing by the milk crate drinking their extras. I stood the class up and let them go to play row by row. I waited for the two boys to finish and left with them to make my way to the staff room.

By the time I got to the staff room most of the staff was there. I got my coffee and sought out Mr Percy who was standing by the window. "I have my request for the television. I've put it down on some paper for you," I said and handed him my written request. "Err, thank you," he replied, "you are the first to make a request. I'll wait until the rest of the staff has had time to hand in their request before I let you know if you will get the time you have requested." He took my piece of paper and put it in his pocket. Just then Tony Telford walked into the room. "Ahhh, just the man I'm waiting for," said Mr Percy, "Mr Telford why did you send that boy Farthingale to Mr Yardley's office?" Tony turned to Mr Percy and said "because Mr Yardley wanted him there, he called out in the assembly and Mr Yardley asked me to take him to his office. Why, is there some sort of problem?"

"Some sort of problem, Mr Telford. Some sort of problem. Mrs Grant is requesting that her office is to be fumigated because of that boy. He has stunk the office out. If you had spoken to the boy you would have known that it wasn't him that had called out in the assembly," said Mr Percy. By this time, the staff room was almost silent and listening to this conversation. "I'm sorry, I'm not sure what you mean," said Tony. "Well the boy who called out said Popeye and Olive Oil, and if you had spoken to the boy you would have realized that he stammers and would not have been able to say those two names outright," said Mr Percy rather indignantly. "Which means the office had to be evacuated and a lot of air fresheners to be used to try to get rid of the smell. The boy was sent home to get changed and have a bath, and Mr Yardley is not a happy person along with Mrs Grant. In future please pay more attention in assembly Mr Telford otherwise the children will take advantage if they think the staff are not watching them." I noted what was being said to Tony and tried to make a mental note that this wouldn't happen to me in the future. Conversion broke out amongst the staff about what people had been doing over the weekend, the new television, the program guide and other small talk until it was all too soon the end of playtime and we all have to go back to our classes.

My class as usual were lined up outside the prefab. The children were getting used to me and I was getting used to them. As I approached them the line was rather straight and quiet, although two boys at the back of the line seemed to be arguing. I went over to them and asked what was going on. "Sir", said one of the boys, "Couldn't Superman beat Batman in a fight?" "Yes I think so," I said, "because Superman has superpowers." "There, I told you so," said one of the boys and with that he punched the other boy in the face. The punch hit the boy in the nose, which started at once to bleed. The class turned to see what was going on. Someone muttered,"Sir shouldn't have sided with Alfie; he always wants to win every argument." I had to act quickly before the situation got more serious. I pointed to one of the girls and said, "Can you please take this boy to the office and get him seen to." Turning to Alfie I said," I will deal with you inside," with no idea what I was going to do with him. I called out to the rest of the class, "Turn to the front and go in one at a time."

The class walked into the class room in silence and to their desks. I told Alfie to stand at the front near my desk and told the rest of the class to sit down and get their maths books out. I still wasn't sure what to do with Alfie then I had an idea. "Now Alfie, you are much bigger than the boy you hit so what would happen if I hit you in the face and made your nose bleed as I am much bigger than you. How would you feel and what would you do?" Alfie looked me up and down and said, "I'd get me dad and he'll sort you out, that's what." "And what happens if, if, what's the boy's name you hit, his dad comes in and sorts you out. What will happen then, eh?" Straight away Alfie came back with an answer, "Well me dad will sort his dad out, that's what will happen. Me dad can sort anyone out around here, even when the police come round he can sort them out as well. But sometimes they put him away for a few months. "Now that I wasn't expecting. I'll have to tread carefully here I thought and go down the path of trying to reason with Alfie. I looked at Alfie and noticed that all the class were watching and listening to find out how I was going to deal with the situation. "Now Alfie," I started, "We should all get along together and that fighting isn't nice and for the rest of the lesson you should sit at the front at the empty desk and think about what you have done and how you could make things better. At the end of the lesson I want you to tell me how you can make things better. OK!" All of a sudden Alfie burst into tears and balled out "You won't tell me dad will you, he'll belt me for fighting and I don't want that to happen. You won't tell him will you, please." Now there was a surprise, it took me off guard and I started to feel sorry for him. "Just sit there at the front and do your maths and I'll think it over." A tearful "Yes sir," came back and he went over to the desk at the front and sat down. "Can someone get Alfie's math books out of his desk please and pass them forward to him." This was done in the silent class room. I went through the maths exercise with examples on the board and then the children had to complete the exercise in their books. Just as the children started in walked Janet, the girl who had taken the injured boy, whose name I was told was Matthew, came into the class room. I made a mental note that I must get to know all the children's names before the end of this week. I did intend to get to know them all by the end of last week but that didn't happen. It's very hard when certain children are very nondescript and quiet. You always get to know the names of those children who are loud and forward.

"How's Matthew?" I asked. "Miss said that he will live and that he will be staying with her until dinner time then he will be going home as Miss isn't sure if his nose is broken or not." said Janet. "Miss said that she will see you at dinner time and explain things," went on Janet. "Thank you Janet, "I said," Now get you maths books out and I will show you what we are doing in this lesson." For the next thirty minutes the class worked in almost silence and I walked round checking each child's work and explaining various things if they were stuck with their work. "Finish the sum you are doing and pass your books to the front please. Put you text books in your desk and we'll see who is ready to go for lunch." I turned to Alfie and said," Alfie stay where you are and we'll have a quick chat when the class has gone." The children sat in their seats waiting for the bell to go. I took this opportunity to remind them about their behaviour and the television programmes we could be watching. You could almost hear a pin drop, talk about the power of television. The bell went and told the children to stand and lead out row by row, and then I turned to Alfie, who was standing near his desk. "Now then, young man, have you anything to say about your behaviour?" I said. Alfie looked at me with tears in his eyes, "I'm sorry and I'll try to behave and I'll be friends with Matthew and I won't fight with him anymore. Can I go for dinner now sir?" As he had been quite all through the lesson and he seemed to have remorse I said, "OK Alfie, but remember if you fight with him again I'll have to send you to Mr Percy. Go and get your dinner and let this be the end of it." As Alfie went out of the door I turned and got my sandwiches and started out of the door then remembered that Janet has said that Mrs Silby wanted to see me.

I made my way across the playground; the weather looked as though it might rain this afternoon. I must get a wet playtime box as soon as possible as the weather wasn't going to get any better this term. Mrs Silby was in a room near the school entrance as that she was able to see parents easy if the need arose. As I got there she was in the room and when she saw me she got up from her chair and asked me into the room. "Nicola Thompson from my class said that you wanted to see me," I said. "Yes," she said, "Please sit down. Do you want a cup of tea?" "No thanks, I'll get one in the staff room when I have my sandwiches. Why did you want to see me?" I asked. "I understand from Nicola that Alfie Underwood was the one who hit Matthew Armitage. It was quite bad; it took some time before his nose stopped bleeding. He was rather frightened so I saw Mr Percy to say that I thought he should go home and he agreed. I got word to his mother and she picked him up just before the dinner time bell went. He should be fine in the morning and will be back in school. Do you know anything about Alfie Underwood?" she asked. "No," I said, "I have had a word with him and segregated him in the class for the morning and spoke to him before he went to dinner. I explained how wrong it was to fight, especially with boys in our own class. Earlier when we first went into class was a bit worried when I mention his dad. He even started to cry." "Well yes, that's the problem," went on Mrs Silby, "Alfie is looked after by his grandmother, his mother went off a few years ago, and I don't blame her as her husband used to beat her. She has turned up at school in the past with black eyes covered very badly with makeup to hide them and bruises on her arms and legs. However when she left she never took Alfie with her and he has been looked after ever since by his grandmother. His dad turns up every now and again but he seems to blame Alfie for his wife leaving him. Occasionally he tends to be a bit too handy with his fists and Alfie has been in the firing line on a few occasions. Alfie, for some strange reason, adores his dad and defends him so when a bruise appears on his arm he wouldn't tell who'd done it, which makes it very hard for all concerned. Deep down Alfie is a very nice kid but insecure and has to be handled carefully. His dad is the problem. He can be violent especially when he has had a drink and because of that he has been sent to prison a few times. When he is in prison Alfie is a different kid altogether. But when he's out it's a different situation and at the moment he is out of prison." I took this in and considered the situation carefully. "What if I gave Alfie some kind of responsibility in the class? Do you think that might help?" I asked. "It could help," she said, "But think it through first before making any rash decisions. By the way, the boy who was at the end of Alfie's fist, Matthew Armitage, well he is a bit of a Mummy's boy and tends to wind the others up. Because of his small size he thinks that he can get away with things. Obviously today he didn't. He wasn't hurt too bad but when his mother showed up the tears began to roll and she fell for it. She'll be getting him comics, sweets and other things this afternoon to make him feel better. Keep your eye on him in the morning just in case he might try to work some more time off school by goading someone else to hit him. I wouldn't put it past him to try, just for the comics and sweets. Anyway I am keeping you from your lunch but I thought I would have a word with you about these two boys, I checked it with Mr Percy first by the way. Also if you want to have any more details about others in your class just come and see me. If you go to Mr Percy about background of pupils in your class he will only send you to me." "Thank you very much Mrs Silby. I'll take in what you have told me. I'll see how Alfie is this afternoon and in the morning I'll keep my eye on Matthew. Right I better be going to the staff room and get my lunch then I have to get my lessons ready for this afternoon," I replied. "Sylvia," she said, "My name is Sylvia that is when the kids aren't around. Don't forget, anything you want to know about the kids come and see me." "Thanks again," I said and got up and made my way to the staff room.

When I got to the staff room I looked around for a chair to sit on. Better not make the same mistake as last week, I thought, and sit in someone's chair. In the corner were Miss Stark and Mrs Cook who saw me looking around the room. They waved and ushered me to sit with them. I walked over and asked, "Is this anyone's chair?" "Yes, yours," said Miss. Stark with a grin, "Get yourself a cup of tea then come and make yourself comfortable with us." I placed my sandwiches on the chair and went over to the sink to get a cup and make myself a cup of tea. "There's one in the pot and it's just been made," said a voice from the other side of the room. I turned and said thanks to the unknown voice. Again I was very careful which cup to choose, I didn't want to cause any more problems by using someone else's cup. I looked in the cupboard and saw at least half a dozen cups that were all the same. Better get one of those, I thought, at least they are all the same and can't be special. Cup of tea made I went back to my chair. "How are you getting on?" said Mrs Cook, "You have most of the children that I had in my class a few years ago." "Not bad," I said, "But I had a bit of a problem with two of the boys this morning though." "Let me guess; was one of them by chance Alfie Underwood?" I look at her amazed, "How did you know?" "Well," she continued, "It's the start of a new school year for one thing and for a second his dad has just come out of prison the other week. He always tends to be a bit on the aggressive side when his dad's home. His dad has been known to be violent and Alfie is both scared of him and proud of him in a strange way. Something must have happened over the weekend and Alfie takes it out on someone smaller than he is, someone like Matthew Armitage for example. I did ask Mr Percy that those two shouldn't be in the same class as each other as it's such a temptation for Alfie to bully Matthew who won't stand up for himself." "That's exactly right. Alfie hit Matthew about some argument, is Superman stronger than Batman and because Matthew didn't agree with him he hit him, he might have broken his nose. Anyway Matthew's mother came and took him home. I had a talk with Alfie about being friends with each other, especially with children in our own class. He did start crying at the thought of his dad finding out about the incident. Mrs Silby wanted to see me before I came here and she explained some of Alfie's background about his grandmother looking after him." "One of the best things you could do is to try and keep Alfie occupied. Do that and he should be no bother. That's what I did and it works. Just a small job he could do on a regular basis and if he starts to misbehave then the threat of losing that job should be a good deterrent to keep him on the straight and narrow in class." said Mrs Cook. "That's a great idea, could you tell me a quick way of remembering the children's names, four days in and I still can't remember a quarter of the children's names and it's getting embarrassing for me. I can't keep pointing at children and say you," I asked. Miss Stark answered, "Get them to make name place cards for their desks and if you move a child to another part of the class they take their name place card with them. It makes a good art lesson too. Get some A4 cards from the stock cupboard; make sure you only choose two colours, one for girls and one for boys. Get them to measure half way long ways and fold the card so that it can stand up on their desk and you can see it from the front. Make sure they put their names on the front in block capitals properly spaced so it fills the card and then they can decorate the rest of the card in light colours so that their name stands out more. It would be a good idea too if you made one yourself with your name on it and show it to the class what the finished item should look like. It makes a good lesson and if you encourage the children to do their best and take their time it should take the lesson to playtime. Also no more forgetting the children's names unless they start swapping cards with each other then you have problems." "Thanks, that's great. I'll have my lunch, get some card and go over to class and get one done before the bell goes for this afternoon's lessons," I said. So my problem of getting to know the children's names would soon be over. I finished my lunch and asked the way to the stockroom and was told I would have to ask Mr Percy for the key and what I wanted from stock.

I left the staff room and made my way to Mr Percy's room, knocked on his door and waited for the "Come in." He was sat behind his desk reading the morning paper; he looked up and saw me. "Yes, can I help you?" he asked. "Could I get some card from the stock room please, I've been told that you have the key and I need some for my lesson this afternoon," I said. "You are supposed to order stock for the week on a Monday morning and the stock monitors from the top class will deliver it on a Monday afternoon. I suppose that I am at fault for not telling you that earlier. Oh by the way I understand that you had a bit of trouble in your class this morning with Alfie Underwood but Mrs Silby has put you in the picture with that boy and his family background. If you have any trouble with anyone in class that you can't handle send them to me. OK?" he said. "Now here's the key for the stockroom, made sure you lock it afterwards. What was it you wanted?" he asked. "Some coloured card for this afternoon's lesson," I replied. "That will be on the second shelf on the right as you go into the stockroom," he said without having to think about it. I was gob smacked that he knows straight away where the card was. I took the key and thanked him and said that I would be right back as soon as I had the card. I left his room and went to the stock room after he told me where it was. The stock room was on the top floor of the building, same floor as the library and I shuddered and said to myself that I wasn't going to get locked into anymore rooms up here. I found the stockroom and unlocked the door and went in. The light switch was near the door as you went in. I turned the light on and behold it was like a stationary Aladdin's cave. There must have been everything that you would ever need. Now what did Mr Percy say, second shelf on the right as I go in. Yes, there it is, coloured card. I took two lots of twenty sheets of different colours and having a final look around came out and locked the door. I took the key back to Mr Percy. "Did you get the card?" he asked, "And filled the book in?" "Filled the book?" I said. "Yes filled the book in, by the sound of it you didn't. There is a book as you walk in and in it is the record of stock that has been taken out. This is so we can keep a record of how much stock we use and when to re order more stock for which items. Let me see, twenty blue and twenty pink sheets of A four card. I'll make a note of that and fill the book in for you. But next time you do it. "While you are here I haven't seen your report book from last week. All staff must hand in their report books each Monday morning so that I can go through them. As your mentor I have a special interest of how you are getting on with your teaching. You have got your report book, haven't you?" "Err no, I wasn't given one," I said nervously. "You should have been given one when you started last week, but given the theatrical start you made last week, no wonder I forgot to give you one," he said and then went over to a cupboard in the corner and pulled out a thick red hard-backed book came over. "Put your name and class on this. Each day you fill it in outlining the subject and content of each lesson you teach, then on a Monday morning you hand it in and I'll get it back to you at the end of the day so that you can fill it in for that day. Also keep your marking of the pupils books up to date as I might ask for a set of pupil's books and check that they have been marked and that they correspond to the lessons you have put down in your report book. As the first week is always hit and miss regarding finding the levels of the children and as they have just come back from the school holidays and usually have forgotten some basic things in various lessons we don't start the report books until the first full week back at school, which is this week. Here's your book, if you have any problems see me as I am your mentor for this year," and with this he handed over the report book. I thanked him and turned to go when he boomed out," Key please," and the put his hand out for the key. I had forgotten that I was still hold the stock room key, "Oh sorry," I mumbled and handed over the key and left.

I went back to my class room and got to work making a nameplate with my name on it. It took me about 10 minutes or so and the finished product looked quite good. If I got the children started as soon as the register had been taken then it should take them up to playtime to get it finished. I looked at my watch, quarter past six; I must get a new watch soon. It's no good knowing the minutes if the hours are all wrong, but the watch looks good and flash. Never mind, a new watch it must be. Nearly time for the bell, just enough time to go to the loo and back here in time for the start of the afternoon. That afternoon went like a dream. I explained how to make the name plate with examples on the board. Block writing, bubble writing any type of writing so long as it was big and spaced out on the card and could be read from the front of the class. Then the children spent time colouring in the card and I must admit that there were some good pieces of work done by some of the children. Others needed my help and suggestions but before we all knew it playtime came round. Some of the children were so engrossed that they wanted to stay in to finish their cards off. Success, I thought, children wanting to stay in rather than going out to play. The rest of the afternoon went well. No problems with playtime. When the children came back a few still hadn't finished so I decided that we would have story time giving time for those who hadn't finished to finish and the other were to sit and listen to the story. I was quite enjoying reading Robinson Crusoe and it seemed to grab the children's attention. It wasn't too long and the home time bell was ringing. After school had finished I went to find Mr Percy and see how many had filled in the television list and what were the chances that I might be successful for the Friday afternoon slot. As it happen, as I was on my way to the staff room, he was walking down the corridor. "Har, just the man I was looking for," he said, "Just to let you know, your request for the television on a

Friday afternoon is OK. Mrs Peterson will be having it on Tuesday and Friday mornings and then it will be free for the rest of the day. Remember that Mr Sharpe has the music room at dinner time so you will have to get things ready at afternoon playtime if you want to use it." "Thanks fine," I said, "Thank you for letting me know. Can I send for the programme notes that will accompany the programme as they start a week on Friday?" "Yes that will be fine; Mrs Grant will have all the details in the school office. This is a great opportunity for the school you know, having our own colour television for lessons. I don't know why more of our staff hasn't taken up the offer of using it. I suppose they might start using it when those who are to report back about how useful it is. I must get going, have a nice evening," said Mr. Percy. "Yes you too," I replied. I knew that Mrs Grant wouldn't be in her office at this time of the day so I better get in early and see her in the morning and get the notes for the television programme. I had a feeling that this was going to be a good week.

Chapter Five

The next day I was in early so that I could make sure I saw Mrs Grant before school started and order the television notes that I wanted to go with the programme that I had booked. Then I was going to double check with Mr Sharpe that I was going to be OK with the music lesson programmes that I had booked. After all he was the music teacher and I didn't want to step on his toes, so to speak. I would also add that the preparation to the lessons depended on art and craft lessons as according to the outline of the programme which was called "Making Music" the children had to make their own instruments before seeing the lesson on the television. When watching the programme they would then accompany the presenter with the music played. For me it was going to be a win/win situation. Art and craft lesson in the week and then a music lesson, the only problem I could foresee was what type of instruments the children supposed to make and what materials were they going to be made of. I would find all this out when I get the programmes notes sometimes later in the week. The television programme was due to start at the beginning of October and there would be four programmes before half term and then four afterwards. Then it would be a short time before Christmas preparations would start.

Mrs Grant was in her office and I asked if she could send for the notes that I wanted for the television programme. She took a note of what I wanted and said that they would be ordered today. She looked through the television guide and saw that there was a telephone number she could ring which meant that I should have the programme notes by the end of this week. I thanked her and went to the staff room to find Mr Sharpe. He was sat in the corner with a coffee talking to Tony Telford about some up and coming football match that was being played on Saturday. I joined them and, when I could, told Mr Sharpe about my intentions about the television programme and if it would be alright, and as he was the music teacher I didn't want to step on his toes, so to speak. He backed it all the way saying "I wish more teachers would take an interest in music in this school. If you need any help, please ask." I thanked him and left him and Tony to carry on with their discussion about the football match. I looked at my watch, twenty to one. I must get myself a watch, I thought, because one day this one is going to be right and I won't believe it and that could cause me some trouble. Mr Percy came in to do his briefing. "Thank you all for replying to the television timetable. I was hoping more of you would have taken the opportunity but never mind. Those of you who have filled in the timetable have got the slots you wanted and there are more slots to fill for those of you who might change their mind. If you are one of those, see me later, the timetable will be open until the end of this week. There is nothing more to report and as it's nearly time for the bell I suggest you all go and collect your classes from the yard." We all took the hint and started to leave the staff room and go down to the yard to collect our class. When I reached mine, Mark and Terry were at the front standing smart and straight and waiting for me. "Sir," said Mark, "Freddie and Timmy are still away. Can Terry and me collect the milk again, please, sir?" "Er, yes OK. You did a good job of it yesterday. Make sure you do the same again today. You're both staying school dinners today aren't you? I'll mark it in the register. Go and get the milk please. The rest of you into class please," I said. Mark and Terry went rushing off to get the milk. As she went past me Nicola said, "Do you think it was a good idea to send Mark and Terry for the milk again sir?" "You said that yesterday, Nicola, and things seemed OK then. Unless you know something that I don't," I replied. Now this got me thinking, what did she know that I didn't. I followed the class and told them to sit down and take out their reading books while I did the registers. When all this was done I got the children lined up ready to go to assembly. We went across the yard into the main school building and on to the assembly hall. As we walked across the yard I began to think what it might be like in winter, or even when it rains. What do we do then – get wet and cold I suppose. I think I should ask some of the other teachers why my class was outside in the prefab and not in the main school building. Up to now the children seemed to be well behaved, yes there have been a few little incidents, but I'm sure other classes have had the same sort of behaviour. We got to the hall and the children made their way to our place. Other classes made their way to their places and very soon the hall was full and quiet. Just then two children came rushing into the hall, stopped then started walking to our class line. It was Mark and Terry, and when they saw me looking at them they both smiled and went to their place. Nicola's warning came to mind, "Do you think it was a good idea to send Mark and Terry for the milk?" Now, as I thought of it, Freddie and Timmy have the milk back in our class before we set off for assembly, so why do Mark and Terry take so long. I'll have to look into this. Mr Yardley seems to be late this morning I thought, most unlike him. The children were beginning to get fidgety and started to shuffle their feet. Just then Mr Yardley came into the hall from the back, nodded to each member of staff as he passed by and every now and again looked down the children's lines saying, "Yes very good," or "Straighten up there at the end," and so on. He went up on the stage and started with the good news about the new television set that had been delivered yesterday and that various teachers would be using it with their classes very soon. He went on about it being a privilege of being one of the few schools in the town that had been chosen to get a television set, especially a colour television set. He went on to other things but I was thinking about the logistics of my class being out in the prefab having to come to the music room and then having to go back to the class room at the end of the lesson, I dismiss them and then have to go back to the music room to tidy the place up and lock the television set away. Unless they took all the things they needed to go home over to the music room then I could send them home from the music room. Sorted. Mr Sharpe was at his piano ready with the hymn. He played the introduction, popped up from his chair, shouted, "Now," and sat back down to carry on playing the piano while the school started singing the hymn. Again, I got to thinking, one day that will go wrong and the chair will collapse.

As soon as the assembly was finished Mr Percy came over to me and said, "You must have settled in with your class by now so Mr Yardley is going to come and see you teach your children. He'll be in this afternoon and observe your lesson." "Yes, OK, Mr Percy, this afternoon," I said, rather surprised. Well that came out of the blue. I knew that I would be assessed at some time during the term but today well I'd better make a good impression. I know, I'll use a tip that I was given when I was on teaching practice training. Left hand and right hand.

I got the children back to our class room and started the first lesson, maths. After playtime I would teach an English lesson that would be partly repeated this afternoon when Mr Yardley was in the class observing. That way the children should have some idea of getting the answers right when I asked them. I would use the left hand, right hand tip that I had been given. Basically the children will put their hands up when I ask a question. They are told beforehand that if they know the answer to the question then they put their right hand up, right answer right hand, however if they don't know the answer then they put their left hand up so giving the impression that more children know the answers to the questions I'm asking. Anyone watching would think that the children are a lot brighter than they are. I must admit that it worked very well for me when I was being observed when I was on my teaching practice. My tutor even complimented me on how the children were so eager to answer questions when I asked them. If it worked then it should work now. The morning passed rather quickly. The children were primed about this afternoon's lesson when Mr Yardley would be in the room. Nouns, verbs and adjectives was the subject to be taught with a writing exercise to follow. We had a practice in our lesson before dinner and most of the children got the idea of what each was and how to use them. I was sure that they wouldn't forget in the few hours until Mr Yardley was in the room. Anyway, too late now as it was time for dinner, the bell went and the children left to the culinary delights of school dinners

    I went over to the staff room with my packed lunch. I also remembered to bring my own mug so that there would be no confusion of which I should use. My mug was quite distinctive with "I'm backing Britain" slogan over a union flag on the side. I wasn't trying to make a point or back Harold Wilson, our prime minister, it was just that I bought the mug from a shop that was closing down and they were selling them off cheap. So cheap in fact that I went mad and bought four, always come in handy I thought at the time. When I went into the staff room I looked around for a seat. Miss Stark and Mrs Cook were in the corner, saw me, and waved me over to sit in a seat near them. I acknowledged them and went over. I gave my thanks, put my packed lunch on the seat and said, "I'll just go over and get a cup of tea. Do you want one?" They both pointed to the table at two cups of coffee and said, "No thanks, we've already got ours." I went over to the sink and put a teabag into my mug and made my drink. "How's your day going?" asked Miss Stark. "Fine," I said, "Mr Percy. said that Mr. Yardley will be coming into my lesson this afternoon to observe my teaching and I'm a bit nervous about it." "You'll be fine. He'll come in about 1-30 stay about ten to fifteen minutes and go. Make sure the children stand when he comes into the room, he'll expect that. He will want you to ask children questions as you go through the lesson, just to make sure that they are listening and understanding what you are teaching. It's very rare that he stays for the full lesson but if he does just carry on as though he isn't there. When the children are working in their books make sure they do it in silence, he doesn't like it when children are talking when they are supposed to be working. Main thing is, don't worry, it will be all right, if it isn't he'll get Mr. Percy to help you put things right," said Mrs Cook in a supportive way. We spent the next half an hour talking about this and that, where was I living, did I live by myself. Miss Stark asked if I had a girlfriend. I said that I didn't have one in particular and that there was a few of us that went out in a group and the weekend. We were keen ten pin bowlers and also enjoyed watching rugby and football. Mrs Cook said that Ivan Jenkins was a big Welsh rugby union fan and he would go all over to support the international team. Once he missed school on the Monday because he had missed his train after going to see them in France. Mr Yardley wasn't happy but one of the school Governers is a big rugby union fan and sided with Ivan and said he had a valid excuse for missing school that day. Miss Stark started asking me about ten pin bowling and was it easy to play, what sort of shoes did you need, how did you score, how many can play. I was nearly tempted to ask her out for a game at the weekend but then thought better of it. I looked at my watch, nearly a quarter to four, blast this hour hand. A new watch should be on the top of the spending list when I get my first wages I thought. I bid a good day to Mrs Cook and Miss Stark and explained that I would have to get to my class room and get ready for this afternoon's lesson. I picked up my bits and pieces and went over to the sink to wash out my mug. "Are you a big supporter then?" asked Mr Thomas pointing to my mug. At first I didn't know what he was on about then realised that he was pointing to the outside of the mug and the "I'm backing Britain," slogan. "Oooh no, not really, it's just that I got the mug cheap. You see they were selling them off cheap and as I hadn't any mugs I bought some. I'm not a political person, you see. Not that I had anything against Harold Wilson or any other politicians it's just they were cheap." "Steady on, I was just making conversation. I didn't mean to have a political debate about backing Britain, or anything else as it goes," said Mr Thomas with a smile. I muttered, "I need to get back to my class room and get some things ready for this afternoon. Please excuse me." With that I left the staff room and made my way to my class room.

Everything was ready, the bell was ringing and the children were starting to line up outside. As I went out to meet them one of the children called out "Alfie Underwood has been fighting again, sir, and the dinner lady has taken him to Mr Percy." "Yes thank you," I said," Go into class and sit down. Get your reading books out and start silent reading." Now was this a good thing or a bad thing that Alfie was with Mr Percy. Would Mr Percy bring him over to my lesson when Mr Yardley was observing me, but if Alfie was in one of his moods he might disrupt the whole class and that would be bad? Would Mr Percy keep him with him, there was no way of saying at this point in time. I might as well play it by ear. I followed the children into class sat down at my desk and called out the register. I marked Alfie present and asked Janet to take the register back to the office to Mrs Grant. I looked at my watch, twenty five past seven; yes a new watch was definitely needed soon. I told the children to stop reading and close their books. "Remember, we are on our best behaviour this afternoon. Mr Yardley wants to see some good work from you all and also how well you listen and put your hands up to the questions I ask. Don't forget, right hand for right answer and left hand for wrong answer. If you are not sure don't put your hand up. It wouldn't look too good if you all had your hands up all the time," I explained. "Get your Junior English books out and your English exercise book, turn to page twenty six in your book and in your exercise book put down the date and the title of the work we are doing which is Nouns, Verbs and Adjectives. I'll put the title on the board for you to copy," I turned and saw that Janet had walked into the room. "Sir, Mr Percy saw me and said that he will be keeping Alfie in his room until playtime and then he wants to see you at playtime," she said. "Thank you Janet," I said quite relieved that Alfie would be out of the way when Mr Yardley as in the class room observing, "Go to your seat and get your English books out, write the date and the title."

Janet went to her seat, got her books out and just as she was about to start writing Mr Yardley walked into the room. I gestured to the class to stand up, which, to my surprise did straight away and in silence too. Mr Yardley looked at me, then the class and smiled. "Very good children, very good and very smart too. Please sit down. I'll be sitting at the back of the class for a while so please take no notice of me, just carry on with your lesson as you usually do."

With that he went to the back of the class, found himself a chair, sat down and nodded to me. I took that as a sign that I should start the lesson, which I did and the children were very attentive and alert, which was a bit off putting for me. I glanced over to see what Mr Yardley was doing. He seemed to be looking round the class room and writing things down, I'd better get on with the lesson I thought. The introduction of nouns, verb and adjectives went well and then I started to ask questions. "What is a noun?" I asked. A sea of hands went up in front of me. I looked for a right hand that was raised and I must say there were quite a few, definitely more than left hands. "Yes Susan, tell me what a noun is," I said. "It's a naming word, sir, it is the name of a particular person, place or thing," she replied. "Yes, that's right," I said, as I thought to myself a perfect answer in all ways. I then started to ask for examples, again hands were going up all over the class and as always I pick the right hands that were raised. The same went for the definition of verbs, then adjectives. I wrote various words on the blackboard and asked if they were nouns, verbs or adjectives, again hands were going up, some left hands and some right hands, there were only a few with no hands up, which was good in a way. Mr Yardley was still looking round and making notes. Time seemed to be flying by, and then Mr Yardley got up and walked to the front of the class. "That's very good children. I'm pleased to see that so many of you have had your hands up to answer the questions. Now can anyone tell me, is a desk a noun, verb or adjective," he asked. Nice simple question, I thought, and I looked around the class. Nearly all right hands in the air just three with their left hands up. Mr Yardley pointed to Matthew and said, "Yes, you boy, what's the answer?" Matthew looked rather blank that he had been chosen and said, "I don't know, I think I've got the wrong hand up cause I don't know the answer." Mr Yardley looked at me. I had to think quick, "Matthew sometimes gets confused with things but likes to put his hand up to try to answer questions," I said, hoping to sound convincing. Trust him to ask someone who didn't know his left hand from his right. As Mr Yardley was looking at me I noticed a few of the left hands were being put down. Maybe the children were latching on to only put your hand up if you know the answer. "Yes, you," he said pointing to Nicola. "A desk, sir, is a noun and if you put adjectives in front of the noun it will make the noun more descriptive. A desk can't be a verb because it's not a doing word, you can't do a desk, that's right, sir, isn't it," she replied with an angelic smile on her face. Mr Yardley looked surprised with the answer and said, "Yes that's right and a very good answer. Well I'd better not take any more of your time. Can I see you after school please in my office," he said looking at me. "Yes, sir," I said," I'll see you as soon as school is over."

Mr Yardley left and I carried on with the lesson. Someone asked how they had done and I said that I was pleased the way they had all behaved and had answered the questions. Within no time it seemed that the lesson was over and playtime was here. I then remembered that I had to go and see Mr Percy about Alfie. My cup of tea would have to wait. I went to his room and knocked on the door. "Come in," he shouted. I went in and saw that Alfie was sitting at a small desk in the corner writing. "Ah, yes, come in, sit down," he said indicating a chair to sit on, "Alfie and I have had a long conversation about his behaviour and how it affects other people. He has spent the last hour writing letters of apology to those people he has let down. I think that you are on his list to get one as I think you had a word with him yesterday about the incident he had with Matthew Armitage. I'll keep him here until the end of school and if there is any more trouble this week we will have his mother or father in school and let them know what's happening. You did get an incident book with the teacher's pack I gave you along with the time tables and holiday list and things. This must be recorded in the book along with yesterday's incident with Matthew. Your incident book has to be kept up to date and be available should myself or Mr Yardley will want to see it. Understand?" I nodded and looked at Alfie writing at the desk. Anyone seeing him now would almost think he was an angel, well almost an angel. He had that sort of face, a face that could get away with murder. "Is it OK to go and get a cup of tea before break finishes?" I asked. "Oh yes, please do, and don't forget that Mr Yardley want to see you after school. He already has had a word with me about the observation lesson and he wants to talk to you about it. Off you go and get your cup of tea," he said waving his hand for me to leave. As I made my way to the staff room I wondered what Mr Yardley had said to Mr Percy about my teaching. Had Mr Yardley twigged about the right hand left hand con with the answers to the questions? Well, I would soon find out as there was just over an hour to go.

An hour and a quarter later I was making my way to Mr Yardley's room. I knocked on his door and waited for the green light to turn on. It lit up almost immediately and I went in. "Yes, come in and sit down," he said pointing to a chair in front of his desk. Nervously I sat down and waited as he started flicking through some hand written notes and nodding to himself, then he looked at me. "Yes, yes, I think we'll have you out of there," he said, "Not good for you or the children, the sooner the better I think." I thought I was going to faint, this is the end of my teaching after only six days, "Yes, if you think that's for the best. When do you want me to go?" I said, trying to be brave with a stiff upper lip. "I'll have a word with Mr Percy and I think you will be out by the end of Friday this week," he said. He then looked at his notes again, "Oh by the way I was impressed with your teaching this afternoon. The children were very attentive and were also keen to answer your questions when asked. You seemed to have a good rapport already with the children in your class and they seem to like you, which helps. Well if that's it, you can go. I'll put my report about today's lesson in your personal file. Close the door behind you as you go out. Good afternoon." I rose from my seat and went out of the room and closed the door behind me. This was it then, I'd better start looking for another job. Would I be able to get another teaching job if they have got rid of me from this one, what sort of reference would they give me if any? Also all the schools will have their schools fully staffed for this term already. I went back across the yard to my class room, yes my class room. What do I tell the children? Do I tell the children or will that be the job of Mr Percy next Monday when I don't appear in school. I picked up my lunchbox and put it in my briefcase. I better take these as well, I thought, as I put the English exercise books in the brief case as well. I could sit here and mark them now but I wasn't in the mood. I'll do them tonight at home, it will give me something to do. I went to the door and looked around and thought, well it was good while it lasted. I was just starting to enjoy it, starting to get used to the children and their ways although I was still unsure of a few of their names. Maybe, when I leave on Friday, they will still be the unknown names of my class. I looked at my watch, half past ten, and thought maybe that the new watch won't be so high on the agenda after all. I got to the bus stop and realised that I had just missed the bus and the next one would be in fifteen minutes time. Never mind I could wait; I was in no hurry to get home. Fifteen minutes later and bang on time came the bus. There were three others in the queue by now. It stopped and as I was getting on I heard the conductor shout out, "Oh no, it's the frogman. Have you got any more pets with you today then, Sir? Any insects, rodents, reptiles, creepy crawlies or any other of God's creatures in your bag or on your person? And will you expect us to be a money changing service or will you have the right fare this time?" That's all I needed, I looked at him and said, "None of those things you have mentioned, it's just me going to the terminus and yes I have the right money for my fare this time." With that I made my way to an empty seat and sat down. The other passengers got on the bus, found their way to their seats and the bus move off after the conductor rang the bell. He came over to me and I had the one and three pence already for him for my fare. He looked at me and took the fare in silence and gave me my ticket.

Breakfast next morning was, as usual, a marmalade sandwich and a cup of tea although this morning it wasn't rushed as I was up early as I was awake before the alarm had gone off thinking of what I was to do. The journey to school was that morning very nondescript, I was looking out of the window but not seeing things if that makes sense. My mind was on what was going to happen today in school and whatever was happening through the window of the bus was not registering with my mind. I arrived at the school and decided that I would go over to my class room and drop off my bag then go over to the staff room. I wondered if the staff would already know that Friday was going to be my last day, well I would soon find out when I got there. On my way up the stairs to the staff room Tony Telford saw me. "Just the man," he said, "Mr Percy wants to see you straight away. I was just going over to your class room to get you."

"Thanks, Tony," I said, "Did he say what he wanted by any chance?" "No, he just said that he wanted to see you before school starts. It must be important because he's given the morning briefing to Ivan to be read out to the staff. Well I'll get back to the staff room. See you later. Cheers," and with that he made his way back up the stairs. Well this is it, I thought, better get it over with. I made my way to Mr Percy's room and knocked on his door. "Come in," his voice rang out. I went in. He was sitting at his desk, "Yes, come in and sit down," he said, "Do you want a cup of coffee, real coffee?" and he pointed to a cafetiere, which was on a table against the wall, and was giving out such a wonderful smell of coffee. "Much better than the instant muck in the staff room. Please have a cup." He went over and got two cups, "Milk or do you have it black and what about sugar. It's got to be brown sugar in real coffee you know." "Err, yes milk and one sugar," I said rather stunned. Was this the equivalent to the last meal the condemned man has I thought. He placed the cup of coffee on the desk in front of me. "Now down to business," he said, "Mr Yardley saw you yesterday and he's given me his report so that I can have a word with you about it." He lifted a file that was open and inside were some loose pages, Mr Percy lifted one of them up pointed to it with his other hand and said, "This is not on, you know. We can't have this. It's not right for you or the children. Soon the weather will change and it will make things very difficult." I sat there looking at him, not knowing whether to sip my coffee or wait until it had cooled down and drink it in two goes. Hang on; what's he going on about the weather for? I'd better say something, "I have tried my best with the children," I started but before I could continue Mr Percy said "Yes we know and you seem to be doing a good job. Mr Yardley was impressed with your lesson yesterday and how well the children answered the questions especially when he asked about is a desk a noun, verb or adjective and the answer he got from Nicola, was it. The lesson notes are all here and it will be in your personal file. So he has decided that you will move out on Friday as he doesn't want it to go on any longer." I gave him a puzzled look but inside various emotions were building up inside me. Why, if Mr Yardley had given me a good report about my lesson yesterday did I have to move out. I better ask why this was happening as I was feeling angry inside now. "Moving out, Mr Percy, after I seem to get a good report from Mr Yardley. But why?" I asked. "It was only temporary you know; didn't you know that. I'm sure that it was mentioned when you first came here. No, but, yes we had somewhat of a disaster that first day didn't we. Yes, it must have been overlooked. I'm sorry; I thought you knew that it would happen sometime soon. We wanted it done before half term and before the weather started to get bad. It would be rather cold out there, especially if we have a bad winter, and one is forecast this year," he replied. "Mr Johnson will move all your things, you know. You just have to put all your things and the children's books in boxes and he will see to it that they are all moved." He must have seen the confused look on my face, "You don't know, do you," he asked. "Don't know what?" I stammered, "I thought I would be here until my years' probation was over. I didn't know that I would be out by Friday." "Out of your class room, man, your class room. You were only in the prefab until the year four class room was ready. During the last week of the summer holidays the class room had a water leak which made a mess of the electrics in the room and had to be re wired and the floor had to be taken up along with the skirting boards and part of the lower part of the wall had to be re plastered. Then there was the repainting, all of which has just been completed yesterday, so now the class room is ready and waiting. Did you think that you were being sacked and moving out. Oh dear, I'm sorry dear boy, you must have been feeling very insecure, if that's the right word on this occasion. No, your teaching observation that Mr Yardley did yesterday was a pass. You're fine. It's nearly time for the bell. Oh by the way this has come for you. I believe it's the lesson notes for your "Making music" television programme that Mrs Grant sent for you. Last lesson on a Friday afternoon, it's marked down on the television timetable." He gave me the timetable and the notes as I got up from the chair. I then realised that Friday was the day that I was on yard duty. "I'm on yard duty on a Friday," I said, "Would it be alright to swap duty with another member of staff?" "Not many of the staff like having duty on a Friday, so you might just swap the afternoon break so that you can get the television ready for your lesson but it would mean that you still would have to see the children off the premises at home time," he replied. I thanked him and left the room. Outside I didn't know how to feel, relief yes and excitement, not only have I a new class room but lesson notes and time booked for the television on a Friday. Someone up there must be smiling on me. This is going to be a good day I thought, no, this <u>will</u> be a good day I reassured myself.

The bell went and I went over to the prefab to my class who were waiting outside. There was a bit of a problem. Freddie and Timmy were back at school but Mark and Terry wanted to collect the milk as they had been doing it all week. I pointed out that it was Freddie and Timmy's job to get the milk and ordered them to go and get it. I told Mark and Terry that they were the reserve milk monitors and they only get the milk if either Freddie or Timmy were away from school. I told the class to go in and get their reading books out and start reading in silence. I took the register and the dinner register and then told the children the good news that we would be moving class room and the end of the week. Most of the children seemed please although there were a couple that didn't seem too pleased about the move. I also told the children the good news that we would be having the television on a Friday afternoon, following a programme called "Making music." Freddie and Timmy came in with the milk and put the crate in the usual corner, "That was quick," I said, and I looked over to Mark and Terry who just shrugged their shoulders and looked out of the window.

The rest of the week went well with no mishaps along the way. On Friday afternoon I had got some boxes from Mr Johnson and the children put their exercise and text books in them, which mean that for the last lesson in the afternoon it was story time. I had to wear my coat at playtime as it was rather chilly thankfully it wasn't windy. Windy weather has a strange effect on children. They get very excited and silly and if you look at statistics more playground accidents happen when the weather has been windy. This afternoon's break went well; children seemed well behaved although I was at the infants end and away from the older children. Ivan Jenkins was at the other end of the playground with the older children and I couldn't see him having any trouble with those children. After break it was back to the prefab for the last time. We were still ploughing our way through Robison Crusoe, and I felt, like the children must have been thinking, that I should have picked a better book to read to them. Never mind, I had started so I was determined to finish. Home time came at last and I dismissed the children, reminding them that on Monday morning they were to line up at the side of the school with the other class rather than lining up in front of the prefab. As I was the duty teacher for the day I went along with the children to the cloakroom and supervised the children leaving the school. Within ten minutes the place was empty, even most of the staff and made tracks and gone. I went back over to the prefab and started putting my bits and pieces in box when Mr Johnson appeared with his trolley. "I'll get these boxes moved now, if you don't mind", he said, "I'll put them in your new class room and you can sort them out there. Is that box of yours to go with the rest as well?" "Yes, please," I replied," I'll give you a hand with the boxes and I'll come over to the new class room and get some of the books sorted. Is there a big store cupboard in the class room?" "Yes, there's lots of storage room there, much more than here," he said. It didn't take us long and the trolley was loaded. "Anything else to go?" he asked. I looked round the room, "No, that's all I think. Let's go," I said and we made our way over to the main building.

My new class room was on the ground floor with Tony Telford's class next door. On the other side of my class room was the cleaner's store room. One of the first things that struck me was the height of the room itself. Having been used to the prefab these two weeks this class room seemed huge. At the back of the room was a good display area and I had one more blackboard at the front, which could come in handy. "What do you think?" asked Mr Johnson, who saw me looking around the class with awe. "Yes, it's very nice, and big," I replied. "And clean," said Mr Johnson, "And that's the way the cleaners like it. Clean. If you have an art lesson that involves cutting things up and making a mess can you please try and get most of it in the bin. The cleaners only have a certain amount of time to clean the whole school and it doesn't help when they come into a class room that's a complete mess and they have to clean it. So please, try to be tidy. OK?" "Yes, OK, understood. I'll try and make sure that the class room is kept fairly clean at all times," I said. "This is your store cupboard," he said, "I'll unload all your books and things in there. You can then sort them out in your own good time." With that he started to unload the trolley. I went over and helped him putting the boxes on the shelves in the store cupboard." I hope you realise that I have done you a favour today. I don't usually come in until four thirty and then I'm here until eight thirty checking things around the school. You wouldn't believe some of the things I have to repair at the end of the week. If I don't get finished then I come in over the weekend. I don't know how the leak in this class room was missed. I was on holiday in the last week of the school summer holidays and came in on the Friday before school started and there it was, a flooded class room. I say flooded, it was more like a gradual soaking of the floor and walls, but the damage was done and so we had to close the class room and get it all repaired. "Thank you so much Mr Johnson, I owe you," I said smiling, "And if I can return the favour, just let me know. Have a nice weekend." With that he turned and wheeled his trolley out of the class room and was gone. I looked at my watch, twenty to nine. The next bus would be at ten past five, if I left now I should be able to catch it. I had decided that the books could wait until Monday morning. I put my coat on, looked around and thought, "Yes this had been an interesting week," picked up my brief case and left.

Chapter Six

I took the notes for the Making Music programme home and looked through it over the weekend. No point in getting the children to make things unless I have tried making them first. Getting the problems sorted out before going into class. There is nothing worse than having a class room full of children all wanting your attention because the thing they are making has gone wrong and they need some help. There was quite an assortment of instruments that the children could make. Mostly percussion instruments but there were one or two wind instruments to be made. A lot of the shaker instruments needed toilet roll inserts and straight away I could see the problem here. The whole school toilets would be raided by my class and there would be toilet paper all over the place as my children unwound the paper to get to the cardboard insert. I could just imagine what Mr Percy would say yet alone Mr Yardley. The children would have to make the cardboard tubes themselves from thick card, if we have any. If they were making shakers then I would have to get things like dried peas, rice even marbles to place inside the tubes. Each would give a different sound, depending on what they were filled with. Various drums were mentioned, made out of different sized cans with balloons for the drum skin. Another instrument that caught my eye was the singing straws, an instrument made from different sized straws sellotaped together and blown, like pan pipes. Another instrument was made from crown bottle tops with had a hole drilled in them and attached to a cut down broom handle and nailed to it. The instrument was played by either twisting it vigorously or shaking it up and down. Certainly, the acquisition of crown bottle tops should be easy, as they are the metal tops on beer bottles and the children could ask their parent to bring some back from the pub. Reading through the notes I was beginning to realise that this wasn't going to be as easy going as I thought. There were a lot of things to get ready before the lesson and the first television programme was a week on Friday. That means these instruments were to be made and ready for that programme, only two art and craft lessons to complete them all. How would the children decide what instrument they would make. I think that would depend on the child's ability and if I thought they would be capable to make the instrument they chose. I would also need some clean empty tins of various sizes for the body of a drum and balloons to go over the top for the drum skin. I also needed a wet playtime box sorting out before the weather started getting bad and the children were unable to go outside to play. I would have to ask some of the other teachers what sort of stuff they have in their wet playtime box.

Monday came round once again, usual breakfast, two slices of bread and marmalade and a cup of tea, then out for the bus. I thought about getting a morning paper to read on the bus so that I could keep my head down and hopefully get no derogatory remarks from the bus conductor but the newsagents was the other way from the bus stop and that would mean me leaving the house a good ten minutes earlier to get the paper. I thought better of it and decided to run the gauntlet with the bus conductor. To my surprise the bus conductor and driver had changed which meant that I was just another passenger amongst others. It was only when the conductor came to my seat for the fare and said, "Are you taking any of your pets to school today." I looked at him and replied, "No, I decided to leave them at home today. Did your colleague tell you about me and my mishap the other week?" "The whole bloody depot knows about you and your frogs, thanks to the conductor that was on this route when you let them loose on his bus. We couldn't believe it at first until the complaints came in from some of the passengers later on and the bus was late as he had to try to clear all the frogs from the bus before it could continue with its journey. One and three pence is it?" he said as he held out his hand for the fare. As it happens I had the money ready. I gave him the money and he gave me a ticket. I notice that he kept his eye on me the whole journey until I reached the school. As I got off he shouted, "Keep the pets happy," then rang his bell and the bus moved off. I wasn't sure if he meant the frogs or the children.

I dropped my briefcase in my class room and hung my coat up in the store room then went up to the staff room for the weekly Monday morning briefing from Mr Percy. Nothing much was happening this week although Ivan Jenkins was off and his class had been split up and were to be sent to other classes. "The list of children that have been allocated to other classes is here on this paper and I will put the list on the notice board. Please give the children you get from Mr Jenkins' class relevant work to do while they are with you. They will be sent with their own jotters so that Mr Jenkins can see what work they had been doing while they were with you I'm not sure how long Mr Jenkins will be off for, according to his wife he has been up all night with sickness and diarrhoea and as his class room is quite a way from the toilets so it's best he is off. I'll take registration and once that's over I'll send the children to the relevant classes before assembly." Mr Percy looked at me and came over, "As you are new I have only given you one child from Mr Jenkins' class and that's Farthingale. He should be no bother but make sure he has plenty of work to do." And with that he turned to put the list on the notice board. Farthingale I thought, Farthingale. That name rings a bell. "Hard luck, old boy," said Tony Telford, trying not to laugh, "You've got the walking natural gas producer for your class. Hope you've got some pegs and air freshener in your class room as you will need them." With that he turned and went out of the door. That's it, Farthingale, the boy from the assembly last week, the one that caused Mrs Grant to have her office fumigated. I thought his name rang a bell and thinking of bells I looked at my watch, ten to six, time I was off ready to get my class from the yard.

I collected the children from the yard and took them into our "new" class room. I told the children to sit in the same places that they would have had if they were still in the prefab class room. That way I would know who was who, as I still had trouble with some of the names of the children. It's the quiet kids who are no bother in class whose names are hardest to remember. "That's right children, sit down. We'll sort books out after assembly, so sit quiet while I do the register and dinners. Also this week we will start making our instruments for the television programme we are going to follow on a Friday afternoon. That is, if you all behave, otherwise I'll tell Mr Percy that our class doesn't deserve the television lessons and he can give our slot to some other class," I said this with conviction and the children seemed to take notice as they were all sat quiet and well behaved. I thought that I better tell the class that we were going to have someone from another class joining us for the day. Freddie and Timmy delivered the milk in good time and, as I had one child away in my class and we were getting Farthingale, the number of bottles of milk would be right for the class. I looked at my watch, ten past eight, I must get a new watch and soon because one day I might find myself in big trouble using this one. The bell went for assembly. The children lined up across the front of the class room and, with me in front, filed out one by one to the assembly hall. The hall was filling up with various classes and we took our usual place. Mr Percy came in and walked up to me, "You will not be getting Farthingale in your class today as he is away and the rest of the class have already been allocated to other classes. Should Mr Jenkins be away tomorrow and Farthingale comes back he will be with your class until further notice." "Yes, thank you, "I said rather relieved. With assembly over we went back to class and sorted the children's books out before we could make a start with our lessons.

Before long it was lunchtime and after getting a cup of tea from the communal teapot I was invited again to sit with Mrs Cook and Miss Stark. "Did you have a nice weekend, "asked Miss Stark, "Did you go ten pin bowling with your friends? Strange, I thought, what's this with her and wanting to know about ten pin bowling. I thought that she was attached with someone, or is she just making conversation. "Yes, and yes," I replied, "Yes I had a nice weekend and yes I played ten pin bowling. Didn't do much good though, in three games I scored just over a hundred. My best score was 139 which wasn't that good but the rest were having similar games so none of us were great. I spent a lot of time reading through the notes for the television programme I've booked; "Making music" I have to get the children to make their own instruments before we see the programme as they have to play them along with the programme presenter. I'll need all sorts of things, different size tins, paper tubes, straws, balloons, small cardboard boxes and so on. I'm not sure where I can get all the things from." "Have you been told about the resources cupboard near the library?" asked Mrs Cook. "No, "I said. "I can show you after you have eaten your lunch," said Miss Stark. Mrs Cook could see that I was cautious about this offer and said, "I'll come along too, I haven't been in there for a while and there might be some new things in there that I could use. Basically if we have things that we think might be handy for school then we bring it in and put it in the resources cupboard. Mr Sharpe brought in a box of twenty four jam jars, Mr Jenkins brought in some very large flat pack cardboard boxes that we were able to use as flats once they were painted in one of our stage productions. There's all sorts in there that staff have brought in from time to time. I'm sure you might find something that will be handy for you in your lesson. Also get the children to bring things in. Just tell them what you want. Anything that you don't use and could be handy later on and can go in the resources cupboard." "Thank you, that will be nice," I said as I started on my cheese and pickle sandwiches. Miss Stark and Mrs Cook started talking to each other about various relatives of theirs and who had come round that weekend to see them. When there was a lull in the conversation I jumped in and asked, "Is there anything is the resource cupboard that would do for a wet playtime box, as I haven't got one yet and at some time the weather will change and we'll be having indoor playtimes. I've been in other schools on my teaching practice and when they had an indoor playtime the teacher got out a box, referred to as their wet playtime box and the children chose various games that they played with until the end of break." "The best thing to fill a wet playtime box is to go to jumble sales. They usually have plenty of games, jigsaws and things that will keep the children occupied either through break or across dinner time. You could also have a look in second hand shops but they tend to be a bit expensive. Your best bet is the jumble sales as this time of the year, leading up to Christmas, parents are starting clearing out toys and games to make room for the arrival of the new Christmas presents," said Mrs Cook. "If you haven't got anything yet, you could ask Mr Percy for some blank paper that had been torn out of last year's exercise books. It's something we do at the end of the summer term; we go through the children's old exercise books and recover the blank pages to be used at times like wet playtimes. You should have some dice in your maths store. Show the children how to play the game beetle, that always goes down well and if the children are divided into groups of four they will get about two to three games in before the bell goes at the end of break. Are you ready to go up to the resources store room and see what we can get for you to make some instruments?" I said that I was, went over to the sink and washed my mug up and left it on the side to drain then followed the two ladies out, Miss Stark said that she would go and get the key from Mrs Grant and would meet us at the resource cupboard. When she opened the door I was amazed the amount of stuff that was in the room. It was like an Aladdin's cave with shelves filled with bits and pieces, boxes of all sizes, and then I spotted something that would be very handy – cardboard tubes of different sizes. "Just what I need," I said, "Where did they come from?" Mrs Cook looked over and said, "I think that they were what some maps and posters were wrapped around when they sent them in the post. You've struck gold here then as there are quite a few and of different diameters. Did you say that you wanted some balloons and tins, if so there are some over there on that second shelf? Very soon I nearly had all the materials I needed to make a variation of musical instruments. I thanked the two ladies for their help and said that I must get these things to my class room before the afternoon bell went. "I hope you get the instruments finished by Friday," said Miss Stark. "Friday?" I said. "Yes, that's when your programme starts, isn't it? Friday the 27th. The rest of the television programmes start this week," replied Miss Stark. "Oh no, I thought it was next week. I'd better get started with their instruments on Wednesday so they will be ready for Friday," I said. "You do know that you will have to get the class room key along with the store room key for the television, don't you?" asked Mrs Cook. "Mr Percy is very keen on security, especially where the television is concerned," she continued. "Yes thanks," I said, Thanks for all your help. I'd better get all these things down to my class room before the bell goes. Shall I lock up and take the key back to Mrs Grant?" "No, that's OK," replied Miss Stark, "I'll lock up and take the key back. Best of luck with your instruments and with the television programme on Friday."

When I got back to my class room and put the cardboard tubes, tins and balloons in my store cupboard I realised that I would have to go shopping tonight for things to go inside the tubes for the instruments. I started to make a list in my mind, dried peas, lentils, rice, marbles and what else would do I wondered. I had left my programme note book at home, and I'm sure there was something else in there that I had forgotten. Never mind, time for the bell and I should have a good afternoon teaching as now I had the "carrot" for good behaviour – the materials for making the instruments for the Friday programme. If the children behaved then they could choose what instrument they could make but if they misbehaved then I would choose what instrument they would make. This worked very well as the children sailed through the afternoon without a peep. Before home time I asked the children if they could bring in some things that we could use from home. I told them that they could bring in things such as toilet roll tubes, I thought if they take off the paper at home their parents would sort them out not me, beer bottle tops, jars, tins, elastic and any other things they could think of that would make a good instrument. I said that these things would have to be brought in by Wednesday afternoon as that was when we were going to make our instruments for the television programme on Friday, and we all wanted to have an instrument that we could play along with to the programme. There was a lot of nodding and yes sir to this request. This is getting too easy I thought, but the instruments had better work otherwise I was going to be in trouble with the children. Were my expectations too high? Had I sold the idea to them that it was going to be simple to make the instruments and that they would work first time. Now I was beginning to get worried. What if it was all going to fall flat, what was I to do? Stay positive, I told myself, that's the only way; don't let the children see that you are only one step in front of them. Tonight I must make a drum with one of the tins with a balloon to act as the skin, a shaker with a piece of the cardboard tube filled with dried peas and I think I kept the beer bottle tops and a small length of wood to which they could be attached to would make a rattle type instrument. These instruments and others would have to be made and checked that they worked and be ready for Wednesday to show to the children the finished items that they were aiming to make.

On my way home I stopped at the shops and bought rice, lentils, dried peas, dried beans and an inspiration – peanuts. I also thought of using sand as a filling. A packet of elastic bands of various sizes to make a guitar type of instrument and I noticed that there were some tins of cocoa with a plastic lid on them which would make a good shaker as the inside filling would hit the metal base and create a good sound. The cocoa could be stored in a plastic bag for future use. The evening after tea my table was covered with various tins, tubes, elastic bands, balloons tape, paste, beer bottle tops, bits of wood, coloured pens and paint. Hours flew by and just before midnight I assessed my instruments. I had various shakers, different size drums, some instrument made out of the wood and beer bottle tops with holes in the middle that jangled when shaken, and last of all an instrument made from the elastic bands and an old cigar box that was plucked. I had found a selection of old cigar boxes that my father had collected over the years in the back of one of my cupboards. I had kept them thinking they would come in handy and indeed they had. I would get these completed instruments into school in the morning and let the children see them on Wednesday afternoon before our art and craft lesson so they could see the finished articles.

Next morning I was knackered, and when the alarm went off I nearly fell asleep again. I burnt the toast, spilt the milk, dropped one of my "best" plates, snapped my shoe lace and to top it all I couldn't find my door keys. The home-made instruments were stacked up on the table. I found some bags under the stairs and placed them into these bags. I had one of each so that the children could see what they were supposed to be making. I was rushing round, trying to eat my toast and drinking my tea at almost the same time. I looked at my watch, a quarter to eleven, blast this watch, if I don't make a move I'm going to miss the bus. I grabbed my coat, got my brief case and collected the bags rushed out and slammed the door behind me and ran to the bus stop. Just in time I may add, for as I got to the stop the bus was just pulling in. I joined the queue getting on and as I got on one of the bags tore and the instruments fell to the floor then I heard a voice from upstairs shout, "Going to a musical jamboree then, are we?" Oh no my comedic conductor, that's all I need. He came down the stairs while I was still trying to pick the things up. "Here," he said and gave me a new bag from his little cubby hole near the bell. He even bent down and helped me pick some of my instruments up, "Can't have the bus running late while we wait for maestro here to get his orchestra packed up, can we?" I thanked him and made my way to my seat and he followed and put the bag he was holding next to mine. "One and three to the madhouse is it?" he said with a smile. "Yes please," I said, "And thanks for your help back there." He took my money and gave me my ticket and went round the bus collecting other fares.

I got to school and made my way to my class room. I decided to put all the instruments in the store cupboard so that the children did not see them. I wanted it to be a surprise this afternoon also it was my "carrot" for good behaviour in this morning lessons. I hadn't been in the room for more than five minutes when Freddie and Timmy came in with the milk for our class. "Sir," said Timmy, "I've been thinking.

If we keep some of the milk bottles and put different amount of water in each they might make one of them instrument things called a mokaspeel or something like that." I had to think quickly then I realised what he meant, "A glockenspiel," I said, "A glockenspiel, that's very good thinking. Well done. Put the milk in the corner and go out and wait for the bell." With that they put the milk crate in the corner and went out. I was rather pleased that they had come up with that idea with the milk bottles, especially as they weren't the sharpest knives in the drawer. It seemed as though the art and craft lesson on Wednesday afternoon would go well if Freddie and Timmy were so keen then the other children must be as well. I looked at my watch, ten minutes before the bell, just enough time to pop to the staff room and catch up on any news.

As I walked into the room I saw Mr Jenkins in his chair with a cup of tea in his hand. He looked a bit washed out. Mr Percy saw me and came over. "As you can see, Mr Jenkins is back with us so his class will be back with him, although he still looks a bit iffy to me but he says he's OK. He doesn't like being ill, he was saying that it's been years since he was off school with illness. I hope you will take a leaf out of his book on that count. It doesn't do to have teachers off, spoils the continuation of class teaching and disrupts that teachers' class if they have a supply teacher or if the class is split up around the school disrupts all the classes the children go into." With that he turned and went over to talk to at the other side of the room. I don't know if that little talk was a reminder to me that I shouldn't have any time off school unless I was on death's door." Come along people," Mr Percy called out, "The bells due to go any minute, time to collect your classes and I will be taking assembly this morning so you can all leave your classes with me for twenty minutes while you all get your lessons ready, and please don't be late back for your classes. Thank you." I must have looked surprised as I walked out of the staff room as Miss Stark came over and said, "He sometimes does that, must have something to tell the children, anyway it gives us some time to get things ready for the day, How's the instruments doing, did you get any made last night?" "Yes, quite a few," I replied, "Although it took me past midnight before I was finished and I'm feeling a bit delicate this morning so this extra free time is a godsend for me. I also asked the children to fetch any items they thought would make a good instrument and in a moment I'll see if any of them has remembered that." "Well, have a good day," she said and went off to get her class. I made my way to the playground to get my class and as I reached it the bell went and kids were all running in different directions to line up to be taken into their class rooms. A line was forming at my collection point on the yard, with various children with bags with who knows what inside them. Then I saw it, Mark and Terry carrying with a baby's bath between them. I went up to them and asked, "What's that?" as I said the words I realised it was a stupid question as everyone could see that it was a baby's bath. "It's for the musical instrument, sir," said Mark, "We can turn it over and use it as a drum. Makes a good noise sir, 'cos we've tried it. It was that loud we woke the baby up and it started screaming. Mum wasn't very happy though, neither was dad as he was sleeping as well and mum woke him up shouting at us." "That's all well and good but I think it might be too big and too noisy for us to hear the other instruments," I said, " but you better fetch it into class put it in the store cupboard and take it back home tonight." I made my way to the front of the class and led the children into school to the cloakroom and then to our class room. "Put your bags under your desk for the time being and we'll see what you have brought in to make instruments later. Reading books out, silent reading as I take the register," I said to them. That done along with the dinner register and the children were ready for assembly. I led them into the hall where Mr Percy was waiting for the rest of the classes. "Yes you can go," he said looking in my direction. Tony Telford was standing next to me and we both left the hall together. "I'm nipping to the staff room for a fag and cup of tea. Are you coming?" he asked me. "No thanks, I want to get some things sorted before the kids come back from assembly," I said. It was very tempting to go with him but I wanted to find out what the kids had brought into school for our art and craft lesson.

When I got back to the class room I started to have a look in each bag, some had brought jam jars, others tins of all sorts, some toilet roll inserts and there was a couple of plastic lunch boxes. Then I heard it, or should I say, her.
"Bloody stupid if you ask me," said a female voice which was coming from the corridor and was answered by a voice I knew "Can

you kindly keep your voice down, you are in a school," said Mr Yardley. A few seconds later my door flew open and a large well-built woman stood at the doorway and said, "Are you the bloody stupid sod that wants my baby's bathtub?" "Mrs Robinson, please curb your language," spluttered Mr Yardley, "We can't have you swearing on school premises." "Swear, bloody swear, me. I'll give you bloody swearing. This bugger would make a saint swear. How the hell do I bath the baby without his bath? Making sodding instruments, why the hell don't you buy some instead of getting the kids to pinch my baby's bathtub? It's a good job my Albert had to go out before I realised that the kids had pinched the bathtub otherwise he would have come round here to get it and that silly sod wouldn't be standing that's for sure. He would have sorted him out good and proper, getting kids to pinch bathtubs. Not right it isn't." "Have you got the bathtub in question?" Mr Yardley asked me. "How many sodding bathtubs has he got?" shouted Mrs Robinson. "Just the one," I replied mistakenly. "Oh I see, get our Mark to pinch our flaming bathtub did you, thought we didn't wash did you. Bet you didn't get the other kids to pinch their baby's bloody bathtubs, did you?" said a red faced Mrs Robinson. I sensed this might get out of hand if I didn't produce the bathtub soon. I went to the store cupboard and got the tub and handed it over to Mrs Robinson who was too eager to get it off me and as she gripped it with both hands and pulled as I let go. Mr Yardley was standing quite close to Mrs Robinson and I presume that Mrs Robinson's right hand was much stronger that her left because as she gripped the tub and pulled, she pulled to the right and up. Right in the face of Mr Yardley who staggered backwards. I'm not sure if you have been hit in the face by a travelling baby's bathtub but I think it hurts, no, I know it hurts if what Mr Yardley said as it hit him in the face. Mrs Robinson looked horrified and straight away was trying to apologise, "Oh bloody hell, shit and buggery, are you all right?" she asked him. Mr Yardley was groping in his pocket for this handkerchief while his other hand was stemming the blood from his nose. "Dor, I'm not dorl right. Please leave dis school immediately, dorn't come back," said Mr Yardley through his handkerchief. Mrs Robinson didn't need telling twice, she made for the door and was off like a rocket, bathtub in her grasp. I went over to Mr Yardley to give him a hand but as I approached him he stood back and said, "Stay where you are, I shall see you later. Bathtubs indeed," and with that he was off out of the door as well holding his handkerchief to his nose.

I collected the children at the end of assembly and noticed that Tony Telford was speaking with Jimmy Moses who had a piece of paper in his hand. Tony saw me, said something to Jimmy who put the paper in his pocket, and came over to speak to me. "You haven't seen that," he said. "What, Jimmy with that piece of paper," I replied. "Yes, you haven't seen it especially as Ivan has won the bet and he will be most annoyed especially as you stopped the bet last time, which was a great get out clause for Jimmy, as he would have lost a lot of money that time, so, you haven't seen anything and you don't know anything. OK," said Tony in a commanding voice. I just shrugged my shoulders and agreed. I led my class out and back to the class room. As we made our way back to class I wondered what the bet was this time, did Mr Percy scratch his nose like Mr Yardley did, or was it some other oddity like a phrase he said. Although I was curious about this I thought it better that I didn't know or wanted to know. I also wondered how much Ivan had won, again I better not ask as I wasn't supposed to know.

Back in class and I asked the children to get out what they had brought for our art and craft instrument making lesson. Just as they were putting their bags on their desks a voice called out from the store cupboard, "Sir, sir, someone's pinched me bathtub." With that Mark came rushing out of the cupboard and started looking round for his pride and joy. "Your mother came in and has taken it back home. Did you ask her if you could bring it into school, Mark?" I asked. He looked up at me and said, "Err no, I just thought that it would be alright as the baby had a bath last night and wouldn't need one until the weekend as we only have one bath a week in our house, so it wouldn't be used till next week, and it was there doing nothing so I thought it would make a good drum. I did try it out and that's when I woke the baby and she woke dad and he shouted at mum and then he went storming into the kitchen and stood in the dog's dinner cause the dog had dragged it's bowl across the floor and as he was in bare feet the dog food squeezed through his toes which made him shout even more then he said, "sodding hell, this place is like a loony bin, I'm off to the pub and getting pissed," and then……." "Stop!" I said quickly, "Enough, and please don't swear in school, I get the picture." "But that was dad swearing, saying sodding hell and that he was going to the pub to get," but before Mark could carry on I raised my voice and shouted, "Stop !" This had a surprising effect on all the children as they had never heard me shout before. Everything went so quiet you could even hear a pin drop, literally. All eyes were fixed on me, waiting for what I was going to say next. "We do not swear in school, no matter what the reason is, and we do not repeat swear words even though other people might have said them. Is that clear with everyone?" The whole class looked at me and nodded in unison in silence. "Mark, your mother has been into school and has taken the baby's bathtub back home. Now children let me see what you have brought, and those of you who haven't been able to fetch anything you have another day to see if you can find anything suitable. And I mean suitable, I think a bathtub wouldn't be a suitable item to bring in. Anyway we have materials that we can use for those of you who can't find anything," I said. The next ten minutes I went round the class looking at all the different things that had been brought in. That over with and all the items put away we started the morning lessons. At the back of my mind was when was Mr Yardley going to see me and will it affect the television programme on Friday.

The morning seemed to pass by quite quickly, the dinner time bell went and the children went off to get their lunch. It was then I realized that I haven't anything for lunch, rushing round this morning I had forgotten to make myself something for lunch. I couldn't go a full day without having anything at lunchtime and it's far too late to order a school lunch. I know, I thought, I wonder if there is a fish and chip shop somewhere near the school, that's it I'll have fish and chips for lunch. I went up to the staff room and saw Tony Telford in the corner having his lunch. "Sorry to bother you Tony," I said," But is there a fish and chip shop near the school as I didn't have time to make my packed lunch today?" "Yes, there is one about 10 minutes away but if you do get fish and chips don't fetch them back here as Mr. Yardley doesn't allow staff to bring fish and chips back into school. I think he doesn't like the smell that lingers after someone has been having fish and chips. There is a sort of park near the chip shop with a couple of seats where you could eat the fish and chips there. Again don't let Mr. Percy know that you are out there having fish and chips as he would think it most unprofessional for a teacher to be sat at a park bench at dinnertime eating fish and chips. If you just go out of the side entrance to the school, down the street, until you get to the first cut through, go along that, turn left down that street and the chip shop is on the corner. They are not the greatest fish and chips but they will do. There might be a queue so if I were you I should go now, but keep an eye on the time, and don't be late back for school." I thanked Tony, went back to my class room, got my coat and made my way out of school. Tony was right, the chip shop was 10 minutes away from the school; however, there was quite a queue, but the smell of fish and chips and my rumbling tummy I took the chance and joined the queue. Twenty minutes waiting in the queue it was my turn to be served. I ordered fish cake and chips with salt and vinegar and asked for it to be wrapped up. I came out of the shop and look for the park. The park was a rundown field with a child's playground and various seats here and there, some of which had various pieces missing which made them unfit for purpose. I sat down unwrapped my package and tucked in to a surprisingly tasty fish cake and chips. Meal over, I put the paper in the litter bin and made my way back to school. Now I must admit that I am not the greatest navigator and I should have made a note on the route I had taken to the fish shop. I went down the street that I had come up but I had forgotten which cut through I had used and this street had quite a few. I tried the third cut through but when I got to the end it led to people's back gardens, so I had to retrace my steps. After trying two more cut throughs I found the right one looked at my watch, five past seven, if I'm not careful I'm going to be late for school and that would take some explaining. I did manage to get to school with three minutes to spare, I saw Tony in the corridor. "Did you get your fish and chips, and did you enjoy them?" asked Tony," Oh by the way Mr. Percy was asking for you, he said that Mr. Yardley would like to see you after school and asked me if I saw you to give you the message. Have you been a bad boy again? Someone in the staff room said they had seen Mr. Yardley and said that he had what seems to be the start of a black eye. I wonder what he has been up to, anyway I have given you the message, good luck" I thanked Tony as he went off to go and collect his class of the yard. Good luck, yes that's what I needed good luck. I put my coat in a class room and went off to the yard to collect my class just as the bell was starting to ring.

The afternoon passed by too quickly to my liking but before I knew it, it was home time and time for me to see Mr Yardley. I dismissed the children and went up to Mr Yardley's room. Mrs Grant was still in her office and I reported there to her and she said that I should wait in the outer office. She picked up the intercom and said that I was in the outer office. I looked at the traffic lights beside the door. Amber was showing, maybe he was doing something in there and he was going to make me wait. To my surprise the lights went from amber to green within a few minutes. I went over to the door and knocked, "Come in," boomed Mr Yardley. I went in and Mr Yardley was sat in his chair behind his desk. He waved me over and pointed to a spot in front of his desk. I stood there like a naughty boy, perhaps I was. "Why are you asking children in your class to bring bathtubs into school, and what was Mrs Robinson going on about instruments, surely we have instruments in school. You must see Mr Sharpe if you need instruments. We can't have parents coming into school during lesson time to see teachers especially if they are going to use inappropriate language. You were lucky that Mrs Robinson's husband didn't come in for the bathtub, and then there would have been trouble. Last time he was in school it took four policemen to escort him out of the building and it's only a court order that keeps him away now. You were also lucky that I was in the corridor as Mrs Robinson was on her way to your class room. So what have you to say about this matter?" asked Mr Yardley. "Well Mr Yardley," I started, "it's all to do with our television programme on Friday called Making Music, the children have to be inventive and make their own instruments to be used while watching the programme and I asked them to bring in various things that we could use to make an instrument. I gave them examples of toilet tubes, boxes, tins and containers and anything else they thought would make a good instrument. I never considered a baby's bathtub, but Mark got the idea into his head that it would make a good bass drum. We are going to make the instruments in our art and craft lesson tomorrow afternoon and those children who are unable to bring anything in will be able to choose things I have got from the resources cupboard for them to make their own instrument. I didn't expect that this might cause any trouble." I thought that this was a good and concise explanation. "Not toilet roll tubes," he moaned, "Have you let Mr Johnson know what you are doing. I don't want toilet paper all over the place because children from your class have taken the toilet roll tubes from all the toilets and left the paper all over the place. I am holding you responsible for any toilet mishaps between now and Friday." I quickly made a mental note that I should go and find Mr Johnson as soon as Mr Yardley had finished with me and tell him about the toilet rolls. "Yes, Mr Yardley," I said, "Is there anything else you wanted to say to me or should I go now?" "Anything else?" said Mr Yardley in a slow suspicious way, "Is there anything else that I should know about? Should I expect any more parents coming in to collect any more belongs of theirs?" "No, there's nothing else, I'm sure," I said confidently. "Well go, I've got to get off as well. I have to tell my wife that the bruising on my face has been caused by a bath's bathtub of all things. I dread to think what it's going to look like in the morning; most probably I'll have a black eye. What are you waiting for - if there's nothing else, go!" Mr Yardley commanded. I didn't need telling twice. As I passed the traffic lights they went from red to amber.

I had to think, where would Mr Johnson be now at this time, I looked at my watch, half past nine, I really did need a new watch as this was getting silly now knowing how many minutes past the hour the time was but not knowing the hour. I did need to buy one with my first pay packet. I know the cleaners report to him when they come in at four twenty which means he might still be in his small office near the boiler house. Luck was on my side for as I got there he was just locking his door. "Mr Johnson," I shouted," Can I have a moment please?" He turned and saw me, "Yes, certainly, what is it?" he said. I wasn't sure how to phrase it, so I just came straight out with it, "My class are making their own instruments tomorrow and one or two might try to pinch the toilet roll tubes from the toilet rolls." He looked at me and said, "So you're the stupid sod that has helped to create the mess in the toilets at playtime. Toilet paper all over the place and not a toilet roll tube to be seen. A total waste of toilet paper if you ask me, and it's your class that's responsible, is it? If I had my way I would make you and your class tidy up the mess they have made. I'll be telling Mr Yardley, you know. He has to know about these things." I had to think quickly," Mr Yardley has just seen me about the children's homemade instruments and he's sort of reprimanded me about the children getting inappropriate materials and said that I should see you. I'm very sorry about the mess and I'll try to make sure it doesn't happen again. What more can I say?" I was hoping here that he thinks Mr Yardley has seen me about the toilet rolls and thinks that he's sent me to apologise to him about the mess. "Well if Mr Yardley has already seen you about it then there's no more I can do. But please don't let it happen again, and I thought we were getting along fine. I've got to go and check a window catch that's not closing in year three. We can't have the premises open to burglars especially as year three class room is on the ground floor. I'll bid you a goodnight," he said and with that he was off with his bag of tools. A good job I saw him when I did, and before he reported the toilet rolls to Mr Yardley. Not my fault that he jumped to conclusions that Mr Yardley saw me about the toilet rolls and not about a bathtub. I've just got to hope that the two don't mention it to each other. Anyway time for me to collect my coat and bag and get off home. Tomorrow will be the big day for the instrument making.

Chapter Seven

Wednesday morning I awoke before the alarm went off, maybe due to anticipation and the afternoon's art and craft lesson. During the night I had woke up and thought about taking some wall paper paste in for the gluing the instruments together. Luckily, I remembered where I had some, it was a new packet and from what I recalled when I used the same brand before it gave you some time to align the wall paper up before it started to stick and when it did stick that was it. That would be very handy; I could make a batch of glue and divide it up to each table. That was something else I would have to get the class to do, move the desks to make tables of four so that materials could be shared amongst each table. As I had some desks spare they could be put at the back of the room as a drying area. I also had some newspapers that could be put on the desks to protect them from any mess. I had my usual toast and marmalade and a cup of tea, collected all my things and set off for the bus with plenty of time to spare.

I got to school, went to my room and dropped off my things and went up to the staff room. The place was buzzing with groups of staff muttering to each other. I went over to the sink, got my mug, felt the teapot, it was hot so I poured myself a cup. Miss Stark waved me over to sit next to her, which I did. "What's happening?" I asked. "It's Mr Yardley," she said, "Someone has seen him and he has a black eye and bruising on his face and people are making up their own theories of how he got it. Also Mr Johnson was on the warpath last night, something about toilet rolls." Before I could say anything Mr Percy came in and asked for attention. "One moment, if you please staff," he started, "I don't know what people have heard or what people are saying but there was an incident in school yesterday involving a parent and Mr Yardley and the outcome was Mr Yardley slipped and banged his face which has left a black eye and bruising but he is in school today although he has asked not to be disturbed unless it is very urgent. This means that I will be taking the assembly this morning although it will be a short one. Thank you." Miss Stark looked at me and said," I wonder what happened with Mr Yardley and the parent, and how did he slip, was he pushed or was he hit by the parent? Maybe we should know the full facts" Now, this was a case where I should keep my mouth shut and pretend that I knew nothing, and I better try to change the subject. "Yes strange," I said, "I think I've got all the things for this afternoon's lesson, the one where the children are going to be making their own musical instrument. I hope it goes well as they will need them for the television programme on Friday." "Oh, that's good," she said. I looked at my watch, three minutes to eleven, "I'd better go, I've something to check on before I collect the children. Have a good day." She thanked me and I got up, washed my mug and went back to my class room. I looked at the layout of the desks and tried to imagine which desks to put together to make tables to work from as I was quite conscious which children would work well together and which children not to put together. I put the newspapers in the store cupboard along with the packet of paste and then went out to the yard to wait for the bell and collect my class.

I collected the children from the yard as usual, some had brought more things that they thought useful, so I told them to put their items at the back of the class room. I said that I would need four pupils at lunch time to help me set the class room for our art and craft lesson this afternoon. There was a sea of hands shot up, straight away I would use this to my advantage. "I only want those children who can behave and show responsibility so I'll be looking for suitable pupils as we do our lessons this morning." The hands went down and a few moans were heard. I completed registration and we went over to the hall for assembly. Mr Percy was right; it was a short assembly and we were back in class in no time. I asked Freddie if he had brought anything into school from home to make a musical instrument. He said that he hadn't, so I asked if he wanted to make an instrument from some milk bottles as he suggested yesterday. He said that he wanted to so I told him to save six milk bottles from our crate of milk and wash them out so they would be clean and he could use those. The morning went well and some of the children were going out of their way to show how well they were behaving and prompting me every now and again by saying, "Sir, am I behaving?" By the time dinner time came round I chose four to help with the re organising of the class room, they were those who had done their best all morning including Alfie. Some of the children complained that Timmy had already got a job as he was our milk monitor. I said that I had made my mind up and it had been a very hard choice as they had all been good that morning. I made arrangements that the children should come back to the class room at a quarter to one, which should give us a good twenty five minutes to get everything sorted. I would be back at twelve thirty as I had the paste to make and had to get the things out of the store cupboard.

I went up to the staff room with my packed lunch, found a seat near the window and put my lunch on a chair. I went over to get myself a mug of tea and found that no one had made it yet so the ruling was the first one in had to make the tea. I boiled the kettle and put ten tea bags in the pot, that would be one for each member of staff. I gave the pot a good stir and poured myself a mug of tea and went over and sat down. It was nice to have five minutes to yourself but that wasn't to be as the staff room started to fill up. A shout went up, "Who the hell has made this tea?" a voice from the sink. "I did," I said, "Is there anything wrong with it. I thought first one in had to make the tea." "They do but I can nearly stand my spoon up in the tea, it's so bloody strong. How many bags did you put in the pot? We only put five in as a rule," it was Ivan Jenkins talking. "Sorry," I said again, "I'll know next time." I'd better not tell him I had put ten bags in, "Put a drop more water in the pot," I added. I sat there and enjoyed my corned beef and tomato sandwiches; I'd also packed a banana which is one of my favourite fruit. As I sat there I could hear someone talking about Mr Yardley and the black eye and wondering which parent was involved. Time I was going I thought, I looked at my watch, twenty five past nine, time to get back to the class room and start sorting things out.

I got to my class room and started to put the various resources from my cupboard onto my desk. I then looked for a suitable pot to make up the wallpaper paste in and also some jars that I could divide the paste into for each table. I made some drawings on the blackboard showing each instrument and how it was made and what it was filled with. The four children appeared at the door and knocked. "Come in, " I shouted, "Can you please start and put the desks into tables of four, I'll show you in a moment where I want them, then get some newspaper from the cupboard and put it on the desks. Each table should have a collection of coloured pencils, some palettes of paint, water jars, scissors, paint brushes and some paper towels." I made up the paste as the children were sorting out the class room, I looked up and thought that I had made the right decision picking Nicola as she seemed to take charge and started giving out orders to the rest of the children. I looked at the class room layout, my desk would stay at the front and the rest of the desks would make up tables of four, but I also needed the spare desks at the back of the room to act as a drying table. "Can you please make sure that there is enough space between the tables so that there is free movement between them," I said, I looked at my watch, "We have about twenty minutes or so to get the class room sorted, so let's get cracking." I started pointing out where the desks should go and the children moved them in position. As each table was put together Nicola and Janet were putting newspapers down and getting the trays of coloured pencils and putting an assortment of each on the table. In no time at the entire class room had been transformed into an art and craft room. The children stood and waited to be told what to do next. I brought out the bags of rice, lentils, dried peas, peanuts and sand and told the children that each table would have to have a dish of each but put the dishes on the drying table at the back rather than on each table as these dishes would be given out during the lesson. As the paste was ready I asked that it to be divided out into dishes for one for each table. Again, Nicola was quick to start sorting things out, she got some dishes from the store room and laid them out on the drying table and told the others which filling were going onto which dishes. I walked around the class room to make sure I could get around without any difficulty, yes this was fine. I thanked the children and told them that they could go and get ready to line up as the bell would soon be ringing. The children left and I looked round again, yes this looked good and everything is going to be fine I thought. I'd better get on to the yard as the bell would be going in a minutes or so time and I didn't want to be late in starting the lesson as we have a lot of things to get through before they started making their instruments.

I got to the yard before the bell had rung but my class were all lined up ready to go, talk about being keen I thought. I went over to them as the bell rang and seeing that they were all there, brought them into school. The register was on my desk but as the children came into the room they stopped, "Where do we sit?" asked one of the children. Bother, in the re arrangement of the room I had forgot to make a plan of where the children were going to sit, and because the desks were covered in newspaper the children didn't know which desk was which. Think quickly I said to myself. I turned to the children and said, "Because you have all been so good this week you can sit at a table with your friends." At this the children became excited and started to push each other, a quiet voice said, "Are you sure about that, sir?" I looked to my side; it was Nicola. Talk about having your balloon burst, if a kid can spot trouble why didn't I. "Yes, you can sit with your friends, but only four at a table," I turned to Nicola and said, "Yes thanks, but I think it will be alright." The children filled the tables and straight away I could see what Nicola meant. Mark and Terry made their way to the table at the back of the room along with Alfie and another boy, Billy Preston. I looked around the class at some surprising combination of children at the tables. I took the register and asked Susan, who was on the same table as Nicola to take the register back to the office. I said, "I think that I'd better move some of you around, Mark and you go and change places with Jimmy over there and Terry, you change places with Susan there." "But sir, said Mark and Terry in unison, "We've done nothing wrong all week, can't we stay together, you did say that that we could sit at a table with your friends as we have been good all week, and we can help each other with our instruments. Please sir?" It was an impassioned plea and I did say because the class had been good they could sit with their friends. I couldn't go back on my word now otherwise it would be useless giving promises in the future if I didn't mean it. "Well yes, I did say that you all had been good and you could sit with your friends, so for this lesson I'll let you sit together." I caught a glance of Nicola raising her eyes to the ceiling. Susan came back from the office and sat down in her place.

"Can you please get your things you have brought to make your instrument. Please do it quietly and when everyone is ready we will start," I said. The children went over and got the various things they had brought in. I, in turn, went to the cupboard and got the instruments I had made the other night. I showed the class and explained how each one had been made what was inside the shakers to make the different sound they made, how the elastic band guitar was made, the various drums with the balloons and the instrument that was made using the beer bottle tops. I said that I would come round with items that could be used inside the shakers. I pointed to the bags of rice, lentils, dried peas, peanuts and sand and said that I would put a quantity of each on each table. I must have made an impression with the children as they were now extremely keen to start. I asked if they all knew what they were doing and if they had the right things they needed, they all nodded in approval so I said they could start. It only took a minute when a hand went up, "Sir, I need some left handed scissors and there's only right handed scissors on my table. Who's got the left handed scissors, please," said Billy Preston at the back table. Is this a wind up I thought, left handed scissors, I'd better play along. "Who's got the left handed scissors on their table?" I asked the class. "Here they are sir," said Matthew Armitage holding up a pair of scissors. I went over to his table and said, "Thank you Matthew, how do you know they are the left handed scissors?" "Easy sir, "he replied, "They're the ones with green on the plastic handle all the others have red on the handle." I took the scissors from him and passed them over to Billy at his table. So now I knew that there were left handed and right handed scissors and how to tell the difference between them. Who was teaching who here I wondered. Just then another hand went up, "Sir, the scissors won't cut the cardboard rolls, they're too thick" Before I could answer, a voice rang out "Not as thick as you are though." The class started to laugh and I turned round to see who had called out, "Who was that, making a silly remark. And the rest of you, it wasn't funny so stop laughing." Think quickly I thought, the cardboard tubes were too thick for the scissors to cut them, I should have realised that, so what could we do instead. I know, "Children, stop for a moment please. If you have the thick tubes and you can't cut them, then use the card that's on your table. Roll it around the tube as you paste it with the glue and hold it in place with an elastic band until it dries then slide the card from the tube. Here, I'll show you." Using a piece of card and one of the tubes I showed the children what I meant, and it worked. I looked around, most of the children were getting on quite well. "Can the four children who came in at dinner time please give out the fillings for the shakers to those tables that need them," I asked. Nicola, Janet, Timmy and Alfie got up and went to the drying table and gave out the various fillings for the shakers to the tables that needed them in no time at all. Things were going fine; the children were happy and busy and were making progress in what they were doing. I went round the room helping out where needed and offering encouragement to those who were a bit disillusioned they their offering.

As I got near to my desk I saw a pair of scissors on the floor so, naturally, I bent down to pick them up. Just as I was reaching them, pow, a stinging pain in my left buttock. I shot straight up and looked round, rubbing my arse as I turned to face the class. The speed in which this was done surprised the table at the front so much that one of the girls who was just putting her paint brush into the water jar jumped and spilt the jar of water over the table and the other children's work. "Oh sir, look," said David, "The water has gone all over my card that I was colouring." "Quick," I said, "Get some paper towels and mop up the water. Lift your work out of the way. Put the things on the table on another table for the time being until we get this sorted. You two get some more newspaper for the table and put the wet newspaper in the bin. Is there any water on the floor?" The rest of the class was stunned by this outcry and sat in their seats watching the cabaret before their eyes. I looked round the class to see if I could see any guilty faces, "The rest of you get on with your work." My backside was still stinging slightly and I looked around to see what it was that might have hit it. It only took a few minutes and the table was back to normal, complete with a fresh jar of water for the painters. All seemed to be calm on that table now so I started to move round the class room. On another table one of the children needed some help cutting a delicate shape in her card so I offered to help. I took the card and the scissors and bent over and started cutting, just then, pow. This time it was my right buttock and the stinging pain was more intense. I shot upright, and, in my reaction I cut the card in half, much to the dismay to its owner who started crying. I tried rubbing my arse casually while looking round the room. "I'm sorry, can you start again with your cutting out and please stop crying," I said to Susan, the girl who's card I had just cut in half. She sniffed and said that she would try. Just then another child on a different table yelled out. "Who is that making a stupid noise? "I asked. "It's me sir, "a voice said at the other side of the class, "Something has just stung me on my neck." I went over to see but someone else at the opposite cried out and shouted, "I've been stung as well, sir." "Everybody stop, "I shouted, "Who is responsible for this disturbance?" Well that was a dumb thing to ask, as though someone is going to admit to the fact it was them. But who was it. I looked at each table for evidence, but evidence of what? My first suspicion was Mark and Terry, but they were busy making their shaker instruments and something that looked like a cardboard flute. Unless it was a wasp in the class room, but dare I mention that to the children – I think not. Well here goes, "Well if someone is responsible for this disturbance then they will find themselves in serious trouble, and I mean it. Please get on with your work, and quietly, we have to get these finished today and we will be using them during our television programme on Friday." Some of the children had decorated the outsides of their shaker instruments and were starting to add the filling. I told them to experiment with different fillings and listen to the noise they made and when they were happy with the right filling then they had to seal the ends of the tube. Again they had to decide how much filling they put in as to the noise it made. Someone from the table at near the back of the room put their hand up. "Yes Ann, what is it?" I asked. "Please sir, Matthew is taking our nuts from our table. He has already taken the nuts from two other tables and he won't give ours back and we need them." I went over to Matthew's table and saw that there was an empty dish that supposed to have a quantity of nuts in it. I also noted that Matthew was supposed to be making an instrument from a small wooden cigar box and some elastic bands. "Why do you need the nuts, Matthew, when you don't need any filling for your instrument?" I asked. Matthew seemed to be chewing then he started swallowing rather quickly, then he started to choke. I rushed over behind him. "He's been eating all the nuts, sir," said David, "He's like that, eats everything he can. Mrs Cook didn't even have soap at the sink when he was in her class 'cos Matthew used to eat it when no one was looking. One day he went through three bars before Mrs Cook realised he was eating it. I know that day he spent a lot of time at the toilet afterwards."

By this time Matthew was starting to go red in the face, there was only one thing for it, I had to hit him hard in the middle of his back to dislodge the nuts. It worked, but too well as it dislodged the nuts that was causing the trouble but also brought up almost everything he had eaten in the past ten minutes – all over the table. The two children opposite, in order not to get covered in nasty pushed quickly back in their chairs but held onto their desk as well which meant the desks came away from the other two desks that made the table up and created a large gap between them. As all the shared items were in the middle of the table there was now no support for them and everything fell to the floor. The water jar broke, dried peas and nuts were rolling away, the rice, sand and lentils fell into the water, the powdered paint and coloured pencils scattered, other children on other tables jumped up to move away. My main concern was Matthew. There were tears in his eyes and his face was returning to its normal colour and he was no longer choking, although round us was chaos. I salvaged what I could from the table and gave it to the relevant children and started to roll up the newspaper off the desk. "Nicola, Janet, Timmy and Alfie," I said, "Can you please come over here and help, there's a brush and pan in the store cupboard if one of you would get it please. Someone else get some more newspapers, another get a water jar and some more paints. Can you all please put the table as it was. The rest of the class please get on with your work as I'm coming round to see how you are doing." As I bent forward to push one of the desks, pow, another hit on my right buttock. I turned quickly to see who might have done it, although too quickly as Timmy was bringing the water jar to the table and we collided and the water, not the jar thankfully, went over the two children on the next table. I must say Timmy doesn't do a job by half, the water jar was nearly full and the two children got the lot over them. My first priority was the wet children, although my arse was stinging like hell. I told them to move away from the table and take off their cardigans and put them over the radiator to dry and to get some paper towels to dry their hair. Nicola, bless her cotton socks, was putting newspapers over the spillage on the floor to soak up the wet. The chairs were wet but were wiped down and dried. Fortunately, the work on the table had escaped the water and the children were able to continue with their work.

This was not going as I expected it to. Nicola, Janet, Timmy and Alfie had done a good job and the tables were back in operation, at least I had picked kids with some sense. As I walked round the room the instruments were not as I thought they would be. Some children had decorated their shaker tubes very well but others we a bit of a mess. And talking of mess, some tables had spilt the various filling over the table and on to the floor. I stopped at one table and looked at Susan, who had red spots all over her face. "Are you alright?" I asked. "Yes, sir," she replied. "What are all the spots on your face?" I asked. Sheepishly she looked at me and said, "It's paint, sir. He splattered me with paint on his paint brush." She pointed to the boy opposite who also had black spots all over his face, "So I got my own back and did the same to him." "Make sure you get yourselves cleaned up at playtime and," pow, this time the back of my neck was hit, "Who's doing that?" I shouted. It must have come from near the back of the room, Mark and Terry, yes Mark and Terry, it must be them. I walked over to their table but the only thing I could see was a couple of tubes and they were making into shakers and a tube that had holes made in it along the side. They both looked up at me innocently. It must be them but I had no proof, so I just gave them a threatening stare. I decided to cut my losses and bring the lesson to an end. "All those children with a finished instrument put your initials on it and put it on the left hand side of the drying tables at the back of the room. If you have an instrument that's nearly finished put it on the right hand of the drying table. We will do this a table at a time. When your table has been cleared of instruments then please empty the dishes with the rice, lentils nuts and the other fillers in to this metal waste bin. Billy will come round with the bin. Thank you Billy" And then it happened, a dried pea hit the side of the metal bin. I turned and looked towards the back of the room. Everything seemed normal; Mark and Terry were at their desk although Mark was holding his cardboard flute. Could it be him I thought, but looking at the cardboard flute there was no way it could act as a peashooter as the tube was too wide. I gave the bin to Billy who started going round the class and emptying the dishes from each table. I looked at my watch, ten minutes to playtime and the class room was a mess. I looked around the class and saw three other cardboard flutes, none of which would have been suitable as a pea shooter. Table by table the children put their works of art either on the right hand side or on the left hand side of the drying table. Slowly but surely tables were being cleared and paints and pencils put back in their boxes, scissors in their trays. "Nicola, Janet, Timmy and Alfie can you please go round the class and collect the paints, pencils and scissors and put them back in the store cupboard. The pots of paste put on the drying table and empty the water jars in the sink. The rest of you, after the things have been cleared from your tables, put the desks back as they were unless there is paint and newspaper in the space where your desk should be." This made a few spaces in the middle of the class room where desks should be. "And we only have five minutes to playtime," I reminded them. Pandemonium is the word that springs to mind as the children started scraping desks along the floor as they dragged them in position, while others were hovering around the drying table to see what others had done and what their instruments looked like. The class room was a mess with sand, rice, lentils, nuts, dried peas, paint and water in various quantities and in various parts of the floor. There was no alternative than for me to stay in at playtime along with Nicola, Janet, Timmy and Alfie and try to get some of the mess cleaned up before the cleaners came in after school. The four children were only too pleased to be given the responsibility to help put things right. One of them went to get the brush from the store cupboard so the floor could be given a good sweep. I dismissed the class for playtime as soon as the bell rang and the four of us started to sort things out. "Look at this, sir," called Nicola at the drying table. She was holding one of the cardboard flutes and as she turned it to show me it had something shiny down the centre. She gave it to me and I realised that the shiny thing was a metal pea shooter. So that was it. A pea shooter, but who did it belong to I wondered. If Jimmy Moses were here he would give odds of evens if not favourite on Mark Robinson, I'm sure.

It's amazing what can be done in such a short time, especially when everyone works together. Those desks that could be were back in place, most of the floor had been swept of various bits and pieces although the only downside was the paint that had been spilt, newspaper had been used to get some of the wet paint up but that had spread the paint even more around the floor and it had started to dry leaving quite a mess. I had thanked the children and told them to go out and get some fresh air until the end of playtime. Just then I saw Tony Telford walking past the class room. I rushed to the door and called to him, "Have you a moment please, Mr Telford?" Tony stopped and came over and as he did he looked in the class room. "Wow, a bit of a mess, what's been going on here then? A touch of Andy Warhol or Jackson Pollock and their famous floor drip paintings then. I bet Mr Johnson won't share your enthusiasm for such painting." "That's the point, how can I sort things out, the cleaners don't wash the class room floors on a Wednesday evening and I can't leave the floor like this, can I?" I said, desperately. "You have a problem here then, but I might be able to help you. You don't smoke do you, no you don't. Well it just so happens I have a new pack of twenty Players number six tipped cigarettes, just the sort that Mr Johnson smokes which you can buy here and now. See Mr Johnson after school, explain that things got a bit messy this afternoon in your art lesson, and it won't happen again by the way, and is it possible that he can help you by letting you have a bucket and mop to clean the mess, at the same time making sure he sees the unopened pack of Player numbers six in your hand," he said. "But I …" I started. "Listen, Mr Johnson is a bit particular who has his buckets and mops and if you have the cigarettes in your hand and he sees them he most probably say that he will see to it for you later this evening and leave everything to him. Problem sorted." Yes I see," I said, "A bit of bribery then." "No, a friend doing a favour for a friend, that's all. Like I'm doing you a favour, and that's five bob you owe me for the Players. What the heck are those on the desk over there?" said Tony pointing to the table and the drying instruments. "That's what the children were making in this lesson, their own musical instruments to be used on Friday when we have our television programme," I answered. "Well if you ask me, you have let the children have too much choice, you should have let them make the same instrument each, those shaker things, OK with different filling so that they sounded different, but they all do the same. Otherwise, as you have found out today, there is too much mess, but you'll learn. Time for the bell, we must be going. Don't forget my five bob," and with that Tony was off to collect his class.

I collected my class from the yard but when they got back and sat down they soon realised that their desks were not their desks, that is, the desks had been put where desks should be but they didn't belong to the child that sat there. Hands started to go up once they realised this. "Sir, this isn't my desk, its Janet's," "And this isn't mine, it belongs to Jimmy and there's all sorts of things in it," said Matthew. "Leave those things alone," shouted Jimmy, "They're mine and personal." I held my hands up and said, "Stop all of you, let's sort this out quietly. Now, we will go round the class, starting with the desk near the door. Look inside the desk and see who it belongs to, then we will, person by person get the desks moved to their right places." For the next ten minutes or so children were moving desks here and there, but in the end everything was sorted and the class sat there waiting to see what was next. I looked at my watch, twenty to nine, and then I remembered the peashooter. I went over to the drying table to look for the cardboard flute with the peashooter inside it. I held each one in turn to look down the inside but no sign of the peashooter in any of them. The class were looking at me in anticipation, what was I going to say. "Who made these?" I asked. Terry, Michael, John and Mark put their hands up, and Mark had a strange sort of smile, a smile that said yes it was me but can you prove it smile. For me there was only one person in the frame but without any proof I could do nothing. "They are nice and colourful," I had to say something and I'd better pick some of the other things up and make comments about those as well, which I did. I finished off the lesson by reading more of Robinson Crusoe, and, like the children I couldn't wait until the bloody thing was finished. Next time I pick a book to read to the class it would be a much shorter story or a book of short stories. At last the bell rang, it was home time and I dismissed the children with a kind of relief.

With the children gone I made my way to Mr Johnson's small office near the boiler room, twenty Players in my pocket. I knocked on his door. "Yes," his voice cried out, Come in." I opened his door and saw him sitting in an old lounge chair warming himself near an electric fire with a newspaper in his hand and a cup of tea on a small table near the chair. "Err, Mr Johnson, sir," I started, "This afternoon I had an art lesson and I'm afraid that the children have made a bit of a mess with paint on the floor, well not a bit, a lot of mess on the floor and I was wondering if I may borrow a bucket and mop to clean it up. I'm very sorry and I'll clean it up." "A bit of a mess on that nice new floor that has only just been laid. You might have been better off staying in the prefab. "Does Mr Percy know?" he asked me. What, Mr Percy, then he will report it to Mr Yardley and I will be in the doodah, think quick, the Players cigarettes, yes the Players. I put my hand in my pocket and pulled out the cigarettes and started twisting the packet round in my hand. Mr Johnson saw them straight away and his attitude changed. "I don't let staff borrow my mop and buckets usually, and do you know how a new floor should be cleaned with a wet mop, no I don't supposed you do. There's a special knack to it, you know. Put those on the table there and I'll see to it later this evening, and please, next time you are having an art lesson get the children to be more careful. You better get going otherwise you'll miss that bus of yours and the next one will be after five tonight. Good evening," as he said that he smiled and pointed to the door. I took the hint and left. Well, I thought, there's a lot to be learnt in this teaching lark, and today I have learnt a lot, especially how to work around Mr Johnson, something that I hoped I wouldn't have to do too often.

Chapter Eight

The next morning I was in school a bit earlier than usual, as I wanted to see how the children's instruments had turned out now they were dry. I looked them over, not what I was expecting; maybe my expectations were a little too high. Some, when they were drying had gone out of shape; others didn't have enough paste holding them together so they were coming apart at the seams. Out of the whole class I think there was about half a dozen that could be used straight away, maybe a dozen more, with more work, could be salvaged and the rest, well, the bin was the only place for them. What was I going to tell the children? I know, the children whose instruments were fine could help those whose instruments would be binned and they would start again. What did Tony say yesterday, get them to make the same instrument? I went to the store cupboard and saw that there were still plenty of cardboard tubes left. I could cut these down to size and get those who had to make another instrument to make the shaker instrument. I checked that there were enough for each child. Also there was a good supply of rice, lentils, dried peas and sand. After the commotion with Matthew yesterday I left the nuts where they were, I'll take them home with me tonight. It would mean that the class room would have to be set out like yesterday but with only fewer tables. I also would have to be stricter regarding anyone making a mess, especially as Mr Johnson had done a great job of cleaning the floor. I looked at my watch, twenty to eleven, I had time to go and ask Mr Johnson if I could borrow a hacksaw to cut the cardboard tubes to size. When I reached his office I thanked him for the great job he had done with cleaning the floor, this put me in his good books, and then I asked for the hacksaw. I explained what it was for and that the children wouldn't be using it, only me, so there should be any mess. He gladly handed one over and asked that it be returned after school. I took it back to the class room and was able to cut enough cardboard tubes to be used this afternoon. Just in time as it was time to collect the children from the yard.

On the way from the yard to the class room the children were very excited to see how their instruments had turned out. I told them to sit down while I did the registers then I said that some of the instruments needed more work doing to them and some would have to be redone.

We would have another lesson this afternoon sorting them all out as they would be needed for the television programme tomorrow. I asked that the same helpers to come in at the same time at lunchtime and sort the desks and tables out. Some of the children didn't look too happy about having to start all over again but it was time for assembly so we had to get ourselves to the hall. When we got back it was lessons as usual, although they seemed to drag on to lunchtime. For me it was another quick lunch in the staff room and back to my class to supervise the children getting the class room ready for another art and craft lesson. It just so happen that these children, Nicola, Janet, Timmy and Alfie had all completed their instruments and made a very good job of them as well. I explained to them that the children who had to start again were going to make a shaker and that they were going to help them make one. I looked round the class room, water jars, paints, pencils, scissors, and the various fillings for the shakers, plenty of newspaper on the desks, was that it or was there something else that I had missed? Nicola suggested that newspaper be put under the tables so if anything were spilt it would be caught on the newspaper. Brilliant idea I thought and I told her so.

We had finished the class room just in time as the bell rang for afternoon lessons. I told the four helpers to stay in class while I went over to the yard and brought the class in. The children were told to sit in the same place as yesterday. I took the register and then I started to give out the various work from yesterday. "I will have to move children around; those children that haven't been given their work back come and sit at these tables at the front as you will be making a shaker instrument. You can decide what filling to put in them and there will be someone to help you with your work. If your work needs re sticking then please sit on the tables in the middle and those children who just need to finish off painting then sit at the tables at the back. Is there anyone who does not know what they are supposed to be doing?" Silence, I look around the class and saw Mark and Terry at the back, and they saw me. "Mark, can you help the children on that table there and Terry, you help that table over there," I said knowing if they were the ones with the peashooter then they wouldn't dare use it if others could see them, problem kind of sorted. The lesson went much better than the day before although the children seem less enthusiastic than yesterday. I went around from table to table giving help and advice and noticed that the six helpers were doing a fine job helping others. By ten minutes before playtime nearly all the work was finished and placed on the drying table. The helpers cleared the tables efficiently, used newspaper put in the bin, water jars, paints, pencils, scissors, paste, and the various fillings for the shakers were all put back in the store cupboard. Last thing to do was to put the desks back in their rightful places, I wasn't going to have the performance we had yesterday with the desks. The last of the desks was put in place just as the playtime bell rang. I dismissed the class and stood at the front looking round the class room, hardly any mess, the cleaners wouldn't have anything to complain about. Good job Nicola suggested putting the newspaper on the floor under the tables as there had been a couple of spillages and the newspaper saved the floor each time. I went off to the staff room to get a well-deserved cup of tea and some biscuits.

After playtime I thought it was a good idea to go through the children chanting the times tables from the four times table to the twelve times table and then a quick fire question and answer game based on the times tables. To make it more interesting I put girls verses boys on the blackboard with a tick for each right answer under the relevant gender. It's amazing how competitive the children get, and how they turn on each other if someone gets the answer wrong. After fifteen minutes of this and the girls winning the boys eighteen to twelve I decided that we would have the last part of the lesson reading Robinson Crusoe. The bell went for home time. "OK children, home time. Don't forget, Friday is our television debut day. I don't know about you but I am looking forward to it. Goodnight children, off you go" I said. At last, I thought, I'll be able to finish marking books as the children watch the programme and it'll save me some time over the weekend.

I woke up before the alarm went off again maybe due to anticipation of the television lesson this afternoon. However Friday was my duty day so I had to be on the yard from a quarter to nine until the bell went, be on the yard for the two playtimes and last of all be around the cloakroom as the children left for home. I checked the start time of the television programme, it gave me ten minutes to get the children from the yard at the end of playtime, go to our class and pick up the musical instruments they had made and then go up three flights of stairs to the music room get the television out of the store cupboard, plug it in and wait for it to warm up. I washed, shaved got dressed had breakfast and was out in good time. I got to school in good time, dropped my things off in my class room but kept my coat on, went to the staff room and poured myself a cup of tea and took it with me as I went off to do my yard duty. It's usually quiet on the yard in a morning as a few of the children are half asleep and have no intention of running around and most of the rest can't be bothered they just want the bell to go so they can be in school and the warmth. Sometimes parents come on the yard with their child and tell you they were up all night with him or her and could we keep an eye on them just in case. Usually it meant that the child in question didn't want to be in a lesson that day or they had done something wrong the previous day and knew they were going to be in trouble so they had tried it on with their parents. I was told that a parent had seen a teacher on yard duty one morning and asked could their child be excused PE that day as they had a hole in their vest and it was the only one they had and were embarrassed about it. When the bell went the duty teachers had to get the children lined up for their class teacher to collect off the yard and then they took their class into school. This particular Friday things were going well on the yard. Mr Sharpe was the teacher on duty near the school entrance and Mrs Peterson was the third duty teacher for playtime. The bell sounded and the children ran or walked to their lines, Mr Sharpe closed the school gate and walked across to his class and took them into school. Other teachers were collecting their classes as well and by the time I reached my class they were the only ones waiting.

Once in class it was the register, then a quick look at the work that was done yesterday afternoon. The results were very good, this time all the children would have an instrument that they could use, so all the children would be able to take part in the television programme this afternoon. Just a normal Friday morning really, assembly followed by an English lesson, playtime with me on duty, then Maths and then dinnertime. At dinnertime I went to Mrs Grant's office for the music room key. "Mr Sharpe hasn't a music lesson this dinnertime, otherwise he would have the keys. Can you please lock everything away, especially the television, Mr Yardley is very insistent on that. When you fetch the keys back I won't be here but please leave the keys in this top drawer, Mr Yardley will put them back in the key cupboard before he leaves tonight," explained Mrs Grant as she gave me the two keys. I thanked her and left.

The first lesson that afternoon you could almost feel the tension in the air. Ten minutes before the end of the lesson I gave out the musical instruments the children had made. "Leave them on your desks please and we will pick them up after playtime," I said, "And please straight in after playtime, we don't want to miss the start of the programme, do we?" The bell went and we all went out to the yard. I had been told to patrol the end of the yard near the toilets and move children on if they were hanging about. I remembered what Mr Johnson said about the kids peeing into the urinals and it seeping through the wall and as I got nearer the smell got stronger. Stay upwind of the toilets I told myself then I should be alright. Playtime was nearly over when there was a fight and I was the nearest teacher to the two boys. I had to intervene but that might take me past playtime finding out what had happened and why the two boys were fighting and the television programme would start and the class would miss the beginning. I collared the two boys and took them over to Mr Sharpe to ask for his advice. He saw me approaching and said, "You two, not again. I warned you not to go near each other this playtime, and what have you done, disobeyed me. These two are in my class and have been at each other all today, even through the lessons. Leave them with me please, I'll take care of them." As Mr Sharpe walked away with the two boys the bell went and I blew my whistle. Everyone stood still until I blew the whistle a second time, which was the signal for the children to run to their class lines. I have seen a teacher blow the end of playtime whistle and wait for nearly five minutes for everyone to stand still and be quiet before he blew the second whistle for the children to move to their lines. Gets the message across I suppose but not all staff agree with the two whistles.

My class and I went to our class room, the children collected their instruments and I picked up the programme notes book from my bag. I lined the children up and off we went up to the third floor to the music room. I unlocked the door and told the children to sit on the chairs which were in three layers in a semi-circular pattern. I went to the store cupboard at the back of the room and unlocked that door. The television was towards the back of the cupboard on a trolley. I went over to it and pulled, but it didn't move. I moved to the side and pushed, again it didn't move but the trolley nearly tipped over. I then noticed someone at the door, it was Mark Robinson, "Try taking the brakes off, sir," he said pointing to the wheels. I looked down and saw that each wheel had an individual break on it. "Terry and me helped Mr Johnson the other week setting up the television, you'll need that aerial wire over there sir as well, I'll show you where it plugs in," he informed me. With the breaks off the trolley moved quite easily, it was pushed to the front of the class and the various wires were plugged in by Mark and I thanked him told him to sit down and then I switched the set on. It warmed up quickly and I checked it was on the right channel, which it was. We saw a potter's wheel and a hand forming a pot of some kind, and it was in black and white. I looked at the front of the set and wondered if there was a button that I had to press to get a colour picture. Just then the picture changed to a colour one and a voice saying welcome to the schools programmes. The picture faded and the title came up – Making Music. The lady presenter appeared and said, "Good afternoon children." The class in turn replied to her with a good afternoon. They were hooked. I was just about to go to the teachers' desk at the side when what I heard next stunned me. "In the coming weeks, your teachers will be helping you make your own musical instruments made out of various things that you can find around your house. One week we will make musical shakers another week we will concentrate on making drums and yet another week we will see what we can make using elastic bands and boxes. This week we will start by listening to the beat of music. Listen to this piece of music," she said and a piece of music started to play. The children looked at me and I looked at them, each with their various instruments in their hands. "Just listen to the lady and see what she has to say about the beat in music," I said. I went over to the desk and got the lesson programme note book out. Each weekly programme was listed and near the back of the booklet was the section making the instruments, but here two pages were stuck together. I eased them apart and there it read that each week a different instrument was going to be made and the children would then use them alongside the programme. It listed the various things that could be used for each instrument then the following pages, the pages that I had followed, explained how to make the instruments. We had made all the bloody instruments at the same time instead of week by week. A hand went up and a voice said, "Please sir, when are we going to play our instruments with the lady?" What could I say - that I had made a total cock up of everything, that some of these instruments wouldn't be wanted for another five weeks. "Just listen to the lady, yes she wants you all to copy her, she's on about the four beat. Listen, count one, two, three, clap. That's four beat. See, she's going to play some music and you have to clap to the four beat. The colour's nice isn't it?" I said. Gone was the chance of marking books while the children watched the television, I had to keep the children going, somehow. "Put your instruments under the chair, and follow what the lady is telling you to do. We might be using the instruments in the next lesson with the lady, so just for today we will be learning about the beat in music. That's very important when you are playing instruments, being able to get the beat of the music," I explained. The next half hour was like walking through treacle, very difficult. I looked at my watch, ten minutes to go before home time. "Pick your instruments up and we'll take them back to class," I said. Just then there was a shout from the back near the store room, "Sir, the lid's come off three of the shaker things and there's sand and lentils spilt on the floor, what shall we do, it's all over?" There was no way of pushing the television through sand and lentils, it would have to be swept up before I moved it and time was running out. What should I do I thought. I know leave it where it is, lock the class room door, see the children back to our class room, when the bell goes get to the cloak room and supervise the children leaving and then come back with the brush and pan, sweep up the mess and lock the television away in the store room. "Please walk round the mess and try not to spread it about, we're going back to class and you can put your instruments in your desk and then it will be time to go home. Line up outside the door, walking round this way, one at a time," I said, indicating that the children walk around the class away from the spilt mess on the floor and away from the television set. Once outside and lined up I locked the door and led them back to our class room. The children just had time to put their things away when the bell went and I dismissed them and followed children to the cloakroom where I stayed until all the children had left. A bit longer than usual I thought, never mind, back to class for the brush and pan and back to the music room. It took five minutes or so and all the mess was off the floor and in the waste bin.

As I started to unplug the aerial and television wire two men appeared at the door with brown overalls on and one had a clip board in his hand. One knocked and both came in. "This is the one, isn't it Clive? said the man with the clipboard in his hand. "Yes, Albert, this is the one." He turned to me and asked, "Have you been using this television today? I looked at him and said, "Yes, we have been watching a school's television programme this afternoon about music." "Did you notice a variance in the colour spectrum while the programme was playing, you do know about televisions don't you, especially colour television," asked Albert. I looked blankly at him, "No I don't know much about televisions, especially colour televisions. All I know is how to switch them on and how to change channels, oh and how to alter the volume, also I know where to plug the aerial into. Other than that I don't know anything else about them." "Well it's down here on our sheet, isn't it Clive, the variance in the colour spectrum is on the wrong setting, it needs to be changed to the right wave length, and that can only be done in the workshop. When we change the settings we may have to reset some of the valves or if the variance is too great then we will have to upgrade the set and insert new valves. But as I say, this can only be done in the workshop and that's why we are here. It's all here in the paperwork if you want to see it, but if you don't know much about the working of a television set it won't mean much to you. It happens a lot with new televisions they have to be re-set after a few days of use. We'll take it away now and bring it back on Monday morning, we might be able to check it out when we get back to the workshop tonight, otherwise we'll be working on it in the morning to get it ready to bring it back on Monday," said Albert. It would be no good looking at the paperwork about the colour spectrum or whatever Albert was saying, "Have you seen Mr Yardley or Mr Percy before you came up here?" "Oh yes, we saw them and then came up here to collect the television, and we have a paper here that you have to sign saying that you have released the television into our hands, that makes it legal and all that," said Clive as he pointed to the clipboard with various papers on it. "Well if you have seen Mr Yardley and Mr Percy and I sign your papers to make it legal, I suppose it will be alright. Shall I read through the papers first and where do I sign." "If you want to read through them, you can, but look this is what it says. There at the top is the name of our company, here the name of this school, this is the television we are going to take, it just needs Albert to put in the make, model and serial number of the set, he finds that at the back of the set. This piece near the bottom is saying that you have released the television into our care, and here it says that it will be back on Monday morning. But if you want to read through the paper with a fine toothed comb, then please do, but I have just told you basically what it all means," explained Clive. I looked at the paperwork and did look a bit wordy and Clive did explain what it contained so I said, "Where do I sign?" "Just there, there and there," said Clive as he offered me the clipboard. I took it and signed the document in the relevant places. "Do I need a copy?" I asked. "No, a copy will be sent with the invoice on Monday," said Clive, as he took the paper off the clipboard, folded it and put it in his top pocket. Albert and Clive lifted the television from the trolley and Clive said, "Can you open doors for us all the way to our van, which is parked round the back near the boiler house?" "Yes, of course I can, here let me get the door for you, and I'll follow you down the stairs and get the outside doors for you," I said as I went over to the class room door. By the way the two men were walking with the television I realised that it must be quite heavy. A couple of times down the stairs they had to stop and take a breather. When we reached the van Clive asked me to open the back doors for them, which I did. "Thank you for your help," he said to me, "And we will have it back on Monday morning. Enjoy your weekend." "Yes, thank you, you too," I said and thought what nice men. I went back up to the music room, pushed the trolley into the store room, locked it, picked up my brush and pan, and went out and locked the music room up. I went down to my class room and put the brush and pan in the store cupboard and collected my things. On my way out I took the keys back to Mrs Grants office and placed them in her desk drawer as she had told me to. It's been a strange day I thought.

Chapter Nine

My weekend seemed to fly by; I had a lay in on Saturday morning, got up late and walked to the paper shop and bought my paper, went home and had a fry up and started to read my paper while eating it at the table. I went out and did some shopping that would see me fine for most of the following week. Our local football team were playing at home so I thought I would go and watch them in the afternoon. Saturday night I went ten pin bowling. Sunday I had another lay in, skipped breakfast but cooked myself a proper roast dinner with all the trimmings and then spent most of the afternoon marking books. That was one of the things that I had been told that I must keep up to date, the marking of the children's work, especially as I was a probationary teacher for this first year. Teatime was roast beef sandwiches with mustard, which I always enjoy, and then a quick visit to the pub for a swift pint or so, although I got talking to one of the regulars about Saturday's football match and how we should have won if the referee hadn't missed the foul that would have given us the penalty that might have led to some encouragement to the team. As it happens no penalty was given and the dishearten team let two more goals to get past them with a final score of three nil. I did intend to have an early night but by the time I got home and had a bite to eat it was almost the usual time for bed.

Monday morning came all too quickly, the alarm woke me up and I almost turned over and went back to sleep. But no, I was up, shaved, washed and dressed. My usual toast and marmalade and a cup of tea for breakfast then check that I had all the children's books in my bag. When I opened the front door to leave it was starting to rain, so I grabbed my umbrella, I say my umbrella, it was one of my father's finds from the lost property office where he worked and had not been claimed. There was no wonder it hadn't been claimed, I think the owner left it on purpose as it was bright yellow, red and green and rather large. It would be good for two people to shelter from the rain under it, as it was big enough. I didn't intend getting wet so it would have to do. I had to check one more thing if I were going to use the umbrella, the wind. I had used the umbrella once before when it was windy as well as raining and what a job that was, it took me all my time to keep hold of it. Today, thankfully, there was hardly any wind so I decided that it would be OK to use it, at least it will keep me dry. When I got to the bus stop the rain was falling quite heavy, but my umbrella was keeping me dry and it was a good job that I was the only person at the stop because as I stood there I took up three places in the queue. The bus arrived and as it stopped I started to take down the umbrella but the catch was stuck and the thing wouldn't fold up. "Well, Billy Smart, are you taking your tent down and getting on the bus today or what?" said my dismissive conductor. "The catch is stuck," I said trying with all my might to get it to work, "Can you push the topsides down please, that might free it." The conductor came off the bus and tried pressing the top inwards while I was pressing the catch with one hand and pulling the side down with the other. Not being used to such treatment the umbrella gave up with a loud tearing sound and three of the panels gave way. Now it was half an umbrella and half a collection of metal stays. Just then the catch worked and the whole thing folded up, however it folded up with the conductors hand in it. There was some rather choice Anglo Saxon language used by him as he pulled it free. I picked my bag up and what was left of the umbrella and got on the bus. He rang the bell and followed me to my seat. "I'm very sorry about the umbrella and about your hand," I said, "A one and three please." The conductor gave a sort of grunt, took my money and gave me my ticket. For the rest of the journey I thought about what I was to do about the children and their musical instruments and our television programme. They were all very disillusioned last Friday and having to sit there and count and clap instead of using their instruments. This week's lesson was to do with keeping the beat using a drum, so maybe we could make drums in the art and craft lesson on Wednesday afternoon to be used for Friday. I'll have to check what resources we had to make enough drums for everyone to use on Friday. Very soon I was at my stop outside the school. "Take that bloody thing with you," said the conductor pointing to my umbrella with his finger poking out from a handkerchief wrapped round his hand. I picked it up along with my bag and got off the bus.

The rain had nearly stopped as I walked across the playground and into school. I dropped my coat and things off in my class room and went up to the staff room for the Monday morning briefing. Just in time for a quick cup of tea and a sit down but as I was sitting down

Mr Yardley entered the staff room. "Good morning staff," said Mr Yardley who was holding a clipboard with his notes on it. "Can I ask staff to be observant with the pupils in your class as we have three children in year six with chickenpox and we don't want this spreading throughout the school, so if you think someone in your class has it please sent the child to Mrs Silby who will decide whether the child should be sent home? Mr Johnson has informed me that two of the girl's toilets and one in the boy's toilets are blocked and he has fastened the door shut and put a sign saying out of order on the door. Please tell your children that they are not to try to use these toilets. Mr Percy will not be in school on Wednesday as he is out of school on a course at the education centre so I will deal with any problems that he would usually deal with. Has any staff got anything they wish to add?" said Mr Yardley as he looked around the staff room. There was no movement from the staff so Mr Yardley looked at his watch and said, "Five minutes please." This was his way of saying get your backsides out of the staff room and to your classes, the bell is going to ring soon. We all took his hint and started to move, some to the sink to wash out their mugs and others to the door and out.

One my way to collect my class off the yard the rain had stopped altogether and I hoped that it wouldn't rain for the rest of the day otherwise we would be having a wet playtime and I hadn't made up a wet playtime box yet. I must find out if there were going to be any jumble sales in the area next Saturday; they are usually advertised in the local paper during the week. The weather couldn't hold off much longer so I had to get one sorted soon. The bell rang as I approached my class. Most were lined up before the bell as they were getting used to me turning up before the bell was due to go. "Sir, are we going to have another music lesson on the television again this Friday?" asked Susan. A few of the other children were nodding their heads in agreement. "Err yes, we will be having more television lessons on a Friday and we will be using your instruments in some of them," I said being careful not to say which Fridays they will be using their instruments. Thankfully, the bell rang and I waved the children to walk into school to the cloakroom to hang their coats up. I could sense that I would be getting more questions about our music lesson on Friday from the children. Four and a half days to go until then though, enough time to get things organised I thought. Registration, dinners then over to the hall for assembly. I got the children lined up nice and straight and stood at the end with the rest of the staff standing at the end of their classes as well. Tony Telford looked over at me and said in a quiet voice, "How did your television music lesson go on Friday. Did the children's instruments prove a success?" Before I could answer I saw Mr Yardley at the door ready to walk into the hall so I did a quick thumbs up to Tony and turned to look at my class lined up. Mr Yardley walked down the hall, stopping as he did at various classes and saying, "Yes very good, the line is nice and straight, well done." However if your class had a crooked line or someone was talking as he passed, he would look at the class teacher and say, "Why is your class line crooked?" or "Why is that boy talking in your line?" This would bring shame on you, and your class and the rest of the staff were hoping that their class lines were straight and no one was talking in them as Mr Yardley went past. It was another mundane assembly given by Mr Yardley and a heart lifting hymn by Mr Sharpe, who did his usual thing of playing the introduction jumping up off his chair to look over the top of the piano, calling out now for the children to start singing as he swiftly sat down and continued playing. One day, I thought, that chair will give way and then what. Hymn over the classes started to file out of the hall, class by class. I was going to have a quick word with Tony but he was having a word with Mr Percy so I would have to speak to him at playtime.

The first part of the morning passed rather quickly. When it time to give the milk out there was one bottle extra as we had someone off today. I had to choose who to give it to as when I asked who wanted it most of the children's hands went up. I decided that Matthew should have it, mainly because he looked hungry and could do with an extra bottle. Playtime came and I went up to the staff room to have a word with Tony and tell him what a cock up I had made with the television booklet and the pages that were stuck together which meant most of the instruments the children had made were not needed until weeks later. However looking round I couldn't see him anywhere. "Looking for someone?" a voice rang out; it was Ivan Jenkins. "Yes, I was looking for Tony Telford," I said. "He's on yard duty today, if you want to see him go and have a word with him on the yard, he won't mind," answered Ivan. "It's not that important," I replied, and I went over to get my cup of tea and some biscuits. I picked up today's paper and sat in the corner to read it. Why is it when you get engrossed in something time flies, as it did as I was reading the paper, before I knew it, it was the end of playtime.

The rest of the morning past quickly, as did the dinner time and the afternoon. After I had dismissed my class I decided to stay behind and mark the children's books. The maths books are fairly easy to mark, the sum is either right or wrong, a tick or a cross and at the end a comment if it's needed. It's the English composition that takes the time, having to decipher the writing then trying to make sense what the story is about, correcting the spelling and grammar and finally trying to make a constructive comment at the end. It was while marking the books that Mr Percy walked passed my class room, then came back and walked into the room. "Good to see that you are working marking books after school. Do you know that some teachers try to get away with marking books during lesson time while the children get on with something else, not done I'm afraid unless you are marking the book with the child then you can explain where they have gone wrong." he said. Bang goes the idea of me marking books while the children watch the television programme then, I thought, and it would be just my luck for him to come in while I was doing it. "Yes of course, Mr Percy. I try to mark the books before I leave in an evening otherwise I take them home and mark them there," I said. He looked around the class room and commented, "You'll have to get some of the children's work up on the walls, properly mounted of course. Use the display space best you can, when it's parents' night then they will expect at least one piece of work that their child has done displayed on the wall. Sometimes that's not easy but try to make sure that there is something from everyone and if you have four or five pieces of work from the same child space them around don't have them altogether in one area. Don't stay too late. Good evening." He turned and left the room. More work, mounting the children's work, and that's something else I'll have to do, get some work from the children to go on the wall. Maybe this week's art lesson on Wednesday, but no, I'll have to get the children to make some shakers for Friday's television music lesson on Wednesday. I looked at the pile of books left to mark; only another half hour then I'll go home.

If I had known what Tuesday was to bring then the proverb 'The best-laid plans of mice and men oft go astray,' would sprung to mind. Tuesday morning started like most school mornings, with me waking up to the alarm, shaved, washed and dressed then toast and marmalade and a cup of tea. My casual walk to the bus stop, the bus journey to school, popping into my class room to put my bag and coat away and then to the staff room. I saw Tony Telford sitting near the window so I went to join him. "Hi Tony, " I said, "I made a bit of a cock up with those instruments the children made last week for that music programme. In my enthusiasm to get the kids to make those instruments two pages of the television programme book were stuck together, the two pages that lay out that the instruments were to be made over a period of six weeks and not all in one week which I got the children to do. The outcome was that the children didn't need any of the instruments last Friday, which disappointed them somewhat, and they had to sit there and clap to the beat of the music the woman was playing. To make matters worse some of the instruments fell apart and made a hell of a mess on the floor, which I had to clean up afterwards as I didn't want to get into Mr Johnson's bad books, not after last week when they made such a mess on our new class room floor. So, this week we're going to be making the drums all over again as they are needed for this week's lesson." Never mind," he said, "Practice makes perfect, with the kids having another go at making those drums you might get better results this time. Also you should know the pitfalls and avoid them. We've all been there at some time, having high hopes about a lesson and the whole thing falling flat. Put it down to experience and learn from it." That was right I thought, this week the drums could be made a lot better than last week. I thanked Tony and went to get a cup of tea after looking at my watch to see if there was enough time to drink it before the bell went which there was.

Things didn't start to happen until after playtime. On the way into class one of the children made a comment that a police car had pulled up outside the school gates and two policemen had got out and had gone into school towards Mr Yardley's office. It was about ten minutes into our English lesson when Mr Percy came into the room. "Excuse me, but you had a television programme on Friday afternoon, didn't you?" he asked me. "Yes, we had our making music programme, although I had made a mistake with the children and their instruments, as they weren't needed, not the children, the instruments. Anyway this week I think I'll have it sorted and we will have the right instrument to use and…." I was saying but I was stopped. "Can you please go to Mr Yardley's room now. I will look after your class while you are gone. Let me see, Junior English, page 28 verbs, yes, I'll carry on with this page, now go, he's waiting for you," said Mr Percy in a commanding way. I made my way to Mr Yardley's room which was through Mrs Grant's office. I knocked on her door and went in. Mrs Grant was typing a letter and she just looked up at me and said, "Mr Yardley's waiting for you. You have to go straight in," she said, and then went back to her typing. I walked over to the door. The traffic light was on green, so I knocked and waited.

"Come in," shouted Mr Yardley. I walked in and saw two policemen sitting near Mr Yardley's desk drinking tea out of the best china cups. This must be important if the best child cups are out. Was this about the robbery a few weeks ago and they have come to give me a reward I thought. Mr Yardley continued, "Mrs Peterson was to have had a television lesson this morning with her class, but when she went to the store room in the music room there was no television. Mr Percy tells me that you had the television booked for Friday afternoon with your class. Is that right?" "Yes that's right. Two of the pages of the television programme booklet were stuck together which meant that the children didn't need the instruments they had taken with them so this week we will be making more shakers and," "What on earth are you going on about, pages of the booklet stuck together and making more shakers. Did you lock the television away after you used it?" he asked. "They said that it would be back for Monday morning as the variance in the colour spectrum was on the wrong setting, it needed to be changed to the right wave length, and they said that could only be done in the workshop," I explained. "Which men would that be then," asked one of the policemen who had started to take notice what I was saying. "Clive and Albert, the two men who came to collect the television to take to the workshop to alter the variance in the colour spectrum," I replied. "What are you going on about, variance in the colour spectrum, what's all that about?" asked Mr Yardley. "I don't know," I said, "It's what the men said, that it needed changing and that they might have to replace some of the valves. They did say that they would have the television back by Monday morning. They said that they had seen you and that I had to sign the paperwork they had so that they could take the television." "And what paperwork would that be, sir," said the second policeman. "Clive said it was the paperwork that needed to be signed saying that they had permission to take the television away from the school. Mrs Grant should be getting a copy in the post." I said. "So let me get this right, you were in the music room after school on Friday afternoon and before you locked the television away in the store room, two men named Clive and Albert came into the room and said they had to take the television away and that they had seen Mr Yardley but you had to sign a paper saying that you were handing over the television to them," said the first policeman. "They needed some help in getting the television out so I opened the doors for them and also opened the van doors so that they could get it into the back of the van for them," I added. I looked across to Mr Yardley, whose' face was starting to go red with rage. "Do you mean to say that you not only help two villains steal our new television set but you have signed paperwork saying that they have permission from the school to take it away. Constable, will this invalidate our insurance, the fact that a member of the school has signed a document handing the television over to these two villains, "he spluttered. "It depends," said the first policeman, "What exactly did the paperwork say, and was it signed on behalf of the school, did it mention ownership of the television set." I looked over to him and started to realise that I had made a big mistake on a number of levels. "I didn't read the paperwork, Clive explained it to me and asked me to sign it in three places, which I did and he put it in his top pocket in his overalls. I'm sorry, I thought I was doing the right thing," I said apologetically. "Can you recall if there was a name on the paperwork, or was there a name on the van they used, or even a company name on their overalls?" asked policeman number one. "No, I don't think there was a name on the van or their overalls, and as for the paperwork I didn't get to see the top half of the page I signed," I said. "Give me strength," exclaimed Mr Yardley, "So from now on if any villain in the neighbourhood wants anything we have, all they have to do is get a van with no name on it, wear a pair of overalls again with no name on them, carry a clipboard, go to you and you will sign the paperwork allowing them to take whatever they want. I don't know what I am going to tell the Governers about this, especially if our insurance is going to be invalid because of the paper you signed." A strange thought hit me, what am I going to do about our television lesson on Friday with no television. I thought it best not to say anything about that at the moment. "Would you be able to give a description of the two men and would you be able to recognise them again if you saw them?" asked policeman number two. I looked at the two policemen and said," Well they were just average men, they were clean shaven, I think, shortish hair, average build, both about five foot six or seven and they wore overalls." "Did one have a wooden leg?" asked Mr Yardley sarcastically, although I didn't realise it at the time. "No, I don't think so," I said. "Good grief, he doesn't know if they both had two good legs or a wooden leg each, what sort of a witness are you?" asked Mr Yardley. "Calm down please, Mr Yardley," said policeman number one, "We've got all we need for now, we'll be in touch later if we need any more information. We better get back to the station and make out a report. Thank you for the tea." With that the two policemen got up and went out leaving me sitting there in front of Mr Yardley who was shaking his head and muttering to himself. "I got up and said, "I'll better get back to my class if that's OK, Mr Yardley." If looks could kill I would be dead and buried there and then. "Yes you better get back to your class, and don't think this is over because it isn't, I'll see you later. Now go," he said.

I got up and walked out of his office and shut the door, as I did so the traffic lights changed from green to red. Mrs Grant was still at her typewriter typing, she looked up and said, "Everything alright?" How could I reply to that except to say, "Yes, thank you," and I left the room. Everything wasn't alright; I looked at my watch, twenty to four. I thought it best to get back to the safety of my class room, I'm sure that Mr Percy would want to know what happened, or would he be discrete and see me later or would he find out from Mr Yardley when he leaves my class room. What a mess, at least I could change the art lesson tomorrow and get some work to put up on the walls as Mr Percy had suggested, and as for Friday and the making music lesson, that would have to be changed unless I got some ideas from Mr Sharpe on how I could use the musical instruments the children had made in some sort of lesson. It's going to be a case of keeping my head down for a while. What's the rest of the staff going to think when they found out that I have handed over our nice new television over to two burglars, well they weren't burglars as they didn't have to break in, and I helped them take the television away too. When I reached my class room the children were working quietly with Mr Percy walking round the room, stopping here and there looking at different children's work and saying something as he did so. I knocked on the door and walked in, I thought that was the best thing to do, and said, "I'm back Mr Percy, shall I take over now?" He came to the front of the class room, picked up a text book and said, "The children are doing this exercise in their English books, and it has to be in their best handwriting. I said that there will be a reward for the best presented piece of work so when you mark the books please select the best one and send the child to me, with the book, and they will get their reward. Have things been sorted with Mr Yardley and the other people who were with him?" I noticed he mentioned the other people rather than use the word police, which would have ears flapping in the class. "Yes, I think so," I said. "Good, I'll go now, and please don't forget the best piece of work to be sent to me this afternoon," he replied, and with that he went out of the room. Now that was a crafty move, send me the best work this afternoon, which meant that I would have to mark all the books during my lunchtime. At least that would get me out of the staff room and all the banter that there would be when all the staff find out that the new television has been nicked, even worse if they find out it was me that lent a helping hand in its disappearance.

I stopped the lesson with five minutes to go, collected the English books, told the children to put their things away in their desks and said, "Let me see who is the smartest and quietest person sitting in their seat, and don't forget I will be marking your books and the best one will be taking their book to Mr Percy to get a reward from him this afternoon." The reward thing had a great effect on the class as they were all sat there in their seats trying to outdo each other by their silence and stillness. The bell went and I said, "Let's see how quiet you can stand up," and they all stood up in silence and stood by their desks. "Row by row off you go, in silence please," I commanded, and like magic off they went in silence and row by row. As the last child went out I followed and made my way to the staff room. Once there I got my mug, poured myself a cup of tea and took it back to my class room. I put the mug on my desk and got my lunch box from my bag, ham and pickle today and a banana. I sat down and started to go through the English books while I munched away at my lunch.

I finished the marking with ten minutes to spare and I had selected John Harding's book as the best. Just as I was about to go and collect the children from the yard, Tony Telford appeared at my door. "What's all this about the television and you helping the villains to take it," he said. "I understand that Mr Yardley is going to call a Governers meeting this afternoon and try to explain to them what has happened to their precious television set. What really happened, did you help them take it?" "The television lesson was a bit of a disaster, I had skipped a couple of pages in the lesson notes booklet, the pages that said that the instruments would be used in the weeks to come, which meant the children had to sit there and clap their hands at various points in the programme. Some of the instruments got broke and the contents went all over the floor, sand, rice and dried peas which meant the television trolley couldn't move over the mess until it was cleaned up. The programme finished ten minutes before home time and I was on duty on Friday so I decided to lock the class room up and the television could stay where it was until after school, then I could sweep up the mess on the floor and then push the television into the store room and lock it up. Then I would lock the class room up and put the keys back in Mrs Grant's office drawer where I had been told to put them. When I went up to the music room after everyone had gone home I swept the mess off the floor and was about to push the trolley into the store cupboard when two men in overalls came in and said they were to take the television away as they had to alter the variance in the colour spectrum and that could only be done in their workshop. They did say that they would have it back by Monday morning and that they had seen Mr Yardley before coming up to the music room. They even had some paperwork that I had to sign saying that they could take the television away. How was I to know it was all a hoax and that all they were doing is stealing our television," I explained. "You have got yourself in a bit of a pickle," he said, "Are you a member of the union because if you are not careful you might find yourself in big trouble." "I'm not sure, I did sign some papers about a union but I don't know which one, I'll check it out when I go home tonight. Look it's nearly time for the bell, we'd better go and collect the kids off the yard, I don't want to be in any more trouble than I'm already in," I said to him. We both went out over to the yard just as the bell was starting to ring.

As I got to the place on the yard where my class were going to line up, Mr Percy was there waiting for me. "Ah, there you are, I was looking for you in the staff room," he said, "Mr Yardley has told me about your involvement with the television set. He has asked me to tell you that he wants to see you straight after school is over in his office, he will have one or more of the Governers with him. I haven't seen him so agitated like this before, even when someone let all this tyres down on his car he wasn't this bad." Now that was reassuring, not as bad when someone had let all his tyres down. It put me in mind of the story of Daniel going into the den of lions, but thinking of that story, it didn't turn out too bad for Daniel did it. "I've marked the English books from this morning and I have got the best one for you, it is John Harding's book. I'll send him to you straight after registration this afternoon," I said, trying to change the subject from the television set. "Yes, send him to me after registration; I'll give him one of the new pens we sent for last term, that might encourage him to continue to carry on with his best work. Always try to reward those who try their best, it makes the others try harder as well. Don't forget to see Mr Yardley straight after school." And that was that. He turned and went back into school just as the bell started to ring. My class, seeing that I was waiting, rushed to be first in the line which started a pushing and shoving contest between Terry, Tommy and Alfie, and Alfie being the biggest managed to push both Terry and Tommy out of the line. "I'm not having that sort of behaviour in our line," I said, "Now you three go to the back of the line and no more pushing otherwise there will be trouble."

I led the class into school, got them sat down and reading their reading books in silence while I took the register. Once it was done I told the class to close their books and look towards me. When the children saw that I had their English books in my hand, there was a sense of expectancy from them. "Children I have marked this morning's exercise in your English books and Mr Percy told you the best one would get a reward, and the best one was John Harding.

Well done John, now can you take the register back to the office and go to Mr Percy's room and collect your reward," I said. There was a couple of slight moans from various parts of the class room so I added, "It was very hard picking out one of you as nearly all the work you all did was very, very good. But Mr Percy only wanted one and John was the winner." This praise for the rest of them seemed to do the trick as they all calmed down. John came out and took the register and went out to collect his reward. Now, was I going to tell the children that we were not going to have a making music lesson on Friday due to the fact that the school didn't have a television any more, or that we weren't having an art and craft lesson making drums tomorrow. No, I would play it by ear and tell the children that they would be creating some work to decorate the display area on the walls in the art lesson instead of making some more instruments. So this afternoon we were to do some geography and today's lesson was about maps, why they were important and how we use them. After the introduction of the lesson, which was interrupted when John Harding came back holding his new pen up high so that the whole class could see it. "Yes, that's a very nice pen you have been given, now please sit in your seat and follow what we are doing. You haven't missed much, and the rest of you, you might also get a reward for your good work, as John did, if you do your best. Now back to our lesson," I said. I continued with the rest of the introduction and then had some questions and answers. After this I got the children to draw a map of their way to school, showing which streets they walked down and what shops they passed and so on. I found it a good lesson mainly because the children were interested and keen to draw their maps. All too soon it was playtime and I thought it was time to bite the bullet and go and spend the break time in the staff room. I took my mug with me to the staff room and got myself a tea and sat down in the corner of the room.

Miss Stark and Mrs Cook came in went to the sink to get their drink, saw me in the corner and came over to sit next to me. "Hi, you weren't in the staff room at dinner time, you missed all the fuss," said Miss Stark. "No, I had some marking that had to be done as Mr Percy wanted to reward the best piece of work for this afternoon so I had to get it done at dinner time. What was the fuss about?" I asked. "Well Mrs Peterson went with her class to the music room for her television lesson, she had picked the keys up from Mrs Grant, she unlocked the class room door, got her class into the room and went to the store room to get the television out and it wasn't there. It had gone, although the door had been locked," continued Mrs Cook, "She sent one of the children to get Mr Yardley to come and see and when he got to the class room he seemed lost for words, especially when Mrs Peterson had said that both doors had been locked. It's a complete mystery how the television has simply just vanished. One of my children in my class had seen two policemen in school when they had gone to the toilet during lesson time." Now do I own up now and tell them what had really happen or just stay quiet, but as luck would have it a voice from the other side of the staff room called out, "Could Miss Stark and Mrs Cook please go to the playground now as there seems to be an incident involving children from both your classes." They both looked at me and apologised and left for the playground. Saved for the time being but I still had to see Mr Yardley and the governor after school. Playtime over, I collected my class from the yard and took them into our class room. Our last lesson was history, following a series of text books aimed at children aged eight to ten. We were learning about the Roman invasion of Britain and how the Roman way of life spread throughout the country and how it changed life for the indigenous Britain's forever. Most of the children liked this lesson as it involved armies, fighting and strategy and of course everyday living. The children were surprised to find out that the Roman villas had central under floor heating. All too soon the bell went and lesson was over and it was time for me to go and see Mr Yardley.

Once the children had left the class room I collected by bag and coat and made my way up to Mr Yardley's room. I reported to Mrs Grant that I was here to see Mr Yardley who was expecting me. Mrs Grant called Mr Yardley on the intercom to say that I was here and waiting in the outer room. I looked over to the traffic lights on the door frame but they stayed at red. "I think Mr Yardley is waiting for Mr Percy to join him for the meeting," she said, "Could you take a seat and wait please." I'm sure the butterflies in my stomach had butterflies in their stomach as well. Waiting is the worst thing especially when you are not sure which way the meeting is going to go. Fortunately, I wasn't waiting long as Mr Percy arrived, Mrs Grant called Mr Yardley on the intercom and this time he told her to send both of us in. The traffic lights went from red to green.

I followed Mr Percy into the room. Mr Yardley was sat behind his desk and two Governers we at each side of his desk as well. "Come in and please sit down," said Mr Yardley pointing to two empty chairs, one of which was in front of his desk which was meant for me, "these two gentlemen are two of our school Governers, this is Mr Westbrook-Smith who managed to persuade the council to select us to have the colour television and the other gentleman is Governor Mr Myers." "Isn't this the young man that was in the paper a few weeks ago who managed to recover a substantial amount of money, due to his quick thinking, from a robbery that had just taken place in a book makers. And now he is involved in the disappearance of the colour television set from the school," said Mr Westbrook-Smith. I must have looked like a rabbit when it is in the middle of the road at night caught in the headlights of an oncoming car. I was lost for words, my mouth was all dry and I opened it although nothing came out, not even a sound. Mr Percy came to my rescue, "Just tell us all what happened last Friday afternoon regarding the television set." I sat up and composed myself and started, "I had booked a television programme called Making Music which involved the children making their own instruments beforehand ready to play along with the presenter of the programme on the Friday. However I had made a mistake and thought the children had to make all the instruments ready for the first programme, but they didn't need any instruments for the first programme, all they had to do was count and clap to the beat. Unfortunately, some of the instruments got broken and the filling inside them went all over the floor, which meant I was unable to push the television on its trolley into the store room until the floor was swept. As Friday is my duty day and I had to see the children safely out of the cloakroom after school, I locked the music room up while I went and saw all the children safely out and went back with a brush to sweep up all the mess. It was while I was sweeping up that two men called Albert and Clive wearing brown overalls came into the room and said that they had come to take the television set away but they would have it back on Monday morning," "Why did they say they were taking the television away?" asked Mr Myers. "They said they had to alter the variance in the colour spectrum and that could only be done in their workshop, they also added that this was quite common with new colour television sets after they had been running for a week or so. I don't know anything about televisions so I thought this was normal, also they said that they had seen Mr Yardley before coming up to the music room. Seeing that the television set was heavy I offered to give them a hand, which I did, I opened doors for them and the doors on their van," I explained. "Mr Yardley said you signed some paperwork stating that you were handing the television over to the men, is that right?" asked Mr Westbrook-Smith. "Well yes," I said. "Did you read this paperwork first?" said Mr Myers. "No, but Clive told me what it said and that it was normal for such paperwork to be signed by the person handing over the television set. I signed it in three places and he said that a copy would be sent to the school on Monday," I said, "Once the television was loaded in their van I went back up to the music room and put the trolley in the store room and locked the door and then I locked the music room door and went home." "Anything else you wish to ask him?" said Mr Yardley as he looked at each governor and Mr Percy in turn. They all shook their heads then Mr Yardley looked at me, "Can you please wait outside until we talk this through," and he pointed to the door. I got up out of the chair and went out of the room and sat on one of the chairs outside. I noticed the traffic lights on the door frame were on red and that Mrs Grant had gone home.

I was sat outside the room and imagined what a naughty child must feel like, sitting there waiting. I must have been there for about ten minutes or more when the door opened and the two Governers came out, saying their goodbyes to Mr Yardley as they did so. Mr Percy came to the door and asked me to go back in as Mr Yardley wanted to have a word with me. "Yes, come in and sit down please," said Mr Yardley, "Mr Westbrook-Smith was very sympathetic to your explanation of how the television was taken and as he is the chair of Governers we agreed with him. But please be careful in future, especially with school equipment, and if anyone comes to you to take anything away please refer them to me or Mr Percy, even if they say that they have seen us before they came to you. Mr Myers thinks we can get the insurance to cover the loss as they didn't give you the paperwork that you said you had signed, which could have got the insurance company off the hook on paying us for the loss. Do you have anything to say, Mr Percy?" "No thank you headmaster, I think you have covered everything," said Mr Percy. "Good, but before you go, here take this," said Mr Yardley as he gave me an envelope. I took the envelope with a puzzled look on my face. Mr Yardley saw that I wasn't sure about it so he told me, "That's the cleaning bill for my suit from the other weeks little episode regarding your frog and the incident in my office. I told you that you would get the bill and here it is. Please pay it within the next week. Thank you and good evening." As I stood up to leave I said, "Good evening and thank you," and left the room clutching the envelope and in a bit of a daze. I had managed to get out of trouble, thanks to Mr Westbrook-Smith, bless his cotton socks.

Chapter Ten

The next day, Wednesday, started the same as any other school day. The journey into school was uneventful although as I sat on the bus I realised because of Mr Yardley's cleaning bill my intention of buying a new watch went out of the window which meant for another month I would have to put up with a watch that told me the right minutes past or to the hour but not the right hour. I dropped my things off in my class room and went up to the staff room. There was a definite buzz of conversation in the room which is a bit unusual first thing in the morning. I went over to the sink, got my mug and poured myself a cup of tea. I saw Miss Stark waving to me to go over and sit next to her. I waved back and made my way over to sit next to her. Was she going to carry on with the conversation that she started at yesterday's break time about the television before she and Mrs Cook had been called away I wondered. I just got sat down when Mr Percy came into the room and asked for quiet. "As some of you may know by now, our nice new colour television set has been stolen last Friday after school. The theft wasn't realised until Mrs Peterson went with her class to watch a television programme on Tuesday morning. The music room was locked, as was the store room but when she went to the store room the television was missing. Naturally, we called the police as soon as Mrs Peterson let the office know about the theft. Since then they have been making enquiries into how it was taken. Mr Yardley will be telling the whole school about the missing television in assembly this morning. Can staff please take a good look at your classes and see if there are any guilty faces amongst them, if any of the children know anything they might give themselves away? Also if any of the parents tell you anything that might have any bearing on this matter please let myself or Mr Yardley know as soon as possible. Thank you all for your help, and as it's nearly time for the bell please start to go and get your classes," said Mr Percy. Well that was lucky, I thought, he never mentioned me or my part in the missing television. "Did you know what had happened to the television?" asked Miss Stark as we were leaving. "Sort of," I said, "Mr Yardley saw me yesterday as I was the last one to have used the television set with my class on Friday afternoon," which was true, it was the part where I had handed over the television that was missing.

As the staff went out the staff room Mr Percy looked at me and shook his head slightly as I passed by him.

The bell was ringing as I got down to the yard where my class was. As usual there were a few children already lined up waiting for the others to join them. Some of the children were excited and called out to me, "Sir, is it true that our telly has been nicked," and "If the telly has been nicked does that mean we won't be having any more boring music lessons on Friday?" "Mr Yardley will let you all know what has happened in assembly this morning. Please lead in, Matthew, the rest of you follow on," I said. I wondered, should I ask the children if they knew anything about the missing television in registration, as the children walked into school. No leave it to Mr Yardley and then ask them when we come back from assembly. As I thought, there were more questions in the class room from children who wanted to know what had happened to the television set. Again I told them to see what Mr Yardley had to say about it. At last it was assembly and we lined up and went into the hall. Some classes were already there and their teachers stood watching carefully, as Mr Percy had instructed, at their classes with an intense interest in all their pupils. I lined my class up in the usual place and stood at the end and looked at each child in turn to see if there were any tell-tale signs that they might know something. What were the tell-tale signs I wondered, but I did as the rest of the staff were doing looking at the pupils intensely.

Mr Yardley walked down the hall in his usual manner and as he passed me I looked at his face and saw that the black eye was nearly gone but did I detect some make up around the eye and the side of the face. From a distance it wasn't noticeable but close up, as he passed, yes, there was a touch of makeup. I wondered what the children would say if they knew that Mr Yardley wore makeup and the names they would make up for him. These started going round in my head and I started to smile thinking of them when Tony Telford hissed, "Are you alright?" "What, yes, I was just thinking of something," I whispered back. "Well don't let old Yard Brush catch you smiling when he starts, and keep watching your kids, he'll be looking for that from the staff," he replied. With that Mr Yardley was on the stage, "Sit down children," he said. This was unusual as the children never sit down in assembly, although it made it better for the staff to observe not only the children in their own class but children from other classes. "I have something very serious to tell you all. As you know, our school was selected from all the schools in the town, along with a few others, to be given a brand new colour television set so that we could participate with the schools television programmes. I am sorry to have to tell you all that our television has been stolen from our school. Two men came into our school and stole our television from each one of you and our staff, because it is you who are going to miss out without our television set. This was very wrong and we need your help in trying to get it back. If anyone knows anything about this or if you can tell your parents about what has happened, perhaps they might have some information that could lead in getting the television back. If you do have any information, however small then please let your teacher know and if it really important then let Mr Percy or myself know about it. Mr Sharpe, can we have the hymn please, 'Twilight is stealing'," instructed Mr Yardley. From the side, the overhead projector shone the words on the screen while Mr Sharpe played the introduction jumped up from his seat, shouted now, and sat back down as the children started to sing. As I watched the children try to make the most of the hymn, which I had never heard before, I thought about how Mr Yardley had tackled the missing television, how he had said it was their television, each and every one, so that every child would think it had been stolen from them personally.

Back in class after assembly the children were full of it, some had ideas how the television was stolen, others said that they were upset that anyone could steal it from the school, and others called out names that others laughed at. All in all, the children had nothing to offer regarding the theft. I reminded them what Mr Yardley had said about mentioning it to their parents when they went home tonight. From there on, Wednesday morning lessons went on as usual. I told the children that, because we were unable to continue the television programme making music, we would be doing painting in the art lesson this afternoon. I asked for the four people who had helped last week in getting the class room ready for the art and craft lesson to join me again at dinner time and get the class room ready for our art lesson.

I was back in the class room at twelve thirty after having a quick lunch in the staff room. I was thankful that whoever had this class room before me had a good supply of newspapers in the store cupboard. About five minutes later Nicola, Janet, Timmy and Alfie all turned up to help get the class room ready for this afternoon's lesson. I was very impressed with Alfie's behaviour and how determined he was to do his best. Maybe his dad was away and he could relax at home better and not be worried about getting hit by him. "Please make sure that the desks that make up the painting tables come from the same area so that they can be put back in the same place after the lesson. We don't want the same thing that happened last week with the confusion of desks being put back in the wrong place," I said. The four children worked well together and soon the tables were covered with newspaper and water jars along with paints and paint brushes were on the tables. I asked that the coloured pencils along with the ordinary pencils be put on the tables as well. I found an easel in the store room that I placed alongside my desk at the front. The paper for the painting was placed on my desk. A quick look at my watch, ten past eleven, that new watch would have to wait another month as I have to pay Mr Yardley his cleaning bill at the end of this week, anyway nearly time for the bell. I told the four children to go and line up with the rest of the class on the yard. I took a look around the class room then went to collect the children from the yard just as the bell was ringing.

As soon as the registration was out of the way I told the children that the instruments they had made last week were not needed until we had the television back and then if the programme we were following was going to be repeated later in the school year. I explained that we needed some painting to put on display on our walls to cheer the place up and today I was going to show them how to do a landscape painting. I pinned a piece of paper to my easel and got a water jar and a thick paint brush. "I am going to show you how to paint a sky using a wash," I said, "Now watch carefully, first I get my thick paintbrush and dip it into clear water and cover the top third of the paper in clear water, not too much, just enough to wet the paper. Then, quickly, I dip the same brush in the blue paint and starting from the top and working side to side in the wet paper I spread the colour downwards and as it moves closer to the bottom of the wet paper the colour is fading. And there is your sky, a deep blue at the top and a pale blue towards the bottom where the horizon starts. You can then do a wash in the middle third of your painting, but make sure that the water you use is clear, which means you will have to change the water if is any colour in it. It will also mean that there will be a lot of moving about with people changing their water jars so I don't want any trouble from anyone of you. The middle wash you would use a green paint, again but this time starting at the bottom and working your way up to the line of the horizon, which means the deepest green is nearer to you and it gets fader as it joins the horizon. The paper shouldn't take too long to dry, then you can start adding in details in your picture, such as trees, bushes, buildings even people. You could even use the coloured pencils instead of paint for the rest of your picture. Have a think of what you are going to paint and I'll start coming round with the paper." I wasn't sure how much art the children had done last year or what materials they had used which meant that I might be needed here, there and everywhere as the children got into their painting. I must admit, showing the children how to start a painting by doing a wash was working very well. Nearly all the children had got the idea straight away and some good work was being produced and as expected there was a constant trail to the sink to wash out jars and refill them with clean water. On the whole the children were well behaved with a few exceptions when one child would dip a dirty paint brush in a clean jar of water just as another child was about to do a wash on their paper. Before I knew it playtime was upon us, no time to clear up so I told the children that they could carry on after playtime, which sent up a cheer from them all. They all had seemed to have enjoyed this lesson and as it goes, so did I. After I had dismissed the children for playtime I went round the class room looking at the paintings, some of which were very good and then with a feeling of satisfaction I went up to the staff room for my cup of tea.

I walked into the staff room and went straight to the teapot and got my mug and poured myself a cup of tea. I turned to see where to sit when a voice rang out, "Here's the silly bugger that handed over our new colour televisions set over to the tealeaves that made off with it." It was Ivan Jenkins, I'm sure he still had it in for me ever since I sat in his chair at the start of term. All eyes turned to me, I just stood there gob smacked. I had to do something and quickly. There's nothing like the truth to ease your conscience, well that's what my mum used to say when I was pretending to be ill to miss school. "Yes, Ivan's right, I am the silly bugger that handed over our new television set to two men who asked for it," I said. Now you could cut the air with a knife, everyone was waiting for me to carry on. Almost on queue Mr Percy walked into the room and the silence. "What's happening in here then?" he asked. "We were just going to find out what happened to our new television set from Father Christmas here," said Ivan. "Ahh the television set, well, it was a very good con trick by the perpetrators and I think that the majority of you here would have done the same thing as what happened last Friday evening. You're in after school and two men dressed in brown overalls appear at the door saying that they have seen the headmaster and he has sent them up to collect the new television set as they had to alter the variance in the colour spectrum and that could only be done in their workshop, they also added that this was quite common with new colour television sets after they had been running for a week or so. I don't know anything about televisions, and I don't know about you but I suspect that you don't either. So the story is feasible, especially as the men had the paperwork to go with removal of the television set," explained Mr Percy. I just stood there while he was talking and kept nodding my head here and there in agreement. The staff just sat there and listened, I could have kissed Mr Percy on the forehead, but I didn't. Well now the staff knew the whole story and my involvement in it. I took my tea and sat down next to Mrs Cook who said to me, "Well it wasn't your fault that the television set was taken. How were you supposed to know the men were thieves, I might have done the same thing as you. Forget about the whole thing and move on. Put it down to experience." I thanked her and felt relieved that Mr Percy had told the story and not me. The rest of the break time passed rather quickly and it was back to class.

Back in class after break the children finished off their paintings and put them on the table at the back to dry. Along with Nicola, Janet, Timmy and Alfie I allocated three more children to go round and collect all the things off the tables and when they were clear the children moved the desks back to their usual places. With only fifteen minutes left of the lesson it was time for Robinson Crusoe. I must admit, I was looking forward to the ending as much as the children were, not because the book was so exciting, it wasn't, it was because it would be finished. The bell rang at last and I dismissed the children. As I was looking at the paintings the children had done Tony Telford popped into the class room and joined me. "Some of those are quite good," he said," I like the sky in the paintings, how did the children do those, they look great." I explained that they had used a wash to get the sky painted and that some of the children had used other mediums such as the coloured pencils to add various details to the paintings. "Percy Parrott got you off the hook at playtime with the explanation of the missing television set. Ivan was going to rip you to shreds about it as he has a television programme booked on Thursday mornings, he was spiting feathers in the staff room about it at dinner time, some of the things he was calling you were words that he uses on the rugby field, not nice at all," said Tony. "My meeting yesterday with the Governers and Mr Yardley went well especially as Mr Westbrook-Smith was very sympathetic to my explanation of how the television was taken and as he is the chair of Governers the rest agreed with him. This afternoon Mr Percy let the staff know the full story and, as you say, got me off the hook," I said. Tony nodded and said, "Well done, looks like you have a friend in Mr Westbrook-Smith, that's always handy as most Governers don't know members of staff, only their name. Are you staying back to sort your paintings and put them on the wall then?" "No, I'll do it tomorrow evening, I haven't anything on at home and I suppose it will please Mr Percy who has already suggested that I have some kind of display on the wall. At the weekend there is a jumble sale in the church hall near where I am living and I intend to go and see what games I can get for the kids for use at wet playtimes. I've only got some blank paper from old exercise books to use at the moment and the kids will soon get fed up with that, I'm sure." "Try not to get games with plenty of pieces as these will soon go missing after they have been used a couple of times," Tony advised, "And see if they have any kids books such as the Beano or Dandy annuals, they always go down well at wet playtimes. Well time I was going home, I'll see you in the morning."

With that, Tony went, leaving me sorting through the paintings and thinking which one would go where, and which ones would complement each other on the wall. I looked at my watch twenty to eight, I would have to wait at least another month before I could afford another watch, and I must remember to bring in Mr Yardley's money for the cleaning bill this week. I could stay another fifteen minutes and then I'll go and catch my bus.

Chapter Eleven

It was Thursday before half term and sitting there on the bus on the way to school I was thinking that I was lucky to get this far with my teaching considering the various things that had happened to me so far. I was thankful that I could talk to Tony Telford and he had put me straight on a few things, one of which was getting the annuals from the jumble sale. We already had three wet playtimes since I had obtained them and they proved very popular with the children, I wish I could say the same about the games. Already pieces were missing from a few of the games and they would turn up days later in the most unusual places. I kept checking the local paper to see if there were any more jumbles sales being run in the vicinity of where I was living. According to Miss Stark there would be a lot of children's games and books at the jumble sales at this time of the year to make room for the new Christmas presents the children would be getting on Christmas day. I also thought about the Making Music television programme, I had misjudged how much work had to be done before the children even saw the programme. Next time, I will make better preparation and go through the programmes carefully before choosing one, if there were going to be a next time All that would depend on whether or not the insurance was going to pay out for a new television set and if the school thought it was necessary to have one as quite a few of the staff didn't take up the option of using it the first time round. With all these thoughts going round my head the journey was quickly over and I was at the school in good time.

I went to my class room and hung my coat up and unpacked my bag with the books I had marked the night before. I hadn't forgotten Mr Percy's advice to make sure that my marking was up to date. Mr Percy or Mr Yardley could come into my class room at any time and ask to see the children's exercise books. If they weren't up to date then I could be in trouble, especially as I was a probationer. I just had to put the children's marks into my mark book, which was due to be handed in to Mr Percy and the end of the first half term. I looked at my watch just enough time to transfer the marks from last night's marking, I should have taken my mark book home and did it then but I had forgotten to pick it up before I left as I had been talking to Tony Telford about the forth coming football match on Saturday. I managed to finish just as the bell was ringing. I went out to the yard and collected the children. When we got into class the children sat down and got their reading books out and I started calling the register. Mark Robinson and Terry Rogers spotted that the milk wasn't in its usual place in the corner. "Sir, sir, Freddie and Timmy haven't collect our milk yet and it will soon be time for assembly. Can we go and collect it," asked Terry. I looked at the class, no Freddie and Timmy. "Yes, but before you go, what are you both doing for dinner?" I asked. Silly question really because they both stayed school dinners, but I had to ask. Their reply, of course, was that they were staying school dinners. They both got up and made a rush for the door. "Stop !" I said, "No running, especially down the corridor, otherwise you won't collect the milk for this class ever again. Understood?" "No running, yes sir, understood, no running," said Terry. Mark just stood there and nodded. "Right, off you both go and you will join the class in the hall for assembly," I said. About two minutes later Freddie and Timmy walked into the class. "Sorry we are late," said Freddie, "But we missed the bus." "Yes, OK, you nearly missed your mark in the register, Terry and Mark have gone to collect the milk, and I take it you are both school dinners?" I said. "Yes sir," they both answered at once. I gave the register and the class school dinner book to Janet to take to the office and got the rest of the class lined up for assembly.

When we got to the hall there were other classes already lined up. It was a good five minutes before all the classes were there. I saw Mr Yardley waiting outside the hall looking in and waiting until all the classes were ready. As he passed by I saw Mark and Terry coming into the hall and lining up with the rest of our class, as they did so they both looked at me and smiled. This was a bit un-nerving, those two smiling at me, what were they up to, it must be something, but what.

Assembly over, it was back to class and maths. We started the lesson with the children chanting the times tables and then I went round the class asking random times table questions. After that it was doing an exercise from their maths text book on times table sums. I insisted that their work had to be neat and correctly spaced out on the page, for some this was as difficult as the sums were but they knew if the work were untidy I would ask them to do it again only more neatly. Rather than me going around the class to look at the children's work, I had the children bring their book to my desk, where I would mark their work and also check it was being done neatly. It was after five or six children had been to my desk that I noticed a strange smell. The children, when they fetched their work to me at my desk, were now starting to stand a little away from my desk and giving me strange looks. I was trying to work out what the smell was or where it might be coming from I realised that it was time for the milk. "Milk time," I called out. Freddie and Timmy both got up as did Terry and Mark. "We're giving the milk out," said Mark in a threatening way. "It's our job," said Timmy. "Yeah, but you weren't here this morning to collect it, were you," said Terry, "Tell em sir, we're giving the milk out today aren't we?" Diplomacy was needed here," The four of you can give the milk out today," I said, "And Mark and Terry can take the empties back when we have finished." Milk time was over just as the bell rang for playtime. "Put your text books away and put your exercise books on my desk as you go out to play. Thank you, off you go," I said.

It was half way through break time as I was drinking my tea, sitting next to Miss Stark when it hit me. Fish, that's it, fish. "Are you alright?" she asked because I must have said the word 'fish' out loud. "Oh, yes, it was something this morning in my class. Halfway through the lesson I thought that I could smell something familiar and it just hit me what the smell was – fish," I explained. "Was your class room windows open because we do sometimes get the smell of fish wafting in from a fish factory a block away. It all depends which way the wind is blowing. It's worse on a hot summers' day when the wind is blowing in the wrong direction, then you can smell fish. I'd hate to live next door to the factory but I suppose you would get used to it after a while," she said. That must be it, I thought, there was a window open, I'm sure of it, that's where the smell was coming from. "Thanks for that," I said, "That must be it." The rest of the break consisted of small talk, and then it was time to go and collect the children from the yard again.

Back in class it was an English lesson, how adjectives can make stories more interesting. I had prepared a story with no adjectives and the children had to insert their own adjectives in the appropriate places in the story. I explained to them although they all had the same outline story by using different adjectives we would end up with completely different stories from each one of them. I gave them the example start of 'one day' but by using adjectives it could be 'one hot day' or 'one cold November day' or again 'one rainy day' by using adjectives in the story we would end up with different stories. The children were keen to get going with their stories after we had a quick run through with some adjectives we could use in their story. As I got near to my desk there was another smell, completely different from the fish smell of before. I recognised it; it was the same smell that I had smelt on the bus with my encounter with the frogs. No one could have stepped in dog dirt at playtime, surely, but the smell was more pungent than dog dirt. I sat down at my desk, yes it was stronger here. Billy Preston, who's desk was in front of mine and looked up at me and said, "Cor, sir, there's an 'orrible pong in here." I had to agree with him but I said instead, "Never mind about that, get on with your story." I decided to investigate by going round the class room, at the same time trying to smell my way round without giving anything away. It was strongest near my desk that was for sure. There was only one thing for it, don't go near my desk. I walked to the back of the class when there was a strange noise, a sort of scratching noise. Some of the children looked up from their writing, "who was that?" I asked, no answer. The noise started again a few minutes later, this time louder, as though someone was scratching their finger nails over their desk lid. I looked round the class, the children seemed as puzzled as I was with this strange scratching noise. "Everyone stop and put your pens down for a moment," I said, "Who's making that strange noise?" All eyes were on me and then the scratching noise could be heard once more. Billy Preston put his hand up and said, "Sir, it's coming from your desk." I swiftly made my way to my desk and listened. I didn't have long to wait, the scratching sound started again. It was coming from my desk cupboard. With all eyes on me I slowly turned the knob on the door and opened it. It took me by surprise, a ginger furry animal shot out of the cupboard to freedom along with an empty tin of pilchards and then the smell hit me, cat shit. I slammed the door shut to stop the smell; in the meantime the animal was running round the class room like some crazy banshee. The children were either trying to catch the thing or were try to keep the farthest distance away from it. The whole place was in uproar, I was trying to keep order by telling the children to sit down and be quiet, while most of the boys were trying to surround the animal, which by now was identified as a cat, and an extremely fat cat at that. It was obvious that the only thing on the cat's mind was freedom and it was doing everything in its power to get it. I remembered that I had seen some old curtains in my store room, we could try to catch the cat with those. While I asked the boys to try and corner the cat I got one of the curtains out and approached the cat with caution. I managed to throw the curtain over the cat and the boys quickly stood on each corner and the sides thus capturing the cat in the middle. I grabbed hold of the cat through the curtain and turned it over while asking the boys to slowly release the spot they were holding down until finally the cat was in the middle of the curtain and I was holding the rest of the curtain around it, almost like a sack. To say the cat was not happy in this curtain cum sack would have been an understatement. By now it was hissing and meowing and was struggling to find a way out, its claws could be seen poking through the curtain. "Everyone sit down please," I said, "And stay quiet, we don't want a lot of noise otherwise it will frighten the cat."

It was at this point that the class room door opened and Mr Percy walked in. He stopped where he was when he saw me, holding this struggling bundle which was hissing and meowing rather loudly. "Oh, I was going to ask if anyone has seen a ginger cat this morning, but can I assume that is the missing cat in that curtain. Apparently it belongs to Mrs Braithwaite who has reported it to the police because she claimed that it was stolen this morning by two of our pupils on the way to school. How have you got the cat?" he asked. "I think it must have got into the class room at playtime, Mr Percy, one of the windows was open" I said, "And it must have gone into the cupboard and got shut in. When I opened the door it ran out and we have just managed to catch it." I looked over to Mark, Terry, Freddie and Timmy, all of which had their heads down sheepishly. "Maybe the cat just followed the pupils to school and then got lost," I said with conviction. The four boys looked at me with amazement and began to smile slightly. I handed the curtain to Mr Percy, who took it carefully and said, "It might be best to keep it in there until Mrs Braithwaite comes to collect it, unless you have a big box you could put it in." Mr

Percy took the curtain at arm's length which was still moving about erratically and making strange noises and he thanked me and went out of the door, closing it as he left. "I would like a word with four of our pupils at dinner time please. I think they know who they are. Now carry on with your stories."

We packed up three minutes before the dinner time bell rang. I said, "It's been a strange sort of English lesson today and one that I don't want repeating, I hope that your stories will be exciting to read and that you have chosen some good adjectives to make your stories come alive. Mark, Terry, Freddie and Timmy please stay behind as we need to have a little chat before you go to lunch. The rest of you stand, when the bell goes, line by line leave the room after you have placed your English books on my desk." No sooner as I had said this the bell rang. The children stood up and started to go out of the room, placing their English books on my desk as they left. Mark, Terry, Freddie and Timmy were still sat at their desks waiting for me to say something. I indicated that they should sit in the four desks in front of my desk, which they did. It was hard to see who the guilty party was, as all four looked guilty. "Freddie and Timmy, you told me that the reason you were late this morning was because you missed the bus, but a little birdie told me that you live two streets away from the school and you are not on a bus route. Mark and Terry, you went for our milk this morning but took a long time getting it. Now I don't know if you have worked this together or only one of you is responsible for locking the cat in my desk cupboard. Should I take the four of you to Mr Percy and let him decide what to do next or shall I deal with it myself, I wonder," I said. The four started to look worried when I mentioned Mr Percy. It was Terry who spoke first," Can you deal with it please sir, as we are not on Mr Percy's good list, especially after last year when he thought we were responsible for pinching the saddle off his bike, and he didn't notice it as it was dark when he got it out of the bike shed and tried to sit on it, then he realised that there was no saddle on the bike." "So, the four of you have a reputation have you," I started. Mark chipped in, "Terry said he thought it was us, nothing was ever proven but he took it as read that it was us." "Now why would he think that unless he had a good idea it was you, obviously it couldn't have been the only incident that you have all been involved in over the years. Yes, I will deal with it.

First of all the four of you will clean out my desk cupboard as the cat seemed to have had a small accident which has created a horrible smell. Have your dinner first then see Mr Johnson for a bucket and some disinfectant which has a neutralising smell then come back here to class and get the mess cleaned up. I expect everything to be sorted and put right by the end of dinner time. The cat mess should be wrapped up in paper towels and put in the bins outside. Do I make myself clear? "I said. The four of them nodded and said, "Yes sir, thank you sir." "Right, off you go and get your dinner and I'll see you later," I replied. The four stood up and left the room. I felt quiet pleased with myself that I had sorted things myself and in a fair way, anyway time for lunch. I collected my packed lunch from the store room and went up to the staff room.

The staff room was in some sort of uproar, laughter filled the air. As I was getting my tea Tony Telford came up to me and said," Have you heard about old Percy Parrot and his little accident this morning?" I looked at him blankly and thought oh no, now what, but I said, "Mr Percy, no, what accident has he had?" "Well, Mrs Braithwaite came in with a police officer complaining that her cat had been kidnapped by a couple of our pupils because she saw them picking up her cat outside her house and running into the school playground with it and she hasn't seen it since. Because she is always complaining Mr Yardley has told Mrs Grant that if she comes into school Mr Percy has to see her first not him. So, into school she comes along with a police officer and Mrs Grant shows them into Mr Percy's office as she didn't know where he was but couldn't be far as he wasn't down on the timetable for teaching in that period. Apparently old Parrot was only a minute away and he returned carrying a curtain with something in it that was quiet lively and jumping about, any way before Mrs Grant could warn him of his visitors he walked into his office and was surprised to see them, lost part of his grip on the curtain and the thing inside launched itself at the first thing it could see – Percy Parrot. It stuck its claws into his jacket and shall we say, was very loose with its bowels, all down the front of his suit. Mrs Braithwaite shouted, "What the hell have you done to my cat, and why was it in that old curtain. You have given it diarrhoea, you haven't been giving it tinned fish have you, that starts it off." And with that she picked up her cat and left. The policeman didn't know what to say except that the cat excrement smelt rather strong, and as Mrs Braithwaite had gone off without staying to make an official complaint there was no reason for him to be here and he left as well. Mrs Grant agreed with the policeman's comments about the smell when old Percy went into her office to say he was going home to get changed. He is not in a good mood and that might last for days, thankfully its half term as from tomorrow night and by the time we get back he might have calmed down. The only thing is, old Percy has a long memory and he'll not forget this for a long time yet. "Thanks, unfortunate for Mr Percy," I said, "Does he know who is responsible for the kidnapping?" "I don't think so, but he'll be looking into it, I'm sure," replied Tony. "Right," I said, got my cup of tea and took my packed lunch and sat near the window and picked up a newspaper and started to read it, or should I say I started to look as though I was reading it so that hopefully I wouldn't be disturbed. If Mr Percy found out that I knew something about this he just might give me the bill for having his suit cleaned. If that was the case - that new watch of mine was getting further and further away.

I returned to my class room a quarter of an hour before school was to start just to see how the four boys had got on. I walked in but there was no one there, although my desk cupboard was open and the inside was still damp, but it smelt a lot better. It took me a few seconds before I recognised the smell, pine disinfectant; well that was a lot better than pilchards and cat poo. I sat down and started to go through the children's English books and their stories from that morning. I was quite pleased as they were good and some were very good. Just then there was a knock at the door and Mr Johnson came walking in, looking not too happy. "What's this about you telling the kids to put cat shit in my bins? I was sat in my office having a break when I heard them messing about with the bin lid and caught them as they were putting it in my bin - cat shit. When I confronted them they said that you told them to do it." "Please, Mr Johnson, will you not use that word," I pleaded. "I don't know how you want me to dress it up, it's still cat shit, and I don't want it in my bin outside my office, it stinks. They said that you'd told them that they had to collect it and put it in my bin. What are you playing at, getting kids to collect cat shit then telling them to put it in my bin? Not right, that's what it is, not right." I could tell that Mr Johnson was not a happy man at this point in time. I had to get my story across to him now otherwise he would be going to Mr Yardley about it. "I sent the boys to you to get the cleaning materials to clean up the mess and then told them to put the cat shh... poo in an outside bin. I didn't say that it was to be the one outside your office." I explained. "No boys have been to me about cleaning materials today," he replied. That's strange I thought, where did the boys get the cleaning materials from, it's obvious that they have used some because of the pine smell. "I'm very sorry that this has happened and I will have a word with the boys concerned and get to the bottom of it. I'll try and make sure this will never happen again," I said apologetically. "Well make sure you do, I'll be watching out and if it does happen again I'll be straight to Mr Yardley, that's a promise not a warning," said Mr Johnson and then he turned and went out of the room. Things were going from bad to worse, I had to try and get back into Mr Johnson's good books again, that was a goal I have to achieve after half term.

I looked at my watch, five minutes before the bell. I went out onto the yard and saw the four miscreants stood together, so I went up to them. "What's this about you putting the cat poo in Mr Johnson's bin outside his office?" I asked. "You told us, sir," said Terry, "You said put it in the bin outside Mr Johnson's." "No I said put it in the bin outside, I said that you had to go to Mr Johnson and get the cleaning material from him. You were supposed to put it in the bin at the far side of the playground. Oh and yes, where did you get the cleaning materials from? Mr Johnson said you didn't get them from him," I said. "Timmy's mum is a cleaner here and we got the stuff from her cleaning cupboard. We put it all back, honest," explained Terry. So, a misunderstanding, I'd better not press it too much otherwise I could drop myself well and truly in the mess, and there's been too much of that today. "Boys, you did a good job of cleaning my desk, well done. But next time listen carefully to instructions and be sure what you are supposed to do. Now go and line up, the bell should be going soon," I said.

That afternoon seemed to drag very slowly due to the fact that I expected either Mr Yardley or Mr Percy to appear at my class room door and relive that morning's events. By the time it was playtime I was parched and couldn't wait to get to the staff room for my cup of tea. I sat in the same seat as dinner time and picked up the same newspaper. The staff room was filling up and seats taken when Mr Percy walked in wearing a sports jacket and some casual trousers, the first time I had seen him not in a suit. As he was at the table getting a coffee someone made a meowing noise. He spun round, I thought he was about to burst, and yelled, yes yelled, "Who the hell was that bloody comedian. I suppose you all know by now and I bet you all had a good laugh about it at dinner time. When I find out who is responsible for the cat they'd better watch out." With that he stormed out of the staff room leaving everyone stunned; no one had seen him so angry before. It was Ivan that spoke up, "Old Percy is a bit touchy, so my advice to all staff is, don't let the kids find out about what happened otherwise they will take the piss and our lives will be misery. You all know what would happen, he'd be taking assembly and all it would take is one of the kids to meow and everything would take off. We've just seen what happened with us so God know what would happen to the kids. Thankfully, it's half term and this should all be forgotten when we return." There was agreement and the nodding of heads all-round the staff room. After seeing what had happened with Mr Percy and his temper, I made up my mind to lay low the best I could and try to avoid any confrontation with anyone.

Five minutes before the home time bell rang, a boy came to my class with a message. Mr Percy wanted to see me immediately after school in his office. My heart sank, not what I wanted to hear. I thanked the boy and told him that I would be there. The children put their things away a few minutes later and the bell went. I dismissed the class and went up to Mr Percy's office. I knocked on the door and a voice shouted for me to come in. I opened the door and went in. Mr Percy was behind his desk and ushered me to sit down in front of it. He looked up at me and said, "You said that the cat was trapped in your cupboard, is that right?" he asked. "Yes, that's right," I said, honestly, as he didn't say which cupboard, and I thought it was better to be selective with the truth. "You didn't know about the cat until the door was opened, did you?" he asked. "No, I heard a scratching sound and realised it was coming from the cupboard. I opened the door and it sprang out sensing freedom, a child must have closed the door when it was in there," I said, "The only way I could think of catching it was throwing that curtain over it when it was in a corner, as otherwise it would have caused total disruption in the class room as some of the children were frightened of it." "Yes, of course, you did the right thing," said Mr Percy, "You don't know anything about any fish do you?" "Fish," I said, "Has Mrs Braithwaite lost some fish as well?" "No, it's just what she said about her cat and fish. Never mind, it was just a thought," he said, as he sat there looking at me thinking.

Having nothing else to add, I just sat there waiting. Mr Percy scratched his head, rested his elbow on his desk with his chin resting on his hand. "It's all very strange," he continued, "Why would a cat come in through a window at playtime and go into a cupboard?" "May be it smelt mice and went into the cupboard to look for them," I said. Mr Percy sat up at this, "But your class room has only just been renewed. I'd better get on to Mr Johnson and see if he can throw any light on this matter. The last thing we want in school is mice. Yes, you have been a good help, you can go now, but let me know if you see any traces of mice in your class room. Good evening." I got up and left the room leaving Mr Percy sitting at his desk deep in thought. What have I done, if he sees Mr Johnson about the imaginary mice then Mr Johnson might tell him about the boys putting the cat mess in his bin? Oh well, time will tell I suppose.

Chapter Twelve

Half term week passed very quickly, I had managed to get to Blackpool for a few days in a bed and breakfast and see the illuminations, something that we did as a family when I was young and I always told myself that when I started working I would go back to Blackpool and see the illuminations again. Thinking back, the reason we went to Blackpool was because my dad got either free rail tickets or concession tickets as he worked in the lost property office at the railway station. I think he was a bit of a kleptomaniac at heart as he used to bring all sorts of things home with him. I'm not sure why and how but one day he came home with a wooden leg and a stuffed cat. I waited each day for him to come home from work and see what was next in his collection. My mother was not pleased at all and used to say that one day he would be caught and sent to prison, but his answer was that the items had been in the lost property office for over three months and if the owner wanted them then would have collected it before now. He also added that after three months items were usually got rid of, so in a way he was doing the office a favour by bringing them home. I tried to think how someone would lose a wooden leg, or for that matter a stuffed cat. It just shows how careless some people could be. I had managed to get to two jumble sales in the week, bought more children's annuals along with various games that I deemed suitable as they had few parts to them and missing parts could be made easily if they went missing. At one of the jumble sales I had seen and bought a watch to replace the one my father had given me. At last I had a timepiece that would tell me the time not only in minutes but hours as well. I had also got all my marking up to date and the marks put in my mark book.

The second half term is an exciting one as it leads up to Christmas and the children start to get a little bit over the top as the term starts to wind down in December. As I was eating my toast and marmalade I was wondering what this half term would bring. Then I remembered the cat and Mr Percy incident day before half term, surely he would have forgotten all about it, wouldn't he, but Tony Telford said that he had a long memory. Then there was Mr Johnson, I must try to make things up with him somehow, get back on side with him. I collected the children's books and put them in my bag along with my packed lunch and a banana. I looked out of the window, it was starting to rain so I would need my raincoat, also it looked as though it would be set in for the day and the weather forecast on the radio confirmed it. This is going to be a good start to the first day of a new half term, first day back and a wet playtime.

The staff had to assemble in the staff room at eight thirty for Mr Yardley's briefing, ten minutes earlier than a usual Monday morning because it was the first day of a new half term. Most had got there earlier so that they could have a cup of tea or coffee and were sat waiting for the appearance of Mr Yardley. Bang on time in walked Mr Yardley accompanied by Mr Percy, who was dressed in his usual suit, which I thought had cleaned up very well considering what had been down the front of it. Mr Yardley started with the briefing. He welcomed us all back and hoped that we all had a good break and were ready to get back into the fray. There were two new children in the school, both brothers, and their family had just moved into the area. Thankfully neither was going to be in my class, but Tony had one in his class. We were told that the staff playtime schedule was going to stay the same for this half term, which meant that I was still going to be on duty on a Friday. Mr Yardley went on to say that the insurance people were still dragging their feet about the claim on the television set so it looked like the earliest the school would get another television would be next Spring term, and that was only if the insurers paid out. The next item I wasn't expecting, "Will all staff please check their cupboards and store room as Mr Percy thinks that we might have mice in the building," said Mr Yardley, "And it would be advisable not to keep food or any edible things in your cupboards or store room until things are sorted. Mr Johnson knows about it and has said that he will be looking into the matter." I looked at Mr Percy as Mr Yardley was saying this and wondered if Mr Johnson had mentioned the bins and cat mess. "This half term is a nice happy term and the children will start to get excited, so please don't let them get out of hand. We have the Christmas concert for the parents, the children's Christmas party and the staff Christmas night out, all of which will need volunteers to help organise them. If anyone has any ideas where we could go for the staff night out please let Mr Percy know as the venue has to be booked well in advance. Well that's it from me, Mr Percy, anything to add?" said Mr Yardley. Mr Percy took the floor, "Congratulations to Miss Stark, who completed a first aid course last week at the education centre and is now one of the school's first aid officers," he said and there was a round of applause from everyone whilst Miss Stark just sat there rather embarrassed. "There's a few more quid in her pay packet for that," whispered Tony. "What?" I whispered back. "If you are one of the appointed first aiders in the school then you get an increment in your pay, there are now three in school, Mrs Silby, Brian Thomas and now Emma Stark, so if there is an accident when you are on playground duty you'll know who to send for," he whispered. "Sometime during this term the Governers have said they would like to go round the school during a normal school day and see how everything runs. I'm not sure which Governers or how many Governers would come round but please make sure your class rooms are tidy at all times and that your children's work is displayed on the wall. Talking of displays, I notice that some class rooms still haven't got anything on their display boards, so please attend to it this week," said Mr Percy, and he looked across to Tony Telford. "Bugger," whispered Tony, "that means I'll be staying late either tonight or tomorrow putting stuff on the walls. Have you got anything on your walls?" "Yes," I replied, "Those paintings I showed you, the ones the children did with the wash. Get your kids to do something like that, it's easy and doesn't take long and you might get some good results from it. At least you will have something to go on the walls if you haven't already." "Yes, thanks, a good idea, I'll do that this afternoon, and I think I have some handwriting pieces that can go up on the wall as well," he replied. Mr Percy finished his briefing and went out of the room with Mr Yardley. "Well folks, into the battle once more," came the subtle Welsh twang from Ivan Jenkins, as he moved over to the sink and washed his mug out. The rest of the staff took his lead and got up to rinse out their mugs and leave. Tony and I were about the last to depart, yes, into battle, I thought, as we both walked out and made our way to the school yard just as the bell started to ring.

As the rain was very light, the children still lined up in their usual place on the yard. I didn't intend staying there long as I hadn't brought my coat from the class room. It was just a quick jog to my line and then I led the children into school and to the cloakroom where they put their coats on their pegs and then into our class room in line. Our milk was in the corner and Freddie and Timmy were at their desks reading. I got the children sat down and told them to get their reading books out and read in silence as I called the register and did the dinner register. I had a full attendance, something that I had noticed through the last half term, that there were very few absences in my class. Janet took the registers to the office and when she came back I started the English lesson - an essay entitled, 'What I did during my half term break.' I told the children that the best essays would be displayed on the wall and that on Wednesday they could do illustrations to go with their essays. This would mean that nearly all the display area in my class room would be filled with the children's work. There were a couple of groans but on the whole the children were happy to get on with their essays, especially as we talked about using adjectives in our stories to make them more interesting.

The time seemed to fly by as it was time for the milk. The milk monitors went round giving out the bottles of milk and the straws, and I was pleased that I had got a large tin with a lid on it for the milk bottle tops, which was a lot better than the black plastic bag they used to be in. The bell rang for playtime, but rang five times which meant that it was going to be a wet playtime. The children gave a cheer and then hands shot up and some were calling out, "Sir, can I give the games out?" I had put the games in a large cardboard box and the annuals in another; the new games I had bought last week were still at home. I told the children to sort themselves out if they were going to play a game together, then row by row they came out and selected the game they were going to play. Others just wanted to read either the Beano or Dandy annuals. As for the teachers break, the teacher next door would stand in the corridor so that they could look through the windows at the back of each class and make sure the children were behaving while the other teacher went to the loo, if they needed it, and got themselves a cup of tea or coffee after which they would return with their drink and take over from the other teacher looking through the windows. This system worked well, the staff knew what to do and the children knew that they being watched and usually there was no trouble. The children were allowed to go to the toilet a few at a time and the others only went when the first lot got back. Because they were more interested in playing the wet playtime games or reading the annuals, only a few seemed to want the toilet.

The rest of the day went well; it was a wet lunchtime which meant when the children had finished their lunch they came back to their class room and got the wet playtime box out and played games or read the annuals. The dinner ladies patrolled the class rooms making sure that everything was alright and that the children were behaving. I was told that if a child misbehaved at lunchtime, the dinner ladies would report the child to Mr Percy and that child was banned from school dinners and had to be off the school premises until five minutes before the afternoon bell was rung. This was more of a punishment for the parents rather than the child as they were responsible for the supervision of their child as well as feeding them at lunch time. As most of the children were free dinners it was a big blow to the parents having their child missing out on the free lunch. Consequently the children knew they would be in big trouble if a letter was sent home saying they had been banned from school dinner because of their misbehaviour.

After school was over I went round to Tony Telford's class room to see how he had got on with his art lesson. I walked into his class room just as he was looking through the children's paintings. "These have come out better than I thought they would," he said to me, "Certainly a good quick way of knocking out paintings in a hurry, and the kids seem to enjoy it as well." "Do you need any help putting them up on the wall?" I asked. "No, that's fine thanks, I'll stay back tonight and do it myself, I've got some other stuff to go up on the wall as well and I'm not sure yet where to put what with what. Did you have a good break last week, did you go anywhere or do anything?" he asked. I told him about my trip to Blackpool for a few days and the jumble sales where I had bought more stuff for my wet playtime box or should I say boxes. Seeing that he didn't need any help I bid him farewell and returned to my class room, collected my things and went home. As I rode home on the bus I started to think about the Christmas staff night out and what it might be. A dinner and dance maybe, that would mean a new suit or a new jacket and trousers if the dance wasn't that formal. Also, was I expected to take someone with me to be my partner for the night? Were all members of the staff expected to attend the night out or could one drop out without a reason. What else had Mr Yardley said, "A Christmas concert for the parents," what was entailed in that? Were all classes to be involved or just various members of each class, and when would that take place, in the afternoon or in the evening? There were seven and a bit weeks to Christmas and the way time had been going, Christmas would soon be here. That's something that I had noticed, the way time seemed to fly by. At least I was getting used to the children in my class and they were getting used to me.

The next morning, sitting in the staff room drinking my tea along with most of the other staff, Mr Yardley walked in looking like the cat that had got the cream. "Could I have your attention for a moment please," he announced," I have some good news for you all. As you may have read in the local paper over the summer, the council has opened a new ice-rink in the town and has invited various schools to have free sessions during school time over the next five weeks on a Wednesday afternoon. The council is also supplying a bus to take us there and back, so it won't cost the school anything. We will send years two to six to attend these sessions, but we will need some parents to accompany class teachers on these trips, so Mrs Grant is preparing some letters to be sent out to parents of children in your class to ask if they would like to volunteer to help. Mr Percy is working out a timetable of which classes will be going in which weeks. This is a great opportunity for the children to learn new skills. Thank you everyone." And with that he turned and went out of the staff room. "Bloody ice skating," boomed a Welsh accented voice, Ivan Jenkings, "Who does he thinks he has on his staff, bloody Diane Towler and Bernard Ford." I turned to the person next to me, which happened to be Miss Stark, and said "Who are Diane Towler and Bernard Ford?" "You have never heard of Diane Towler and Bernard Ford,? They are the team that won the rhythmic skating at the 1968 Winter Olympics which was held at Le Stade Olympique de Glace in Grenoble, France," she said. I was taken aback, "You seem to know a lot about ice skating," I said. "Yes, there was an ice-skating rink in the town where I came from and I used to go there every Saturday from being quite young and got quite good at it. I love to watch the rhythmic skating, sometimes known as ice dancing, the way the skaters move and their interpretation of the music they dance to. Mr Yardley is right, it will be a good opportunity for the children to learn new skills," she said. Well that put me in my place. The staff were still discussing the ice-skating as we went out to collect the kids.

Tony Telford came up to me and said, "Don't tell the kids about the ice-skating yet, I think Percy Parrot will let them know in assembly this morning." Yes, OK and thanks," I said.

Tony was right, Mr Percy was taking the assembly. He stood there at the centre of the stage waiting for all the classes to come into the hall and line up, unlike Mr Yardley who would wait outside the hall until everyone was in the hall and lined up in silence then he make his entrance like a little Mussolini strutting his stuff. Come to think of it, Mr Yardley distinctly resembled the Italian fascist dictator Mussolini. All he needed was one of those funny hats with the eagles' badge on the front and yes that was it – Mussolini's twin brother. Anyway, back to Mr Percy who was waiting, holding a piece of paper in his hand. Silence descended on the waiting audience, who were wondering what the piece of paper in his was that seemed so precious in his hand. We all waited with bated breath. "I have here in my hand a letter from the council inviting this school to take part in skating lessons for each class over the next five weeks," he said. He continued, "Your teacher will be informed when you are going. If anyone misbehaves then they won't be going." He then went on to tell the children that there was a lot of lost property from last term in Mrs Silby's room, so if anyone had lost something last half term they should go and see if it was there. There were other notices that he also read out then it was time for the hymn. Today it was one of the popular hymns that the children liked, you could tell that they liked it due to fact that they all sang rather loudly, whether they were in tune or not, and sounded happy about it. Hymn over it was time to get back to class. As I was taking my class out of the hall, Mr Percy approached me and said that he wanted to see me at playtime. "Now what?" I thought. Yesterday went alright and nothing has happened today, unless Mr Johnson has let him know about the children from my class and the cat mess in his bins. Mr Percy must have let Mr Johnson know about the 'mice' for Mr Johnson to be doing something about them and so in turn he might have told Mr Percy about the bins. Well, I'd find out in just over an hour's time.

When we got back to class the children were very excited about the ice-skating. I asked the class how many have been ice-skating before, not many hands went up. How many could ice-skate I asked them, even less hands. How was this going to work, I thought, if most of the children were unable to skate. I knew the basics of skating, how to walk on the ice, how to start and how to stop, after a fashion I must say. I could skate forward but I hadn't mastered skating backwards, so I suppose I was just one up from a beginner. I'd better keep that information from the children as at the moment I didn't know if I was supposed to go on the ice with the children. I started the maths lesson, reminding the children of what Mr Percy had said about those children who misbehaved wouldn't be able to go ice skating. A perfect carrot for good behaviour. I only hoped that my class would be one of the last to go skating then the threat of missing out could be used to my advantage. All too soon the lesson was over, the milk had been given out and the empties collected back in, then the crate sent back with Freddie and Timmy. The bell rang for playtime and I went off to Mr Percy's office not knowing what to expect.

I got to his office and knocked on the door. A voice called out for me to come in. I went in and Mr Percy was sat at his desk with various papers and what looked like staff time tables. He looked up and said, "Yes, please sit down. Did you get a drink before you came up?" "No, I came straight up to your office when the bell went, just as you told me to," I replied. "Sorry, there's some tea that's just been made in the pot over there, help yourself to a cup if you want," he said, pointing to a tray with a teapot and cups on it on the side desk. This is strange I thought, obviously I can't be in trouble if he's offering me tea. I went over to the tray and poured myself a tea. Just then there was a knock on the door, Mr Percy called out, "Come in." In walked Miss Stark. "Get yourself a cup of tea, if you want one," said Mr Percy. She came over and I poured her a cup of tea and she put in milk and sugar. "Sit down, both of you," said Mr Percy, "I suppose you are both wondering why I have called you here? Well both your classes will be going to the ice arena on Thursday afternoon. I am getting Mrs Grant to get letters typed up to send to parents asking permission to take their children ice-skating, which they'll have to sign and return by Thursday. If a child doesn't return the letter then they don't go ice-skating. Also there will be some letters to various parents in your class inviting them to join you; these are parents who have helped out on trips in the past and are very good with the children. I have decided to send two different year classes together so that the older children will help the younger children on the ice rink. As Miss Stark has her first aid certificate and you are a probationary teacher I thought it would be good to put your two classes together. Before Thursday you may like to get the two classes together and pair the children up so that they know who their partner will be when they get to the ice arena. How does this sound to you?" "Yes," I said, "it sounds good to me and it will give the children in my class an ideal opportunity to show how responsible they can be towards the younger children." "And it's fine by me, "said Miss Stark, "We can both skate, so we will be on the ice as well as the children. You did say that you could skate, didn't you? "I can skate, just. I wouldn't say that I was a good skater, matter of fact I'm just a beginner," I admitted.

As we sat there drinking our tea, Mr Percy went through the timetable for the ice skating and asked Miss Starks opinion. The thought of Ivan Jenkings teaming up with Paul Sharpe was quite amusing, especially if they both fell on the ice at the same time they might crack it. I looked at my watch, Mr Percy noticed that and looked at his and said, "Sorry, it's nearly the end of break but thank you for your time. This meeting had to be called quickly so that we can get the paperwork moving. Please arrange amongst yourselves when you can combine your classes before Thursday afternoon. I'm sure Miss Stark will go through the safety aspects of the trip and what will be expected at the ice arena. Thank you both once more." We both left and on the way back down to the playground we decided that we would put the two classes together on Wednesday afternoon in my class room as it was a bigger room than hers. Well this was a turn up, and I thought that I was going to get dropped in the mire.

The rest of the day went well. The letters that Mrs Grant had typed arrived just after afternoon playtime. I explained to the children that their parents had to sign the letter and return it back to me by Thursday at the latest, otherwise no signed letter - no visit to the ice arena. They all nodded in agreement, also I had four letters for the parents who usually helped with school trips, and they were the parents of Susan, Janet, John and Terry. Those parents were going to meet with us on Thursday dinner time so that the children could see who else was going ice-skating. In a way I was quite excited, although I wasn't certain about going on the ice myself as I was sure that I would show myself up not only in front of the children but also in front of Miss Stark. After a few more pages of Robinson Crusoe it was the home time bell. As the children filed out of the room I gave out the letters saying, "Bring it back in the morning if you can, signed by one of your parents please." Once the children had gone I popped round to Tony Telford's class room to have a chat with him. On entering his class room I was impressed with his display work on the wall. He came out of his store cupboard with some more display work. "You've made a good job with those paintings and they go well together with those pieces of writing next to them. Have you heard, I'm going ice-skating on Thursday, my class with Miss Starks class," I told him. "That sounds good," he said, "only be careful." "I can skate, well just about skate. I should be alright on the ice, I think," I replied. "No, not be careful on the ice, I mean be careful off the ice," he said. I was puzzled, "What do you mean, be careful off the ice? "Well, just be careful, Emma, or Miss Stark as you like to call her, broke up with her boyfriend of three years last week during half term and she might be looking for a replacement. How old are you twenty six or so?" I nodded. he continued, "she is only twenty four, and, well, you know, she might start getting interested in you, as you are free and single. You are free and single, aren't you? "Yes, I am free and single as you put it, but I'm not interested. Yes, she's a nice girl and all that but as far as I'm concerned she is just a work colleague. Thanks for the warning though. I came here to see you to ask about the Christmas staff night out. How does it work and do we all have to attend?" "Well, previous years Mr Percy has arranged a dinner and dance mainly because both he and Mr Yardley and their wives are big ballroom dancers and that sort of night out is right up their street. Last year some of the staff sort of complained as quite a lot of the staff can't ballroom dance. Mr Percy wasn't happy but said that this year someone else could organise the night out, hence the comment yesterday from Mr Yardley about letting Mr Percy know what we all wanted to do for a night out," explained Tony. "I don't dance either, but I was thinking, it's apparent that a number of the staff like to have a bet, if Jimmy Moses is anything to go by, so what about a staff night out at the Casino that has opened recently? I understand that you get a deal from them: a three course dinner and then some chips to play on the roulette tables. That could be better than dancing - and you could win some money at the same time," I said. "That's a bloody good idea, I'm sure most of the staff would be up for that instead of a boring dinner and dance. Can you get more details such as what the meal would be, the cost, the time, what nights would be available around Christmas time, you know all that kind of stuff. I've never been to a Casino and I don't think many of the staff would have either so it would be a new experience for us all," he said. I told him that I would get the information from the Casino at the weekend and thanked him for the warning me about Miss Stark. I went back to my class room, picked up my things and went home.

The next morning at registration the ice-skating letters were being returned, nearly all the class had them signed and returned. The letters that were sent to the four parents were returned as well, although one of the parents said that she would be unable to help out this time but would we consider her to help in the future. I made a point of telling those children who hadn't brought back their letters that unless I had them by tomorrow morning they wouldn't be able to go ice-skating with the rest of the class and that they would have to stay in school and join another class for the afternoon. I nearly thought of saying that they would join Mr Jenkins's class for the afternoon, knowing that he had a reputation throughout the school as being rather strict with his class, but that might backfire on me so I kept quiet. The thought of missing out on the ice-skating because of misbehaviour was marvellous, the children didn't put a foot wrong, even when someone spilt their milk over Alfie Underwood's work by accident he just said, "Never mind," and asked for a cloth to wipe up the mess himself. Now that wouldn't have happened if there was no ice-skating trip in the offing. Normally he would have just lashed out and caused a scene, but no, today he was totally laid back about it. "We should have these ice-skating trips every day," I thought.

At break time I was just settling down with my cup of tea and was about to read the paper when Miss Stark came over with her drink and sat beside me. I looked up and smiled, as I did so I could see Tony Telford looking my way from the other side of the staff room. He smiled as he put his thumb up, which knocked the smile off my face. "Anything wrong?" asked Miss Stark. "Er, no, sorry. I was just thinking, er what do we do about transport, have we got to arrange that or what?" I asked nervously. "No, all that is sorted. I've got most of my consent letters back from the children and the four parents have also sent their letters back as well. What about your children and parents, have you got their letters back as well?" she asked. "The mums of Susan, Janet and Terry have said that they can come but John's mum says she can't come this time but would like to be considered to help next time. Most of the children have brought in their letters, I'm only waiting for six more," I said. "That's good," she replied, "Susan, Janet and Terry go home for dinner so can you ask if their mums can come into school this afternoon for a meeting straight after registration, that would be helpful but not essential. We'll get both classes in your class room after registration and go through what will happen at the ice arena tomorrow afternoon. Mr Percy has given me a leaflet from the ice arena of what they are offering and how long we will be on the ice and where we have to go to collect our skates and all that. I'll give you a copy later." She was definitely taking charge here I thought, but after all I was just the probationary teacher and should be thankful that she was taking charge. I'd just do as I'm told then nothing could go wrong. I looked across to where Tony Telford was sitting and when he saw me looking over he smiled again and put this thumb up. I told Miss Stark that I had to go and get some things ready for the next lesson so needed to go before the bell went at the end of break. She seemed OK with that and said that she would see me at dinner time. I told myself that I would take my time getting to the staff room at dinner time.

The lesson after break flew by, the children working their little socks off, all the time trying to please me with their efforts. It seemed very soon that it was time for dinner. As the children went out of the class room I reminded Susan, Janet and Terry to ask their mums if they could come back to school with them for a meeting about the ice-skating trip tomorrow. I decided to mark the children's books before I went up to the staff room, then have my packed lunch and after that come back to the class room and get the desks pushed to the side of the room so that all the children would have to sit in the middle of the room for the meeting. I managed to finish the marking by half past twelve and then made my way to the staff room with my packed lunch. I got my mug and poured myself some tea, looked around and saw an empty seat in the corner and went over and sat in it. Just as I was biting into my first sandwich I heard Miss Stark, "Oh, there you are, I've been looking for you. I thought you had stayed for a school dinner as you weren't in the staff room earlier. Mrs Peterson, can I kindly ask you to move as I want to have a chat regarding our ice-skating trip tomorrow?" Mrs Peterson, who was sitting in the seat next to me, got up and moved to the other side of the staff room and Miss Stark sat down. She had some papers in her hand, "Here's the itinerary for the trip," she said, "We leave school at one thirty so we will have to make sure we get the registers done quickly, and arrive at the ice arena at one fifty five. The children are not on the ice until twenty past two, but we have to make sure that they all have their ice skates on and fastened. That will be our job, helped of course by the parents. We are then on the ice until ten past three. For the first twenty minutes we will be having some coaching from the arena staff about the basics of ice-skating and then the children are let loose on the ice, unless there are some that need more help, and the ice coaches will be there to give it. We can couple the children up, an older child with a younger child. I have your class list and as I have taught them in the past I have matched them up with children in my class. How does this sound to you?" she asked. What more could I say as she seemed to have covered all bases, "That's great. I'll get my class room ready for our meeting this afternoon, so I'll just finish my lunch and get back down there," I said. "Yes, you finish your lunch and I'll come down and help you get things set up," she said. She then got up and went over to get herself a cup of tea. From the corner of my eye I saw Tony Telford looking my way, and smiling. He had his thumb up again. I'd like to tell him what he could do with that thumb, I thought.

I didn't expect Miss Stark to come down to my class room as I wanted space away from her, especially knowing what Tony had told me that she might be looking for a replacement boyfriend and I might be in the frame. We moved the desks to the side of the room, making a big space in the middle, big enough for the two classes to sit down. "I think I'm going to enjoy going to the ice arena with you," she said to me, "You seem to be more adventurous than the rest of the staff." How could I answer that I thought. I know, I'll change the subject quickly. "Oh, it's nearly time for the bell and I think I've left something in the staff room. I'd better go up and get it. I'll see you straight after registration," and with that I left the class room. I went up to the staff room just in case she was watching me. Just as I was approaching the door Tony Telford came out and saw me and smiled. "Everything going alright?" he asked. "Yes fine," I answered, "But I took note of what you said about Miss Stark breaking up with her boyfriend and I'm keeping my distance. That's why I've come up to the staff room, to get away from her." Tony just laughed and turned to go down the corridor and down the stairs, I followed. I made my way to the yard and waited for the bell to go. I stood where my class would line up and three parents came over to join me. "We're the parents of Janet, Susan and Terry. I'm Terry's mum, Tracy. This is Angela, Susan's mum and Maureen Janet's mum, we've come for the meeting about the ice-skating tomorrow," said Maureen "I'm pleased to meet you, and thanks for coming along and helping," I said, "I'm Mr Tredwell." A few minutes later the bell rang and the children lined up. I led them into school, followed by their parents.

After registration had been taken, Miss Stark and her class, along with four more parents, came to my class room and we had the children join mine sitting on the floor. "Nice you see Miss Stark's class joining my class and I hope we're all going to get along together. Miss Stark is going to tell us what is going to happen at the ice arena tomorrow so can everyone listen carefully and if you have any questions, please save them for the end. So it's over to Miss Stark," I said. For the next ten minutes or so Miss Stark explained what was to happen, "Lining up to get your ice skates, getting the adults to tie the laces, as these were to be tight to prevent accidents, listening to the ice coaches and doing what they told them, getting their shoes back and then lining up for the bus." The children were paired up, one child from one class paired up with another from the other class. The children were also told which adult was going to be in their group, so if they had any problems at the arena they were to go to that adult for help. I suggested that the children wear gloves to protect their hands, and Miss Stark backed up that idea. The children sat there and took it all in with only a few minor questions at the end. With all the details covered, the meeting was over and we both thanked the parents, adding that we would see them tomorrow at one o'clock then they left, along with Miss Stark and her class. I got the children to put the desks back in their usual places and we continued with normal lessons for the rest of the afternoon. After school I decided to make a quick getaway just in case Miss Stark put in an appearance. I was still thinking about what Tony Telford had said about Miss Stark looking for another replacement boyfriend.

Thursday mornings registration I had one pupil away, Matthew Armitage. He'd seemed alright yesterday I thought, so I asked the class if anyone knew why he might be away. David Hinchcliffe said that at playtime after the meeting, Matthew said he didn't want to go ice-skating in case he fell and hurt himself. I thought that was a shame because Matthew would have gained a lot out if it he had gone ice skating, mainly self-confidence, which he tended to lack. All the letters had been returned, except Matthew's, so that side of things were sorted. At break time Miss Stark sat next to me and asked if all the letters were back. I told her about Matthew and she said that she wasn't surprised. She then went through the final details with me; I suspected that she would do this again at lunch time as well. At the end of break as I was about to lead my children in from the yard, Tony Telford's class walked past and as he passed me Tony said, "You seem to be getting on fine," and he smiled. Before I could reply he was going through the door and into school along with his class. The rest of the morning passed quickly and just before the children went for dinner I reminded them that they had to line up quickly at ten past one, before the bell rang and we would get their coats and into class for registration and then we would be ready to go and catch the bus along with Miss Stark's class. I went up to the staff room with my packed lunch, got my cup of tea and tried to sit in a chair that was occupied on both sides but no - all of the vacant chairs had spaces in between so that's where I sat, in a chair that had an empty seat at one side or the other. About ten minutes later Miss Stark came in got her drink, looked around the staff room, saw me and came over and sat beside me. She put her drink on the small table in front of us and started to get her sandwiches out of her lunch box, "I've got you a list of the paired up children in both our classes," she said, "And I've allocated the different groups to the adults. Of course we will have more children in our group than the parents. I'm looking forward to ice-skating myself, what about you?" "Yes, I'm looking forward to it too," I answered, "It will be different from normal classes and I'll get the chance to see how the children behave out of school." "Yes, it can be an eye-opener to see how they behave, but usually on the whole they are quite good. If I thought that there was going to be a child that might kick off then I would have had a word with Mr Percy. I taught most of your class a couple of years ago and apart from one or two lively children they are a good class, once you get to know them. Lively children," she said. That was a good word for it, if it weren't frogs then it was cats or should I say a cat, and that was just in the first half of the term, but what would be next I thought. We spent the rest of the lunch break talking about ice-skating, taking part in it, even watching it on the television and wondered how the children were going to react to it, as nearly all of them hadn't skated before. The time soon passed and it was just past one o'clock, time to go and get the children, we both set out from the staff room together and down to the yard.

All of the children were waiting there in line, along with the three parents. As they were all there, I led them into school and our class room and told them to sit down whilst I did the register. I asked if anyone wanted to go the toilet before we left and about half a dozen said that they did. I told them to go and meet us in the cloakroom where the rest of the class would be getting their coats. Ten minutes later we were with Miss Stark's class outside the school gates waiting for the bus to come. Whilst waiting, I told my class that they'd be sitting towards the rear of the bus and Miss Stark's class would be sat at the front half of the bus. We only had to wait a few minutes for the bus, then the children quickly got on and we were off. Once at the arena the children got off the bus and lined up and Miss Stark checked us in with the reception before leading us to the area where we got our skates. The children had to take their shoes off and when it was their turn they handed them over in return for a pair of skates after telling the assistant what size their shoes were. Then they had to sit on a nearby bench and put their skates on and wait until one of the teachers or one of the parents went over and fastened their skates up, making sure that they were a tight fit. Then it was time for the adults to get their skates, although only two of the parents wanted to go on the ice.

That was it then; Miss Stark led at the front whilst I was at the end of the line and we headed off towards the ice rink where there were two tutors waiting for us. The children had to line up behind the barrier whilst they were told a safety drill by the tutors explaining to them what to do if they fell, which way to skate round the rink, where to go if they thought they were hurt. Then they were told how to get on to the ice and how to start walking on the ice and then, if they could, start to skate. They were also told that it was easier to hold a partner's hand for support as each held each other up. Miss Stark then told the children that the parent helpers were going to be at different points around the ice arena should they need help off the ice and that she and I, along with the two parents would be on the ice skating round to help anyone in need. That was basically it. We needn't have worried though, because the children took to the ice like ducks to water and I noticed that most were in the couples that Miss Stark had assigned them to, but one couple stood out, that of Alfie and a small boy who had a slight limp. I was amazed at how kind and helpful Alfie was with the boy and the encouragement he was giving him. He could have gone off and skated with others from his own class but no, he stayed with the boy, helping him all the way. There were a few falls, well many falls, but the children just shrugged them off and carried on skating. Those that did fall heavily went to one of the parents at the side, helped by their skating partner, for a quick burst of reassurance and then they were back out on the ice.

Miss Stark skated around the arena like a professional, whilst I wobbled about on the ice unsure of where and when I was going to fall. She skated up to me and got hold of my hand, "Come on," she said, "We're going round the rink. Hold tight." That was it, I didn't have time to say anything, and before I knew it we were skating round the rink with me hanging on to her hand like grim death to keep my balance. Once around the rink and then we stopped near a group of our children who seemed to be stuck. "Hold hands with your partner," Miss Stark said, "Like this." Once more she had hold of my hand and was showing the children how hold each other up while skating forward. A couple of the children laughed as Miss Stark skated round with me hanging on trying to keep my balance. "That's all there is to it," she said, "Now you try." The children needed no more encouragement as they moved off, slowly at first, but soon they had the idea and were off.

As with all good lessons, the time simply flew by and it was time to go off the ice and get changed back into their own shoes. I was pleased how many said thank you to the ice arena staff. We were all lined up ready to go when Susan in my class realised that she had dropped one of her gloves, saw it over near the benches and ran to pick it up. However she tripped, fell forward and, somehow, put her arm out to break the fall but in doing so caught it on the bench and gave such a yell that everyone in place would have heard it. Both Miss Stark and Susan's mother rushed over to her to find out how bad it was. One of the arena staff came over as well and the four of them went into the arena's first aid room, leaving me and the other parents waiting with the children. "Will she be alright sir?" asked some of the children. "Yes, I think so," I said, "She's with her mother and Miss Stark will check her arm, she shouldn't be long." Five minutes, that's how long she was although it seemed longer. The children were getting fidgety waiting. Miss Stark waved me over away from the children, "I think Susan has broken her arm so the arena staff have rung for an ambulance to take her to hospital. Her mother will go along with her, she'll wait here with Susan for the ambulance so we can get back to school. We'll just tell the children as far as we know she is alright but has to go to hospital for a check-up," said Miss Stark. "We'll have to make out an accident report when we get back to school. Did any of the children see what happened?" I asked. "We'll sort that out back at school," she said, "The bus will be waiting and we don't want to be late back." Off we went, the bus was waiting and the journey back was rather quiet, most of the conversation was about Susan and her accident and some were saying how many times they had fallen on the ice. We got back to school, returned to our class rooms and had ten minutes of Robinson Crusoe then it was time for the bell and home. I went round to Miss Stark's class room just as she was leaving. "I was just coming to your class room," she said, "We'd better go and tell Mr Percy about Susan, it's just a formality but he has to know."

We both went up to his room and knocked on the door. "Come in," he shouted. We both went in and were invited to sit down. Miss

Stark told him about Susan Harris and the fall and that her mother was there and had taken her to the hospital. She said that she would complete the accident report in the morning after she had any witness reports from the children. Mr Percy said it was a good job that her mother was there and was able to go with her to the hospital, he also wanted to know how the trip went in general and had there been any trouble from any of the children. We both agreed that the children behaved very well and were very respectful to the arena staff at all times. That pleased Mr Percy and he remarked that the rest of the classes had something to live up to. He thanked us both for the preparatory work that we had put in to make the trip a success and if there were an extra lessons going he would consider our classes. As there was no more to be said we left and went back to our class rooms but on the way down Miss Stark asked me, "Do you fancy going for a drink sometime?" What was I to say, she had caught me unawares, "I'm busy at the moment, when were you thinking of?" I said. "Maybe one Saturday evening, or if you prefer we could have a meal somewhere, it's up to you," she said. "Yes, good, let me think it over," I said, "I'm not sure what's happening over the next few weeks." With that, she went her way to her class room and I went mine. What did Tony say, she was looking for a replacement boyfriend, was I that replacement I wondered?

The next morning in the staff room there was some kind of discussion as I walked in. I went over to the sink to get a cup of tea and as I was walking to an empty chair a voice said, "Well, we've heard that one of the kids has broken their arm at the ice rink yesterday," and another voice said "I said it was dangerous going to the ice rink with all those kids. Next time it might be one of the staff who has an accident, then what?" Before I could answer any of the questions Mr Percy walked in and the questions were directed at him before he had chance to say anything. He then said, "Will you all please be quiet and listen for a moment. Yes there was an accident at the ice arena yesterday and a child has broken her arm. The accident had nothing to do with the ice or skating. The girl in question fell as the class was about to go and catch the bus. As she fell she hit a bench and that's how the arm was broken and it was fortunate, in a way, that her mother was one of the parents helping with the trip so she accompanied her to the hospital. The ice-skating was, from what I hear, a great success and all the children enjoyed the experience. I hope that the rest of the classes have the same results - apart from the accident," explained Mr Percy. "I would also like to add that staff don't have to go on the ice if they don't want to, but it helps both for the children and the staff at the arena. Other schools have been going to the ice arena for a while now and I don't think there have been many accidents, only a few knocks and bruises. If any member of staff has any complaints then come and see me in my office and I'll try to get them sorted." With that he went out of the staff room, which now was very quiet. "Well that told us," said Ivan Jenkins, "I had no intention of going on the ice in the first place." "Good job, because if you fell on the ice you'd crack it," said Paul Sharpe as the rest of the staff laughed. Ivan just snorted, got out of his chair, put his mug on the sink and stormed out, slamming the door as he left, which caused more laughter.

Chapter Thirteen

The weeks were flying by; the ice-skating lessons were going well with the various classes attending each week, and fortunately there were no more accidents. It was the briefing on the first Monday in December; Mr Yardley reminded staff that classes could start getting ready for the Christmas concert, which would give us about two and a half weeks to prepare for it. The concert would be on the evening of Tuesday 16th December, the children's Christmas party would be on Thursday 18th December, the day before the school broke up for the Christmas holidays. The staff night out was going to be on Friday 19th December at the Casino, a venue that most of the staff agreed on and the rest of the staff fell into line with. Mr Yardley said that Mr Percy would make the draw for the concert at lunch time and everyone started nodding. I wasn't sure what that meant but I would find out at lunch time. As I was going down the stairs to collect my children from the yard I caught up with Tony Telford and asked him about the draw for the concert. He looked at me and smiled, "Well, each year one class has to do a nativity play in the concert. No one ever wants to do it so Mr Percy draws a name out of the hat and that person's class has to do a nativity play. Also in the draw is the order of appearance of classes for the concert, again some members of staff always wanted to be first on and others last on, so Mr Percy had the idea of drawing positions from a hat. Over the past few years that has worked and the staff seem happy with it," he said. "Right," I said, "I'm not sure what my class could do in the concert, I'll just have to wait and see what position my class gets and take it from there." I reached the yard just as the bell was ringing and the children were starting to line up. As I was waiting for the rest of the class to join us I thought it best not to say anything about the Christmas concert to the children until the afternoon.

When I got to the staff room at lunchtime all the staff were there, which meant that there were only three spare chairs left. All the staff were eating and chatting to each other and there was a sense of expectancy in the air. At about twenty past twelve Mr Percy walked in holding a hat in one hand and strips of paper in the other. As he walked in there was a cheer from various parts of the staff room. "Thank you," he said, "Time for the draw for the Christmas concert. I see that most of you have finished your lunch. In this hand I have all the teachers' names and may I ask Mrs Peterson to fold them up please and while doing so check that all the staff names are on them, and then write down the order of names as they come out of the hat" Mrs Peterson looked at each strip of paper then she folded it into four and placed it in the hat. The noise in the staff room subsided then at last all the names were in the hat. This was it, very soon I would know in which position my class would be in the concert. "The first name out will be responsible for our nativity play and that will be the finalé of the concert," said Mr Percy, "And that name is," he paused to add to the tension, "is Mr Tredwell." All eyes were on me, I didn't know whether to be pleased or not, but looking round the rest of the staff were obviously very pleased. Was there something that I didn't know about here? "Right, yes, thank you," I said, not knowing how I should react to this honour. Mr Percy continued with the draw and Mrs Peterson wrote down the order in which the names came out of the hat. "Well, that's the concert order done, can staff please let me know what their class will be doing in the concert before the end of this week. Thank you," said Mr Percy and then he took his hat, the strips of paper and the list of the concert running order and went out.

The staff room was a buzz of chatter, different members of staff saying what they intended to do in the concert. I just sat there, thinking, when Miss Stark came over and said, "Well done, all you have to do now is find a nativity play that you could use, either that or you could write your own, that would impress both Mr Percy and Mr Yardley especially as you are a probationary teacher," she said with a smile. Now that was something, write my own nativity play, yes that would go down well on my record. "Do any of the Governors come to the Christmas concert?" I asked. "Yes, usually nearly all of the Governors come to see it and last year the Lord and Lady Mayor came and we had photos in the local paper. I think they only came because Ivan Jenkins used to play rugby with the Lord Mayor many years ago and they have kept in touch for years, so Ivan pulled in a favour to get him here," she said. "Have a word with Paul Sharpe, he could give you some good ideas about nativity plays, certainly he'll help you the music, if you are going to have any. I see from the draw that my class are second on the list, which is good because after they have performed I can get them back to class and changed so that they are ready to go home with their parents at the end. I'm afraid that your class are on last so when they have finished they will have to get changed before you can let them go home. There'll be parents waiting outside your class room and telling their child to get a move on and hurry up. You won't be finished until maybe a good half an hour after the concert," she continued. "Thanks," I said, "I'll see if I can find a nativity play to use and I'll see Paul about the music. I've some things I want to sort out in my class room before the bell goes so I'm sorry but I'll have to leave you, and thanks again." I got up, rinsed out my mug and left it on the sink unit then went out to my class room, not that I had anything to sort out.

I got back to my class room and sat at my desk, thinking. Maybe I could write a nativity play myself, add a different slant on the story, or maybe get the children to help write the play, yes that could work. I'd have to find out which children would be good in which parts, I'd also have to get all the children in the class to take part, giving each one a role to play. I started jotting down ideas, first the scenes then the characters that would be in each scene then what music I would need. Already the play was starting to formulate in my mind; it would take up some time but it would be worth it. As I was sat there thinking, the bell rang, so I quickly got up and went off to the yard to collect my class.

After registration I told the children that our class would be performing the nativity play at the school concert and I wanted everyone to take part in it. There was a mixed reaction from the children, some seemed excited but others tutted and put on their bored expression on their face. "We are going to do a nativity play that we are going to write ourselves, so I want you all to start thinking what characters are going to be in it and what they might say," I told them. For the next ten minutes I told them the nativity story but I pointed out why Mary and Joseph had to go to Bethlehem, the need for registration for the Roman emperor and the amount of money that would be raised by knowing how many people could be taxed, which meant how big an invading army could be, using the tax money to pay for it. Next I gave them some paper and got them to write the nativity story in their own words which we could maybe put together to add to our play. The children were interested in the background to the story, which many people don't know. This was right up my street as I'd studied history at college, with an interest in Roman history and the Roman Empire. The children worked well and happily and asked quite a few interesting question as they worked. They worked so well that it was playtime before we knew it. I collected the papers and the children went out to play and I went to the staff room.

I got my tea and sat down and was joined by Tony Telford. "Well done," he said, "getting the nativity play. Do you have any idea what you are going to do?" "Well, I thought that my class and I could write a nativity play, that way they would all be involved in it in some way. I've made a start by getting them to write their own version of a nativity story. I'm not sure which children would be good at which parts in the play, I need something to try them out first, if that makes sense," I said. "I've got some play books in my class room that you can borrow, there's enough for one between two. You can get them to read out the parts, the books have six short plays with six or seven characters in them. Get the children to take it in turn to read out a play, telling them to project their voice and be expressive. It makes for a good lesson and you'll soon know which children to be in the main parts of your play," said Tony, "I'll send the play books to you straight after playtime then you can have a go with them until home time. Keep the books for as long as you need them. I'll go and dig them out for you now." With that he got up and went out, leaving me sat there thinking. I was sat there still thinking as staff around me were getting up and leaving. I looked at my watch, nearly time for the end of break so I got up and followed.

Tony was as good as his word; the books arrived a few minutes after we were back in class. I gave the books out one between two. I looked through my copy, six short plays each about eight pages long and each with about six or seven characters in them. I explained to the children that we were going to read the plays out loud to the rest of the class. Starting with the desk nearest the door and moving along the front the children played the character in the list, so the first child played the first character; the second child played the second character and so on. Before we started on the first play I read out loud the first page playing all the characters myself but putting on different expressive voices for different characters. As the plays were comical and funny, my interpretation of the characters added to the humour with led to uproar in the class. I had to remind the children to keep the noise level down a bit as we might disturb other classes. The lesson was a great success, both myself and the children enjoyed the plays and the laughter but with every enjoyable lesson it had to come to an end. The children asked if they could do the lesson again the following day, to which I replied that we would see. The bell rang and the children left. Once they had gone I started to go through the nativity stories, some good, some bad, and some just understandable. I might have confused them by talking so much about the Romans and invasion armies, still I had some outline to work with. I got a blank piece of paper and started writing, the different slant would be that the story starts in Rome with the emperor Caesar Augustus and his generals planning to invade various countries and discussing how many men they will need, how many of those would be soldiers, how many cooks, armourers, slaves and how many supplies they would need and where was the money coming from. This scene wouldn't need much scripting apart from the two main characters, so children who couldn't learn many lines could be Roman officers who'd just nod and agree at various times. The only downside I could see was the costumes needed for this scene. I sat there writing away until Mr Johnson appeared at the door, "Still here?" he said. I looked up surprised, "Er, yes. I'm just planning the play for the school concert, I didn't realise the time, it simply flies by when you're busy," I replied. "So you have got the nativity play have you," he said smiling, "Always happens. Oh I haven't seen any mice or caught any in my traps, but keep a look out will you." With that he went on his way, I started to think, "How does he know that my class is going to perform the nativity play in the school concert?" I looked at my watch, another half an hour then I was off home.

The next day I had the scenes all set for the play and wrote them on the blackboard, then I explained them to the children, how many characters would be in each scene and how we would use the stage along with lighting so that some of the scenes would only use half the stage thus cutting down on scenery and characters. In our English lesson I suggested that we would write the scenes together as a class and that each child would have an input so it would be a class play written and performed by our class. The children all thought this was a great idea and were keen to get started. Our first lesson concentrated on the first scene which started in Rome with the emperor Caesar Augustus and his generals discussing invasion plans of other countries and the idea of taxing those countries already conquered to pay the expense of invading other countries. I picked John Harding to be the emperor and three other boys to be the generals and had them stood at the front of the class to act out the scene Their classmates were ready to add to the dialogue which was written down as we went along. It was pointed out that there no girls in the scene, so I asked what part some girls could play in the scene and it was suggested that the emperor should have a wife and she should have her girl slaves. With these in place, the pupils were not sure what they might say in the scene, so these were put on hold until later. These English lessons continued to the end of the week, by which time the whole play was almost finished. I promised the children that I would get the script typed out over the weekend and that we would start to rehearse the next week which would give us six days before the performance. Alongside that, I got the children to draw what they thought each scene might look like on stage to help us work out what scenery would be needed, which would have to be made next week. Then there were the costumes to be sorted. For these, I asked the children if any of their parents would be able to help make them. I knew that Mrs Harris and Mrs Harding were always keen to help and if we had a few more that would a great help. I was feeling confident that everything was going so well.

Whilst I was on yard duty on Friday afternoon walking round the yard making sure that the children were playing well together, Miss Stark came out and joined me. "Hi stranger," she said, "We haven't seen you in the staff room since the concert draw. Everything alright?" "Yes, things are fine," I replied, "I've just been very busy with the nativity play with my class." "Which book are you using? Did you get the one from Mr Percy, and by the way he has a couple that staff that you could use?" she said. "He has, oh I didn't know that, but it doesn't matter as we've written our own play, the children and I, and this weekend I'm typing it out and next week we will start rehearsals in the class room. So by the end of the week I hope to have the hall and practice on the stage," I said. "Well, I've just come out to see how you are and if you needed any help with the play. My class are only singing a few songs, one of which requires actions performed by the children which is great fun for them and the audience. I am on second, which means the children can go and join the audience then I can give you some help, as yours is the finalé of the concert," she said. "Well, I might be needing some help, getting the children ready with costumes, getting the scenery ready and that sort of thing. Can I see you Monday morning break time and we can talk it over. I'll give you a copy of the script and a copy which characters the children will be playing, that isn't fully sorted yet," I said. "Thanks," she replied, "I'll see you Monday morning at break time and I can't wait to read the script," she said, "I'd better get in, but I thought I would just let you know that I'll help with anything you want." With that she turned and went back into school leaving me thinking whether or not I was doing the right thing.

Whilst I was on duty after the home time bell had gone, stood by the cloakroom making sure everyone was leaving safely, Mr Percy came up to me and asked if everything was alright. I was a little puzzled and said, "Yes." He saw that I didn't quite know what he was referring to so he asked about the concert and the nativity play. I explained that the class and I were writing the play and it was finished and I was typing it up over the weekend so that we could start rehearsals next week starting on Monday. He was a bit surprised at that but said if there was anything that I wanted then just to see him and then left. As all the children had gone, I went to see if Tony Telford was still in his class room. When I got there he was packing his bag and looked ready to leave then he saw me. "Now then, can I help the budding Shakespeare?" he said sarcastically. "I've been thinking, on Monday, how did Mr Johnson know that my class were doing the nativity play at the school concert? He wasn't in the staff room when the draw was done, yet he knew straight after school," I asked. "Well to be honest, and don't let people know that I told you, but you have been stitched up with the nativity play for the concert," he answered, "Nobody ever wants to do it so it was decided a few years back that the new teacher would be responsible for the nativity play. Mr Johnson knew that and that's how he knew that you would be doing it. Mr Percy has the new teacher's slip of paper in his hand before the draw so it looks like he has drawn it from the hat but all the time it's in his hand. You've surprised all the staff the way you've gone about writing the play with your class. Mr Percy has stood back to let you get on with it, although he has asked me to keep an eye on you and if you needed help to let him know," said Tony sounding apologetic. "Well, in that case I will need help with the scenery and the lighting. Are you be up for that?" I asked. "Sure," he said, "I'm the teacher who has been responsible for the school plays in the past and I always work the lights for any of the performances that happen on the stage. We pride ourselves in having a good stage that is well kitted out, along with the stage lighting, also one or two of the staff could also give a hand if you need them, so don't be afraid to ask. By the way, how long will this play of yours last," he asked. "We haven't timed it yet, but it could be about thirty to forty minutes," I answered. "How long," he stammered. "About thirty to forty minutes," I repeated. "Bloody hell, I bet Mr Percy doesn't know that. In previous years, the nativity play has lasted about ten minutes and that included the carols that the kids sing in the play. How come it's so long?" he asked.

"Well I've put in the background to how it all starts, that is, with Caesar Augustus and his invasion plans in the middle east and how he intends to fund them, then on to the Annunciation with the angel to Mary and then to Joseph with leads to the road to Bethlehem and so on," I said. "Where have you got all the information from to write the play in such a short time?" he asked. "I did Roman history along with religious studies at college when I was training to be a teacher, it's also something that I am interested in, so writing the play was quite easy really and I wanted to put it all into perspective instead of the usual Mary, Joseph and the baby in the manger type nativity," I explained. "Well it's going to be different, that's for sure. Let's keep it to ourselves so it will be a big surprise for not only for the parents but for the rest of the staff when they see it. Has anyone else said they will help with the play?" he asked. "Yes Miss Stark came to me today while I was on yard duty and said that she would help with the costumes and getting the children ready on the night, also one or two of the parents are willing to make costumes as well," I said. "You have been a busy boy, haven't you? Well I'm ready to get off home, so I'll see you on Monday morning. Don't work too hard over the weekend," he said and then started to pick his things up and went out of the door. So I'd been stitched up to do the nativity play had I. Well, they were going to get a nativity play that they would remember for a long time to come, I thought.

Monday morning came around rather too quickly than I wanted, but I had managed to get the script written which I had dropped off with Mrs Grant to get copied for the class to be picked up later that day. I had a carbon copy of the script to work with that day with the class. Mr Yardley gave his briefing in the staff room before school started, there was nothing much happening but he did want our mark books up to date and handing in at the end of the week. Thankfully, mine was up to date with only this week to add to it. At registration I told the class that we would have our normal lessons in the morning but the afternoons this week we would concentrate on our nativity play, learning the script and also making some of the costumes and scenery.

Billy Preston put his hand up, "Sir, I've been thinking, to make our nativity play that extra special, what about having a real donkey. That's never been done before in the nativity play. It's always been kids with donkey heads on playing the donkey, but to have a real donkey would be great." "Yes, it would be great," I said not thinking it through, "it would make our play that much different. Now let's stand and get ready for assembly." The rest of the morning passed without incident. At break time Miss Stark sat next to me and I told her that the play had been completed and Mrs Grant was making copies for me to give to the class. I explained the different scenes and what sort of costumes would be needed, along with the sort of scenery that could be used. We agreed to meet at dinner time and go through the play and I said that I would be grateful for any suggestions she might have.

At about half past eleven that morning a child knocked on my class room door with a pile of papers, "These are from Mrs Grant," the child said and put them down on my desk and left. "Well children, we have our scripts for our play, which means that those who have speaking parts will be able to take their script home and learn their part," I told the class. There was a cheer from nearly everyone. I thanked them and told them that they had to finish their morning's work otherwise we would have to continue the lesson during the afternoon. That did the trick, their heads were down and they were busily writing away at their work - even Alfie and Matthew were working away. Dinner time came and all the work was finished, so I told the class we would make a start reading through the play, then act out various scenes in the class room. The children left the class room for their lunch with happy expectant faces, which rather pleased me.

I went up to the staff room to eat my packed lunch and get myself a drink. Halfway through eating my lunch, Miss Stark came and sat down beside me. She had her packed lunch with her and started to eat it and she asked, "Have you the script with you?" "No, I thought we'd have our lunch here in the staff room then go down to my class room and go through the script, making a list of the costumes needed. I've already started the list but I'm not sure where I can get some of the costumes from," I said. "We have a costume store room behind the stage. I'm sure there'll be plenty of stuff we can use from there, and there might be some scenery that could come in useful. The stage has two sets of curtains, the outer ones and then there's another set half way in so that you could have your final elaborate scene set at the back of the stage while the other scenes are acted out on the front half of the stage. Tony Telford usually does the lighting for our stage performances," she said. Things were certainly coming together.

As soon as we had eaten our lunch we made our way to my class room and went through the script. Miss Stark was reading through it whilst I was going through the scenes and the costumes and scenery needed for each one. Once she'd finished reading it she looked at me in astonishment and said, "This is wonderful, better than the nativity plays that we've had in the past, and you say that you are hoping to have every member of your class in the play." "That's right," I said, "and don't forget, the children have also helped to write the play themselves. I explained the scene then asked them what might have been said between the characters, which we then wrote down. It's been a joint effort which has given the children some pride in their work." Miss Stark looked at me in amazement and said, "What a great idea! Have you shown Mr Percy your play?" "No, but he knows that I'm writing one, and as far as I know none of the other staff know except Tony and he says he will help with the production. I would like it to be a surprise for both the parents and staff, so can you keep it a secret please. The children and I will be working on the play every afternoon this week. If they are not rehearsing the lines then they'll be making parts of costumes or making scenery. I might have to see if I can come in on Sunday afternoon to finish things off, that's if it is OK with Mr Johnson," I said. "You are keen if you want to come in on a Sunday afternoon. I'll help after school this week if there is anything that you want doing," she said. "Yes, thanks, that will be fine," I answered. For the rest of the lunch time we went through the scenes and added to the list of costumes and scenery that might be needed. Soon it was time for the bell, so we both went out to collect our children from the yard.

The children were keen to get into class and make a start with the play. Once registration was over I gave out the scripts, one between two, and allocated various parts to different children but pointed out that these parts were just for the read-through and didn't mean that those children would actually be playing those parts on the night of the performance. The children accepted that and each scene had another set of children reading the parts. Then I had an idea - what about the children suggesting who should play which part in the play. We could then have another read-through with those nominated children reading those parts. The children could be changed if it didn't sound right. I put this to the class and they all seemed to agree with the idea.

Just before the playtime bell rang, I got the children to push the desks to the side of the room so that we had a space in the middle of the room in which we could start to rehearse as though they were on the stage. After playtime, as the class room was ready, we went straight into the first scene, the players in the middle of the room whilst the rest of the children sat round watching. I had to remind Caesar Augustus that he was the emperor and was in charge so he had to act as though he was. His other generals had to be aware of the fact that Caesar Augustus could have them killed if they disagreed with him, so they had to suck up to him. With that in mind, the children acted very well. I had to keep reminding the actors to project their voices as they wouldn't be heard at the back of the hall from the stage. Very soon it was home time. The class and I were agreed that those that had acted scene one would be the ones for the part on the night, so they were allowed to take their scripts home with them to learn them. The desks were put back in place, the bell rang and the children went home.

A few minutes later Miss Stark came into the room and asked how things had gone. I told her what we had done and that the parts for the first scene were sorted, it was just the costumes and scenery to be allocated to that scene. We both made a list of what was needed for this and other scenes and she said that she would see what she could find at home which might be useful. I said that I was going to have an early night as today had been quiet exhausting and I wanted to be ready for tomorrow. She agreed that was a good idea and she left whilst I got my things together and then I also left. Today's been a good day, I thought, and things are falling into place.

The next morning in the staff room Mr Percy came in with a pile of papers in his hand. "I'm sorry but I should have given these forms out to you all yesterday. These have to be filled in today and returned back to the office before home time. They are application forms to be filled in for membership for the Casino. We have to be members before we are allowed in and it takes forty eight hours for the Casino to process the forms. I don't want to have any problems on our night out when we go there a week on Friday so I thought we better get these done as soon as possible. The membership is free and of course you can use them after our night out there," he said and then started to give out the forms. "I forgot to mention. You'll need to take two, one for you and one for your wife, that is those with wives and if others are bringing a friend then please take one for your friend. They'll have to be filled in tonight and brought back in the morning," said Mr Percy, "Also someone has suggested to book a minibus to take us all there and back, so to see if it's a viable proposition, could staff let me know how many would use it then I can cost it out and let you all know what the charge would be. Thank you." "Have you got a suit for the do?" Tony asked me as he walked towards the sink to wash his mug. I looked at him and said, "A suit, no I haven't got a suit. Is it necessary for the Casino?" I asked. "Well yes, it is a formal do and there is a dress code at the Casino. They don't let just anyone in you know, that's why we all have to be members before we go. You'd better get yourself kitted up with a suit, that's if you still want to go," he answered. "Right," I said. That got me thinking, where was I going to get a suit from, maybe I could borrow one just for that night. It would be pointless buying a suit that I was only going to use a couple of nights a year. Now, I thought, who did I know that was my size and who would have a formal suit. I'd have to think about that later as I had other things to do, especially where the nativity play was concerned.

As the week progressed so did the nativity play, as well as the costumes and scenery making. I would have the children in scene groups in various parts of the class room acting out their parts at the same time. It sounded like a confused mess but each group knew what they were doing and got on with their scene. By Thursday afternoon we managed to have a complete run-through of the play.

I was impressed as most of the children had learnt their parts off by heart and were rather confident with their lines. I told the class that I would see if we could do a rehearsal tomorrow afternoon in the hall on the stage, the full play minus the scenery. The costumes were coming along well too, thanks to the help from Miss Stark and from three of the parents that had come in on Wednesday afternoon and had taken various costumes home to make and said they would return them on Friday afternoon. I saw Tony Telford after school with a suggested lighting plan for the stage for each scene. He went through it and made some alterations to the plan, which was fine by me as he was the expert in these things. I asked about the possibility of a costume rehearsal on stage with scenery on Monday afternoon along with Miss Stark. He told me that I would have to ask Mr Percy about that and he would see Mr Yardley for permission, although he thought that there shouldn't be a problem. Mr Yardley would take one class and Mr Percy would take the other. Tony also let slip that both Mr Yardley and Mr Percy were both intrigued to see how I had done with this nativity project so they would both stand in for Miss Stark and Tony on Monday afternoon. That would be my first job in the morning, seeing Mr Percy and asking permission for the rehearsal on Monday afternoon. I thanked Tony and left, went to my class room and collected my things and then went home. On the way home I thought of someone who might help me regarding a suit and I was almost certain that I had his phone number in my address book at home.

After I'd had my tea I looked for my address book and after half an hour found it. I'm not the world's tidiest person and that's why it took so long. I wrote down the phone number and went to the phone box at the end of the street to ring him. I dialled the number and waited. A voice answered and I asked, "Now then, how are you doing?" "Jot, is that you? How are you doing?" said the voice. "Are you still working for Collins and if so, do you have a spare suit I could borrow for a night. I need a formal suit as we're going on a works do to a Casino and as I don't have one and can't afford to buy one I thought that I might borrow one from you, as we're both the same size and weight. You do have a spare suit, don't you?" I asked. "Yes, it's part and parcel for the job, two suits. Yes, you can borrow one, I'll let you have the best one. How can I get it to you?" he asked. "Can you drop it off at my mothers and I'll pick it up on Saturday afternoon. I'll get it back to her the week after so you can pick it up then. I'll be spending some time with my mother over Christmas so we'll have to get together and go out for a drink or two, as I owe you for this favour. Everything else alright?" I asked. "Yes, everything is fine. Did you hear that Smithy got married in November and he's moved away from the area?" the voice said. "Yes, I'd heard that. Look I'll have to go. Thanks for the suit, I'll take good care of it, and as I said we'll catch up at Christmas. See you later, bye," I said and hung up. Well that was that; suit sorted for the school do - so one less thing to worry about. I went back home and read through the play again, tweaking one or two small points.

It was just after registration next morning, Billy Preston put his hand up and I pointed to him and said, "Yes." He said, "Sir, I've managed to get one, and it's not that old. He was born at the start of this year but we can borrow him for the night." Confused, I looked at him, "What have you managed to get that's not quite a year old?" I asked. "A donkey sir, a donkey. He's very tame as he's a pet at the moment, but I've been told we can't ride him, he doesn't like that but he's very good otherwise. He's well behaved and Mr Smith said he would pick him up at the end of our concert," said Billy in a voice of satisfaction and achievement. The rest of the class, hearing this news, were ecstatic with someone calling out "This will be the best play the school has ever seen, with a live donkey on stage." That swung it for me, I had to agree that this would be the best play the school has seen, so I gave Billy the nod that we would use the donkey in the play but it would have to be our class secret, even Miss Stark and Mr Telford shouldn't know until the night of the performance. We had to go to assembly and as I led the class into the hall each and every one had an expression on their faces like a cat that had got the cream. Even Tony Telford noticed and whispered to me, "What the hell have you done to your class, they all look so smug. Would I be wasting my time in trying to ask one of them what's going on?" "Yes you would and they wouldn't tell you anyway, so don't try," I whispered back.

The rest of the day went well. In the afternoon, the parents who'd taken the costumes home returned with them and we had a fitting session with their help which went extremely well. Names were put on the various costumes and then put in the store cupboard. After school, once I'd completed my duty in the cloakroom, Miss Stark came into my class room with some costumes that she'd taken from the stage store room the other day and she'd altered and also to have a look at the costumes the parents had made. "Is that all the costumes done and sorted now?" she asked after putting the costumes she had brought with the rest of them in the store room. "Yes, along with yours that's the last," I said, "'I've got permission from Mr Johnson to come into school on Sunday afternoon between two and four. Tony said he could come in and go through the lighting plan for the play, and to make sure all the lights are in working order. Is there any chance you could also come in for part of the time to give a hand, that way we would know exactly what we should be doing on Monday afternoon during the dress rehearsal? Oh, and I have permission from Mr Percy that you and Tony can help with the dress rehearsal as well on Monday afternoon."

"Yes I'll come in on Sunday to help you both, it'll be just after two o'clock," she answered. I thanked her and we both made our way out, going in different directions when we walked through the school gates. When I got home there was an envelope on the mat. When I picked it up and opened it I couldn't believe my eyes. It was a cheque from the bookies and a letter thanking me in my part helping to try to stop the robbery all those months back, reward money for my help.

I had a little sleep in on the Saturday morning and a late breakfast, then I went to ring my mother to check that Stuart, my friend with the suit, had dropped it off and if she'd be at home this afternoon so that I could pick it up. She confirmed both, yes the suit had been dropped off and yes, she would be in that afternoon. So, it would be a bus ride into the town centre, then to the railway station to get my ticket and then a rail journey of about an hour and a half. Last time I'd made the journey home was at half term after I'd spent a few days in Blackpool and I had taken my mother some Blackpool rock, a treat that she likes, seaside rock - and even better if it came from Blackpool. Before I left I had a quick sandwich and a cup of tea and then I was on my way. I got to my mother's house at one thirty and as soon as I walked in she was offering tea and cakes. I sat down while she made the tea, I looked around the room and noticed new curtains at the windows. When she came in carrying a tray with the tea and cakes I commented on the new curtains. She said that she'd got them for winter as they were double lined and would keep out the cold. She went out to the spare bedroom and came back with a black suit inside a plastic see-through suit bag. "Stuart dropped this round before he went to work this morning. He said they were quite busy especially as it's getting towards winter and people start catching things. He said that they were much busier than this time last year," she told me. We sat talking for a few hours, then I asked her if it would be alright to come home for Christmas and then go back just after New Year. She though it would be a good idea as she had nothing planned, although my married sister usually came down on Boxing Day with her husband and two kids, stayed for lunch and then went home just before tea time. A family Christmas tradition so to speak,. My mother said that she was looking forward to Christmas now that I was going to be around for the holidays. I was pressed into having something to eat, my mother opening a tin of salmon, a treat normally set aside for special days, and I suppose this was a special day for my mother, a visit from me. Before I left I told her about my reward and gave her twenty pounds to treat herself with, although at first she didn't want to take it, but I insisted that she have it. With our goodbyes said, I left and went back to my home, along with the suit. I arrived home just after eight in the evening, went upstairs and hung the suit up in the plastic bag in the wardrobe, looked at the clock and decided that I could manage a couple of hours in the pub.

It was strange to be in school on a Sunday afternoon, no children or staff about, the quietness of the place. I had to go and report to Mr Johnson's office at two o'clock and he would let me in the school and the hall. I was a little early but so was he and as we went to the main doors Tony and Miss Stark were walking across the playground to meet us. When we got into the hall Mr Johnson told us that we had to be out at four o'clock prompt as he had another appointment later and didn't want to be late for it. In the meantime he would be getting on with some work in the school that wasn't able to be done during the week because the children were about. He left us to it, Tony got the lighting controls out of the stage store room and connected them up, which meant that he could control all the stage lights while standing just to the side of the stage near the front. I had a copy of the script for each of us which we could mark down costumes and scenery needed.

Most of the scenery that was going to be used was already on the stage. The three of us went through each scene and which pieces of scenery would be needed and where on stage it would be placed. Each piece had the scene number marked on the back and we were able to mark the stage floor where each piece would be placed on the night of the play. Just to be sure, Tony suggested that we had a stage map of each scene with the scenery marked on it, which was a good idea. The three of us worked well and about an hour and three quarters later we had the play sorted. Come Monday afternoon we would know if our hard work was going to pay off.

Just as Tony was putting the lighting controls away Mr Johnson came into the hall and asked if we'd finished. I told him we had and thanked him very much for his help and as I passed by him I slipped a packet of Players Number Six cigarettes in his hand, to which he said he was most thankful. I thanked Tony and Miss Stark for their time and help, then the three of us went our separate ways.

Monday morning went well, nothing much in the briefing as this was the last week of term. Mr Yardley gave out the membership cards for the Casino that had arrived in the post that morning. He reminded us not to forget them on Friday evening when we went to the Casino. He also hoped that all classes would be ready for the concert on Tuesday evening and that the hall would be off limits that afternoon as my class were doing a dress rehearsal in there. Also, in case anyone had forgotten, the school Christmas Party was on Thursday afternoon with a visit from Santa who was coming round to each class group. He mentioned that he hadn't received some mark books from various members of staff and requested them by the end of the day. As I went down to the yard to collect my class I asked Tony about Santa coming around the class groups at the party. "That's Mr Johnson dressed up, all the kids know that but it adds to the fun of it," he told me. He also said that my class would be joining his for the party in his class room, and that we would have to get the class room ready on Thursday dinner time. He said he would see me later about the set-up, just get the concert out of the way first.

Chapter Fourteen

Our first lesson after assembly was maths, but I promised that we'd have a run through of our nativity after playtime. I checked with the three children whose parents had come in on Wednesday that they would be here that afternoon for the dress rehearsal and they said that they'd be there. The excitement in the class was electric, the children couldn't wait for the read-through after break, the only thing that was slightly bothering me was the donkey. Was it a mistake or would it be a sensation? Billy did say that it was a pet and very tame and I assumed that it was used to children, as it was a pet. That afternoon we would rehearse as though it is there with us, Mary and Joseph will have to pretend they were leading it around but they would have to try to remember its length as they walked it around the stage.

Playtime came and went and it was back into class to do the read-through. Most knew their lines off by heart but I said they'd better have their scripts open on the desk just in case there were any last minutes changes. By the end of the lesson both myself and the children were happy. The bell rang to end the mornings' lessons, so after dismissing the children I went up to the staff room with my packed lunch got my drink and sat down in the usual corner. Miss Stark came in a few minutes later and sat beside me, followed by Tony Telford who sat the other side of me. "Are the children ready for this afternoon and the dress rehearsal?" he asked. "Yes, and the three parents are coming to give a hand as well. We had a run through this morning and most of the children know all their lines, which is good. Shall we all meet in the hall after registration and the first thing to do will be to get the children in to their costumes? We could get the children to group themselves around the hall and practice their scene, and then practice the scene on the stage. The more they practice together the better it will be. Tony, can we go through the lighting as the scenes are played out on stage, then that will give the children some idea how it will be on the night. Miss Stark can you take charge of the costumes, there will be the parents to help as well," I said. Miss Stark said she would and that she would have her sewing kit with her just in case there were some adjustments to be made. Tony said he would have his lighting script with him, a script he added to the nativity script which told him which lights to turn on and off and the appropriate time. Both Tony and Miss Stark said that they would go straight to the hall as Mr Yardley and Mr Percy would be taking their classes, along with doing the register at the start of the lesson. I'd made a scenery map showing what was needed for each scene and where it was to go. I gave a copy to Tony and Miss Stark just to keep them in the picture. After I'd eaten my lunch and had my drink I said that I'd go to the hall and start to get things ready, both Tony and Miss Stark said they'd come along soon to give me a hand. When I walked into the hall I started to imagine what it was going to be like the following evening. Chairs would be put out in the afternoon, with a space down the centre to allow classes to move back and forth to the stage for their performances. Mrs Grant would be printing out the programme for the concert this afternoon, giving information of the running order, and on the back page the Christmas carol 'We wish you a merry Christmas' for all the audience to join in with. "Yes, I'm going to put on a nativity play that they won't forget," I thought.

I collected my class from the yard almost as soon as the bell had rung. The three parents were there so I asked them to go straight to the hall and told them that we'd be there after registration. Once in class the children sat down in their places whilst I called the register. Billy Preston wasn't here, calamity! He was Joseph and one of the main parts, we couldn't have a nativity play without Joseph. "Has anyone seen Billy Preston?" I asked the class. "He went home for dinner today, sir," said Michael Spicer. This was a disaster, who could I put in his place, who would be able to learn his lines in time for tomorrow. Just then a voice called out, "Sir, here he is." The class looked to the corridor window and there walking towards our door was Billy Preston. He came in and approached my desk, "Sorry I'm late sir but I was just checking on the donkey for the concert. Mr Smith said that I could pick him up at six o'clock and it's just a ten minute walk from his house. He wanted to know what time the concert would end so I said about half past eight. Mr Smith said he would come round and take the donkey home. Was that alright sir?" "Yes, well done. We can keep the donkey here in the class room until it's needed for the play at about eight o'clock. We may have to be careful and put newspaper down on the floor though; just in case and because it will be here early the rest of the school won't see it until it makes its appearance in the play, which should be a big surprise for everyone. Everyone get your scripts, stand up and line up at the door," I said.

Once in the hall, the children were organised in their scene groups and spread themselves around the hall to practice their lines and when called, went and changed into their costumes. Each scene was rehearsed on stage with the scenery in place. One of the children thought it was a good idea that a few of the actors who had little or no lines could help with moving the scenery on stage until it was their scene. I thought that was a good idea too so looking down the script I made a note of those with only one or two lines or even no lines who were then appointed stage hands. Nicola Thompson, who I thought would have been a good person to play Mary, asked if she could be the narrator as she didn't think that she was very good at acting but good at reading. So she was our narrator and when I heard her on the microphone it was a good choice as she had a very expressive voice and took her time as she read the script. One of the things that usually happens when someone reads a script using a microphone is that they tend to read too quickly, but that wasn't the case with Nicola. I also noticed that she would look to see if the next scene were ready to start and if it weren't she read a little slower, giving us more time to get things ready. We managed to go through the whole play with some scenes having to be done twice. We worked through playtime which was the children's idea and by ten to four we called it a day.

Costumes were fitted and completed, scenery and backstage helpers were confident with their roles, our parents said they would come into school at half past six o'clock the next day to help get the children ready. Miss Stark said she would help after her class had done their piece in the concert; Tony had to be in the hall all the time as he was operating the lights for the whole concert. The children made sure their names were on the costumes and we took them back to our class room. The delicate costumes were on coat hangers and were put in the store room, the remainder were put on the tables at the back of the class, which we normally used for drying our paintings on. I told the children that we would have normal lessons in the morning and then in the afternoon we would have another read through of the play. Various children commented that they couldn't wait for the concert but I reminded them to keep it a secret about the donkey in our play.

Tuesday was here at last,. The day went by without any mishaps, which was a surprise considering the high the children were on. Mr Johnson had put all the chairs out in the hall for the concert in the afternoon, helped by some children from year six. At home time I told the children to be back by no later than ten to seven, which should give us enough time to get ready for the play. Miss Stark and Tony Telford came into my class room at twenty past four to check that everything was going smoothly. I said that I would treat them both to fish and chips from the chip shop round the corner for the help that they'd had given me. Miss Stark asked if I could call in to the shop round the corner from the chip shop and get a small loaf so that we could have bread and butter with our fish and chips. She said that there was some butter in the 'fridge in the staff room. I went off to get the fish and chips, this time I hoped that I would remember how to get back to school without getting lost. When I got to the chip shop after getting the loaf of bread, there was quite a big queue. Fish and chips was obviously a good meal for teatime with the people round there I thought.

I got back to the staff room at about ten past five. The tea was in the pot ready and waiting, Miss Stark made the bread and butter whilst I put the fish and chips on plates. Tony had already got the tomato sauce and vinegar on the table. Tony said that he had set the stage for scene one whilst I was away at the chip shop. My class was going to be the only class that was going to use the full stage, the rest of the other classes were doing their pieces on the floor in front of the stage or in front of the curtains on the stage. As we ate the meal we discussed the concert and how the children were to get on and off the stage. The stage had a door at the back and one at the side, both of which could be used by actors going on and off the stage. The door at the side led into the corridor and the door at the back led into the costume store room. The costume store room had another door which meant that actors could assemble in there waiting for their cues to go onstage. All in all, the school was very lucky to have such an asset, but I suspected that it wasn't used to its full potential. We had practiced with the children which area they would be in to go on the stage, even our scripts were marked as to the stage entrances the children would make. Things had been checked and double checked that afternoon and I had a run through of the nativity play and the children were almost word perfect - and that was without looking at their scripts. One or two forgot the start of their lines but one of the other children gave them the first couple of words and then they were off with the lines. I was impressed that the children were helping each other, not only impressed but encouraged, like our lesson at the ice arena.

It had just gone six o'clock and Miss Stark and Tony were in my room going through the last minute details of the nativity play. A couple of children came in and asked if they could get their costumes from the store cupboard, as these children were the Magi or Wise Men, Miss Stark said she would give them a hand in getting ready as the costumes were exotic and rather tricky to put one by ones-self. Slowly but surely the children started to drift in, each one getting his or her costume and getting changed into it. Then at six twenty in walks Billy Preston followed by a small grey donkey on a lead. "This is the donkey, sir. His name is Chewy and he's very friendly. Mr Smith said he will come to school at half past eight and pick him up. He also said that we haven't to ride him as he hasn't been broken in yet," said Billy. "Well I hope no one tries to ride him, can you put some newspaper on the floor over there and tie him up to the radiator. Will he need anything to drink?" I asked. "No sir, he's been fed and watered, that's why I'm a bit late. I'll get changed and then stay with Chewy all the time until Mr Smith comes to collect him at the end," said Billy. Miss Stark had gone out of the class room to get some safety pins from the staff room when Billy had made his appearance with Chewy. She walked into the class room with the safety pins and saw Chewy. "That's a donkey," she said pointing to Chewy. In all our rehearsals neither I, nor the children, had ever mentioned the fact that we were going to have a real donkey in the play, I hadn't even mentioned it to Tony. The reaction on Miss Stark's face was sheer bewilderment, the same reaction I was hoping to get from everyone who was going to be watching the play. "Yes, that's a donkey and his name is Chewy and he is going to be in our play tonight," I said, "I did mention that our play would have a different slant to it." "Yes, but a real donkey in the play. Does Mr Percy or Mr Yardley know about this?" she asked as she walked over the Chewy and started stroking him. "I might have forgotten to mention it, but it's too late now," I said, "Anyway it's almost done now and nobody, except you, has seen Chewy and if you want you can say that you knew nothing about it." She agreed to keep quiet about Chewy then she said that she would have to go and get her class ready but she would come back and help to get my children ready for the play after her class's performance. Miss Stark left to go to her class and my class were now nearly all here getting changed into their costumes. Chewy was the main star of the show, even in the class room. It was quite difficult to keep the children away as they all wanted to stroke him. "See, sir," said Billy, "Chewy is very tame and he likes all the attention." I had to admit, he was right on that score. Chewy was enjoying all the attention, then I notice Billy giving Chewy something to eat. "What's that you're giving Chewy?" I asked Billy. "Peppermints sir, he likes them and he's allowed to eat them, I checked with Mr Smith," said Billy. Yes, Chewy was enjoying the mints. The four parents that were helping walked into the class room together and they just stopped and looked across the room at Chewy. One of them pointed and said, "It's a donkey." "Yes ladies, it's a donkey and his name is Chewy and that's the donkey that Mary and Joseph take to Bethlehem to go and get registered," I explained, "You can stroke him if you want to, he's quiet tame." They went over and started to stroke Chewy who seemed to like all the attention he was getting.

All the children were now here and I checked that each one would be taken home by their parent after the concert, or that they were going to be taken home with someone. When I looked at my watch, it was five minutes to seven, so the concert would be starting very soon. I asked the parents if they could keep an eye on the class whilst I went to the hall for a quick word with Mr Telford to check the everything was in place for our play. When I got there, Mr Percy came up and asked if things for the nativity were alright, and I told him they were. I approached Tony, who was sitting at his lighting control unit, surrounded by various bits of papers, and the nativity scrip prominent in the left hand corner of the desk.

"What's all this about a donkey?" he whispered," "Miss Stark told me you have a bloody donkey in the play. It certainly wasn't at the rehearsal yesterday." "Shush," I said, "Don't give the game away, you haven't told anyone else have you? It's supposed to be a big surprise for everyone." "Surprise, it will be a bloody shock for everyone. A donkey, what were you thinking of," he whispered back. I told him that I'd better get back to my class room and check that the children were ready.

Back in the class room the children were in their costumes and stroking the donkey, which seemed quite happy with the attention he was getting. I told the children to sit in their places and go through their lines whilst we waited for our turn in the concert. Going round the class room I tried to give each child encouragement by chatting to them about their part and asking if they had any questions they wanted to ask. I spoke to the parents about their role and checked that they had a copy of their script which was slightly different from the children's script as it had the stage directions on it, telling which children were going onto the stage from which side. I noticed, as I went past the waste paper bin, that there were a couple of empty liquorice allsorts boxes in it, well I had said that the children could eat sweets while we waited to perform, but they must have eaten them quickly as I was only away for about ten minutes and I hadn't seen anyone eating them before I went to the hall.

I made my way over to Chewy, who was stood very calmly on the newspaper, with Billy Preston stroking him. I gave Chewy a stroke and I must admit he was rather a nice donkey, not that I know many donkeys. "Where does he sleep?" I asked Billy. "In the front room of Mr Smith's house, along with his mother," replied Billy. "In the front room with Mr Smith's mother?" I said rather shocked. "No, in the front room with Chewy's mother. The two donkeys live in the front room of Mr Smith's house," replied Billy. I decided that I wouldn't take the conversation any further. Just then Miss Stark walked into the room and came over. "Well my class has done their bit and are sitting on the chairs at the back of the hall. Tony's class are singing their Christmas songs and will soon be finished. He's going to send a child over here to your class room when Paul Sharpe's class are on as they are second to last on the running order, then it's your class. Are all the children ready?" she asked. I replied, "Yes, all ready and eager to get on with it. Now are you sure you will be OK with Mary and Joseph and Chewy outside the hall doors ready for their big entrance. Mary and Joseph have a scene on stage, they'll join you outside the hall after their scene, so you will be with Chewy until they come and join you. I'll be backstage acting as a prompt and making sure everyone goes on and off at the right time. The parents will be with the children both at the stage door from the costume store room or at the stage door in the corridor. They have a list of children in their group and when it's time for them to go on the stage."

Twenty minutes later a boy popped his head into the room and said, "Mr Telford said that it's time for your class to get ready on stage, sir." "Thank you," I said to the boy, then I turned to the class, "This is it children. Let's go and give them a nativity play they won't forget. Now into your groups, and when we get to the stage go into the places we rehearsed yesterday. Nicola, have you got your narrators script to read out?" I asked. "Yes sir," she replied.

We went down the corridor and up the stairs to the first floor where the hall was. When we got there I slowly opened the door at the back and peeped in. The stage area was brightly lit whilst the rest of the hall was in semi-darkness; at the front, all lit up was Paul Sharpe's class singing away. I remembered that Tony said he would put a couple of lights on when Mary and Joseph walked down the aisle to the stage which, looking how dark it was, was a good idea. The children were all in place, the stage set for the first scene. Paul's class finished their song and Mr Percy stood up and went to the middle of the floor and announced that it was time for the nativity play which was going to be performed by Mr Tredwell's class, a play that had also been written by the class, along with Mr Tredwell himself. He sat down, and Nicola, who was stood at the side of the stage with a microphone, set the background for the first scene, Caesar Augustus's invasion office in Rome. I was operating the curtains and when they opened I could hear the "Ooohs and Aahs" from the audience and when the scene was over there was applause. The play was going great, the audience applauding after each scene, which seemed to encourage the children even more to give a better performance. I managed to take a peep at the front row of the audience and saw Mr Percy then Mr Yardley, Mr Westbrook-Smith,

Mr Myers, Mrs Grant, and then some others that I assumed were more Governers, who all seemed to be enjoying the play.

Time for the big entrance, Mary and Joseph had done their annunciation scene with the angel and had gone to the back of the hall via the corridor to meet up with Miss Stark while the next scene was being performed. Both Mary and Joseph had to do a quick change into their 'walking with donkey' robes on. The dimmed hall lights were switched on, which was the cue for Mary and Joseph, and of course Chewy, to make their way to the stage. The effect on the audience was electric, "Look, it's a donkey, a real donkey," were most of the comments being said. Mary was first to walk up the stage steps, then Joseph leading Chewy, who at first didn't want to know about going up the steps and just stood still, which Joseph wasn't expecting and he nearly fell back down the steps as he was holding the donkey's bridle strap. I was watching from the side of the stage and almost panicked. What was I to do, especially if Chewy refused to go up the steps. I think I made the right choice in picking Billy to play Joseph as he got something out of his pocket and placed it under Chewy's nose. Almost immediately Chewy raised his head and followed Billy up the steps, which earned him applause from the audience. Mary and Joseph went round the stage knocking on the inn doors and finding no room, until the last one offered the stable. End of scene, curtains close and the scenery was quickly changed to that of a stable, complete with manger and straw, curtains open, next scene. Mary with the new baby, Joseph standing by, Chewy in the background tied to a piece of scenery that was supposed to be part of the stable, and then a visit from the shepherds, all was going well. Until that was, when Chewy noticed that the baby was in a manger of hay. Well, no donkey can resist a free meal, the piece of scenery offered no resistance when Chewy pulled on it, and it came away with Chewy dragging it across the stage. Billy was on the other side of the stage when it happened so he was unable to get to Chewy when he started to eat the hay, nudging the baby Jesus out of the manger and on to the floor. Mary didn't panic she just said, 'Oh dear,' then picked the doll up, rocked it and said, 'Never mind, you're alright now.' The audience was loving this. Billy went over to Chewy and tried pulling him away from the hay, no luck. Then he put his hand in his pocket and placed it over Chewy's nose which stopped him eating the hay and he followed Billy to the back of the stage and the scene continued.

Our final scene took place in the stable with the visit of the Magi or Wise Men which caused some muttering in the audience, 'There's five kings' and 'Shouldn't there be only three kings.' The performers ignored the various comments and continued with the scene although there was some commotion coming from the shepherds at the back. "Look out, don't step in it," whispered one shepherd to another. "There's a lot more over there," whispered another and all the while the scene was being acted out at the front of the stage. I wondered what was going on, then I saw it and smelt it, Chewy was standing there as another discharge from his rear rained down on the stage. Oh no, Chewy had diarrhoea. It came to me in a flash, the empty liquorice allsorts boxes in the paper bin, someone must have fed Chewy liquorice allsorts. Thankfully, no one in the hall could see what I was seeing and once the scene was over all the cast came on stage and I had to manipulate children around so that no one stepped into any of the mess. We finished with 'Silent Night' and the audience clapped and cheered the children who took quite a few bows. One of the biggest cheers was when Billy brought Chewy, who fortunately behaved himself, to the front of the stage. Mr Yardley took to the floor and thanked the audience for coming and all the staff and their classes for a wonderful concert and a special thanks to my class and the nativity play.

That was it, a nativity play that would be remembered for some time to come. Tony and Miss Stark came up onto the stage and said that they'd help me getting the children changed. Mr Yardley and all the VIP's came forward to shake my hand and thanked me for a thoughtful nativity play. Mr Westbrook-Smith asked about the five kings with the three gifts, so I pointed out that in the bible there is no mention of how many kings or wise men there were, just that they brought three gifts, and having five kings meant more parts for the children to play. I returned to the stage, most of the children had gone with Miss Stark and the parents back to my class room. Chewy was finishing off the hay in the centre of the stage so I asked Billy to bring him down the steps. Billy took the bridle and led Chewy to the steps then he stopped at the top and wouldn't move. I took hold of the bridle and pulled but Chewy pulled backwards, Billy tried pushing from the back while I pulled from the front, still nothing. Then Billy said something that chilled my bones, "Can donkeys go downstairs and steps?" Something that I hadn't checked, then I remembered that I had read somewhere that cows can't go downstairs, they can go up but not down. Don't say donkeys are the same, I thought.

As nearly all the parents, staff and children had gone, Mr Johnson came into the hall with his chair trolley to remove the chairs. He saw Billy and myself on stage along with Chewy and made his way to the stage. He walked up the steps and came up on the stage, "A bloody donkey! I did hear some of the kids talking about a donkey but I thought it was a wind-up," said Mr Johnson. Then he saw the accident on the stage floor, "And bloody donkey crap on the stage. I hope you don't think that I'm going to clean that up do you! I do have my limits you know; I'm a caretaker - not a bloody zoo keeper, donkeys indeed. I hope you don't do a play about Hannibal otherwise we'll have bloody elephants on the stage crapping all over," he said. "Who's Hannibal?" asked Billy. "Never mind that Billy, when did Mr Smith say he was picking Chewy up?" I asked. Before Billy could answer, Tony and Miss Stark came into the hall accompanied by a stranger and walked up to the stage. "That's Mr Smith, sir," said Billy pointing to the stranger. "Having trouble are we?" asked Mr Smith laughing, "You do know that donkeys can go up steps but don't like to come down them, don't you. No of course you don't. And it looks as though you have some manure for your roses, courtesy of Chewy. I usually charge a shilling a bag but I'll let you have that lot for nothing. Now the trick is to guide him down carefully as he can't see the steps when he puts his head down, that's why donkeys don't like going down steps. Watch" As soon as Mr Smith went on the stage and said his name Chewy came over and nudged his side in a friendly way. Mr Smith led Chewy to the steps and talked to him as he led him down, "There," he said, "nothing to it when you know how. Come on Chewy, time to go home to bed." "Thank you very much for letting us borrow Chewy, Mr Smith," I said, "He's been the star of the show." "Anytime, sir, anytime, I'm pleased to be of service," he answered and with that Mr Smith walked out of the hall followed by Chewy. I could just see Chewy in my imagination in the front room of Mr Smith's house laying down on some hay along with the older donkey. I was brought back down to earth when Mr Johnson said that he would get me a bucket and spade along with a mop and bucket to clear the mess off the stage. Billy said he would stay and help, but I wouldn't let him as his mother was waiting at the back of the hall to take him home, so I thanked him and told him to go home. Tony and Miss Stark volunteered their services and very soon we had the stage cleaned down, much to the delight of Mr Johnson who was clearing the chairs away as we cleaned the stage.

We were told to leave the buckets on stage, along with the spade and mop by Mr Johnson and he would clear them away afterwards. "Well done," said Tony, "you got your wish, a nativity play that will be remembered for a long time to come." "Yes, well done," said Miss Stark, "but you do realise that you've set the level for future plays in the school." "Well to be honest I couldn't have done it without the help from the two of you, so on Friday let me buy you your drinks at the staff do at the Casino, my treat," I answered. With that the three of us left the hall and made our way to our class rooms, collected our things and went off home.

Chapter Fifteen

I was feeling on top of the world when I walked into the staff room the next morning. I'd caught the earlier bus to school so that I'd have an extra fifteen minutes drinking my tea and reading the morning paper. As various members of staff came into the staff room, they congratulated me on my class's performance of the nativity play and also for taking the chance and having a live donkey on stage. I didn't tell them about the donkey's little accident and having to clean it up. Later Mr Percy came in, followed, by Mr Yardley which was unusual as he only made an appearance on a Monday morning for the briefing. "Could I have your attention for a moment please," asked Mr Yardley, "I've just come in to say many thanks to all staff for the wonderful concert last night; the Governers have asked me to send their congratulations to the staff and especially to Mr Tredwell and his class. It certainly was an unusual nativity play, what with Caesar Augustus's invasion plans and the five kings at the end, and he says that the children help to write it," and with that he gave a round of applause with the staff joining in. I felt embarrassed and proud at the same time. I had been determined to produce a play that would be remembered and I think that I'd achieved that. Mr Yardley went on, "Tomorrow is the children's Christmas party in the afternoon and as usual class rooms that are next to each can join together for joint parties. It makes it easier when cleaning up at the end, also, having two classes in one class room means less space for any horseplay from the children. I have ordered ice-cream for all the classes and these will be delivered just before afternoon playtime. Father Christmas will also be making a visit during the party, but please don't let the children get too excited. Don't forget to remind your children to bring in the party food for their parties. It wouldn't be much of a party if there was no food to eat. Thank you again all and have a nice day." At that he left the staff room. Mr Percy came over to me and said how much he'd enjoyed the play and was pleased that all the children in the class had some part to play. After that other members of staff came over and said that they had enjoyed it as well. I looked for Tony Telford and saw him near the sink, so I went over and asked him a favour; could I borrow his bike at lunchtime so that I could go to the bank and get some money out, and also asked him where the nearest branch of my bank was. He explained that there was a bank about five minutes bike ride away and yes I could borrow his bike. That was sorted then. I should have drawn some money out last Saturday when I'd paid the reward money cheque in. Even if the cheque hadn't cleared I could still draw twenty pounds out, but it would leave only a few pounds in my account until the cheque was cleared.

At break time as I was walked into the staff room I could hear talking about my nativity play, mainly from Ivan Jenkins who seemed to be complaining about something. I got my mug of tea and looked for an empty seat to sit on when Paul Sharpe said to Ivan, "Go on then, he's here now, you ask him." I looked across at Ivan who was looking straight at me, and the rest of the staff started to go quiet. Ivan said, "Your nativity play was a bit long last night, not that I'm complaining about the length of it, but what was all that about Caesar Augustus's invasion office in Rome, the angel appearing to Joseph, I thought it just appeared to Mary and at the end the five kings?" The staff were waiting for my explanation so off I went. I told Ivan that Rome wanted to know how much tax they would get so that they could fund more invasions, hence the registration of all the people, the angel appeared to Joseph to let him know what was going to happen to Mary and lastly there are no mention of three kings in the bible only the words 'some Wise Men,' therefore it could have been two or even six Wise Men or Kings, we don't know. I mentioned that Mr Westbrook-Smith had asked the same question about the five Kings and that I had given him the same answer. That put Ivan in his place, especially when some of the staff said well done to me, which didn't do Ivan any favours. He just got up and stormed out of the staff room, humiliated. I sat down next to Tony who said that I was treading on thin ice, showing Ivan up in front of the staff, and that I should be careful as he had a long memory. For the rest of the break time Tony and I talked about the Christmas party in his class room and how the children could make some Christmas decorations that afternoon to be used at the party the following day. Tony then gave me some advice, "Don't eat anything that isn't shop wrapped, no matter how tempting it looks. We have our staff night out on Friday evening and it wouldn't be good if you miss it because you got food poisoning at the kids Christmas party." I told him that I would bear that in mind.

Just before lunchtime I told the children that they would be making Christmas decoration for the party in Mr Telford's class room on Thursday afternoon. I asked for the usual art monitors to help get the class room ready at ten to one. I had found templates in my store cupboard of various Christmas decorations which I intended to use with the children. Bells of different sizes, holly leaves, angels, garlands and other such things, I also found paper strips with glue on one end which you had to lick and stick to make paper chains. As the children went out for lunch they all seemed happy and excited about the prospect of making the Christmas decorations for the party. As soon as the children had left for their lunch I went to Tony Telford's class room to ask him where his bike was. He was just about to go to the staff room to have his lunch when I reached his room. He explained where his bike was and gave me the key to the bike lock and told me to make sure that I locked the bike up securely before I went into the bank. I told him that I would and should be back before one o'clock with just enough time to eat my packed lunch.

I got to the bank at just gone twenty past twelve and locked the bike up to the drain pipe outside the bank. Just as I was approaching the bank doors I saw a car parked nearby with three men sitting in it. One of the men looked familiar; I'd seen him somewhere before but couldn't remember where. I decided to walk past the bank and do a bit of window shopping but at the same time trying to see the make and model and registration number of the car and then write it down on a piece of paper. Then it hit me, it was Harry, the man with the snooker cue case from the bookmaker robbery, although I wasn't sure about the other two in the car with him. I looked around, and then I saw it, a telephone box. I casually made my way to the telephone box and rang 999, all the time watching the car. The girl at the other asked which emergency service I wanted and I said Police. I was put through to the Police Emergency Service and explained what I could see. I explained about the bookmaker robbery a few months earlier and that I now recognised one of the men in the waiting car as one of the bookmaker robbers. I gave all the information I had on my piece of paper and then gave details of who I was, my name and address, and how I had helped the Police in the bookmaker robbery, The girl said that I was to do nothing to alert the men but to go along with my usual business and they would check it out and be in touch with me later. I let her know that I was a teacher at Cromwell Street Mixed Infants and Juniors and would be back at school by one o'clock. She thanked me and then hung up. I looked at my watch, twenty five to one already. I went into the bank, fortunately it wasn't too busy so I got served quite quickly, that is after having to verify my bank book by showing the Teller my driving licence, my electric bill and my teacher's union card. I went a bit overboard and drew twenty five pounds instead of twenty, "After all, it's Christmas," I thought.

I got back to school at just past one o'clock and put Tony's bike back and collected my packed lunch then went to the staff room and got myself a cup of tea. I saw a spare chair next to Tony and sat there. "Here's the key for your bike lock, I've put your bike back where it belongs and it's locked up. Thanks very much. I'm going to have the children making Christmas decorations for tomorrow afternoon, is there anything you need them to do?" I asked. "No, that'll be fine if they make the decorations. We could get the class room ready tomorrow dinner time with the help of a few of the kids," he replied. Now I didn't know whether or not to mention the incident outside the bank, but then thought better of it and kept quiet. I only just managed to finish my lunch when it was time to go and collect the children from the yard as the bell was ringing. I then remembered that I'd asked the art monitors to go to the class room at ten to one to get it ready for the art lesson that afternoon.

I went to the yard and the class was lined up. I led them into school to our class room and to my surprise it was all laid out for the art lesson. I asked the art monitors to come to my desk as the other children sat down. I thanked them for getting the class room ready but told them that they shouldn't have done it without me being there, so in future they would have to wait for me before they start to get anything ready. I called the register and everyone was present; it's amazing that there were few or no absentees when the last week of the autumn term arrived. I started the art lesson by showing the children the templates and how to use them, also the different coloured card and tissue paper that was available for them to use. I also told them that if they wanted they could design their own decorations. For the next hour and a half the children were engaged in manufacturing decorations of various sizes, shapes and colours. The tables making the paper chains were competing with each other as to how they could make the longest chain. I had to remind them that the paper chains had to go round the class room not round the school, which caused some laughter from the children. Break time came and went and we spent the next ten minutes of the lesson finishing off and tidying away. Now it was time to make a list of which child was bringing what food to the Christmas party. I told the children that the sandwiches had to be well wrapped up and if possible put in a biscuit tin of something similar that was air tight. The sandwich list comprised of meat paste, egg, (although I wasn't too happy about that due to the smell of boiled egg sandwiches), jam, cheese, and one child said that they were bring salmon sandwiches, another said sardine sandwiches. Also on the list was cakes and biscuits together with crisps, but I made a point that there were to be no nuts at all as they could be dangerous.

Once that was done it was time for story time, 'Robinson Crusoe' had finally been finished and I had started to read 'Stig of the dump' which the children were enjoying much better than 'Robison Crusoe.' I'd only had time for half a chapter when Mr Percy knocked on my class room door and walked in. "Sorry for the interruption, but Mr Yardley would like to see you immediately in his office. I'll take over your class while you go and see him," he said. I was stunned, as was the class, "Yes, I'll go now. I'm reading this with the class and we're on page 35," I said then gave him my book and left. Do I run up the stairs to Mr Yardley's office or take my time and walk - no take your time, I thought. Now why would he want to see me immediately, surely it wasn't about Chewy from last night; he hasn't fallen ill with all the sweets and liquorice the children had given him. No, Mr Smith had said his name was Chewy because he was always looking for something to eat and chew. Maybe Mr Johnson had complained about the mess on the stage, yes that could be it. When I got to Mrs Grants office she buzzed the intercom and told Mr Yardley that I was in the outer office. The traffic lights on Mr Yardley's door frame changed from red to green at once. I knocked on the door and "Come in" was called out. I went in and Mr Yardley was sitting at his desk. In the two chairs against the wall were a police sergeant and a man in a gaberdine coat, above them a moose's head hanging on the wall. "These two police officers would like to have a word with you and have asked that I stay in the room with you," said Mr Yardley. I noticed that the police sergeant was looking at me as thought he was trying to remember something.

The man in the gabardine coat began the conversation, "My name is DCI Jarvis and this is Sergeant Brown and we would like a statement from you about what you saw this lunchtime." Sergeant Brown had his note book out and was ready to take notes whilst Mr Yardley looked at me with interest. "Well," I began, "I had to get some money from the bank and to get there I borrowed a colleagues bike. I was just locking it up outside the bank when I saw a car with three men in it. At first I took no notice but when I looked again the man in the back looked familiar so instead of going straight into the bank I walked a few shops away looking in the windows as though I was window shopping, whilst all the time I was taking notes about the car, its make, colour and number plates and also tried to get a description of the men in the car. I then saw the phone box on the corner of the street and decided to ring Nine, Nine, Nine and told the operator what I had seen and gave all the details I'd written down. I still have them if you want them. After that I went into the bank and drew some money out and then came back to school. Was the information useful to you?" "Yes sir, very useful," said DCI Jarvis, "As a matter of fact you've prevented an armed robbery outside that bank. We had a tip off that a robbery was going to take place somewhere in the town today but we didn't know where and when and we didn't have the manpower to cover all the banks, but when we got your information we knew exactly where it was going to be. The banks get delivery of extra money, due to the Christmas holiday next week, so they get a double delivery of money from the security company. We were able to swap the security personnel with our own men and we had unmarked police cars at strategic points around the bank with some of our men armed. We waited and at half past one the security van pulled up outside the bank as usual and our officer went round the back of the van and tapped the back and the security box was passed out, empty of course. The robbers made their move and jumped out of their car armed with sawn off shotguns at which point our lads broke cover and surrounded the area whilst the getaway car was trapped in by three of our cars. The robbers gave up straight away and are now being questioned at our police station.

Because they've been caught in the act they'll be facing a long prison sentence. If we'd caught them in their car before the attempt then they would have been charged with possession of firearms, which would only have been a short prison sentence. So it's thanks to you that three dangerous criminals have been caught and will be going down for a long time." I didn't know what to say. I looked over at Mr Yardley who was smiling and nodding his head. "One more thing," said DCI Jarvis, "The press and television have got the story of the attempted robbery and it will be public very soon but there's no mention of your part in all this and we would like to keep it that way, so please don't tell anyone what you did. You haven't told anyone, have you?" he asked. "No, I nearly did but thought better of it," I replied. "Thank you once more, sir, "said DCI Jarvis, "There should be a reward as you prevented a lot of money being stolen this afternoon, I'm sure the bank or the insurance company will be in touch with you about it. We've given them your details." "Will I have to go to court," I asked. "No sir, I don't think you will be needed. I think it will be noted as information obtained," said DCI Jarvis.

Sergeant Brown looked at me and said, "The penny's just dropped! You're the teacher that Mrs Braithwaite thought was a kidnapped child in the library back in September and because there wasn't a kidnapped child I didn't win the five pounds back at the station." DCI Jarvis just looked at Sergeant Brown and said "Yes, we'd better be going, there's a lot of paperwork to complete from this afternoon. Thank you Mr Yardley for your time and thank you sir, your quick observation has save quite a lot of money. Merry Christmas both." Then they made their way out of the office whilst I just sat there waiting for Mr Yardley to say something. "Amazing, simply amazing," he said to me, "It's been quite a week for you. First your outstanding nativity play and now this, preventing an armed robbery. I can't think what might happen next, we haven't had a probationary teacher like you before. As the police officer said, you can't tell anyone about what happened and your role in stopping the robbery. I have of course let Mr Percy know but that's it, no one else in the school will know. Understand?" "Yes, sir, understood," I replied. Just then the home time bell rang and I look at Mr Yardley. "Don't worry, Mr Percy will see your children out, he's done it before," said Mr Yardley with a hint of sarcasm. "All the tickets for the Casino have come and they will be given out in the morning to the staff, I've never been to a Casino before and I'm looking forward to it. Have you been to one before?" he asked. "Yes, once or twice when I was on holiday at the Casino on Blackpool pleasure beach a few years ago," I said, "Can I go now, sir, I need to sort some things out about tomorrow's Christmas party with Mr Telford before he goes home." "Yes, yes of course, off you go," he instructed me. I got up and left saying, "Good evening," as I left.

When I got back to my class room, the children had gone but Mr Percy was still there. "Well done," he said, "Only Mr Yardley you and I know what happened and I understand the Police want it that way." "That's right, "I answered, "and as far as I can see there's no need for anyone else to know, so I'm happy to keep it that way. I have to go and see Mr Telford about the party tomorrow, so if you would excuse me I'll be off." I picked up the party food list and went to see Tony Telford in his class room where he was sat at his desk. "Hi," he said, "I came looking for you at home time but Mr Percy was looking after your class. Is everything alright, someone said you were with Mr Yardley." Yes I'm fine," I answered, "Mr Yardley wanted to see me about some observation lessons in the next term and what preparations I would have to make, some of which could be done over the Christmas holidays. Anyway about this party tomorrow, I have a food list from the children, looks like we are going to have plenty of meat paste; cheese, jam and egg sandwiches - and one child said she'd be bringing salmon sandwiches." "That would be Ann Carter, her mum likes to think she's a cut above the others," said Tony, "Plenty of buns and biscuits, oh did you mention no nuts. One kid nearly choked the other year with a peanut, frightened the life out of one of the teachers that did. We'll be having four parents helping us with the food and things. At dinner time we'll get the class room ready, mine for the food and we'll use yours for the party games. We'll play musical chairs, statues, pass the parcel. I'll get the parcels made at home tonight, and any other games you can think of. Organisation, that's the word, organisation. If we have good organisation then everything should run just fine." We went through some other things for the party then decided it was time to go home as we would have a bit of a job on hand tidying up after tomorrow's party.

Thursday morning and in the staff room before the start of school Mr Percy was giving out the Casino tickets. We'd paid for them about four weeks ago and I was thankful that I was going by myself as I wouldn't have been able to afford two tickets. I thought about yesterday's attempted bank robbery and wondered about the reward money and how much it might be, I was hopeful that it might be the same as the reward from the bookmakers robbery which had been quite substantial and was going to pay for Christmas gifts and a holiday in summer, if I didn't spend the lot before then. I made my way down the stairs and out to the playground where, waiting for the bell to ring, children clutching their party tins were standing around asking each other what was in their tin. First job after registration was to get the children to write their names on a sticky label and put it on their tins then they would know which tin was theirs. The bell rang and the children lined up and as it was a bit nippy I got my children into school as soon as possible and into the class room.

I was just about to close my class room door when I heard a raised voice coming from the corridor. "I want my sodding tin back. I don't give a bugger if it's the Christmas party, she's got my cakes, they're not for her, they are my cakes and I want them back!" I looked for the owner of the voice and saw it was a large woman outside Tony Telford's class room. I called out, "Can I help you?" "It's him, in there, he's got my cakes, and the little sod has brought them to school. I said I would get her some but she's got mine and I want them back," she said in a rather loud voice. Tony popped his head out of his class room and called to me, "It's alright, I'm sorting it. I'm just trying to find the right tin," then to the woman, "Can you please keep your voice down and refrain from swearing, we don't allow swearing in school." "All right, but bloody hurry up will you. I've got places to go and people to see and I can do without this pratting around. Taking my bloody cakes indeed. Who the hell does she think she is," said the woman. I thought it best to get back into my class room where I would be safe and I'd see Tony later. Because it was the second to last day of term there was no assembly, so we had a Christmas quiz and I told the children it would be girls versus the boys. That brought a mixed reaction from the children; the girls complained that there were three more boys than girls, so the boys would score more points than the girls. I said that I had a way of making it fair at the end of the quiz. I had no idea how I could work out a system of the three extra boys, but deep down I knew that the girls were better than the boys so if they won the quiz it wouldn't matter about the extra boys, I just had to make sure that they won. The quiz consisted of all sorts of questions relating to Christmas such as characters in the various pantomimes, Christmas carols, Christmas customs around the world, almost any question that you could ask about Christmas. As I'd thought, the girls won the quiz by a very large margin, much to the annoyance of the boys. Unfortunately, the girls rubbed in their victory by pointing out to the boys that the boys had three extra players on their side, which caused some friction between the boys and the girls. It was milk time and the monitors distributed it, reluctantly to the girls at first, but the threat of missing the party that afternoon was enough to put them back on track. The playtime bell rang and the children went out to play and I made my way up to the staff room to find out what had been going on outside Tony's class room this morning.

I walked into the staff room and saw that there was an empty chair next to Tony. I got my mug, poured myself a tea and sat down next to him. "What was all that about outside your class room this morning, and who was that woman?" I asked. "That was Mrs Grindell, someone who is not supposed to be in the school building as she can be dangerous, that's why I wouldn't let her into my class room," said Tony. "Well what was all that about her cakes, she seemed a bit concerned about them," I asked. "Her cakes are made with pounds shillings and pence," he said in a low voice. That didn't make sense, pounds shillings and pence, what was all that about, so I asked him, "Pounds, shillings and pence, I don't get it, are they worth some money or something?" What's the notation we use on the blackboard for pounds shillings and pence when we are doing maths?" Tony said. "It's the pound sign, a s and a d," I replied. "And the pound sign is what in Latin, you're the history guy," he said. "Well as far as I can remember it derives from a capital "L", representing libra, the basic unit of weight in the Roman Empire, which in turn is derived from the Latin name for scales or a balance,"

I answered. "So what have you got in letters for pounds shillings and pence then," said Tony smiling. I thought for a few seconds and said, "LSD. You don't mean that the cakes she was after contained LSD do you. We'd better tell Mr Percy and let him know." "Well that's the thing. When the cake tin was found and opened it contained ordinary shop bought cakes. Her kid had swapped the cakes over unbeknown to the mother so if I'd sent for Mr Percy and he'd looked in the cake tin he would have found ordinary shop bought cakes, so what could he do then, apart from telling Mrs Grindell that she wasn't supposed to be on the school premises," said Tony. "What happened to the cakes with the LSD in them?" I asked. "Her daughter whispered something to her which I couldn't hear, and then she went off home muttering about bloody parties," explained Tony. After that we talked through the rest of break time about how the children would be seated in his class room for the party. As I walked to the yard to collect my class at the end of break time I wondered what other things about the school and parents I would be finding out in the months to come.

When we got back to class I had the children design and make a Christmas card for their parents and I stretched the lesson out so that it would finish at lunch time. If a child had been quick at making their card then I suggested they make one for their Nan or another relation that would like a card from them. That worked a treat and kept the children busy most of the time. At last it was lunchtime; the children went to get their lunch and I collected my packed lunch and went off to the staff room. It was only going to be a short lunch for most of the teachers as they were all going back to their class rooms to prepare the rooms for the Christmas parties. I was sat next to Tony eating my packed lunch when Miss Stark came in and came over to sit in the empty chair next to me. "Here," she said, "I've got you a present for this afternoon." She then handed me paper bag. Tony said, "Open it then, see what you have got." I didn't know what to say but I opened the bag and inside was an apron. I looked at it and gave a her a puzzled look. "It's for this afternoon, you'll need it," laughed Miss Stark. Tony looked at it and said, "I forgot to say that you will need some kind of covering over your suit as things sometimes get messy. That's fantastic and it'll keep your suit clean, I hope." I thanked Miss Stark and the three of us discussed the Christmas parties. Mr Percy came in and told all the staff that the jelly and ice cream would be delivered to each party at about two o'clock. The kitchen staff had made the jellies and the ice creams had been delivered that morning. Tony said that they would be safe to eat, if I wanted one but he warned me again not to eat anything offered to me unless it was shop wrapped and sealed. We finished our lunch and made our way to our class rooms. Miss Stark came down the stairs with us and said that her class would be in with Mrs Cook's class for the party and that her class room would be used for the party games.

I helped Tony moving desks around to make three long tables then we covered them with banquet paper which Tony had obtained. These were rolls of paper much like wall paper but much wider and went from one end of the table to the other in one sheet. Tony suggested that we take the register in our own class rooms then my class would join Tony's class, bringing their own chairs with them, for the party. I collected the children's party tins from my class room and brought them into Tony's class room while he started to fill some water jugs he had obtained from the kitchens, with water diluted orange squash. He pointed to packets of paper cups and asked me to put them on the table, one at each place. After that I had to put paper plates at each place. He suggested that we mix the classes so we put the tins on the tables, one from Tony's class followed by one from my class and so on, also we had to make sure the children were also mixed, boys and girls alternately in the places. Ten minutes before the bell was due to go, four parents knocked on the class room door and one said, "We're here to help with the party. Is there anything we can do? Tony explained how the afternoon was planned out and that the children could have the orange squash but had to stay in their place and raise their hand up for a refill, but the refills had to be within reason. When the children go to their places, they would place their sandwiches and buns on the plates in the middle of the table and the tins would then be placed on the desks at the back of the room. The children would be told that the sandwiches were to be shared and had to be eaten first before they started on the buns and cakes. Bags of crisps were also to be put on paper plates in the middle of the table so that children could help themselves and take a few to put on their plates. We adults would move about the room keeping order and making sure the children weren't getting out of hand. At about two o'clock we had to be ready to start giving out the jelly and ice cream, then, at about two fifteen the classes would move into my class room for the party games. Tony saw that the parents had brought aprons with them and said," I see that you've helped with Christmas parties before then," and laughed. "Yes," said one of the parents, "better to be safe than sorry." Tony went on to explain what would happen next, two would stay in Tony's class room and two would go into my class room. The two in Tony's class room would start to tidy up the room best they could. Tony had brought in a big cardboard box into which the waste could be deposited. Tony looked at his watch and said, "This is it folks, time for the chimps tea party," and looking at me he said, "Don't forget your apron, you'll need it." Both Tony and I went off to the playground whilst the parents were making the finishing touches in Tony's class room.

The children were lining up even before the bell had rung, one or two had their party outfits on and others had paper hats on their heads. As we were stood there waiting for the bell, Mr Percy came out and gave me a box of Christmas crackers to give to the children. "There should be one each in there," he said as he moved from class to class as the bell started to ring for the end of lunch time. Tony came over holding his box of Christmas crackers and said, "Have you got ten shillings? I bought four boxes of chocolates for the parents that are helping us this afternoon and it cost me a pound so I thought we would split it fifty- fifty. I assume that's alright with you?" "Yes, that's a good idea, I'll give you the money at break time," I said as I lead my children into school. Registration was taken and we waited for Janet, who took the register to the office, to come back before we went to Mr Telford's class room. The children carried their chairs as we moved class rooms. The children had to wait at the front of the class as Tony went along the table and called a name and that child then had to go with their chair and sit in that space at the table. Once everyone was seated, the Christmas crackers were distributed to each child and then children were told to open their tins and place the food on the plates in the middle of the table. Tony and I realised that there would be a few children that wouldn't have brought anything to the party so they were placed alongside those children who had heavy tins indicating that their tins were full and far too much food inside for one child to consume the whole lot. Once all the tins had been emptied the children were told to put the tins at the back of the room, out of the way but not to forget where they'd put them. Then they were allowed to start.

Christmas crackers were pulled and paper hats were placed on heads, even Tony, the parents and me all had paper hats on. As they were eating Tony, the parents and I went round pouring orange squash into paper cups. Looking around the class room I was astounded how many sandwiches were on the tables, sandwiches of all shapes and sizes. Some had been cut into squares and others into triangles, and then there were the sausage rolls, buns and cakes. Tony had to make an announcement that he didn't want to see more than one sausage roll on children's plates and warned children not to be greedy and make sure the food was shared equally. It was quite an eye opener for me seeing children eating with their mouths open, not a pretty sight, others eating while talking and spraying bits of sandwiches everywhere, some children grabbing at the food as though they hadn't eaten for months yet it was just over an hour ago when they'd finished their lunch. I notice a pile of sandwiches that no one except one child was eating. The sandwiches that had been cut into nice triangular shapes but the filling was a dark brown. I went over to Tony and mentioned them to him. "That's Harry Trueman in my class, as far as I know he always brings Marmite sandwiches to the Christmas party. None of the other kids like them but he loves them, so he has them all to himself. Occasionally a kid will try one and spit it out. Have a look under the table, I bet you'll find a bitten Marmite sandwich there," he told me. I casually walked past the table again and glanced under it and yes, there was the bitten Marmite sandwich lying there.

The children were munching through the food. Tony had told them to eat the sandwiches before they could start on the buns and cakes. I was looking at a plate of tempting buns; one of the children saw me and asked if I wanted one. It was a good job Tony was watching because I nearly reached over to take one but he caught my eye and shook his head, mouthing the word no. I thanked the child and made an excuse that I had a dietary problem and was unable to eat buns. I made my way to Tony who said, "You nearly fell for it then, didn't you. Remember, if it's not shop wrapped you don't eat it." "But those buns look so good," I said. "Yes they do, but they have five dogs and three cats in their house and the mother doesn't wash her hands very often, so be warned - looks can be deceiving," he replied. I realised that I'd had a narrow escape, and then the door opened and in walked one of the dinner ladies with a trolley full of portions of jelly and ice cream. The children cheered and all the adults quickly gave them out to each child. Tony came over and said, "You can have a portion of jelly and ice cream, we know who made them and they're safe to eat and we have been included to have a portion." I took my portion and tried to remember the last time I'd had jelly and ice cream, realising that it was years ago. Mr Johnson made an appearance, or should I say Santa made an appearance, he came into the class room wishing everyone a 'Happy Christmas' and hoped he would get the children's Christmas lists right, and then he was gone. A few were saying that he wasn't the real Santa only Mr Johnson dressed up. You can't fool kids. As I was at the back of the room a small girl started to get out of her seat so I went over and said, "No stay where you are, don't leave your seat," but she still started again to get up and again I told her no. The third time she got up and before I could say anything she tried to push past me but too late, she was sick all over my front. One of the parents, seeing what happened came over quickly and took the child out to the toilet. Tony nipped into his store cupboard and came back with a bucket of sawdust to put on the floor whilst I just looked down my front at the mess, good job I had the apron on, Miss Stark must have known something like that might happen. "Take that bloody thing off," whispered Tony, "Fold it up carefully to keep the mess in and put it on the cardboard box at the front near my desk." After he'd scattered the sawdust on the floor he told the children that we were going into my class room to play some games.

Once in my class room I had the children sit in two big circles and we played 'pass the parcel' with a difference. When the music stopped the child with the parcel had to sit out and the child on their right removed a layer of paper from the parcel. With two circles we had two games on the go at the same time, and as Tony had six parcels we managed to play three sessions of the game. After that it was a game of 'statues' which I stretched out until playtime. Whilst all this was going on, Tony and a couple of the parents were tidying his class room. I was so relieved to go to the staff room with Tony and the parents and get a cup of tea. Looking around the staff room other members of staff looked haggard, suffering from the effect of the Christmas parties I'm sure. After break Tony asked me to have a few more games in my class room then we could get the children to put the desks and chairs back in their usual places in the class rooms and also to get the party tins back to the rightful owners. By the time home time came around, the class rooms were almost back to normal, the children all had their tins back and the parents who had helped us were given their boxes of chocolates for which they were thankful. Once the children had gone home I went back into Tony's class room and asked, "Is it usually like that, the Christmas party?" "Today was classed as very good, only one child sick, no food fights, no one peeing in the corner, yes today was classed as a good Christmas party as things go," answered Tony. "Here, pop this in a bucket of water with some disinfectant overnight when you get home and then wash it, it will be as good as new," he said as he gave me the cardboard box with the vomit-stained apron in it. "One more day to go. I think that Mr Percy will have a film in the hall for the whole school in the morning whilst the staff clear their rooms, although we have to take it in turns to spend some time in the hall with him in case the kids get restless, but that doesn't happen very often as the kids enjoy the films he shows," said Tony. "Sounds good," I said, "and what happens in the afternoon?" "Mr Yardley has an assembly half an hour before play time, he likes to go through the true meaning of Christmas and all that. So before and after that get your 'wet playtime' box out or have a quiz or something with the kids, keep them occupied until home time. If you sort out the kids work that has been on the wall or paintings they have done through this term and let them take them home, it means less stuff for the bins and anyway the kids like to take their work home. Come on, we've been here long enough, time to go home, it's a big night tomorrow, I'm looking forward to the Casino," he said. I went back to my class room collected my things and went home.

Chapter Sixteen

Well, it was here at last, the last day of my first term at Cromwell Street Mixed Infants and Juniors and I was on duty. As I sat at the table eating my toast and marmalade I was thinking how the children in my class had changed over the past three and a half months or so. They were beginning to get to know me and I was getting to know them. I also wondered what it might have been like at St Ninians, the nice posh school I had dreams of going to, and if my teaching methods would have been any different. Get the day over with and then tonight enjoy a night at the Casino, along with the meal, which means I'd better not have a lot for tea, just a snack. I looked at the clock; if I didn't get a move on I'll be late for my duty, and on the last day too. I quickly got my things together and set off for the bus. Riding the bus to school I started thinking of the three course meal at the Casino. Prawn cocktail for starters followed by medium rare steak and chips with onion rings and mushrooms and to finish with - a black forest gateau. The meal had been ordered a few weeks ago when the Casino trip was booked. We'd been given a menu and had to put in the order for the meal we wanted. As I've always liked steak, I ordered that. Also, so that staff could have a drink, a minibus had been ordered and a map was drawn of where staff lived and which way the minibus would pick each one of us up. I was going to be the last on the route, which meant that I would be first off when we were coming back. All that had been paid for a month or so ago, so the only expense tonight would be the drinks and our betting money. I had drawn twenty five pounds out of the bank as I had promised Tony and Miss Stark that I would pay for the drinks, their reward for helping me with the nativity play over the past week. I wasn't sure when to go and stay with my mother for the Christmas holidays and just how long to stay. I was soon at the bus stop for the school and I had enough time to go to the staff room and get a cup of tea before going on duty in the yard before school started.

As it was the last day of term the children were allowed to bring in their toys or should I say a toy to keep them occupied during the day. Morning assembly would now be in the place of the last lesson of the afternoon, so that straight after assembly the children would go home. The teacher's main job today would be to keep the children occupied which would be a trying time as most children were excited and looking forward to Christmas. Walking round the yard I was surprised by how mild the weather was, yes, you needed your coat and gloves but we hadn't had any snow yet and only a few frosty mornings. According to the met office there could be a white Christmas this year. I tried to think back when the last white Christmas was and I recalled that some parts of the country had snow at Christmas in 1966 and before that was, I think, 1964. My thoughts were broken when a child came up to me and asked if I was looking forward to Christmas and asked what presents was I getting. I said that I didn't know, it would be up to Santa. She gave me a funny look and said. "You don't believe in Santa Claus, do you, that's for kids." I asked how old she was and she told me she was seven, and with that she went off to play with her friends. Seven, I thought, and she doesn't believe in Santa any more - what's the world coming to. Our kids are growing up too fast. The bell rang and the children started to line up in their classes.

I stayed on the yard until all the teachers had come to collect their classes then I went to my class who were all stood waiting for me. I led them to the cloakroom to hang up their coats and then to our class room. Registration was called, along with the dinner register, and then I thought we could have some play reading as I still had the play books from Mr Telford's class. The children enjoyed this lesson, especially as we made a space by moving some desks out of the way and used that as our stage so that the children could act out the plays as well as reading them. We were so engrossed in the lesson that I didn't realise that time was flying by until Timmy asked if we were going to have the milk that morning as it was nearly break time. I told the children to sit in their places and the milk was given out. No sooner had the children had finished the milk and returned their empties to the crate when the break time bell rang. I collected my coat and followed the children out to the yard. Playground duty can be interesting at times, with children coming up to you and telling you interesting facts, even though they're not in your class. For example, once when I was on duty a girl of about seven came up and told me that a boy shouldn't be wearing a jacket with a picture of a spliff on the back. I didn't understand what she was on about, "Spliff," I said, "what's that?" She told me, "You know sir a spliff, a joint, a reefer, wacky baccy. Oh sir, if you want any I know where to go and you won't get ripped off and it's good stuff too," and with that she went skipping off to join her friends without a care in the world. Sometimes you felt as though you were just keeping the peace, especially when there was a sense of tension in the air, but on the whole it could be rewarding. The bell rang and I blew my whistle, the children had to stop what they were doing and stand in silence, then a second whistle was blown which was the sign for the children to walk to their class lines in silence. My class were last into school as I was the teacher on duty and had to see that the other classes were in before my class moved. I had to get the children to class and then to the hall as Mr Percy was going to show the school a film whilst teachers could clear their rooms.

Once in the class room I had a pile of various papers, some art pictures that the children had made this past term and another pile of written work. I would give them out to the children during the afternoon and tell them that if they didn't want to take them home then they could put them in the waste bin. Some of the pictures didn't have a name on them so it would be a case of holding up the picture and asking, "Who does this belong to?" Most of the children would want to take their works of art home to show their parents, while others wouldn't be bothered and would put them in the bin. There were some pieces that I wanted to keep and those were put away for future use. Soon it was almost dinnertime and teachers had to go and collect their classes from the hall before the dinner time bell rang. As it was Christmas, the staff were invited to join the children in the dining hall for Christmas dinner. The staff were sat at a table just for themselves, as at other times it was expected that individual members of staff would each sit at a table with the children, mainly to help keep order but with so many staff in the dining room at one time the children knew that they had to behave. As school dinners went, the Christmas meal was very good and had a good selection of vegetables, including sprouts, which weren't popular with the children. The sweet was jelly and cream for the children whilst the staff were treated to Christmas pudding and white sauce. I was told that the sauce was supposed to have been made with brandy, quite how much I didn't know as I was unable to taste it, so it couldn't have been much brandy. After that it was up to the staff room where

Mr Percy had brought in a coffee percolator and treated the staff to 'real' ground coffee. To make the Christmas feeling complete, Ivan Jenkins took out a cigar and lit it. The smell of a cigar always reminds me of Christmas. My father also enjoyed his cigar along with a glass of brandy after our Christmas dinner at home.

I had to leave the staff room ten minutes before the bell rang as I was on playground duty and to be honest I was glad to go early as most of the conversation was about what Christmas presents different members of staff were buying for their partners and how much they were paying or they were discussing tonight's visit to the Casino. Some of the staff thought that eleven pm was too late to be leaving the Casino, whilst others thought it was too early. It just goes to show that you can please some of the people some of the time but you can't please all the people all of the time. Personally, I thought that eleven pm was a good time to leave, especially if you'd lost all of your money early on the roulette tables or one-armed bandits or to give them their correct titles slot machines or fruit machines. Walking round the yard, a couple of children from the infant class came and walked with me. "One of the bigger children is saying that there is no Santa Claus. Is that true sir?" one of the children asked me. That put me in a strange situation, should I say yes and in years to come the child would remember that her teacher lied about Santa, or should I say no, there's no Santa and from then on spoil her Christmas. "If you believe in Santa then carry on believing in him, it's part of the magic of Christmas. Maybe the older ones don't believe in magic anymore," I said, with conviction. That was accepted by the children, who thanked me and ran off to join their other friends at the far side of the yard. I started thinking about my childhood and how I'd always looked forward to Christmas morning to see what Santa had brought me, never thinking that all the presents had been bought by my parents. That bubble had been burst when I was about eight or nine when a friend of mine put me straight about Santa Claus. At first I didn't want to believe him, but the evidence he put forward as to there being no Santa swayed me, although deep down I was hoping it wasn't true. The following Christmas I found some of my presents on top of my parents wardrobe two weeks before Christmas and realised that my friend had been telling the truth about Santa and my age of innocence began to crumble. Just as I was getting deeper in thought the bell rang and I had to blow my whistle, once for the children to stop moving about and stop talking and twice for them to make their way to their class lines. Again, my class were the last ones to go in to school.

The last registration was taken for this term and before the register was taken back to the office I had to fill in various boxes in the register showing the attendance for each child and how many times they had been absent in this half term, I noticed that Matthew Armitage had a poor record for Tuesday afternoons, which was when we had our PE lesson, and those Tuesdays he was present he tried to make excuses why he shouldn't take part in the lesson. If he was off then his mum always seemed to send in a note saying why he had been away. It didn't help that he went home at lunchtime either. While all this was going on, the children were playing with their games or drawing and some were playing paper games such as battleships and noughts and crosses. On the whole the children were behaving quite well, although there was a couple of incidents of cheating in some of the games they were playing and the arguments got rather heated. If I hadn't have been there, fighting might have broken out. Someone who surprised me was Alfie, who sat alone by himself at the back of the class with some card that I had given him. He had a set of coloured pencils and had told me that he wanted to make a special Christmas card, and there he sat, at the back working away at his card. If I approached him he would cover it up with his arm so as not to let me see it.

The time was ticking away and five minutes before break time I told the children to put their things away and if they were taking their pictures and written work home to leave them on their desks so that they could pick them up when we came back from assembly. I decided that the children could go out before the bell rang as I was on duty and would be on the yard with them. As my class ran around the yard, the bell rang and other classes started to fill up the yard and playing various chasing games. After break time the children were taken by their teacher to the hall for the last assembly of the term. Mr Yardley was on good form, telling the children to behave and help their parents during the holidays and not be a nuisance around the home. Mr Sharpe was asked to play some Christmas carols to end the assembly and the whole school joined in, including the teachers. After assembly it was back to class, the children collecting their things and then on to the cloakroom where I stood supervising the orderly exit of the children. As they were leaving some were calling out "Happy Christmas" or "Have a nice holiday sir' and "See you next year," all of them were in fine spirits.

Once the cloakrooms were clear, I went back to my class room to pick up my things and decided that I wasn't going to stay long as the bus for the Casino would be picking me up at just gone seven o'clock and I wanted to relax in a nice hot bath before then. When I got into my class room there was something on my desk. A pupil had made a Christmas card. On the front was a picture of a Christmas tree with baubles and presents underneath it, at the top it read 'To Sir.' Inside it read, 'To sir, I hope you have a nice Christmas and get lots of presents. You are the bestest teacher in the school and I like you. I'm sorry I have been naughty at times but I'll try to be good next term. Best wishes from Alfie Underwood.' I stood there looking at the card, "I have made a difference," I thought.

"Don't you want to go home or are you staying?" Tony shouted at me from the corridor. I thought about showing him the card but instead I called out, "No, I've just got something to do before I leave. I'll see you tonight at the Casino, and don't forget that the drinks are on me." "How could I forget that!" he remarked then walked away. I got my bag and pulled out a box of chocolates wrapped in Christmas paper along with a Christmas card, on both it read 'To the cleaners, thank you for all your hard work in my class room. Best wishes, Mr Tredwell,' and put them on my desk. As I did so, I recalled being told when I was at college that the caretaker and cleaners are the backbone of the school, keep them happy and you won't go wrong.

When I arrived home I felt that I needed to unwind and what better than to have a hot bath. I put my briefcase in the cupboard under the stairs out of sight so as not to remind me of school during the holidays. I was a bit peckish so a cheese sandwich was on the cards before my bath. I ate my sandwich whilst the bath was running and took my cup of coffee into the bath room to drink while soaking in the bath. Before getting into the bath I got my clothes ready, a new shirt, which was still in its' packing, socks, clip on bow tie and, of course, Stuarts black three piece suit still in the plastic suit bag. Before getting in the bath I shaved using a new blade in my razor so that I would get a close shave then I got in the bath. Laying in the bath was sheer bliss listening to Radio One and 'What's new.' Although I liked Radio One, I still preferred the pirate radio station Radio Caroline, even though it had officially ended last year in August. I kept an eye on the time, I didn't want to rush and yet it was so nice just to relax in the hot water. In the end I had to force myself to make a move and get out and get dried. Standing in my bedroom in my underwear and socks I was having trouble with the new shirt. Why do they put so many pins in a new shirt, just when I thought I had them all and started to put the shirt on, a pin let itself known at the back of my neck by sticking in me. Lucky for me it didn't break the skin and start bleeding, but it set me off using some choice language. I checked the shirt again looking for any more rogue pins and found none.

Once it was on I looked in the mirror, the fit was good but it was very creased, then I remembered that I'd dropped my iron last weekend when I was ironing my school shirts and it had stopped working. I'd better keep my jacket on and with the waistcoat on there wasn't much shirt to see, so hopefully no one would notice the creases. Time for Stuarts' suit, so I pulled the bag off the suit and the smell hit me. I should have hung the suit up without the suit bag, too late now. I looked around for something that might hide the smell and there it was – 'Old Spice' aftershave. I stood there splashing 'Old Spice' all over the suit, hoping that the smell would go away. I put the suit on; the smell was still there, so more 'Old Spice' was needed. I just hoped that the smell would be gone by the time we got to the Casino. I would have to put my large overcoat on when I got into the mini bus and hope that the ladies were wearing strong perfume and not notice the pong coming from me. I put the clip-on bow tie on and looked in the mirror. I must admit that I looked rather smart, the suit fitted well and there were only a few small creases in the shirt that could be seen, and even then only if you looked closely. I'd be a good catch for any woman that had no sense of smell, I thought. I went downstairs and got my wallet out of my school jacket and put twenty five pounds inside and checked that I had my ticket for the Casino in the wallet then tucked the wallet into the inside pocked of the jacket. My black shoes had been shined last night ready for tonight and they set the suit off to perfection. I looked at my watch, I'd better be going, I thought. I put my long overcoat on, a quick sniff, and then I rushed upstairs to my bedroom and a final splash of 'Old Spice' all over me and the suit. I walked down the stairs, sniffing as I walked and convinced myself that everything was going to be alright. The minibus was scheduled to pick me up at the end of the street, which it did five minutes later.

As I was the last one on the bus, the only seat left was the one at the front near the driver, which suited me fine, although the driver looked at me strangely a bit later on when he gave a little sniffed as if I'd trodden in something. We arrived at the Casino half an hour later and gathered in the reception area with Mr Percy at the front talking to the girl behind the reception desk. He turned to us and said, "Can you please have your tickets ready and leave your coats here. The girls will give you a cloakroom ticket for your coat, then when everyone's ready we can go upstairs to the restaurant." "He thinks we're still in school," said a voice behind me. I turned and saw Tony Telford with his partner. He looked at me and smiled then said, "Bloody hell have you got shares in Old Spice, you must have used a bucket full." Oh no, I thought, it's not that obvious is it? I'd better keep my distance from the others if I could. It was my turn to give in my ticket and I handed over my overcoat to the girl behind the counter. She took the coat, wrinkled her nose and then passed the coat over to the girl who was responsible for taking the coats into the back and hanging them up. "Elsie, coat," she said as a girl came forward, presumably Elsie, "Hang this in the corner away from the others," and then she passed me a numbered cloakroom plastic disc.

When we were all ready, we made our way to the restaurant and, as always, Mr Percy had a seating plan for us all and started pointing to where he wanted people to sit. Fortunately, I was placed at the end of the table so there was no one on my left, but he had put Miss Stark on my right hand side with Tony Telford and his partner opposite us. Mr Percy said to Miss Stark and myself that he'd put us together because we'd both come without a partner and thought it would be company for the both of us. Tony looked across the table and smiled and when Miss Stark wasn't looking gave me the thumbs up sign. Tony introduced his wife, Margaret, to Miss Stark and me and we all shook hands and we introduced ourselves to her. Miss Stark whispered to me that I should call her Emma and she would call me John, "We're not in school now," she added. Mr Percy came round the table to say that our menus had been given in last week and the waitresses would come round and ask what our meal was then serve it. He also said that we'd been given complimentary bottles of wine, one bottle per four people and we had to decide in fours if we wanted red or white wine. I wasn't bothered whether I had red or white, neither was Tony, so the ladies chose white. The wine waiter came over and when he saw me said, "Jot, what are you doing here?" Tony and Emma both looked at me then the waiter. I said, "Richie, I'm on a night out with the staff I work with. I didn't know you were working here, how long has it been?" "Must be three or four years. Look we'll have to catch up properly at some other time, I'll get shot if I don't get a move on. Enjoy your night." "Thanks we will, and it's white wine please," I said and he opened a bottle of white wine and poured a little into Tony's glass. Tony tasted it and said, "Yes, that's good, thank you," then Richie poured wine out for the four of us and left the bottle in the middle and moved further up the table. Tony and Emma were still looking at me then Tony said "Jot?" I looked at both of them, embarrassed, "Yes, Jot, that's what they called me when I left school, my initials John Oliver Tredwell. Richie and me were good friends and even worked together at one time, then I went off to teacher training college and lost touch." "You're a dark horse, you are," said Tony laughing, "Jot, indeed."

  The waitresses came round with the starter, most of us had selected the pawn cocktail. Part of tonight's deal included a ten shilling bet on the roulette tables. It seemed that very few of the staff had ever been to a Casino before yet alone placed a bet on roulette. As some of the staff were still eating their starter I excused myself and went to the gaming floor and got a leaflet explaining how to play roulette and how to place bets. I took it back to our table and started to explain how it all worked. The leaflet showed how chips were placed on the numbers or part of the numbers and what odds were give on where you placed your chip. I had to stop as our next course was started to be given out by the waitresses. I noticed that our bottle of wine was empty so I called Richie over and ordered another bottle. As we were eating our meal we chatted about the past term and various incidents that had happened. Tony got told off by his wife when he started telling the story of Farthingale and how Mrs Grants office had to be fumigated after Tony had left him there to wait for Mr Yardley. I mentioned Alfie Underwood and how much he had changed since the start of term; I nearly mentioned his Christmas card to me then decided not to. Emma was interested to know how I got the donkey off the stage the other night and I had to explain how Mr Smith had managed it. I looked down the table and the rest of the staff were chatting away enjoying their meals. Next came the sweet followed by coffee, I looked at my watch, nine forty five, which meant that we would have about an hour on the gaming floor. I went over to Richie along with other members of staff that had bought more wine or drinks and paid him. Behind me in the queue to pay was Mike Charlesworth, he looked at me and said, "Strange aftershave you've got on, a heavy smell of Old Spice with an undercurrent of embalming fluid." Trust a chemistry teacher to come out with something like that. All I could reply to him was, "Oh really, maybe I've put too much on tonight." Fortunately, it was me next in the queue, so I paid Richie for the wine and said that I would get in touch with him soon and we could arrange to meet up for a drink.

Most of the staff made their way to the roulette tables, which were starting to fill up. The ten shilling bet consisted of one chip. I explained that depending on where you put the chip would depend what odds you would be paid out. I told the staff to get a roulette playing leaflet which were stacked on the end of the tables and study it, so that they were fairly clear on how to bet on the tables. Tony, Margaret and Emma stayed with me and said that they would watch me first before committing their chip to the table. I decided to put my chip on the line dividing 23 and 24 and explained that if either number came up I'd win and the pay-out would be eighteen to one. The wheel spun and the ball was rolled in, it went round and round and jumped in and out of various slots until the wheel slowed down and the ball rested in twenty four. The croupier paid me nine pounds and I left my betting chip on the table in the same place. Tony pointed out that the chip was still there. I explained that if I wanted I could take that chip and put it anywhere I wanted as it was still mine but I had decided to 'let it ride,' as the saying goes. The wheel was spun again and the ball bounced about on the wheel and something caught my attention on another table and didn't hear the croupier say the number. Tony poked me in the ribs and said, "You lucky bugger, it's come up again, bloody twenty four." I turned and looked, twenty four again, this time I took my chip off the table as the croupier paid me another nine pounds.

The rest of the staff were no so lucky with their ten shilling chips. Some bought more chips this time, but at a lesser value, one shilling each and most either got a pound or two pounds worth. Tony, Margaret and Emma were not so lucky with their chips and Margaret and Emma decided to go to the bar for a drink. Mike Charlesworth came and joined Tony and myself and said, "That aftershave is getting no better, still has a hit of embalming fluid about it." "Funny you should say that Mike, but I've been smelling a strange smell all evening," said Tony then looking at me said, "You've been heavy handed with the Old Spice, but there's some else in it as well." I just looked blank and shrugged my shoulders. Looking at the table I said, "What are the odds of winning on the table?" Tony said thirty six to one but Mike said thirty seven to one when you included the zero. I put it to them, "What if we can reduce the odds to four to one?" They both looked at me and asked how. I explained, "Pick a central number and place a chip on its four corners, then you are betting on nine numbers which makes it a one in four chance that one of the numbers will come up." I went further, "If you put a chip on the number as well, then the dividing line of the corresponding numbers, you'll have a good pay-out if your middle number comes up. Look, I'll show you on the leaflet. Let's take thirty two, one chip on thirty two, a chip on each corner and a chip on each dividing line, so we have covered nine numbers which will use nine chips." They both looked at the leaflet and both said, "Let's give it a go." Tony and Mike got twenty one shilling chips and we all put nine chips on and around thirty two. The wheel spun and twenty eight came out which paid us nine shillings, the odds being nine to one. "Same again," I said and they both agreed. The wheel spun and when it stopped Tony couldn't believe it, thirty two. The croupier paid us seven pounds four shillings each. I suggested that we ask for value chips and the croupier gave us seven one pound chips and four one shilling chips. "Put the value chips in your pocket and cash them up at the end," I told them. We played on with the shilling chips until they were gone. Emma and Margaret came to join us as we were walking to the cashiers to cash in our chips. We stood in the queue waiting for our turn, I put my hand in my jacket pocket to get my chips and as I pulled my hand out a business card fell to the floor. Mike Charlesworth bent down and picked it up, "What's this," he asked, "Collins Undertakers! No wonder I could smell embalming fluid, it's on your suit. Are you moonlighting as an Undertaker's assistant in the evenings and at the weekend?" Tony and Emma just stood there looking at me waiting for my reply. What could I say except the truth, I had borrowed the suit which belonged to a friend named Stuart who, yes, worked in an Undertakers and I hadn't taken it out of the suit bag until this evening, hence the smell of embalming fluid. I'd panicked and tried to hide the smell with Old Spice and nearly got away with it, and might have done so had it not been for Mike Charlesworth and his good sense of smell. Tony looked at me and said, "I've said it before and I'll say it again, you're a dark horse, you are," and he, Emma and Mike started laughing. The cashier looked at us from behind his counter and asked if we were cashing up or standing there waiting for a bus. The three of us cashed in, I'd won twenty five pounds and Tony and Mike seven pounds each, but I warned them both that, "We've been lucky tonight, other nights could be much different so you should only bring money you can afford to lose."

Mr Percy saw us and came over, "I'm sorry to say that we'll have to make our way out as the minibus will be here soon to take us home." We all started to make our way down to reception to get our coats and when we were all together Mr Percy nipped outside and came back a few minutes later to inform us all that the bus had arrived. On the way to the bus Emma asked what I was doing over Christmas and I explained that I was going to my mothers and didn't know when I'd be back. I said that I thought it would be same seats in the bus on the way back so I would have to sit in the front. She opened her bag and quickly wrote down something on an envelope and passed it to me, "Here," she said, "here's my telephone number. We could go for a drink or something if you are free." "Yes, thanks, that would be nice," I said and I actually meant it, it would be nice.

We all climbed onto the bus, in the same seats as requested by Mr Percy. Mr Yardley asked if everyone had enjoyed the evening and there was a resounding "Yes!" from everyone. He also gave thanks to the person who had suggested coming to the Casino for the night out. I sat there and smiled. Half an hour later I was getting off the bus with members of staff shouting, "Happy Christmas," and "All the best," with me replying, "Thanks - and all the best to you all." I shut the door and the bus drove off. I put my hand in my pocket and pulled the envelope out and looked what Emma had written. It said 'Emma' then her phone number followed by, "Have a nice Christmas. Love Emma."

Chapter Seventeen

It's nice to wake up in a morning when you're ready to wake up and not be woken up by an strident alarm clock urging you to get up. This was such a morning, the first day of the Christmas holidays and I was awake not knowing what time it was or bothered about what time it was. I laid there and thought about the previous night and how nice it was to see Richie again and recalling our holiday in Blackpool. It was thanks to him that I'd first visited a Casino there. Strange, I thought, that he'd ended up with a job working in a Casino. I also thought that now I have a membership card for the Casino I might start going there, maybe once a month or so. My system of betting, cutting the odds down to four to one had paid off last night and I wondered if it would pay off in the future. I realise that roulette was a game of luck and if there was a system to beat the odds then Casinos would have to close down. As there seem to be more Casinos opening around the country then my system, like everyone else's, would depend on luck and nothing more. I started thinking how well Tony, Margaret, Emma and I got on. We'd talked, joked and made fun of each other and Tony and I had won at the tables, which was the icing on the cake. I realised then that I referred to Miss Stark as Emma and not Miss Stark, now why was that? I thought of the envelope that she'd given me and that she'd signed it 'Love, Emma' and not just 'Emma.' I wondered about Alfie Underwood and what Mrs Silby had told me about his dad and that when he was in prison Alfie seemed like a different child, and for the past six weeks Alfie had behaved well in school, which would indicate that dad must be at Her Majesty's pleasure. I was very flattered by his Christmas card to me and I felt proud that I might have made a difference in his life. My thoughts went back to Emma and the 'phone number on the envelope. When should I ring though, maybe later today. If I rang it would be just to arrange for us to go out for a drink, I wasn't going to be the replacement boyfriend, as Tony had warned me that she was looking for. I closed my eyes and fell asleep. When I woke up again I made the effort and got out of bed and looked at the clock, ten to eleven, now that was a late sleep in, something that I hadn't done for months.

A couple of Christmas cards had arrived in the post, one from my sister and her family and one from my mother. I remembered the card from Alfie and got it out of my bag and I put all three on the mantelpiece along with the card that the Salvation Army had sent me as I'd made a donation earlier in the year and they were now asking if I could send them another donation for Christmas. I went into the kitchen and looked in the fridge, two rashers of bacon and one egg - just enough for a sandwich. After cooking the bacon and egg I sat at the table and made a shopping list. I would go to my mother's on Monday afternoon and stay maybe until the Saturday. As Christmas Day was on Wednesday that would mean on Thursday my sister and her family would be round and would spend most of the day and expecting my mother to lay on a big spread for dinner. I always thought that this was a bit unfair but my mother said that she enjoyed it. This had started the first Christmas after my father had died and had continued ever since. Maybe it was a bit unfair on my part as well as I'd always gone home for Christmas, staying for a week or more, with my mother doing most of the cooking all the time. Because my sister and her family came round on Boxing Day our Christmas Day main meal was a small chicken and all the trimmings with tea, consisting of leftovers with chips, which I cooked. Boxing Day was the turkey and ham with roast potatoes, carrots, sprouts, broccoli, mashed potato, Yorkshire pudding, Cranbury sauce and gravy, good to say that there was plenty of meat left over for sandwiches for the next two days, although my mother always insisted that my sister take some home for their meals. All this thinking of food, I double checked my shopping list and worked out what I might have for the different meals I would be having here. I then thought about ringing Emma and going for a meal at the Berni Inn in town. Saturday before Christmas it would be extremely busy, but Sunday night, I wondered. Last night I had twenty five pounds in my wallet and I had won twenty five pounds on the roulette table and I had bought two bottles of wine which cost four pounds ten shillings, so I had forty five pounds ten shillings. I began to think about the armed bank robbery and what the reward might be. I'd read somewhere that there had been a reward of two hundred and sixty thousand pounds offered for information leading to the arrests of the robbers and return of the money on the great train robbery of 1963, but the money they stole was two point six million pounds which meant the reward was ten per cent. If that was the case, then how much money would have been in the security van on the day of the robbery? The police did say that the security van would have carried double the amount it usually did because of the Christmas holiday. "Better not to get too far ahead of yourself," I thought, "you might only end up with a thank you letter from the bank and the police and that's it."

That afternoon whilst out shopping I popped into a telephone box and rang Emma. As the 'phone was ringing I wasn't sure what to say then a voice said, "Hello." "Hello," I said, "Is that Emma?" "No, I'm sorry, she's not here at the moment, this is her mother speaking, who's calling," said the voice. "It's John, John Tredwell, I'm a colleague from school. She asked me to give her a call, and, er, well I just thought, well I was passing a 'phone box and, well I, I just thought I would give her a call. It's nothing important, I just thought she might like to go for a drink, but if she's not there, well, when might she be in?" I asked. "As I said she's not here at the moment but she will be back later on, if you'd like to ring later this afternoon, I'll tell her that you rang. John Tredwell you say," she said. "Yes, that's right. I'll call back later if that's alright. Thank you, Bye," I replied and then I put the 'phone down. I then got thinking, What am I doing? I asked myself, but it's only a drink, I answered. I remembered what Tony had said to me, "She's looking for a replacement boyfriend," so was I going to be that replacement boyfriend. Just then there was a knocking on the side of the 'phone box and as I turned to see who it was, a woman was pointing at the telephone and shouting, "Are you going to use that thing or what? I want to make an important call and you've been in there for the past ten minutes." I picked up Emma's envelope with her telephone number on it and put it in my pocket then came out of the telephone box, holding the door open for the woman and apologised as she moved in. The woman just grunted something inaudible as she stepped in the box and started to get some change out of her purse and then picked up the telephone receiver. I walked away to continue with my shopping.

I sat down to a plate of sausage, egg beans and chips for tea and had decided to go to the pub that evening for a drink or two as there wasn't much on the television. After tea I went and got changed into a smart but casual jacket and trousers. I checked that I had my wallet and some change in my pocket. I opened the front door and it was snowing, enough to start lying on the road. I went to get my raincoat and umbrella. I wasn't keen taking the umbrella but it looked as though the snow was set to continue and I suppose that the umbrella would keep most of the snow off me. As I started walking down the street I realised that I hadn't picked up Emma's envelope with her telephone number on it, so I went back home to collect it. At first I couldn't remember what I'd done with it, then I recalled that I'd put it in my trouser pocket so I nipped upstairs to retrieve it. Instead of putting the envelope in my pocket I wrote the number down in my note book which I usually carried with me. I set off again, the snow was coming down faster now and I thought that I wouldn't stay too long in the pub due to the weather. I stopped at the 'phone box at the top of the street and rang Emma. The same voice answered, "Hello," she said. "Hello, it's John Tredwell again, could I speak to Emma please," I asked. "I'm sorry, she's just gone out again, but I told her that you had rung this afternoon and she asked if you could ring again after eight thirty tonight. Would that be alright?" she asked me. Well what could I say, "Er, yes. I think I can ring later, say after eight thirty tonight. Thank you, good bye," I said. "Ok, I'll tell her that you rang again and that you'll ring back later. Goodbye," said Emma's mother and with that she put the 'phone down. I stood in the 'phone box and thought of the situation that I was getting myself in. All I wanted to do was go for a bite to eat and a chat and in one day I've rung her twice and said that I'd ring her a third time. What would she think of it, I wondered, never mind what she thinks, I'm off to the pub for a pint.

The pub was more crowded than usual on a Saturday night; well it was Christmas I suppose. I managed to push my way to the bar and order a pint and while the bar maid was pulling it I looked around. Lots of people but no one I knew, so I paid for my drink and moved to a small table near the corner. I took my coat off and rested the umbrella with the coat on a spare chair at the table. I sat at the table and planned the next week in my mind. I would go to my mother's on Monday and maybe come home on Saturday the 28th but what would I do for the next week at home, maybe some school work for the next term. "Anyone sitting there, mate," a voice asked. I looked up and saw a middle aged man with a woman, "No, it's no one's seat and I'm not expecting anyone, so please sit there if you want to," I replied. "Thanks," the man said, "Looks like the snow could be quite deep when we leave here tonight, it's really coming down now, so fast that you can't see across the road. Just think, we might have to stay here the night. How about that love?" he said looking at the woman. "No thanks," she said, "I want you to check the weather in half an hour's time and if it's still snowing we're going home. I don't want to be stuck in this pub all night." The man replied, "I was just joking about staying here all night if the weather was too bad." He looked at me, "Tell her mate, we wouldn't stay her all night if the snow got too deep, would we?" "I don't think that they'd be allowed to do that, what with all these people in here all night," I said trying to calm the woman down. The man started, "I don't understand you," he said to her, "we come out for a drink and you want me to check the weather as though I'm some bloke from the met office and don't start getting awkward about the crack about staying here all night, I was just joking, you spoil our night out before it's started. I don't know why we come out, I really don't."

I looked around once more and I couldn't see any one I knew and I had the feeling that this couple would continue arguing all night and seeing that my glass was empty decided it was time to go home. I stood up, put my coat on and picked up my umbrella then wished the man and woman a "Merry Christmas" and made my way to the door, leaving them both still arguing about the weather. Once outside I could see that they were right, you couldn't see across the road due to the amount of snow that was falling. I looked at my watch; it was nearly eight thirty as I approached the telephone box I'd used earlier. I stopped outside it and wondered should I ring Emma again or should I give it a miss. Oh, sod it, I thought, and went inside the 'phone box. I pulled out my note book, found the number and rang it. "Hello," said a by now familiar voice. "Is Emma there?" I asked. "Well, yes, she came in not five minutes ago. Wait a moment and I'll get her for you. It is John, isn't it?" she said. "Yes, it's John," I replied and waited. In the background I could hear her calling for Emma, 'It's that John calling again for you, he's hanging on the 'phone.' I could hear steps and then, "Hello, Emma here, is that

John?" she asked. "Yes, it's John here, I was just wondering if you would like to go for a meal and a drink at the Berni Inn tomorrow night at about seven, if I can get it booked?" I said. "Seven," she said, "Seven, yes that should be alright if you can get it booked for then." "OK, I'll try and get it booked and let you know tomorrow. I'll come and pick you up in a taxi, but I don't know your address, what is it?" I asked. She told me and I wrote it down in my notebook. Just then the pips started to go and I fumbled in my pocket but there was no change so I just had time to say, "The pips are going and I haven't any more change, I'll ring you tomorrow just after lunchtime. Bye." The phone went dead before Emma could say anything. Well that was that. I'd try and get a table at the Berni Inn for seven o'clock. As I walked home in the snow I was still not sure if I was doing the right thing, Tony's words were still going round my head, "She's looking for a replacement boyfriend. Was that me?" I thought.

By the time I arrived home, the snow was beginning to be getting thick on the ground. I decided to watch a bit of television, 'Match of the Day,' whilst I had some supper with a small whisky as a night cap. The next day I expected more snow but it seemed that all the snow had fallen before midnight but what was on the ground was now frozen. I made myself some breakfast and looked through one of last week's newspapers for the telephone number of the Berni Inn, which had been an advertisement in one of the papers. Why is it that you can never find what you are looking for, it took me three times to look through the papers before I found the information that I needed. I jotted down the number and I also looked for the telephone number of a nearby taxi company. For the rest of the morning I just took it easy and relaxed and caught up with some reading. I went out to the telephone box at about twelve o'clock, the paths were very slippery and I was careful not to fall. Once inside the telephone box I rang the Berni Inn and managed to book a table for seven that evening. The manager said that I was lucky as a party of ten had just rung in to cancel their booking at six forty five due to the weather. I then rang Emma and got 'you know who' on the 'phone, "Hello," she said, "Who's calling?" "Hello," I said, "Is Emma there, please?" "Yes, just a moment, is that John?" she asked. "Yes, it's John here, I said that I'd ring today," I added. She put the 'phone down and went to get Emma whilst I waited. This time I had a pocket full of change so that

I wouldn't be caught out with the pips going for time's up. "Hello, John, it's Emma," said Emma. "Hi Emma, I've managed to get the table booked for seven this evening, I was lucky as a party of ten had cancelled their booking for six forty five. What time shall I pick you up?" I asked. "Well, I have something to do this afternoon but I can be ready for about a quarter past six if that's alright?" she said. "Yes, sure," I said, "I'll be round for a quarter past six tonight and if we are early we can have a drink before the meal. See you later, bye for now." "Yes, thanks, see you later too," she said. My next job was to book a taxi, fortunately I'd made a note of a taxi company near to my house so I rang them and booked a taxi to pick me up at five to six as I reckoned that the journey to Emma's would take about twenty minutes. As I walked back home I started thinking that Emma had been quite busy over the past day or so and that her mother gave no indication of either she was or what she'd been doing, but it had nothing to do with me I thought.

I had got half way home then I realised that I hadn't rung Stuart to tell him that I was going home in the morning and I would bring the suit with me. I went back to the 'phone box and rang him. The phone rang four times and then Stuart answered it. "Hi Stuart, it's Jot here. Just to let you know that I'm coming home to my mother's in the morning and I'll have your suit with me. When do you want to pick it up or shall I drop it off to you?" I said. "Brilliant," he said, "I'm pleased you rang. Can you bring the suit to Collins by eleven o'clock, it's quite urgent." "Yes, no problem, and let me know what I owe you for the use of the suit." I said. "Oh, that's alright, I'll have to think of something," he said and started laughing. "I'll see you at eleven or earlier in the morning. Take care. Bye," I said and put the phone down. I thought I'd better let my mother know I'd be coming home early as all she knew was that I could be home on the Monday but no time had been mentioned. I rang our next door neighbour, Mrs Taylor, as my mother didn't have a phone. I asked if she would give a message to my mother to say that I would be catching the early train and would be home at about ten in the morning. Once on the phone with Mrs Taylor you couldn't get off as she like to talk and ask how you are getting on, and as she knew that I'd been teaching she wanted to know all about the school and the children. As I'd nothing else to do we had a good long chat and I kept topping the call box with sixpences until, at last, I was all out of news. I thanked her again for taking the message and said that I'd call round to see her when I was home.

On the way home I bought a Sunday newspaper to read that afternoon after lunch. I'd decided to have a Vesta Curry followed by Angel Delight for lunch, something that I enjoyed. I read the newspaper then indulged myself with a nice long hot bath while listening to John Peel on Radio One which started at three pm, and when Alan Freeman came on at five o'clock with 'Pick of the Pops' then it was time to make a move and get out of the bath. I thought about wearing the same shirt from Friday when I'd gone to the Casino but then though better of it. I was sure I had another new shirt somewhere in one of my drawers. Why is it that you can never find something you are looking for but when you are not looking for it then it turns up? That was the shirt, a good twenty minutes trying to find it. When I did find it I wasn't sure if it would go with my jacket and trousers. I unpacked the shirt from its plastic covering and pulled all the pins out, and, remembering what had happened on Friday I doubled checked the collar, and yes, found a small pin at the back of the collar. Once fully dressed I looked in the mirror, yes that will do, I thought. I splashed myself cautiously all over with Old Spice, no smell of embalming fluid to hide this time, so I was not over generous. I put my overcoat on, checked that I had my wallet; I took twenty pound out of the wallet and put it on the mantelpiece which meant that I had twenty five pounds ten shilling left in the wallet. There was a knock on the front door, my taxi had arrived. I gave the man Emma's address and explained that we were going to the Berni Inn in the town. The driver asked if we would want him to pick us up after the meal as trying to get a taxi later on could mean a long wait, seeing this was the last Sunday before Christmas and a lot of people were out celebrating early. I said that I would ask Emma after we picked her up from her house. The taxi pulled up outside of her house exactly at a quarter past six and I got out and rang the doorbell and waited. No answer. I rang the bell again, still no answer. I tried a third time and rang the bell three or four times and waited. I looked over to the taxi driver and I shrugged my shoulders at him. "Where is she?" I thought. I had said that I'd pick her up at a quarter past six. I decided to knock rather hard on the door. This time I could hear some movement in the hall way inside. The door opened, "Oh hello, have you been waiting long?" asked Emma, "You haven't been pressing the doorbell have you? It doesn't work," and she started laughing. "Well, after pressing it four times and getting no reply I was thinking maybe I had the wrong time," I said, rather relieved. I must say that Emma looked very nice and attractive and I just seemed to stare at her. "Is there anything wrong?" she asked. "No," I said, "You look very nice," and then changing the subject I said, "The taxi driver has asked if we want him to pick us up later this evening as it might be difficult trying to book a taxi later on, being Christmas and all that." "Yes, that'll be a good idea," she said.

On the way we discussed what time we would want the taxi to come back and pick us up. I said that if we have the table from seven then it would be booked again later in the evening, so I reckoned that we would have about an hour and a half at the most at the table. As I had to be up early in the morning to catch my train home I asked if it would be alright if the taxi picked us up at nine thirty. Emma agreed that nine thirty would be a good time to leave, so we asked the driver to come back for us then, which he said he would. We got to the Berni Inn at a quarter to seven and went straight to the restaurant area and booked in. As the previous clients had booked the table for quarter to seven and had cancelled the booking, the table was empty and we were directed to it. We took our coats off and put them on the backs of our chairs. We were both given a menu and I asked for the wine menu which the waiter gave to me. I asked Emma what wine she would like and she said it was up to me as she liked both red and white wine. I said that we would compromise and I chose a bottle of Mateus Rosé and Emma agreed with the choice. I looked at the menu, the starter was melon boat with maraschino cherry or prawn cocktail followed by the main course of steak, gammon steak or plaice all with chips and peas, the dessert was Black Forest gateau or a choice from the cheese board and to finish - Irish coffee with After Eight mints.

We both chose the prawn cocktail, then the steak and Black Forest gateau. I waved to the waiter who came over and took our order. I asked if we could have the wine straight away and within a couple of minutes it was on our table and poured out. I looked at

Emma and raised my glass, "Merry Christmas and a Happy New Year," I said. She reciprocated and we clinked glasses and took a sip. I looked around the restaurant at the Tudor-looking false oak beams and white walls. It was very busy in the restaurant and looking through to the bar it seemed very full in there too.

I looked at Emma and thought, what do I talk about, and what do I say? Before I could say anything Emma started the conversation, "Well, has your first term at Cromwell Street School been up to your expectations?" "I didn't know what my expectations were, I was just pleased to have a job teaching, but it's a lot different from teaching practice when you knew that you were only teaching for a few weeks. Now I'm teaching all the time and having to keep records of the children's work and progression," I answered. "You'll get used to it, main thing is to have a routine each week and try to stick to it, so you keep your marking up to date along with the record keeping then you won't fall behind. Also remember that you have Mr Percy to fall back on if you need help, he's your mentor and then there are the other members of staff who will help you out if you need them. We've all been there at some time or other and there's nothing wrong in admitting that you need help at times," she said to me. What she was saying to me made total sense and I thought she was talking from experience. Before we could carry on with the conversation the waiter brought our prawn cocktails, not as well presented as those at the Casino but very tasty and Emma agreed. For the rest of the meal we talked about this and that, the weather and if the snow would last for Christmas, what the children from school may be getting for Christmas and so on. Then came the crunch, Emma asked what I was doing for Christmas and the rest of the holidays. I said that I was going home in the morning and would be staying at my mother's until maybe three days after Christmas before coming back to my house. I also said that I had no plans for the New Year, which, having said so, I thought it might have been a mistake to say it. Emma told me that she would be spending all the holiday at home with her parents and told me the family traditions they had regarding Christmas and the New Year. Before the conversation got any deeper the waiter came over and asked if we could move to the bar area as the table would be needed, after it had been wiped down, for the next customers. He also gave me the bill for the meal and pointed where I had to pay. We thanked him and stood, got our coats and moved over to pay the bill before going to the bar area, which by now was quite full. I looked at my watch, twenty five minutes before the taxi arrived so we both had another glass of wine from the bar and chatted again before going outside to wait for the taxi.

On the way home Emma told me what some of the staff would be doing during their Christmas holiday as they did the same each year. Mr Yardley and his wife went to a hotel in Scotland and spent Christmas and the New Year there. Ivan Jenkins went back home to Wales, Mrs Peterson always spent her Christmas Day and Boxing Day with her son and family, Paul Sharpe helped out at the Salvation Army hostel on Christmas Day, serving dinners to the homeless and needy. In no time we arrived at Emma's house, she thanked me very much for the meal and night out and wished me all the best and before she got out of the taxi gave me a peck on the cheek and told me to take care. I thanked her for the nice night and said I'd ring her during the holiday. She shut the taxi door and walked to her front door; I asked the taxi driver to wait whilst she'd gone into the house before moving off. As we were driving back to my house I realised that I should have walked Emma to her front door instead of just sitting in the taxi watching her go in, too late now though. I got home and had a whisky nightcap and reviewed the night in my mind. Yes, it had been a nice night but what do I do next, do I take it further, would Emma want me to take it further. Was I going to be the replacement boyfriend as Tony had said, did I want to be the replacement boyfriend, I thought. I finished the whisky and went to bed.

I was up early next morning, got myself a quick breakfast and then packed a few clothes, along with Stuart's suit and was at the station for a quarter to eight in time to catch the eight o'clock train. I got myself a newspaper to read on the train. It was still cold although there'd been no more snow since Saturday evening. I made myself comfortable on the train and settled in to read the paper. It was an uneventful journey and we arrived at our destination bang on time at nine thirty. I caught a bus and was at my mother's by ten o'clock. She was pleased to see me, as she always was, and I put my things in my room, the room that I always had when I lived there and I still consider it as my room, as does my mother. When I came downstairs my mother had a cup of tea ready for me, along with some biscuits. I explained that I had to take the suit back to Stuart at Collins Undertakers and we might go for a pub lunch, so I didn't know what time I'd be back. I asked if she wanted anything bringing whilst I was out but she didn't. I was told that it was one of my favourite meals for tea - sausage, egg, beans and chips - and to follow, Angel Delight.

Stuart said to drop the suit off at eleven o'clock, but I was a bit early. Instead of going through the front door I went round the back through a side door and into the office at the far end of the building. Pam, the office clerk, was typing something at her desk. She looked up and said, "Hi Jot, Stuart said that you'd be coming round this morning. He'll be glad to see you, and you are early too, that's good. I'll let Mr Collins know that you are here." She got up from her desk and went through to the outer office as she went she called out for Stuart. A couple of minutes later Stuart appeared and said, "Come on mate, get the suit on, we have to be out in twenty minutes and I'll have to show you how to hold and carry a coffin." I looked at him blankly and said, "A coffin, what do you mean a coffin. I'm just returning your suit." "Er yes, you did say when you borrowed the suit that I should let you know what you owed me, well we are a few down and I told Mr Collins that you could be a temporary pall-bearer today to help us out. We usually borrow pall-bearers from other Undertakers when we are short and they borrow pall bearers from us, but being Christmas, we all have a lot on and there are no spare pall-bearers to be had. Come through to the back and meet the others and we'll show you the ropes," he told me. I had no choice, and after all, I did owed him. Stuart took me through the office to the coffin room where at the back there were two men dressed in black suits waiting. "This is my friend Jot, or John as he is known to others; he's going to be helping us today with the four funerals. We just have to show him how we lift and carry the coffins," explained Stuart. He then introduced me to the other two pall-bearers, "This is Chris and that's Mike. The driver of the hearse is Dave who helps with the initial lift of the coffin, as does Mr Collins." The two nodded and said they were pleased to meet me.

There was a coffin placed on a couple of trestles in the middle of the room. Stuart asked if I were left or right handed, I said right. He told me that I would be on the left hand side of the coffin so that my right shoulder would take the weight of the coffin and to keep the coffin as close as possible to my body. As the four of us stood round the coffin, Stuart explained that we faced the coffin, bowed and then placed our, in my case, right hand under the coffin and lifted it to shoulder height and turned inward so that our shoulders were under the coffin and we then placed the weight on them. We had to ensure that we had a firm grip of the underside and side of the coffin and, when raising the coffin to shoulder height, got a hand underneath it as you brought it onto your shoulder. We had to do the reverse when placing the coffin down. I was told not to use the handles at the side of the coffin as they were usually for show only and not weight bearing. Also you had to make sure that the pall-bearer on the other side of the coffin was about the same height as you. The shorter pall-bearers are at the front, which would be Stuart and myself as we were both the same height, and when the coffin is lifted onto the shoulder, there will be someone at each end to assist with the lift, the Undertaker and the driver of the hearse. Also it is traditional to carry a coffin so that the body travels feet first. When carried into a crematorium the coffin must be placed feet facing forward onto the catafalque (the platform on which it must be placed).

Many coffins are shaped, so that the feet end is the more tapered end. The same goes for a church where at the end of the service the coffin is turned round so that the deceased goes out of the church feet first. There was a lot to take in but Stuart said not to worry, after the first funeral I would get used to it. He then told me to go and get changed in to the suit that I had brought back. I went to the changing room at the back and changed then returned to the coffin room. Stuart looked at me and said, "Bloody hell, are you a walking advert for Old Spice, it's a bit strong," turning to one of the others he said," Chris go and get some embalming fluid and sprinkle it on his suit to kill the smell of the Old Spice." A few minutes later Mr Collins came in and shook my hand and thanked me for helping them out at such short notice. He then asked Stuart if he had explained to me what to do and how to carry the coffin. Just then Dave the driver of the hearse came in and introduced himself to me and shook hands.

He turned to Mr Collins and said the hearse was loaded with the two coffins. I looked at Stuart and said, "Two coffins?" He explained that the hearse had a compartment under the coffin on show and that the coffin underneath would be for the next funeral so that the hearse didn't have to come all the way back to the Undertaker's premises for the next funeral.

The four funerals that day went well and I played my part as the stand in pall-bearer, fortunately without any hitches. Mr Collins was impressed and asked if he could call on me again if he were short-handed as the absent pall- bearer would be back at work the following morning. I explained that I was only home for a while but if he were short-handed again I would definitely think about it. He also paid me for a day's work, which was good. Stuart said that he would see me in the pub later on at about eight o'clock and then we would have a big catch up over the past year's events or so. I changed back into my own clothes and put Stuart's suit back into its bag, said goodbye to my new friends and made my way back home. I bought an evening newspaper and a bar of Fry's Turkish Delight for my mother, one of her favourite bars of chocolate. When I got home my mother asked how everything had gone, apparently she'd known that Stuart was going to ask me to be a pall-bearer but she hadn't wanted to let me know. I told her that things went well and Mr Collins had asked if he could call on me again as a stand in pall-bearer, and of course he'd paid me for the day's work. I gave her the bar of chocolate and she was very pleased, then she started making the tea. I told her that I was going out later with Stuart to do some catching up with him.

I sat reading the paper whilst my mother made the tea, my favourite - sausage, egg, beans and chips and to follow, Angel Delight. We sat at the table and chatted as we ate. I mentioned that if my teaching didn't work out I could always be a pall-bearer and work my way up to be an Undertaker. My mother didn't know if I was joking or being serious, I laughed and said that it was worth thinking about. After tea I watched the news on the television then got myself ready to go out. I told my mother that I might be home late but that I had my key and I would try not to wake her when I came in.

I arrived at the Kings Arms at ten to eight and ordered a pint and waited at the bar for Stuart to turn up. Stuart was always either early or late, but never on time. Tonight he was late, getting here at five past eight. I bought him a pint and we went and sat down at a table near the window. I started by saying that the weather here was better than the weather from where I'd just come from, I had left snow and ice and here there was no sign of it, although the weather forecast said there might be snow for Christmas. I told him that I'd enjoyed today and that being a pall-bearer was a lot different from teaching, and you didn't get the person in the box answering back - unlike teaching. I went through the school term with him, the stolen television set, the donkey in the nativity play and how it wouldn't come off the stage, my involvement in the bookmaker robbery and the reward and I even mention my part with the information in the armed security van robbery but I asked him to keep quiet about it as the case was still ongoing with the police. He was quite amazed that I still had a job teaching with all the various things that had happened to me and then said that I should put a bit more time in with Mr Collins as it could be a good fall-back job should the teaching collapse. I also mention that I'd seen Richie at the Casino as the three of us had spent a holiday together in Blackpool, and it was there that we all had our first taste of Casinos. I told him of my win on the roulette table, "You didn't use the thirty two and the four corners did you?" he asked. "Yes, and the line in between, and thirty two came out twice, one after the other. All in all I came away with twenty five pounds in winnings," I said. I then asked about various friends we used to go around with in the past and what were they up to now. The night flew by and we managed to get through quite a few drinks,. By the end of the night we were merry but not drunk. We agreed to meet up again at the end of the week, maybe Friday evening but I would leave him a message for him at Collins during the week, confirming the day and the time. We left the pub and said our goodbyes and went our separate ways home. It was a cold night but pleasant and I had that nice warm feeling inside me.

The next day, Christmas Eve, my mother didn't wake me so I had a long sleep in. By the time I'd washed and shaved and gone downstairs it was past ten o'clock. I got myself some toast and made a pot of tea for mother and myself. She asked if I had any plans for the day, but I hadn't and asked if she wanted any help with the shopping, I did asked if she knew what I could get for my sister and her husband as well as the two children for Christmas. Mum said that maybe a doll for Jane and that Michael liked to play with soldiers, as for my sister and her husband, perfume for her and aftershave for him. That was sorted, and as for my mother I thought a litre bottle of brandy and half a dozen bottles of Babycham. Something she liked to drink but I had to make sure she didn't know anything about what I intended to buy her. The chicken for Christmas Day and the turkey and ham for Boxing Day had been ordered at the local butchers and the vegetables from the nearby greengrocers. I asked mum what drinks she wanted over Christmas as she wasn't a big drinker, just a nightcap each evening sort of person. She suggested that we get some beers, half a bottle of whisky and half a bottle of gin, some bottles of lemonade, some orange juice and some tonic water. I told her that I would pay for the drinks and the food as I'd had a big win at the casino last Friday evening on the staff night out. That led to an argument, so I also reminded her that I had been given a reward for my information in the bookmaker's robbery and I was relatively well off at the moment. That seemed to calm her down, but she kept saying, 'Well, if you're sure you can afford it,' I told her that I could afford it and that it was my treat.

We made our way to the local shops just after lunch and picked up the meat and vegetables and brought them home. I then went back into town to buy my Christmas presents, first on the list was the perfume and aftershave, so I went to Boots to see what I could find. The assistant suggested 'Sea Jade Perfume Moisturizing Iced Cologne' by Yardley for my sister Helen and a bottle of 'Hai Karate' aftershave for her husband Dave. I went along with the suggestion and bought them both. Then I went to Woolworth's to buy the children their toys, a doll for Jane and soldiers for Michael. I wondered around looking at all the different toys on offer, and then I saw it, a doll called 'Chatty Cathy,' a doll that talked when you pulled a string on her back. That would be ideal for six year old Jane. Next, four year old Michael and soldiers but I changed my mind - not soldiers but a soldier, 'G.I. Joe,' an action soldier that had bendy arms and legs. I caught the bus home and I started thinking of Jane with 'Chatty Cathy' and I wondered how long it would be before my sister threatened to throw it in the bin if it didn't shut up talking. I decided that I would drop the presents off at home and then go to Tesco's to get the drinks. As I was buying quite a lot of drink I took my mother's shopping trolley with me. Walking round Tesco's I not only got the drinks but added some cherry brandy and a bottle of port so that we could make up port and lemon, also some tins of 'Watney's Red Barrel' and tins of 'Double Diamond.' I put a couple of bottles of Asti Spumante in the trolley and got some packets of crisps, nuts and pork scratchings. It would be nice to have plenty of drinks in, along with the nibbles just in case someone came round to see us. I didn't forget my mother's litre of Brandy along with the six bottles of Babycham. At the check-out I was pleased that I had the foresight to bring my mother's shopping trolley along as it was now nearly full and quite heavy. Once I was home I had to make sure that my mother didn't see the Babycham and Brandy, which she didn't, and I quickly took them to my room to be wrapped in Christmas paper for the morning. When my mother saw the shopping trolley and all the things I'd bought she wanted to pay for some of it but I refused to take anything, I just said that it was my treat and a way of saying thank you for having me here at Christmas.

Whilst we were having tea, my mother said that she wanted to go to midnight mass but she wanted to go early as they had carols before the mass. I said that would be nice and I'd go with her. The church was about twenty minutes away and I began to think of Christmas time years ago when my father was alive and how we'd go to Christmas midnight mass together and come back in the early hours of the morning, through silent streets with the road and pavements glistening with the frost, getting home and having to wait until morning to unwrap our presents. My mother looked at me and asked, "Are you thinking of years ago when we all would go to midnight mass together, and how your father would join loudly in the singing of the carols but he didn't know some of the words so he made up words to fit, and how the people around us would be put off and stop singing themselves. We couldn't shut him up, but he was happy in his own sweet way, mind you the amount of whisky he drank beforehand didn't help." We both sat there at the table, thinking, with tears in our eyes, just remembering.

We got to the church at half past eleven and it was nearly half full. We were given a hymn book each as we went in and my mother recognised a few of the congregation and waved to them. We sat about ten rows from the front and within minutes the singing started. Mother gave me a nudge in the ribs as a sign that I should be singing and rather having bruised ribs I had no choice than to sing along to each carol. In actual fact I enjoyed singing and in no time at all it was time for the mass. By that time, the church was full, with people standing at the back as there was nowhere to sit. During the mass, mother continually encouraged me to sing by a dig in the ribs and an hour and a quarter later mass was over. We came out of the church and various members of the congregation wished us and each other a Merry Christmas. My mother stood and spoke to a number of people and explained that I was home for the holidays. Eventually we started to make our way back home. The weather was getting cold and it was starting to freeze, making the road and pavement glisten the way it did all those years ago. Twenty minutes later we were home and I suggested that we have a drink before going to bed. Coffee with a good dollop of whiskey! We both wished each other a Merry Christmas and sat by the fire looking into the flames and thinking. We finished our drink and both of us decided it was time for bed.

I got up early, before my mother and prepared breakfast, a boiled egg and a slice of toast, along with a Buck's Fizz made with the Asti Spumante and orange juice and I took it up to her bedroom. "Good morning and a Merry Christmas," I said. "Merry Christmas to you too. I can't remember the last time I had breakfast in bed," she replied. "Well, you enjoy it. I've lit the fire and filled the coal scuttle, and I'll see you later when you decide to get up," I said. I went downstairs and had my breakfast and then watched the television. On the BBC at twenty five past nine there was a message from the American Apollo Eight space-ship from its orbit round the moon. The astronaut William Anders read the first ten verses of Genesis from the bible. I sat there and was fascinated that this message was coming all the way from the moon on Christmas morning. After it had finished I looked in the Radio Times to see what was on the television for the rest of the day. At half past eleven it was a programme called 'Meet the Kids' children who were in hospital and that afternoon after the Queen's speech we were spoilt for choice. The BBC had 'Billy

Smarts Circus' and ITV had 'The Kelvin Hall Circus' and for those culture people there was the Royal Ballet on BBC Two at the same time. That evening it was 'Christmas Night with the Stars' with 'Some like it hot,' as the main feature film later on. I turned the television off and put the radio on and it was Eric Robinson with 'Melodies for Christmas' playing, which was nice. Mother came down a bit later on with a wrapped present for me. I gave her the present I'd wrapped earlier and we both sat there unwrapping our presents. My mother had got me a blue pullover and a book, 'Octopussy' and The Living Daylights,' the 14th and final James Bond book written by Ian Fleming. When she'd unwrapped her present she thanked me and said that I shouldn't have bought such a big bottle - but she liked it all the same.

We sat talking, catching up on people and relatives, where they were and what they were doing, also the various people from the church and the ones who had passed away over the year. Although I'd been back home at half term we didn't talk as such and this was a chance to catch up. Mother asked me about my teaching, about the teachers and about the children. She also asked if there was any girl that had caught my eye. I didn't know whether to mention Emma or not, after all she was just a colleague. Before long it was time to prepare the dinner and as we were the only two, mother decided that dinner would be served at about two o'clock so we both had another Bucks Fizz and relaxed a bit more. Christmas Day went well, the dinner was, as always, very good and we had enough chicken left over for chicken and chips for tea. We played cards for quite a while after getting bored with the circus in the afternoon. We both enjoyed the film 'Some like it hot' and as our glasses kept getting refilled by the time the film had finished we were ready for our beds.

Boxing Day started with a couple of aspirin, toast and marmalade and a cup of tea. I was surprised that mother had no after-effects from the previous night, maybe it was just that I'm not used to drinking any more. The turkey was already in the oven when I got up and all the vegetables were ready, along with the ham. I've always admired the way my mother had everything under control and knew exactly when to start cooking which meats and vegetables so that everything would be ready at the same time. I was ordered out of the kitchen because, as mother put it, I would be in the way and under her feet. I went back into the living room and started to read my book. My mother knew that I was a big James Bond fan and I must have mentioned this final James Bond book the last time I was home at half term. At one o'clock my sister Helen and her husband Dave and the two children Jane and Michael arrived and for the next ten minutes we were all sat around opening presents and showing each other what we'd got. Helen and I got the table ready, as we had always done in the past at Christmas.

A yell came from the kitchen, "Ten minutes," which was mother informing us that we had to get our hands washed and start helping moving food from the kitchen to the table. I brought out the bottle of Asti Spumante and poured it into the glasses, whilst the children had lemonade. Eventually all the food was laid out on the table and I was told to sit at the head of the table and carve the turkey, a task that my father had undertaken in years past. For the next half an hour or so there was little conversation, just the sound of people eating and enjoying their food.

After the meal, Helen and I did the washing up whilst the children played with their new toys. At three o'clock we all sat around the television and listened to the Queen's Christmas message. Dave said that they'd better be going home around four o'clock as the weather forecast wasn't good and predicted that it might snow. I said that I'd left the snow behind on Monday morning, and added how strange it was that sixty odd miles could make so much difference with the weather. Jane had spent the last hour or so with her new 'Chatty Cathy' doll which continually repeated the phrases, "I love you," and "Tell me a story," as she pulled the string in the doll's back. Dave whispered to me, "Why the hell didn't you get her something that worked with batteries, that way we could have taken them out and had some peace and quiet." Michael was playing with his 'GI Joe,' bending its arms and legs into all sort of positions and making shooting noises with the toy guns that accompanied the toy. My mother went into the kitchen and parcelled up the left-over turkey and ham and told Helen that it would make nice sandwiches for their tea. For some reason she went out the back way to put some rubbish in the bin and the first we knew about this was when she was shouting for us to come and help her. Dave, Helen and I went rushing out to see what had happened, "Careful," said Dave, "it's thick ice out here." My mother was laid on the ground near the dustbin, "Help," she said, "I think I've done something to my arm and my leg hurts if I try to move it. I was only putting some rubbish in the dustbin and I slipped on the ice, twisted my leg and my arm hit that small wall there." She pointed to a six inch wall holding back the rockery. "We can't leave her here," said Helen, "You and Dave carefully lift her into the house and get her sat down, I think we'd better call and ambulance as there's no way we can get her in the car like this. Nip next door and ask Mrs Taylor if you can use her 'phone." Once mother was settled in a chair I went round to Mrs Taylor's and rang for an ambulance, explaining what had happened to mother. Twenty minutes later the ambulance came and mother was assessed and a wheelchair was brought in to transport her into the ambulance. Helen and I were able to go with mother to the hospital whilst Dave took the kids home - with mother reminding him to take the parcel of meat for their sandwiches later on.

Helen and I sat in the waiting room whilst mother had gone for an X-Ray. There were only a couple of people in 'A and E,' much to the relief of the staff I thought. "When are you going back?" asked Helen. "I was going back on Saturday, why?" I said. "Well, we'll just have to see what happens to mother, she may need looking after, which means could you look after her until you are due back at school? I could look after her when Jane and Michael are at school." That meant that any plans I'd made for the holiday were now changed. I'd been thinking about taking Emma out again before school started. I thought that I'd better give her a ring and let her know what had happened. I put my hand in my inside pocket for my note book with my telephone numbers in it. It wasn't there. I started thinking about the last time I had it, which was Sunday afternoon when I rang Emma, then I went back to the telephone box to ring Stuart. That was the last time I'd used it. Had I left it in the telephone box I wondered? It also meant that I wouldn't be able to ring Richie as his number was in the book as well.

About forty five minutes later a doctor came to see us. He explained that mother had sustained a humerus fracture, that is the upper arm, and it did not require surgery as the bone wasn't out of place so he had it plastered and said that she had to keep her arm in a sling in order to minimize movement and allow it to heal properly. In most cases, the mobility will return to the joint after the fracture healed. As regards her leg, she had a ruptured Achilles tendon and they'd put a pot on it for the moment and would check it out in a week's time. He asked if there would be someone at home with her over the next month or so. Helen looked at me and then at the doctor, but before she could speak I said that I would look after her for the next ten days then my sister would take over as I had to get back to work. I also said that I would come back at weekends to look after mother until she was able to look after herself. The doctor was happy with the situation and said that mother would be out in a few minutes, along with her paperwork explaining what to do regarding pain control and also a letter for her next appointment. He said that she would have some painkillers given to her and that she could borrow a hospital wheelchair, but one of us would have to sign for it. If we wanted to go straight home when mother re-joined us, the nurse at reception would get us a taxi that specialised in transporting wheelchairs in the back. Ten minutes later mother came rolling in with an orderly pushing her wheelchair; Helen had ordered the taxi and was told it would be with us in fifteen minutes. When it arrived I suggested that we drop Helen off at home before we went back to mothers. She asked if I would be able to manage when we got home and I said yes. After dropping Helen off I thought that this definitely wasn't how my Christmas holiday was supposed to turn out.

Chapter Eighteen

Once home I managed to push the wheelchair into the house and into the living room. The fire was still in, just, so I put more coal in the grate and asked mother if she wanted a drink. She said that she was dying for a good cup of tea and a sandwich, any sandwich, she didn't care. Whilst the kettle was boiling I looked at the settee and suggested that mother sleep on that for the first night as it would be better for her to be sleeping in a sitting position rather than laying down in her bed. Helen had said that she would come round in the morning and help mother with washing and such like. I made the tea and some sandwiches and went upstairs to get some pillows and a couple of eiderdowns. I pushed the wheelchair against the settee and mother shuffled and managed to get herself from the wheelchair onto the settee. For the next half hour we drank out tea and ate the sandwiches and spoke about what we were going to do whilst she was incapacitated. I told mother that I had agreed with Helen that I would stay there until a day before I had to go back when school started and then Helen would stay with her when her children were at school. I said that I would tell Mrs Taylor what had happened as she would certainly want to be involved in helping out. She and mother were almost like sisters and had been neighbours for at least thirty odd years living down this same street. The ground floor of my mother's house was all on one level, there were no steps to manoeuvre and also, my father bless his cotton socks, had a downstairs toilet installed which included a washbasin. The toilet had a grab rail alongside it which had been installed because my grandmother used to stay with us and had difficulty getting on and off the toilet. Before I went to bed, mother wanted to use the toilet. I put the wheelchair as close as possible to the settee and helped mother to shuffle along to sit on it. I pushed her along to the toilet and once inside managed to get the chair within reach of the grab rail, from there on mother said that she could manage. Whilst she was in there I banked up the fire so that the living room would be nice and warm throughout the night. I heard mother shout to say that she was finished so I went to bring her back to the settee. Without going into too much detail she said that she had managed, which was a big problem sorted. I made sure that she was as comfortable as was possible, put a glass of water and some painkillers on a table close to hand and then went off to bed.

I didn't sleep very well that night, thinking about my mother and how she was going to cope, what meals I would be getting ready, what needed doing around the house and so on. Then, later on in the night, I started thinking about how to try and get in touch with Emma. I still couldn't recall what had happened to my note book with all my telephone numbers in it. Similarly, how could I call Richie, he had given me his phone number at the casino and told me to contact him some time, unless Stuart had his number. Once mother was settled, one day next week I'd pop around to Collins Undertakers and see Stuart to arrange a night out, which would have to be a short night out as I'd have to be back for mother. Later on, at about five thirty, I was dreaming that Mr Yardley had me in his office and was asking why I was late for school and dressed in my pyjamas - the rest of the staff along with the Governers were there as well. It was so vivid that it woke me up with a start, and it took me a few seconds to realise where I was. I looked over to the clock, half past five, I got up and went downstairs and looked in at mother. She was fast asleep with a pillow at either side of her keeping her propped up. Quietly I raked the fire and put more coal on it and then went back to bed. The next time I woke up it was ten past eight, so I got out of bed and into the bathroom for a wash, I'd shave later I thought. I also noticed that it was quite chilly and the bathroom window was frosted over on the outside. Having got dressed, I went downstairs where mother was awake and reading Tuesday's newspaper. I asked if she'd slept well and she answered yes and no, she also said that she had to take some painkillers in the night to help her get to sleep. She asked me to take her to the toilet in the wheelchair, which I did and whilst she was there I stoked the fire and then started making the breakfast. Porridge followed by bacon, egg, sausage and tomato and a round of toast. The porridge was nearly done when she asked me to take her back to the settee, I made sure she was comfortable then I served the porridge. When I told her what was to follow she asked me to cut it all up for her as she was only one handed. After breakfast, which went extremely well, mother asked if I could let Mrs Taylor know what had happened so I nipped round and saw Mrs Taylor and told her about mother and her injuries and she insisted that she come to see my mother, which she did. "Oh Elsie, how are you? How did it happen? Do you want anything? Is there anything I can do?" said Mrs Taylor as soon as she came into the room. "I've got everything that I need at the moment, Maud, thank you. John's looking after me very well and when he goes back to school Helen said that she'll be coming round to look after me, so I should be alright," replied my mother. I left the two of them talking about Christmas and what had been happening the past few days and went upstairs to the bath room for a shave.

When I went back downstairs, Mrs Taylor had made a pot of tea and told me there was cup for me if I wanted it. I apologised to her for not offering to make a cup of tea as soon as she came in, my excuse was that when you live by yourself you forget those sorts of things. Mrs Taylor said that we could use her 'phone any time of the day or night if necessary, just to knock on her door. Mrs Taylor lived on her own, her husband had died three years before my father. Her sons, one in Australia and one in New Zealand were unable to get home for the funeral so both mum and dad helped Mrs Taylor get through her dark days. Two years after losing her husband, her son in New Zealand had drowned whilst swimming, which was very sad as Mrs Taylor was unable to go over for his funeral but his brother was able to arrange things from Australia and attend the funeral himself in New Zealand. That seemed to have established a bond between Mrs Taylor and our family which was made stronger when she came with us on holiday a couple of times. "John, can you cut some ham and turkey to give to Maud for her tea. There should be lots to spare, and can you put a drop of port in a small bottle for her as well," asked my mother. I went into the kitchen and cut some turkey and ham and then wrapped it in some tin foil before finding a small bottle for the port then took it into the living room. Mrs Taylor was thanking my mother for her Christmas presents of a hat and matching gloves and said that they would be ideal in this cold weather that we were experiencing. "Your mother said that you're staying here until you have to go back to school; you can call on me anytime to help out, don't be afraid to ask, and the same goes for the use of the 'phone," said Mrs Taylor. She checked that mother didn't need anything before she returned home.

After she had gone I talked with mother about getting a

'phone installed as this little incident had shown how necessary a 'phone was and both Helen and I could call on a regular basis to check up on how she was keeping. I said that I'd pay for it and both Helen and I would feel much happier that we could keep in touch with her as well as mother keeping in touch with us. Eventually mother agreed and I said I would try to get it set up before I returned to my home.

Over the next few days mother and I had a daily routine set up, from early morning to late evening. Some of the tasks were a little delicate, so Mrs Taylor would come in and help mother with those. I was getting used to shopping and cooking for two, and cleaning and dusting - with advice from mother how it should be done. I even went to the launderette, with strict instructions from mother to get two machines, one for the light coloured clothes and one for the dark washing. I didn't tell her that back home I put all the washing in one machine, apart from my best shirts. On a couple of occasions I took mother out in the wheelchair for some fresh air and a visit to the shops. I could tell that she wasn't happy sitting there with a blanket over her legs being pushed about, but soon cheered up when she saw some of her friends who stopped and chatted. Although it was still very cold and we had frost at night there was no snow, so going to the shops with the wheelchair made a nice change from sitting in the house all day. Mrs Taylor had been invited round a few times for her tea and stayed afterwards, the three of us playing cards until about nine then Mrs Taylor went home after having a nightcap. We even gambled when we played cards, using matchsticks as our currency.

A few days later, a letter came from the hospital for mother telling her that she had an appointment for New Year's Eve at eleven o'clock. I got everything set in place; I made a booking with the taxi company we had used to bring us home on Boxing Day with the vehicle that could accommodate the wheelchair. I had also filled in the application forms for the telephone company to install a 'phone, explaining that a 'phone was now essential due to my mother's condition. I agreed to pay the twenty pounds to have it installed and a year's line rental at fourteen pounds. Although my mother objected, I insisted saying that I still had quite a bit of the reward money in the bank. I also told her that I might be getting another reward because of my involvement in the armed robbery just before Christmas, but that she hadn't to let anyone know about it as the case hadn't gone to court yet, not even Helen or Mrs Taylor.

New Year's Eve and we were both up early ready for the appointment at eleven o'clock. Helen came round and Dave and the kids popped in just to say hello and wish my mother good luck at the hospital, then went home leaving Helen to accompany us to the hospital. I'd ordered the taxi so that we would be in good time for the appointment. We still had to rely on the wheelchair to get mother about as she was still unable to put her foot down on the ground. We went to reception and the assistant booked us in and directed us to the Outpatients department where we had to wait for our turn. A nurse appeared and called mother's name out. I got up to push her wheelchair and Helen and I followed the nurse to a side room and went inside. The doctor, who was sitting at his desk stood up when we entered, then introduced himself and shook our hands. He asked mother how she was feeling and how the past few days had been. Mother said that she was fed up with the cast on her leg and that she'd be pleased when she was able to stand on her own two feet, and also that the cast on her arm was a nuisance and heavy. The doctor explained that the cast on the leg was going to be removed and replaced by bandages and a support boot which was something like a ski boot, and would enable mother to stand and walk whilst wearing it. Also, it could be removed at night, prior to her going to bed, which pleased mother. The cast on her arm was also going to be removed, then the arm X-rayed to check that the bone was mending before a lighter cast would be put on. That would then be reviewed in a fortnight, and if all were well the arm would no longer need a cast but would still need a support sling. The cast on the leg was removed and the doctor examined the leg, asking mother to move it in different directions and to push against his hand and he kept asking if it was painful as she did the different moves. He then told her that she would have to start walking using the boot so as to exercise the leg and start to strengthen the ruptured Achilles tendon. The nurse cleaned the leg and put bandages around it and fitted the boot, showing mother, Helen and me how to fasten and remove it. She also showed us how to replace the bandages on the leg and gave us a supply of them, telling us that the bandages could be washed and used again. Mother stood up and put some weight on the boot, with me holding her arm. She took a few small steps which pleased both her and the doctor. Once the doctor was happy that mother seemed alright with the boot it was time for mother to go to the X-ray department and get the plaster on her arm removed and the arm X-rayed. We all thanked the doctor and went out, following the nurse to the X-ray department. Once that was done we had to sit in the waiting room for the X-ray results. Mother said that she'd walk to the taxi and Helen and I said she was not to start walking on the leg until we got home. Half an hour later we were on our way from the hospital in the taxi, via Helen's house to drop her off, then continue home. I was adamant that mother sit in the wheelchair from the taxi to inside her house. Once inside she stood up carefully and put her weight on the boot and moved into the kitchen, "Let's have a cup of tea," she said. "Yes, we'll have a cup of tea, but you're not making it. Go and sit down and I'll made the tea and a sandwich for the two of us," I said. I could see that mother was going to try and get back to normal, although her damaged arm would almost certainly prevent it, so I told her to take things easy and not to rush things otherwise it would take longer for things to heal.

Later that afternoon Stuart called round to see if I was going out to the pub to celebrate New Year's Eve as there was an extension to half past twelve to see the New Year in. He said that we'd have to there early as it would soon get full and once that had happened then no more people would be allowed in. When he saw mother he realised that I had my hands full but she insisted that if I wanted to go out then I could. I compromised, I told Stuart that I would go out with him and come back home at about ten thirty to see to mother. I knew that Stuart wouldn't be alone as he had many friends that went into the Kings Arms, so I wouldn't feel guilty about leaving before midnight. He was asked by mother if he wanted to stay for tea but said that he would get off. We arranged to meet at seven o'clock. Mother insisted that before he went that he had a drink with us, an offer that he couldn't refuse. Mother told me to get the brandy out and the three of us toasted the coming of the New Year. After Stuart had gone I got the tea ready; salmon sandwiches, a special treat that was only had three or four times a year, yet when mother went to the supermarket she looked for the tinned salmon to see if it was on offer.

I'd told her that when it was on offer to buy it and eat it and enjoy it and not to save it just for special occasions. I had time to get a bath before going out. I checked that my mother had everything she needed and that I would be home at about ten forty and if she were up for it we could see the New Year in together.

I got to the Kings Arms at ten to seven and was surprised to see that Stuart was early and had managed to get a small table at the side of the room and on it were two drinks waiting, one for him and one for me. I went over and sat down, he pointed to my drink, lifted his up and said, "Cheers," then downed nearly half a pint. "I was waiting for that," he said and smiled. He said that he hadn't realised how much mother had relied on me since her accident. I said that I didn't mind and that Helen was going to be looking after her when I went back to school. I explained that things would be a lot better now that mother had been told that she could start to walk with her boot on. We talked about friends, past and present, what they were doing now, how many had got married, how many had children, things like that. As we talked we had a few more pints then Stuart asked me if I had my eye on anyone special. That took me by surprise and I wasn't ready for such a question. I went to avoid the answer by trying to change the subject. Stuart saw right past that, "So there is someone then?" he said. I tried to tell Stuart that I wasn't sure. "What do you mean you're not sure! When it comes to girls you've always been the same, slow on the uptake. Look at the girl who fancied the pants off you when we were on holiday in Blackpool, you dithered about and when you decided that you liked her it was too late; she'd gone off with someone else. That wasn't the only time you missed out - there was the time when..." I interrupted him before he could continue, "Yes, I know, you don't have to remind me. It's just that another teacher told me that she'd broken up with her long term boyfriend and was looking for a replacement, and that might be me," I explained. "What does that matter if you are a 'replacement boyfriend' as you say, the bottom line is do you like her and does she like you," he said. "Well, we seem to get along well at school and she has helped me out on a few occasions, helping with my nativity play in the school concert. The other Sunday I took her out for a meal and we got along alright, actually I thought the time went past too quickly," I said. "So the teacher that told you she was looking for a replacement boyfriend, is he trying to put you off, is he on the prowl or what?" said Stuart. "No, he's happily married and I don't think he's like that. I think he thought he was being friendly warning me," I said. "Well, if you like her and she likes you, what are you waiting for? Enjoy each other's company and if it leads to something very good, then great, and if it doesn't, then never mind. So long as you've enjoyed yourselves you can put it down to experience," said Stuart. We were joined by Chris and Mike, the pall-bearers from Collins Undertakers, and Mike got a round in. For the rest of the evening we all talked about football, work, rugby, work, other things and more work. There was no getting away from it; work seemed to come up in the conversation more than once. At half past ten I said that I had to go. Stuart explained to Chris and Mike why I was leaving early and about mother's situation. They both wished me all the best for the New Year and hoped that they'd see me again. I told Stuart that I'd be in touch before I went back at the end of the holidays. I had to elbow my way out of the pub and ask the doorman to be let out as people were being stopped from coming in as the pub was now full. On the way home I thought about what Stuart had said, "What does it matter if I were the replacement boyfriend, if we were both happy, so what." Yes, so what, we'd been happy when we had the meal at the Casino and at the Berni Inn. What did someone say to me at college, "Wake up and smell the roses." So, yes that was it, maybe it was time that I woke up?

When I got home, mother was watching television with Mrs Taylor and they both wanted to see the New Year in together, she said that Cilla Black was just about to start her programme and then just after midnight Jimmy Logan appeared in a New Year's special from Scotland. I asked if they wanted their drinks topping up and went and got one for myself. One of Cilla Black's guests was Matt Monro who sang, 'My kind of girl,' which got me thinking about Emma who was my kind of girl. I must have fallen asleep because the next thing I knew was Mrs Taylor shaking me and insisting that we all sing 'Auld lang syne' as the New Year rang out on the television. Both Mrs Taylor and I held mother's hand as we sang and when we were finished we toasted each other, hoping that the following year would be a happy, healthy, wealthy and peaceful one for us all. When we were finished we sat down and watched Jimmy Logan for about half an hour by which time we'd had enough and decided that it was time for bed. Mrs Taylor helped mother upstairs and I followed and removed her boot then left Mrs Taylor to help mother into the bed. Once that was done she came downstairs told me that mother was settled and went off home.

The next morning I went into mother's bedroom and put her boot on then helped her to the bathroom. She told me how much better it felt during the night not having a heavy plaster on her leg. She said that she'd be able to get dressed herself so I left her to it. Mother had invited Helen, Dave and the children for New Year's Day dinner, starting at one o'clock. We'd been out and bought two chickens, so that the adults could have a chicken leg each. I said that I'd get the vegetables ready and mother would supervise the cooking, which made her feel useful. Living by myself I'd got to enjoy cooking, although I wasn't used to cooking for six, make that seven, as mother had invited Mrs Taylor round for dinner sometime last night and she'd accepted the offer. Mother explained to me that it was all about timing when you were cooking; knowing when to put what on the cooker so that everything was ready at the same time. For afters we were having apple-pie and cream, the pie was going into the warm oven as we served the dinner so that it would be warm for us to eat afterwards, remembering to turn the oven off when we put the pie in otherwise it would burn.

Helen and her family arrived at a quarter to one and she helped me get the table ready. Mrs Taylor and mother were sat on the settee talking and Helen was pleased to see mother looking relaxed. I was in the kitchen when a voice said, "Tell me a story," then "I love you," I looked round and saw Jane with her 'Chatty Cathy' doll. Dave came up and told Jane to go back into the living room and sit down then he turned to me and said, "That bloody doll you bought her is a flaming nuisance and she takes it everywhere with her. I did think about cutting the string that you pull to make it talk, but Helen was against it. I just wish it had batteries then I could have taken them out." I apologised just as Helen came into the kitchen. "Is he still complaining about Jane's doll," she asked, "It's a very nice doll and Jane loves it. It was a very nice present you bought her, and Michael enjoys his toy as well. You've done well this year with your present giving. Dave, get out of the kitchen and get the kids to wash their hands. John and I will start to put out the dinner." Once all the dinner had been served I remembered the apple pie and popped it into the warm oven, remembering to make sure the oven was off. We all sat round the table enjoying the food. Mrs Taylor complimented me on the cooking and I said that it was mother who'd made sure everything was right. I told Helen that I'd be going back home on Sunday as school started on Monday. She said that she'd call in on Monday and attend to mother, then said to mother that she should stay in bed until she arrived which wouldn't be until after she'd dropped the children off at school. Helen asked if mother would be able to take her boot off at bedtime by herself then Mrs Taylor said that she would come in and assist mother to get to bed and asked if we would show her how to get the boot off so that she could help with that. Mother was content with that, so too was Helen and Mrs Taylor was pleased that she could help. The apple pie and cream went down a treat, and then it was followed by coffee and some After Eight mints. Whilst Helen and Dave washed up, I watched Laurel and Hardy on the television along with mother, Mrs Taylor and the children,

Whether it's because I live by myself, I found that that I got bored with people after a few hours company so I was rather pleased that Helen and her family decided to go home just after four, o'clock as did Mrs Taylor. Mother and I had the house to ourselves and the quiet was so peaceful, "Just listen to the quiet," mother said, "Isn't it nice?" I had to agree with her, the quiet was nice. We started talking and I happened to mention what Stuart had said about Emma that if I like her and she liked me why not make a go of it. I also told mother what Tony Telford had said about Emma looking for a replacement boyfriend. Mother listened carefully and said that if we liked each other why not just be friends and enjoy each other's company and if anything else became of it so be it. She also added how did Tony know she was looking for a replacement boyfriend? We talked until it was time for tea, there was still a lot of chicken left so we had chicken sandwiches with Branston pickle and because it was New Year's Day we both had a can of Double Diamond each. The evening passed quickly and soon we were both dropping off to sleep while sitting through a 'Gala Performance from Sadler's Wells Opera at the London Coliseum' on the television. We both had a nightcap and I helped mother to bed, taking off her boot and then making sure she was alright. I went to my room and undressed and got into bed. I didn't feel tired and just laid there thinking what mother had said about Emma, about her being a friend and how I liked her company. Maybe we could be just that, friends with no attachment, both free agents to do as we pleased. At least I'd have someone to go with me when I wanted to go to the pictures or the theatre or even the odd meal. I could still meet up with the football lads for a drink, although they liked to drink a little too much at times. I started thinking about the next term and what I was going to do with my class. Eventually I drifted off to sleep and started having weird dreams about two television men leading a donkey and taking Emma away after I signed some papers.

Over the next four days, time seemed to fly by. A couple of days after New Year the telephone men came to install the telephone, which for me was a relief as it meant that I'd be able to ring mother on a regular basis. The men explained to mother how the 'phone worked and gave her a telephone directory and showed her the page outlining how much calls cost as they said that older people didn't realise how much money they could spend on long distance calls over a period of ten minutes. Once they'd left, mother was eager to use her new 'toy' so she called Helen, after first looking up her number in the directory. She told her that the 'phone had been installed and gave her the number and then put the 'phone down. I was puzzled and asked why she didn't have a longer conversation with Helen. She said that the man had said it would cost a lot of money to stay on the 'phone for a long time. I explained that to call Helen was classed as a local call and that it would cost two pence for six minutes during the day and two pence for twelve minutes in the evenings and weekends. I rang Helen back and explained what had happened and then mother took over and talked to Helen for about ten minutes. After she put the receiver down I said that the call had cost four pence. She then started looking through the telephone directory for her name, so I had to explain that her name would be in the new telephone directory when it came out in April, so if she wanted her friends to ring her she'd have to let them know her 'phone number. On the Saturday we both went out to do the shopping and I insisted that she ride in the wheelchair, although she tried to tell me that she could walk using her boot. I refused to back down saying, "What would happen if your leg started to hurt whilst we were in the supermarket. How would she get home then?" I won the argument and the shopping was done with mother in her wheelchair. On Saturday evening Stuart and I went to the pub for a drink for the last time until I was back home, maybe next time at half term. I told him that when I got back to school I would ask Emma out a bit more often and see where it might go from there. He told me that he was thinking of asking Pam, the office clerk, out for a meal next week or maybe a trip to the pictures, he wasn't sure. I wished him luck and he wished the same for me. We called it a day at twenty past ten and left the pub, Stuart going one way and me the other, promising each other that we would keep in touch.

Sunday, my last day, mother insisted that she'd make a full Sunday lunch for the two of us after I'd prepared the vegetables. Mother had started using her arm more often, it was still in its cast but she was able to grasp things in her hand, the sling taking the weight of the arm and the cast. I could see that she was going to be alright looking after herself after I was gone. After all, there was always Mrs Taylor next door and Helen at the other end of the 'phone if things went wrong. After lunch I washed up and put all the things away and made sure that everything in the kitchen was neat and tidy. My train left at four that afternoon and I should be home at about six o'clock. Mother told me to cut some roast beef to take for my tea when I got home and I had to remember to take the bottle of milk I'd bought the previous day along with some bread. I packed my bag and at quarter past three said my goodbyes and went off to catch my train. Travelling home on the train I thought about the past two weeks and how things had worked out and I wondered what Emma's Christmas holidays had been like, maybe I'd find out the next day.

Chapter Nineteen

I was up early next morning. I'd gone to bed early the previous night as the house was so cold with me having not been there for the past two weeks and the only place that was comfortable and warm was in my bed - with a hot water bottle. I slept very well through the night; how great it was to be back in my own bed again. As I sat having my breakfast I made a note of what I needed from the shops after school. I was out of nearly everything; it had been a good job that I had brought home the bottle of milk and the bread from my mothers. There was enough roast beef to make some sandwiches for my lunch and I'd found some mustard to add to them. I had decided that this morning in the English lesson I'd have the children write about what they'd got for Christmas and that afternoon they could make drawings of their various gifts. Maths could be about addition of money, what presents had cost and making shopping lists of Christmas items and adding them up. Then today we'd get Christmas out of the way because usually all the children talk about on the first day back is what they got for Christmas, which would be a way of releasing that excitement. Tomorrow we'd be able to move on with other things. I looked out of the window and saw that it had been frosty overnight and I noticed that there were still patches of snow here and there on the garden. It was much colder here than at mothers. The landlord had told me to make sure the outside tap was well insulated from the frost otherwise it would freeze and possibly cause a burst water pipe. I'd taken that advice onboard and at the first signs of frost in early December had bought some insulation and made sure that the tap was well protected.

I looked at the clock, time for a quick visit to the toilet then I was off for the bus. The journey to school on the bus was quite uneventful, I looked out of the window and saw numerous houses with the Christmas tree lights on. I felt that it was a waste of time putting a tree and festive decorations up if you lived by yourself and didn't get many visitors. Then there was the mess if you had a real tree, the pine needles on the carpet. Very different if you were married and had children; then it was essential that you had Christmas decorations and a tree. Very soon I arrived at the school. I walked over to my class room and put my coat and bag in the store cupboard and went up to the staff room. I walked in and wished everyone a Happy New Year but I was faced with a room with sad faces and a few half-hearted Happy New Year responses back. Mr Percy saw me and got out of his chair and came over to me. "Can you come with me please," he asked in a very serious tone. I was confused and in awe and replied, "Er, yes, why what's going on?" "This way please, to my room. You'll find out there," he said still in the serious tone.

We went to his room, past Mrs Grant, who looked at me with a sorrowful look on her face but didn't say anything as we passed by. Mr Percy opened his door and went to his desk and pointed to a chair indicating where I should sit. He looked at me then looked down to his desk then back to me. He's going to tell me something bad I thought, so I broke the ice by saying "Can I ask, what's all this about?" "I wanted to tell you this away from the rest of the staff. Mr Yardley will be telling them during his briefing in a few minutes time. I understand that you have been away for the whole of the Christmas holidays. Is that right?" he asked. "Yes, I went and stayed with my mother but unfortunately she had an accident on Boxing Day and fractured her humerus and tore her Achilles tendon which made her almost immobile for nearly a week as both were plastered, so I had to stay and look after her. My sister is looking after her now as her children are back at school and she's making the time to see to her needs during the day. Why, what's happened?" I asked. "You won't have had access to any of the local papers whilst you've been away then?" said Mr Percy. "No, and I haven't been able to ring anyone as I had lost my notebook with all my 'phone numbers in it," I replied. "Well I'm sorry to say there had been an incident regarding one of your pupils and it was reported in the local paper on Friday. As you haven't had access to it you won't know what has happened," he said. By now I was starting to fear the worst and my heart was beating rather fast. I started sweating and I said, "What do you mean there has been an incident?" "On New Year's Day, Alfie Underwood's father went round to take him away from his grandmother who has been looking after Alfie for the past two years under a court order. There seems to have been a fight between Mr Underwood and his mother, Alfie's grandmother. A very serious fight during which Alfie ran to try to stop it but his father lashed out knocking Alfie into the fireplace where he hit his head on the hearth and lost consciousness. His grandmother had screamed and Mr Underwood hit her and according to the police she had a heart attack due to all the stress. Fortunately, a neighbour had heard the noise and rang the police. Mr Underwood did a runner before the police got there and they found his mother clutching her chest and Alfie lying in the hearth. They were both taken to the hospital and I'm afraid that they have had to operate on Alfie as they found that he had a fractured skull and a bleed on the brain. As far as we know he's got through the operation but is seriously ill in the intensive care unit. His grandmother is also in the intensive care unit where she is likely to be for about three weeks. The police are still looking for Mr Underwood who is considered very dangerous; they have also said that Mrs Underwood, Alfie's grandmother, has spoken very highly of you and how Alfie thinks the world of you. They are concerned that Mr Underwood could construe that you are trying to take his place and could come looking for you. So, over the next few weeks I must urge you to be careful where you go and what you do and if you see anything suspicious then let the police know. They also said they'll be having a word with you today after school," explained Mr Percy.

I just sat there looking at his desk, what could I say? "Will the hospital allow visitors?" I asked. "No, not this week and I think the rules are that only family members are allowed to visit the intensive care unit," said Mr Percy, "Look, you've had a shock, do you want to take some time out? I'll take your class for registration and you stay in the staff room and have some coffee, and if you want more time out I can teach up to dinner time." "Will Alfie be coming back when he's well?" I asked. "The hospital has said that after the operation Alfie will be poorly for quite a long time and as his grandmother is ill too he might be fostered out, maybe not in this area, so there's a good possibility that we won't see him again here at Cromwell Street School," replied Mr Percy. "Will the children be told what has happened to Alfie, and could we send him a card signed by all the class?" I asked. "It's likely that some of the children would already know as it was reported in the local paper, but Mr Yardley is going to tell all the children in assembly this morning just to make sure that the true events are known as there are various rumours going around about what happened already. And yes, it would be a good idea to send him a card from his class mates. Look, you go to the staff room and stay there until the end of assembly and if you still think you need some more time out let me know. I'll have to go now as the bell will be ringing soon and I'll pick your class up from the yard," said Mr Percy. I thanked him and left his office and as I passed Mrs Grant she looked at me and said that she was sorry about what had happened.

By the time I got to the staff room the staff had left to collect their classes, although Mr Yardley was still there. He came over and asked if Mr Percy had told me the whole story about Alfie. I said yes he had, and he said that things like this sometimes happen and there is nothing we can do when it does, but sometimes we can see signs beforehand and help prevent things happening. That is what being a good teacher is, to see the signs beforehand. He also said that I'd done my best according to Alfie's grandmother and that was something to be proud of. He then told me to get a cup of coffee and sit down for a while, and stay until assembly was over then collect my class from the hall, and then he left the staff room. I went over to the sink and collected my mug and made myself a cup of strong coffee then sat down. I sat there staring into space thinking of Alfie, how at first he was quick tempered and would lash out, how he nearly broke Matthew Armitage's nose all due to the argument about was Superman stronger than Batman, and how Alfie had changed after I gave him various jobs to do in the class room. I started to wonder what would happen to him when he came out of hospital. Would his grandmother still be able to look after him? I also wondered what the police would say to me when they came to see me after school today. I started to wonder what sort of Christmas Emma had, I'd try and catch up with her at playtime and explain why I hadn't rung ring her through the holidays. I finished my coffee and went down to my class room. As I stood at my desk I looked over at Alfie's desk and thought about removing it and close the gap with the other desks, but that was a bit final so I decided to leave it where it was for the time being. I looked at my watch; assembly would soon be over so I went to the hall and waited outside until it was finished then I was ready to collect my class.

I walked into the hall to my usual place alongside my class

and waited until it was our turn to leave to go back to our class room. The whole atmosphere in the hall was different. It was so quiet, no chatter or whispering from the children, just silence and that was the same from all the classes. Even the staff were quiet as they left, they didn't have to say anything to their classes as they left the hall, they just pointed to the way out to the first child in the queue and the rest followed in silence. My class was the same, I just pointed to the door and the class led out with me walking alongside them. When we got to the class room the children went in and sat down in silence, waiting for me to say something. "You will all know about Alfie by now and it's very sad what happened to him. This afternoon we will all make some get well cards for him and I'll send them along to the hospital and I'm sure they will make him happy when he sees them. But first we have our work to do so in this lesson I want you all to write about your Christmas holiday, what you did, where you went, who you saw and what you got for Christmas. Don't forget to add plenty of adjectives to help describe your story. You might want to write about Christmas Day only and that's fine," I said. The children got their books out and started their stories, I went round the class helping here and there and asking about the different stories that were being written. That kept the children occupied until milk time and Tommy and Freddie distributed it along with the straws. "Sir, the old milk bottle tops are still here, they were supposed to be given in at the end of term," said Freddie as he brought a plastic bin with a sealed top on it out of the store room. "Who collects them?" I asked. "We take them to Mr Johnson and he has a big sack to put all the class milk bottle tops in and then someone from the 'Dogs for the blind' collects them," said Tommy. "Well take the bin along with the empties and see if he could take then today," I asked, "And say that I'm sorry but I didn't know that they had to be in by the end of term." The English books were collected and the children lined up waiting for the playtime bell to ring. Once it did I let the children straight out to play and I went up to the staff room.

The girls from the top class were still in the staff room making the tea. When they saw me they finished off and left, whilst I got my mug and poured myself a cup of tea and sat down. Gradually the staff came in and got their own tea and sat down, I was waiting to see Emma and explain why I hadn't rung her over the holidays. Tony

Telford came in, got his tea and came over to sit next to me. "How's things? "he asked. "Well it was a complete shock to me about Alfie Underwood," I replied. I kept looking at the door every time it opened and Tony noticed this. "Are you expecting someone?" he asked. "No, well yes sort of. I was hoping to have a quick word with Miss Stark, there's something that I have to explain to her," I said. "Well you'll have to shout very loud then," he laughed. I looked at him blankly and said, "What do you mean?" "Well she's not in, she's off at the moment, something to do with her teeth I think," said Tony. "Oh, right, it can wait I suppose," I said. "You're a dark horse, you are," he said. I looked at him, thinking, does he know about me taking Emma for a meal, "What do you mean, me a dark horse," I asked. "You on the roulette table on our night out, working that system of yours and winning, Ivan was very impressed and apparently he has been back a few times, using that system and has won," explained Tony. "I must tell him that it's only luck, there is no system, if there were the Casinos would all go bankrupt if people had systems that won. I don't want to be responsible if he starts losing money using my so called 'system,'" I said. "Apart from that, did you have a good Christmas and New Year?" he asked. I explained how my Christmas went and what happened about mother's accident and how I'd had to look after her until yesterday then that my sister was to look after her and about me getting a telephone installed for her so that I could keep in touch. Tony told me that I had been a busy boy and that his Christmas was like many others, quite nondescript. Very soon break was over and we were back downstairs collecting our classes from the playground. Once in class we had a maths lesson that took us up to dinner time.

After the class had left to get their lunch I got my roast beef and mustard sandwiches from my bag and went to see Mrs Grant. She was still in her office when I got there. "Excuse me, Mrs Grant," I said, "but is it possible that you could give me Miss Stark's 'phone number please, I need to speak to her." "I'm sorry but I can't give teachers telephone numbers out to other people without their permission," she said. She must have seen how disappointed I was because she said, "I'll give her a ring and see if it's alright for me to give you her number. Come back later this dinner time and I might have it then, unless she doesn't want you to have it, of course," and as she said that she smiled at me. I could feel myself blushing and thanked her then left for the staff room. Once there I saw a vacant chair next to Ivan so I got my cup of tea and went over to sit next to him. He was reading a newspaper and glanced up when I sat next to him. I wasn't really sure how to approach the subject so I just came out with it, "Tony has said that you have been back to the Casino and had some wins and that you used what Tony called 'my system.' Can I just say that I've lost a lot of money using that so called system of mine. Roulette is a game of luck. One night I saw the same number come up three consecutive times, now what's the chances of that?" Ivan looked at me and said, "I like the way that you can put four chips on the table and cover nine numbers. I know that it's all about chance and luck and be assured I'm not gambling with money I can't afford. I thank you for your concern but I'm not turning into a gambling man - my wife wouldn't let me. Now, can I read my paper in peace?" Without saying anything more he started reading the newspaper, so I took the hint and went to sit next to Tony Telford and started eating my lunch. I told him about the children wanting to make cards for Alfie, which was planned for that afternoon, although I wasn't sure if I could get them to the hospital ward for him. I told him about my stint of being a pall-bearer, a returned favour for borrowing a black suit for our night out. I looked at my watch, nearly one o'clock, I apologised to Tony and said that there was something I had to do before school started and went out of the staff room. I went straight up to Mrs Grant's office where she was sitting at her desk, she smiled and gave me a piece of paper and said that Miss Stark would be pleased to get a 'phone call from me.

That afternoon the children made get well cards for Alfie. Someone, Nicola I think, suggested that we send one to Alfie's grandmother to help to make her feel better, which we did. All the time I kept looking at the empty desk where Alfie had sat and I could almost imagine him working on a get well card. Once these were done we had a lesson on geography which carried on after playtime and then for the last ten minutes or so it was story time with 'Stig of the dump' which I'd almost finished. I remembered that it was one of Alfie's favourite stories so I made a mental reminder to send him a copy of the book when he was a bit better. Just before the bell rang a child came to my class room with a message from Mr Percy to remind me to go to his room after school had finished. At last the bell rang. I was glad that the school day had finished, it had been a hard day. I'd made my mind up about moving Alfie's desk, I know that morning I'd felt that moving it might be a bit final but through the day it had been a distraction for me and I think for some of the children so before going up to see Mr Percy I moved the desk to the back of the room and pushed the two either side of it together. I then gathered up my coat and bag and went over to Mr Percy's office.

I knocked on his door and a voice shouted, "Come in!" which I did. Mr Percy was at his desk and DCI Jarvis was seated in the chair near the desk. Mr Percy asked me to sit and DCI Jarvis looked at me and said, "Mr Tredwell, nice to see you again. Mr Percy has asked me to pop in and have a word with you about Mr Charles Underwood or Charlie Underwood as he is known. I understand that you had been away for the Christmas holidays and wouldn't have seen the local papers. Mr Yardley has told you what has happened and we can let you know some more information that Mrs Underwood has told us. On New Year's Day Charlie Underwood went round to his mother's after consuming a large amount of alcohol and demanded that he take Alfie away with him. This was the first time that he had been round to his mother's house since Christmas Day when he dropped off a Christmas present for Alfie and he only stayed ten minutes or so. Mrs Underwood said that Alfie was quite upset that his dad didn't stay longer but his dad was in a bad mood and said he was going to the pub and would be back later, which he wasn't, which upset Alfie even more. On the day in question Charlie walked into his mother's house and demanded that Alfie was going away with him. Mrs Underwood seeing that Charlie was in no fit state to take Alfie refused. Alfie was upstairs at this point and came down to see what the noise was. As he came running into the room his dad had Mrs Underwood pinned against the wall and was slapping her telling her that she wasn't going to stop him, Alfie went running to stop his dad and Charlie spun round and pushed Alfie away with such force that he struck his head on the hearth. Mrs Underwood screamed and started fighting back and Charlie punched her. It seems that the stress of all this caused her to have a heart attack and she collapsed. Charlie just ran out of the house without giving aid to either of them. A neighbour saw him run out of the house in a distressed state and went in and found both Mrs Underwood and Alfie and she rushed back home to ring for an ambulance and the police. Another neighbour had already rung for the police a few minutes earlier. In the hospital, after she had been seen to and was able to talk, Mrs Underwood mentioned that Alfie had said to his dad how much he had liked his teacher and how he had helped him. While he was assaulting Mrs Underwood Charlie had said that he would 'fix that bloody teacher as well.' So, Mr Tredwell, as Mr Underwood is still at large and dangerous it would be advisable for you not to go to places by yourself until he is caught. We will keep you informed of the situation and let you know when we catch him. We think he knows what you look like as one of the parents said he was at the Christmas concert and you did the nativity play with the children. You do realise how serious this situation is, don't you?" "Well yes, I think so," I said, "What are the chances that you'll catch him soon?" "We have had a tip off that he might be staying with some villains he met in prison and he is staying only a few days with each, but time is running out and I'm sure he will be caught soon," said DCI Jarvis. "Changing the subject, is there any news regarding the armed robbery just before Christmas, will there be a reward?" I asked. "Those we nicked are awaiting trial and when they are convicted then you should be awarded a reward as the banks say that information leading to the conviction of criminals will be rewarded. At the moment I can't say when the court case will be but they are being held in remand," he replied.

"Well I think that DCI Jarvis has explained everything very well, don't you?" asked Mr Percy. "Yes, thank you very much. I'll be careful what I do and where I go until I hear from you, DCI Jarvis," I said. The DCI said that would be fine and said he had to get back to the station; he wished us well and left. Mr Percy asked if my day had gone well and I said that it had been hard at times, seeing Alfie's desk, and I said that I was going to move it so it wouldn't cause a distraction. Mr Percy agreed with me and said that was a good idea. As there was nothing more to say I got up and bid Mr Percy a good evening then left and went to catch my bus.

The journey home on the bus was a bit un-nerving; I looked around the passengers to see if any one of them were looking at me in a suspicious way. Then I realised that I didn't know what Charlie

Underwood looked like so if someone were looking at me, how would I know it was him. I called into the supermarket before going home from the bus stop and did a bit of a shop. One of the things I did buy was half a bottle of whisky, I knew I was going to need a nightcap to help me sleep and whisky tended to make me sleepy after two or three tots. Once home I couldn't be bothered with a large tea so I made myself sausage, egg, beans and chips with Angel Delight to follow. Comfort food as my mother would say, and yes, I really enjoyed it. I switched the television on just for some background noise. Crossroads was on, I was about to turn to the BBC when the card on the mantlepiece caught my eye. It was the one Alfie had made for me. I picked it up and looked at the picture on the front, a Christmas tree with baubles and presents underneath it. At the top it read 'To Sir.' I turned the card over and inside it read 'To Sir, I hope you have a nice Christmas and get lots of presents. You are the bestest teacher in the school and I like you. I'm sorry I have been naughty at times but I'll try to be good next term. Best wishes from Alfie Underwood' I stood there looking at the card and thought of Alfie in that intensive hospital ward by himself. As I read it over again a tear came to my eye as I wondered if we would ever see him again at Cromwell Street School. I don't know how long I stood there with the card in my hand, thinking. Then I remembered I had to ring Emma, I went to my jacket and got the piece of paper Mrs Grant had given me with Emma's 'phone number on it. As I lifted the jacket up there was something near the pocket at the bottom of the jacket inside the lining. I felt around and it seemed like a note book. I checked the inside pocket and saw that the lining around the pocket had torn, which meant that my notebook had fallen through the lining, so I hadn't lost it after all. I had all my 'phone numbers back again. I put the book on the mantelpiece and made a mental note that I would get another note book and copy out all the telephone numbers so that I would have a duplicate should I lose one. I made sure that I had plenty of change for the 'phone box, put my coat and scarf on and made my way to the end of the street.

As I walked to the 'phone box I wasn't sure what I was going to say to Emma. I supposed that I should apologise first for not ringing during the holidays then go on to explain that I'd lost my notebook with all my telephone numbers in it. Also I should explain why I'd spent all the holidays with my mother, due to her accident. Then I should ask about her, had she enjoyed her holidays, did she go anywhere, how were her parents, or was that being too personal. Tony said that she was off school because it was 'something to do with her teeth.' Should I mention that I wondered, well, we'll find out soon enough, I thought as I opened the 'phone box and started to dial the number that was on the piece of paper Mrs Grant had given me. As the number was ringing I put my change on the side ready to push money into the phone's cash box. "Hello," said a voice as I pushed my money in, "Hello," I said, "is Emma there please, it's John Tredwell speaking." "Emma has had an operation at the hospital this morning to remove her wisdom teeth and she's having difficulty in speaking. This is her mother, just a moment I'll see if she'll come to the telephone." I waited as she put the phone down, now what was I going to say. A muffled "Yes," was said at the other end of the telephone. "Hi Emma, it's John, er, sorry to hear about your operation I'm also sorry I haven't rung you through the holidays but I lost my notebook with all my telephone numbers in it and I've only just got your number today from Mrs Grant. Would you like me to come and see you?" I asked, then thought – what am I doing? Again there was a muffled sound but this time it said no, then there was quiet as the telephone receiver was being passed to her mother, "Hello, John, it's Emma's mother here. Emma is having trouble speaking and she's in a lot of pain at the moment, also she doesn't want anyone to see her as she's badly bruised and it looks as though she might have a couple of black eyes later and she's very self-conscious about her looks. Could you ring back in a few days' time, then she might be able to speak to you properly. She's nodding here in agreement. Will that be alright?" her mother asked. "Yes," I said, "I'll ring back on Wednesday if that's alright. Thank you and good night. "Yes, thank you and good night," she replied and then put her 'phone down. Well, that explained the teeth problem, now I'll ring mother and see how she was. I thought it best not to mention Alfie at the moment. Mother had some good news for me; she was going to have physiotherapy on her Achilles tendon and her arm later that week and Helen would be there to see how it was done so that she'd be able to help her with the exercises during the week when the physiotherapist wasn't there. I said that it was good news and that I would be back home at half term in February and stay a few days with mother. I hung up and was just collecting my change when there was the sound of a coin banging on the 'phone box window, which made me jump. I quickly turned round to see an angry man glaring at me from the outside; I just froze on the spot. "Well, are you getting out of the sodding 'phone box or what! I'm waiting to make a very important call!" he shouted. I picked up my notebook and carefully opened the door and apologised to the man who pushed past me and picked up the receiver and started to make his call. I was so relieved, that could have been Mr Underwood, Alfie's dad, I thought. I made my way back home as quickly as I could without running. Once home I poured myself a large whisky and sat in the chair without taking off my coat, still having thoughts of what might have happened if that had been Charlie Underwood and what he might have done to me.

I'd had a restless night dreaming about Charlie Underwood chasing me down the street, then chasing me round my class room, then into the hall and on the stage and somehow me in a 'phone box on the stage with all the school looking on and Charlie trying to get inside the 'phone box with me. It seemed so real that I shouted out and woke myself up. I looked at my bedside clock, ten to three; from there I was in and out of sleep until the alarm clock woke me up. I shaved, washed and dressed in almost automatic mode, made my breakfast and had an extra strong coffee to try to fully wake me up. I nearly fell asleep on the bus; it was only thanks to the observant bus conductor shouting down the bus, "Wakey wakey Rip Van Winkle, it's your stop!" otherwise I would have gone past the bus stop with noticing. As I got off I thanked him and he looked at me and said, "Take more water with it next time," and laughed as he rang the bell and the bus left. I went over to my class room and put my coat and bag in the store room and went up to the staff room. I got myself a coffee and sat next to Tony Telford. He looked at me and said, "You look a bit rough, had a bad night?" I replied, "Sort of, I was having nightmares about someone trying to hurt me and it kept waking me up." "Who was he?" he asked. " Oh never mind, it's just something that's happened and it has been playing on my mind and I suppose having a drink before going to bed last night didn't help," I said. I felt that I couldn't tell him what the police had told me last night about the possibility of Charlie Underwood trying to get to me. Mr Percy came into the staff room and looked around the room, seeing that all the staff were in the room, he asked for quiet and reminded the staff that Parent's Night was to be the Wednesday before half-term and also could staff think about a school concert for Easter. He then thanked staff for their co-operation with the children from Miss Stark's class. I looked at Tony and he told me that her class had been split up after registration and sent to various classes around the school for the day, with work set by Mr Percy. The same children would go to the same class each day until Miss Stark returned to school. Tony explained that I didn't get any sent to me because I wasn't in the briefing yesterday as I'd been with Mr Percy and maybe it was because I was a probationary teacher. Mr Percy came over and asked if I'd have a word with him at playtime in his office. Now what? I thought.

The first half of the morning went well; the children hadn't made any comment about the removal of Alfie's desk from the front row although when the milk was given out there was a spare bottle left, Alfie's. I decided to give it to the child that had tried the hardest during the morning, which was John Harding, so he got the extra bottle of milk. I asked Tommy to tell Mr Johnson that we only needed twenty eight bottles of milk instead of twenty nine until further notice, next time they collected the milk. After the children went out for playtime I went to Mr Percy's office and knocked on his door. I was invited in and told to sit down and asked if I wanted a cup of coffee, which I accepted. He poured a cup and gave it to me and sat down at his desk with his cup of coffee. He looked at me and said that I didn't look too good and was I alright. I explained about my restless night and the nightmares and he said that it was understandable considering the circumstances.

The reason he wanted to see me was to explain the Parent's Night and what was expected of us by the parents. Letters would be sent out to the parents informing them when the night would be and asking that if they were going to attend, and what time did they want to see teachers. Before the children went home that evening they would have to get all their exercise books out on their desk so that the parents could look through them and ask questions about the work they were doing. It was essential that all the work was up to date with the marking and that our mark books were also up to date with, along with the spelling test results and reading levels. We should also be able to say how their child had behaved in class and outside on the playground. Mr Percy said he was telling me that now so that I'd be prepared when the Parent's Night came around as he was my mentor. He also told me that Mr Yardley would be observing one of my lessons sometime during this term, but I would be told when a few days before the observation. I asked about the Easter concert and he told me that it was on the last week of that term and usually the children make Easter hats, the best from each class parading them at the concert. Mr Sharpe has his choir singing various songs and classes are invited to select children to read poetry in the concert. Parents are invited to support the children and there's a small cost for the tickets which helped to raise a bit of money for the school funds. I finished my coffee and thanked Mr Percy for his help and left his office just as the bell was ringing for the end of playtime.

As I was walking my class back to the class room I was thinking about the Easter concert. Once back in the class room I asked the children about last year's concert. Nicola had read some poetry she'd written, which was no surprise to me; some of the other girls had read poetry that they'd chosen from poetry books in the class room. A dozen of the children said they had made some Easter hats decorated with Easter chicks and paraded with them in the hall in front of an audience. I was surprised that there had been only three boys in the concert, so I asked why. They me that the concert was all girls stuff and that they didn't like parading in hats, "It was all right when we were little," one boy said. "All the class was there because we had to sing some songs," said another child. I looked at the class and asked, "Did you all enjoy the nativity play you did at the Christmas concert?" There was a resounding "Yes" from the children. That got me thinking about having a different Easter concert, although the rest of the staff would have to agree it, as would Mr Percy and Mr Yardley. The rest of the day passed as normal, but the Easter concert was on my mind in the background.

That evening I thought about the Easter concert again and came up with the idea of a pantomime. There was no reason why a pantomime couldn't be performed at any time of the year. I thought of all the different pantomimes, then wrote down the titles on a piece of paper. Once that was done I wrote the plot of each next to the titles. Eventually I decided that Aladdin would be the best pantomime to perform as a scene could be written in there where the wash house put on an Easter fashion parade using children from the different classes showing off their Easter hats and various clothes that they'd 'found' in the laundry. I would ask Paul Sharpe to see if he could find some music that would go well whilst the fashion parade was being performed. I also thought of having a member of staff to take the main part so that they could hold it all together. "That's it!" I thought, "if a member of staff plays Widow Twankey, they'd be on stage for most of the time and the children would only have short lines to learn and the more children that were in it the better." The only other character to have a lot of lines to learn would be Aladdin himself and I was certain there'd be a child in year five or six who would be capable of having the part. I went to bed that night full of enthusiasm and hoped that the staff would be in favour of such an idea.

I got to school early the next morning and after dropping my things off in my class room I went round to see Paul Sharpe and ran my pantomime idea past him. He was in his class room sat at his desk when I went in. I spoke about having had the idea for an Easter pantomime with him and he seemed taken with the idea, especially the part with the Easter fashion parade. He said that children could perform in the pantomime without having to say a word. I asked if he could find suitable music for the fashion show and maybe some songs to be included as the pantomime progressed. The more we both talked about it the better it became. I had a list of the scenes and Paul started to suggest songs that could be sung in the various scenes. We both decided that we'd take responsibility to write and direct the pantomime and also ask if any staff members would like to join the team as we would need scenery building and backstage staff to be ready to help on the night of the performance. I looked at my watch, time to put it to the staff in the staff room before the morning bell rang. When we both entered the staff room, Mr Percy was there as well as the rest of the staff. I'd agreed with Paul that he'd do the talking as I was a probationer and I might not get the response that Paul would get. I must admit that Paul was very good at selling our Aladdin pantomime idea to the staff. As he went through the scene with the fashion parade there were a lot of head nodding from the staff. Mr Percy said he liked the idea but would leave it for all the staff to think it over and decide if they wanted a pantomime at Easter. There was one comment that was made out loud and that was from Ivan who said, "Bloody stupid pantomimes! I hate them at the best of times, now you want to do them at Easter, they're bad enough at Christmas. All that "It's behind you" rubbish." Someone called out, "Old misery guts! Bet you wouldn't say that if it was being performed by the Welsh Rugby Team," and everyone laughed, even Ivan. Mr Percy said that staff would have to decide by Friday if it was to go ahead. All Paul and I could do was to wait for Friday and the decision, but in the meantime we could both start preparation with the scenes, how many characters in each one, where the scene was set, what props we would need for each scene and finally how long would it take to get the thing written. Yes, it was going to be a busy term if it was decided the pantomime was to go ahead and there was also the Parent's Night to think about as well.

Chapter Twenty

As I travelled on the bus to school the next morning I was still thinking about the pantomime and the different scenes. I knew that it would be a lot of work for me but I was really looking forward to it, should the staff agree to the pantomime in principle. When I got to school I dropped my things off and went up to the staff room and was told to go to Mr Percy's office straight away. "Now what's happened?" I though as I walked up the stairs to his office. The door was open and he saw me approaching so he waved me in and told me to sit down. He was behind his desk looking for some paper whilst I sat waiting and wondering why he'd sent for me. "Do you have the get well cards the children made for Alfie Underwood?" he asked. "Yes, I was going to ask what I should do with them. I think at the moment the hospital will only allow family visitors to the intensive care wards," I said. "The hospital has been in touch with us and has asked would it be possible for Alfie's teacher visit him, possibly today. I have spoken to Mr Yardley about it and he is in agreement with me that you and Mrs Silby go and see him this afternoon and you can take the get well cards with you. I'll take your class for the afternoon lessons whilst you're at the hospital. They've also said that Alfie is very ill and may not recognise you or Mrs Silby and as yet he hasn't spoken to anyone. Seeing you might help, as according to his grandmother you are his favourite teacher," explained Mr Percy. I was quite shocked to hear how ill Alfie was and wasn't sure what I was going to say to him whilst I was there. Maybe it was a good idea that Mrs Silby was coming along with me, she might know what to say to Alfie. "Have your lunch here in school and then you and Mrs Silby can go at about one o'clock. There are no rules about visiting time and how long you can stay in the intensive ward, but if you can get back before the end of the school day and give me a report of how you both got on I'd be grateful. You just have time to get yourself a coffee in the staff room before school starts," he said. On that note I took it that it was time for me to leave, so I went down to the staff room and got my coffee.

I sat there thinking when Tony came over and said, "A penny for your thoughts." I looked up and gave him a half-hearted smile. I told him about the hospital visit that afternoon and he wished me the best of luck. I asked him what he thought of the Easter pantomime as I would need his skill with the stage lighting. He said that he would fall in line with the rest of the staff, if the majority wanted it then he would go along with it too. I didn't know whether to put my case more forcefully to him that we should give it a go but it was almost time for the bell and staff were already going to collect their children from the yard. On the way down I started thinking about Alfie again and what was I going to talk about. I decided that I would tell the children where I was going that afternoon and I would be taking their get well cards along with me. The morning went along well, the children seemed pleased that I was going to see Alfie and I said that I would read each card to him. At break time I went to see Mrs Silby who had already been asked by Mr Percy to accompany me to the hospital. I said that we would travel by bus into the town then on to the hospital. I mentioned that the children had made him some get well cards and I'd bought one myself on Monday evening when I was out shopping. After break whilst the children were working, I made sure that my class room was tidy, especially if Mr Percy was going to be teaching in it that afternoon. I also pinned some more of the children's up to date work on the wall, just in case he recognised that the older displays that had been on the wall a few months.

Dinnertime came and I went up to the staff room and got myself a cup of tea and sat down to eat my cheese and pickle sandwiches. Tony Telford saw me and asked if it was alright if he joined me, which I thought a bit strange him having to ask for permission. "I'm sorry if I was a bit offish this morning, I've been thinking," he said, "This pantomime might be a good idea as I never look forward to the Easter concert and having the kids display Easter hats to the parents and sing some old, weird songs. I don't think the kids enjoy it either. Have you got a pantomime that you are going to use or what?" "Well no, I haven't got a pantomime. I thought that Paul Sharpe and I could write one then we would use local places in the script and we could use as many or as few actors in it, depending on how many children volunteer to take part in it. I thought that a teacher could be used to say the majority of the lines then the children wouldn't have many to learn, it would be just a case of when to say them. We could use more script writers if you want to come aboard. We could share the scenes between ourselves or we could sit together and write the scene together as we go along. That's how I wrote the nativity play at Christmas, the class were told what the scene was then I told them to imagine what the characters would say to each other and we built up the scenes that way. So, are you going to be a participant? Incidentally, I'll also ask Miss Stark when she comes back if she wants to join us, it worked at Christmas very well," I said. I could see Tony thinking it through, "Yes, OK, I'll give it a go. Let me know what I have to do and I'll also take care of the lighting on the stage," he said. "That's great," I said, then looked at my watch, "Look, I'd better be going, but thanks for your support. I'll see you tomorrow. Cheers." I got up and washed my mug at the sink and went off to my class room to collect my coat and the get well cards from my bag. I popped up to see Mrs Grant to see if she had a big envelope to put the cards in and she had. She wished me luck and that I had to send her good wishes to Alfie and to tell him to get better soon. I went down to collect Mrs Silby and then we set off for the hospital.

We chatted on the way to town on the bus. She said that she had been expecting something like this to happen in the Underwood family. She blamed Charlie for all the trouble that had happened, his love of drink was the main culprit. It was a well-known fact that he'd hit his wife on numerous occasions and that he'd been sent to prison a few times until his wife had had enough and left home, leaving Alfie with him. It was at that time that Charlie's mother decided to step in and look after the child herself, but Charlie would turn up drunk and try to take the child back. In the end the grandmother had to get a court order stopping him taking the child away. He would still go around to see Alfie, but if he were drunk he got violent and would lash out at anyone who was near, which sometimes was Alfie. In a strange way Alfie was fond of his father but also very frighten of him and on occasions he bore the bruises but would never tell who'd done it to him, so there were never any charges levelled. I sat there listening to what Mrs Silby had to say and tried to imagine what it would have been like for me if my father had come in drunk and started hitting Helen and me or even my mother. Why do these people do it I wondered? Along with the get well cards I'd brought along the class reader, 'Stig of the dump,' which was my copy of the book that I was going to give to Alfie.

We got to the hospital and went to the intensive care ward where we were met by the ward matron who explained that Alfie was conscious but hadn't said anything since coming round from the operation. She told us that we could stay for about a quarter of an hour and that Mrs Underwood was going to join us. She was being brought from her ward in a wheelchair. It would be the third time that she had been brought to see Alfie. The matron led us into the side room where Alfie was. I didn't know what to expect as I walked in. Alfie was in bed with pillows supporting him up and there were various wires connecting him to some machines at the side of his bed. Alfie himself was just staring straight ahead, his head was bandaged and his arms were resting on the blanket in front of him. There was a chair either side of the bed that had been put there for Mrs Silby and me. The matron said that we should talk to him as normal, although he hadn't made any replies to questions yet and that if we wanted anything we just had to see one of the nurses on the ward. I looked at Mrs Silby and she looked at me as we both sat down on the chairs. "Hello Alfie, it's Mr Tredwell and Mrs Silby. Our class have sent you some get well cards for you; do you want me to read them out to you?" I said. There was no reaction from Alfie, he just stared straight ahead.

I gave half the cards to Mrs Silby and we took it in turns to read them out to Alfie. After that I said that we would put the cards on the side and the nurses might put them around the room for him. I remembered the class reader, so I took it out and told Alfie that I would read the next chapter to him. Again there was no reaction from Alfie, which for me, was very sad as I'd hoped that we might have got some recognition from him, a smile or even a glance in my direction from his eyes, but nothing. After I'd read a chapter of 'Stig of the dump,' Mrs Silby told Alfie what sort of Christmas she'd had and anything new that was going on in school, anything that might have got a reaction from Alfie, but still nothing. I looked at my watch just as the matron was pushing Mrs Underwood into the room. I stood up and she asked the matron to push her chair to me, then she shook my hand and thanked me for helping Alfie over the past school term. She looked at Alfie with a tear in her eye and moved her chair closer to the bed to hold his hand. Mrs Silby and I were just going out of the room when a small voice said, "Thank you sir," it came from

Alfie. The matron looked at me and said, "Thank you, that's what we needed and you have helped a great deal." I didn't know what to say, I was so pleased I'd been able to help. On the way out the matron said that I could visit again if I wished, to which I said I would and she said for me to ring before I came, just to ensure that Alfie wasn't undergoing any treatment.

On the bus back to school, Mrs Silby said that our visit was just what Alfie needed to help start his recuperation, although it seemed it could be a long stay in hospital for him. We got to school just as the afternoon break was starting, so I was able to inform the staff together with Mr Yardley and Mr Percy how Alfie was getting on and how he responded to Mrs Silby and me. I asked Mr Percy if I could take my class for the last lesson, which he agreed to and I was able to tell the children about my visit and how Alfie appreciated his get well cards, I didn't tell them that he just laid there hardly reacting to anything. They asked if he was coming back to school and I said that I didn't know. I finished the lesson with 'Stig of the dump.' After school had finished I stayed behind and started working on the pantomime's scene one as I was hoping to show the staff the scene on Friday if they voted for the pantomime as the Easter concert. I was lost in thought when a voice called out, "Are you staying here all night or what?" I looked up and saw Mr Johnson standing in the doorway, "It's gone five you know," he said, "Isn't it time you were off home or are you going to stay here all night so that you'll be here early in the morning." I gathered my papers together and thanked him and said that I'd be gone in five minutes. I got my coat and put the papers in my bag and said good night to Mr Johnson who replied, "Mind how you go!"

Once outside, it was quite cold, "Maybe we might get some snow tonight," I thought, then I saw the bus pulling away from the bus stop. That meant I'd have to wait a good twenty minutes for the next one, so to keep warm I would walk to the next bus stop down the road. I set off thinking about the pantomime then thinking about that afternoon's visit to the hospital. I also wondered if the staff would vote for the pantomime. All of a sudden, as I walked past a very large hedge, a hand shot out and grabbed my arm and dragged me into a garden, a hand covered my mouth and a voice said, "Keep quiet and things will be OK." I nodded and muffled a yes from under the hand. "I'm not going to hurt you, Mr Tredwell, that's your name isn't it?" the voice said. I nodded a yes and he removed his hand from around my mouth. "In case you don't know, I'm Charlie Underwood and I've been watching you. I saw you this afternoon and followed you to the hospital with that Silby woman. I take it that you went to see my lad?" I nodded. He continued, "As I said I'm not going to hurt you, whatever you may have read in the papers or have been told by others. My lad thinks very highly of you and I know you have helped him in his schooling and things and the way he talks about you when I'm with him, and I thank you for that. What happened at New Year was down to me and the drink. Once I'm drunk I don't know what I am doing some of the time. I only pushed the lad when he tried to stop me hitting my mum, but he fell and bashed his head on the hearth and then mother had the heart attack. I panicked and ran, then the next thing I know is that the police are after me for attempted murder. I didn't go around to my mum's to murder anyone; it was all a misunderstanding and now I'm on the run. Some mates have let me stay with them for a night and no longer and some of the time I've been sleeping rough, but in this weather it'll be the death of me." I looked at him and there were tears in his eyes and he seemed genuine in what he had said.

"Look, Mr Underwood, I suggest that you turn yourself in to the police and tell them what you've just told me, I'm sure they'll drop the attempted murder charge when they hear what you have to say. This afternoon I went to see Alfie and I can tell you that he is starting to get better after having an operation for his fractured skull; he spoke to me and I also saw your mother who's getting better. If you sort all this mess out with the police they might let you go and see them both in hospital," I said. He looked at me and I could tell he was mulling it over in his mind. "It's going to be a very cold night and we might have snow as well. At least in the police station you'll be warm and they'll give you something to eat. If you decide not to turn yourself in I won't mention our meeting this evening, but it's up to you," I said. He put his hand out to shake my hand, thanked me and half walked, half ran down the street. I looked at my watch; the bus was due in a few minutes time which meant that I would have to rush for the bus stop. Riding home on the bus I wondered what Mr

Underwood would do.

After I got off the bus I popped into the fish and chip shop and ordered fish and chips with peas, I'd have to pop them in the oven when I got home but I was looking forward to my tea. Once tea was over I went out to the 'phone box and rang Emma. Her mother answered the 'phone and said that she would get her. I waited and once she answered I asked how she was. She told me that she'd started to eat some solid food again but her face was still badly swollen and bruised. I told her about my visit to the hospital and about the idea of a pantomime for the Easter concert. She thought the pantomime idea was great and she would back it and also help out with anything that needed doing. I told her that was the news I was hoping to hear as I needed someone in charge of costumes. We chatted for nearly half an hour with me feeding the telephone box with change, and then I asked if I could go round and see her. She asked could I wait until the weekend at the earliest and I agreed, I asked if I could ring on Friday evening and she told me that would be alright. On the way home from the telephone box I thought about what my mother had said. If we liked each other then why not just be friends and enjoy each other's company and if anything else became of it so be it. I decided to have an early night, although once in bed I found it hard to sleep as I was thinking about the pantomime again but after a while I dropped off to sleep.

Thursday morning and Mr Percy came into the staff room for a quick briefing before school to tell us all that the school nurse was making a visit that morning and that she would visit each class in turn. I looked at Tony and asked him what happens. He said that she would knock on my class room door and ask for the children to see her in the corridor. She would inspect the children's heads for lice and if she found any then the child would be given a letter to be taken home to explain to the parents what they had to do to get rid of the lice. He told me that the kids referred to the nurse as 'Nitty Nora the flea explorer' he also said to expect in the days to follow to see some children's hair tinged delicately brown as those had been the highly-infected cases, in other words lice had been detected and the tint was iodine which, for the lice, signalled their demise. That morning, just after eleven o'clock, the knock came at my door. The nurse came in and confirmed which class we were then asked for the children to be sent to her a row at a time to the corridor. There were whispers round the class of, 'It's Nitty Nora.' I asked for quiet and told the class to carry on with their work as the children went out row by row. As children returned there were whispers of who had got a letter from the nurse, again I asked for quiet. After she'd finished she came into the class room and had a quick word with me and gave me a list of my class with ticks against those who had been given a letter from her. I was asked to have a look at it and then give the letter to Mrs Grant at dinner time who would then put it in the class file. After she'd gone I looked through the list. Six children had been given letters, some I expected, but a couple of children on the list I didn't. The children were restless and pointing out who had got the letters. I tried to calm everyone down by saying that anyone could catch nits and that they could easily be cured. I told them that in the First World War in the trenches on the battlefield nearly all the soldiers had lice and nits, but it didn't stop them from being soldiers.

On the Friday, the staff agreed to the pantomime idea so Paul and I met up at break time and discussed the scenes once more, Tony Telford came along as well and said that he would like to help with the writing. By the end of break we had most of the scenes set and decided that we would write the scenes together around a table, that way we weren't relying on one person to think up the ideas and the plot. We were in agreement that a teacher would have to be the mainstay of the pantomime and the children would have limited or short lines to say. That way we could have more children participating and the scene where the children have a fashion show using the clothes from the laundry and their own made Easter hats would mean many non- speaking parts which might encourage more children to join in. We set a date for half term for the writing of the whole pantomime and music to be finished. That was it, we could start auditions from children in any class in the school and then after half term we would start rehearsals.

As I was going out to the playground to collect my class, Mr Percy met me and told me that the police had rung him and told him that Charlie Underwood had handed himself in at a police station yesterday. I thanked him for letting me know and as I walked to my class I wondered if it was anything to do with what I'd had said to Charlie on Wednesday evening.

On Saturday dinner time I rang Emma and we had a chat during which I told her about the pantomime and that it was being written by Paul Sharpe, Tony Telford and me. She said that she'd like to be involved as well, then, out of the blue; she invited me for tea on Sunday afternoon and said that we could talk about the pantomime then. I accepted the invitation and said I'd see her on Sunday afternoon. The next day I went round to Emma's after first buying some flowers and a bottle of wine. When she saw them she told me that I shouldn't have but that she appreciated them all the same. I notice that she was wearing a lot more facial makeup than usual and she explained that her face was still bruised slightly, but with the make up it was less noticeable now and I agreed with her. I was introduced to the family, her father Jack and her mother Elsie who were pleased to meet me as Emma had mentioned me often to them. We had a wonderful tea and the wine went well with it. Afterwards, Emma and I went to the front room and just talked whilst Jack and Elsie watched television in the sitting room. We talked about anything and everything, school, the pupils, the staff, then where we had been on holidays in the past, where we would like to go in the future. The time passed quickly and then it was time for me to go home. We went into the sitting room where I thanked Jack and Elsie for the tea and Emma showed me to the door. I thanked her and said I would see her in school in the morning and wished her a good evening. She reached over and gave me a kiss on the cheek and wished me a good evening. As I walked down the garden path she stood at the door and waved me good bye. I waved back and had a good feeling within me.

Over the next few weeks Paul, Tony, Emma and I worked on the pantomime script. Some of the jokes were dropped and more were added, the main point of them being funny and to appeal to the children, although some would sound corny to the adults. By the time half term came around, the pantomime was finished and Paul had found suitable songs to be included in it. We'd held some auditions and we'd found our Aladdin, a boy from year six who had a fantastic memory who had learnt the first scene in two days and was almost word perfect. Just before half term we had the Parent's Night, which for me was a new experience. I had to fill in a form for each parent I met, and on it I had to tick that the parents had seen their child's books and seen their work displayed on the wall. I had also explained where they were with their reading and finally asked them if they had any questions about their child's education. Most of the children's parents in my class attended and after two and a half hours I was exhausted. My forms had to go to Mr Percy who would look through them and keep them in my file in his office. I was pleased when half term came and I could have a break. Going to spend time with mother would be an ideal break from school things. I made arrangements to take Emma for a meal on the Saturday before we came back to school.

I went over to my mothers on the Saturday afternoon and got to her house in time for tea. I was quite surprised to see that the plaster cast that had been on her arm had been removed and she was starting to use her arm, although she still had to have the sling to rest it from time to time. She had also stopped using the boot on the Achilles tendon, although she'd been told that if her tendon started bothering her again she would have to use it for a while. I called Stuart and Richie and we made arrangements to meet up on the Sunday for a drink. It was good for the three of us catching up, especially with Richie. Stuart and I hadn't had a catch up with Richie for a few years, apart from the few minutes in the Casino at Christmas. I went round to Helen's and spent the day with her and the children 'Chatty Cathy' was still going strong and Jane was still very fond of it. For the rest of the week I just chilled out, got out of bed when I wanted to and I'm afraid that my mother spoilt me throughout the week cooking me my favourite meals. I had taken the pantomime script with me and for a couple of afternoons I went through it and thought about stage lighting, scenery, costumes and so on. I was determined that the pantomime was going to be a success.

I went back home on the Saturday morning and rang Emma and arranged a meal at the Berni Inn that we'd visited before for that evening. I picked her up in a taxi and we spent a nice evening together. We both discussed the pantomime; she was as keen as I was to make sure that it would be a success. She had some ideas about the costumes and how they could be made and which of the parents would come along and help. By the time I'd dropped her off at her house we had the pantomime sorted.

Monday morning, before the briefing, Mr Yardley sent for me and asked how things were going with the pantomime. I explained that the script was finished, the music sorted, the costumes were ready to be made, the scenery making would start soon, some auditions had been done and the main parts had been taken, apart from the part of Widow Twankey which was to be played by a member of staff but no one had volunteered for the part.

In his briefing in the staff room Mr Yardley mentioned the pantomime and hoped that staff would help out where possible, he also said he was pleased that it was an all school project. After the briefing I saw Paul Sharpe, Emma and Tony Telford and asked if we could have a meeting at dinnertime to organise a timetable of rehearsals for different scenes for the children. I suggested that at each rehearsal two members of staff would be present then we could take it in turns to be there and not to have to be at every rehearsal.

By Wednesday, the role of Widow Twankey still hadn't been filled. Mr Percy asked for someone to take the part and help out, but no one volunteered. "The person to play the part is obvious," exclaimed Ivan Jenkins, "Mr Tredwell! He wrote it, why not star in it as well?" Trouble was, he got backing from the other members of staff, who sat there nodding and agreeing. Well, if that's what they thought why not, "If no one else wants to do it, I'll do it then," I said. There was a relieved cheer from the rest of the staff and a couple of them shouted, "Well done!"

The next five weeks were very intensive; teaching during the day, marking books, keeping my mark book up to date, listening to children reading, then at break times, dinner times and after school, pantomime rehearsals. At the weekends I was making props and pieces of scenery. A couple of weekends I took Emma out for a 'thank you' meal for all her help, which was a pleasant relief from all the pressure of work. We'd agreed to perform the pantomime on the Tuesday of the last week of term. Mrs Grant had seen to the tickets which were available during the previous week.

We had a dress rehearsal on the Sunday afternoon with the full cast and an audience of parents who had brought the children along with Mr Johnson. The children were used to me performing the part of Widow Twankey but without costume, but today though they and the audience would be seeing me in my stage outfit. Along with the audience, Paul, Tony, Emma and I would judge the reaction from them all. I was in a separate room and changed into my costume, Emma put on my make up. By the time she was finished I didn't recognise myself in the mirror. I was able to get backstage without anyone seeing me and waited for my cue. Aladdin said, "Where's my mother?" and I walked on stage saying, "Here I am."

The whole place erupted in laughter which last for two or three minutes at least, I had to whisper to Aladdin to wait for the laughter to die down before saying his next line. As the pantomime progressed and more laughter came, the cast began to settle in and enjoy the performance as much as the audience did. The scene that got the audience in a frenzy was the party scene where Widow Twankey sees a servant carrying a cream pie and says, "That looks nice, can I have it?" The servant looks at the audience and asks, "Shall I let her have it?" and of course they all shout "YES!" but undaunted he asks the same question again and again. They all shouted, "YES!" again – and then 'splat,' the cake was thrust into Widow Twankey's face. The audience participation was fantastic, even Mr Johnson was joining in and shouting. That sketch was played out five times, each time the person with the pie asking the audience should he let her have it and the audience getting louder and louder. At the end of the rehearsal we all sat around, cast and staff and discussed how we thought it went. Apart from a few minor changes and suggestions from a couple of the children we decided that it was good to go.

Monday morning in the staff room Mr Yardley hadn't much to say in his briefing but he said that he hoped the pantomime on Tuesday would go well and that Mr Johnson had already told him how much he had enjoyed it yesterday at the dress rehearsal. Tuesday morning in the staff room Mr Percy said that all the tickets had been sold and more parents were asking would there be another performance. I said that we might be able to have a second performance on Thursday but I would have to send a letter out to the parents of the children in the pantomime asking if they could bring them on Thursday evening for a second performance. I had sent a similar letter out the previous week for the Tuesday's performance to ensure that the parents would collect their children after the performance.

We had a run through of the pantomime in the afternoon and arranged for the children to get back to school for half past six for the performance at seven o'clock. We had good support from the parents, with many of them helping get the children ready backstage. By ten to seven the hall was full. Mr Yardley and Mr Percy were on the front row along with Mr West-Brook Smith and Mr Myers and some of the other Governers that I hadn't seen before. At seven the lights dimmed and the curtain went up. Aladdin was centre stage setting the scene about his mother and the laundry she owned, then he said the line, "Where's my mother?" From the side of the stage I could almost feel the anticipation from the audience, and then I walked on to the stage.

We got a similar reaction to what we'd had on Sunday at the dress rehearsal, laughter from everyone in the room, even Mr Yardley and Mr Percy were laughing. When it got to the party scene and I asked for the pie, the whole place erupted - adults as well as the kids who were shouting their hearts out, and when I got splattered with the pie there were riotous cheers and applause. When the performance ended we got a five minute standing ovation. Mr Yardley stood up and congratulated all the cast and all those that had been involved in the production and announced that there was going to be a second performance on Thursday, which got more applause.

Thursday and the pantomime was another sell out, some tickets had been bought by parents that had seen Tuesday's performance. When Emma was applying my makeup I asked her what she was doing for the Easter holidays. She said that it was her mum and dads fiftieth birthdays and their thirtieth wedding anniversary, so they were all going on holiday to Holland for the two weeks as it was there where her parents had their short honeymoon all those years ago. I said, "That should be nice and I hope that they'll have a great time there."

Next morning Mr Yardley congratulated all those connected with the second performance of the pantomime which he thought was better than the first, even though the first one had been very good. Paul, Tony, Emma and I smiled at each, other pleased that it had been a success. Then, out of the blue, Mr Yardley produced four bottles of Asti Spumante and said that it was a present from the Governers for all our hard work. The rest of the staff gave a round of applause as he gave each one of us a bottle.

That night, as I lay in my bed, I thought about Alfie and wondered where he was as he'd been moved from the hospital in town to a hospital that dealt with head injuries. I also felt very pleased with myself for thinking up the idea of staging the pantomime and then wondered to myself, "What will the next term bring?"

Chapter Twenty One

The Easter holidays went well, although time seemed to have flown by, as it passed all too quickly. I went home to take mother to the Easter services at the church, as we'd done ever since I was small, then after a few days at home Stuart and I went for a small holiday to the Isle of Man. We had asked Richie to come with us but he had to work over Easter as it was a busy time for him. I got back to my house on the Sunday before school started and spent all that day planning what I was to teach for the coming weeks. Sometime over the next term Mr Yardley would do a final observation lesson with me and my class then he had to write a report of which I would be given a copy and a copy would be placed in my personal file. The weather was starting to get warmer and I hoped that there would be fewer wet playtimes than last term. I'd made a note to myself that I would have to go to more jumble sales for some more games and get my 'wet playtime' box topped up.

Monday morning and Mr Yardley was giving his briefing in the staff room. He welcomed us all back and hoped that it would be a good term for us all. He told us it would be busy term with school trips, a sports day and the school fete, which was the biggest money maker for the school funds. He then went on to mention various pieces of paperwork that we had to complete during this term. After the briefing many of the staff were catching up with holiday talk, where they'd been and what they'd seen. I went over and asked Emma if she'd had a good time in Holland with her parents. Unfortunately, she'd caught a heavy cold and had a miserable first week trying to cure it while travelling from place to place in Holland with her parents. At one point it was so bad that she spent two days in bed in a hotel; she said that she was pleased to get home. I felt guilty about telling her that I'd had a good time on the Isle of Man so decided not to. I looked at my watch, time to collect the children from the playground. As I got up and walked over to the door, other members of staff started doing the same, taking their cue from me.

The children were stood in line waiting for me and the bell to ring. They all looked happy and seemed pleased to see me and started asking what they would be doing in class today. Once the children were in class I got them writing a story of what they'd done during their Easter holidays. There were a few moans and groans and comments such as, 'We do this every time we start a new term,' which in fact they did. I let the children know that Alfie had been moved to a hospital in another town so that they would be able to look after him better as he needed specialist treatment for his injuries. Someone suggested that we send him some more get well cards to remind him that we hadn't forgotten him, so I said that we could do that during the afternoon art lesson. The rest of the morning passed and soon it was dinner time. After I'd dismissed the children I went up to the staff room with my packed lunch, got a cup of tea and sat next to Emma. I didn't know whether to mention her holiday in Holland but she mentioned it herself. It seemed that her parents had friends in Holland who they'd kept in touch with and always promised that they would go and visit them. As they'd honeymooned in Holland thirty years ago they thought it would be a good idea to celebrate their thirtieth wedding anniversary there over the Easter Holiday.

Emma told us where they went in Holland and what they saw; she was very pleased to have seen the Night Watch, a painting by Rembrandt which was on display in the Rijksmuseum in Amsterdam, and whilst in Amsterdam she took the opportunity to visit the house of Anne Frank. I told her that Stuart and I had managed to spend a few days away on the Isle of Man and for the rest of the time I was at home with mother. After lunch, the children made get well cards for Alfie which I put in a big envelope and told the children that they would be sent off to Alfie.

The weeks passed and soon Mr Percy asked all the staff to start thinking about their class school trip and where they wanted to go. We were given a choice of venues, stately homes such as Ragley Hall and Soho House or a trip to the coast to Flamborough Head; also classes could join with other classes for the trip. I saw Tony Telford and asked if our classes could join up for the trip and he suggested that Paul Sharpe might like to join us as well, that way the three classes would only need two coaches. The three of us hadn't been to Flamborough Head before and we thought it would be a good place to visit, particularly as there were no amusements there and if we checked on the tide times we would go when the tide was almost out, so it would give us a good four hours on the beach. We also researched the history of the place as well as the geography of the area so that we could get some worksheets made for the children to complete whilst they were there. The trip was to take place after half term, but the weeks leading up to half term we had class tests to do and I also had another class observation by Mr Yardley. Again, the lesson was prepared in the morning for the observation by him in the afternoon.

I used the same question and answer format with the children; if they knew the answer to a question then they put their right hand up if they didn't know the answer they put their left hand up, it had worked before so there was no reason that it wouldn't work again. When the time came round for the observation lesson, Mr Yardley sat at the back of the class room making notes for the whole lesson then thanked me and left. When I had to see him after school he said that I had passed and that he was impressed how the children were eager to answer the questions that I'd asked and that every child I picked had the right answer. "Strange," he said, "that it was always a child with their right hand up." He had twigged but didn't say anything else about it except did I have anything to ask him, which I didn't. All I had to do now was to finish the school year and my probation period would be over, and then I would be a fully fledged teacher.

Half term came and I was going home to see my mother for a few days. Over the past few weeks I'd telephoned her three or four times a week to check on her progress regarding her arm and her Achilles tendon. I also made arrangements to take Emma out on a couple of day trips during the week; we'd been going out for meals each weekend and were enjoying each other's company. However, on the Saturday morning things changed. I received a letter from the security company that had the attempted robbery from its van before Christmas. They wanted me to go to their offices in the town on Monday morning which meant that I wouldn't be going to mothers on Sunday; I would have to go there on Monday afternoon. My intention was to stay from Sunday to Wednesday, four days, but now I would go on Monday afternoon and come back either Wednesday evening or Thursday sometime. I was also meeting Stuart on Sunday evening for a drink, so I had to ring him and let him know that my plans had changed and that I would ring him when I got to mothers. I rang and let my mother know that I wouldn't be arriving until Monday afternoon instead of Sunday. All through the weekend I wondered why I had to go to the security company on Monday morning.

Monday morning came round at long last; my appointment was for ten o'clock. I wore my suit and took the letter with me and arrived ten minutes early. The receptionist at the office took me through to see one of the managers, who in turn took me to see more managers. I was asked if I wanted a coffee, which I accepted. Sitting in a fine office in front of three pin-striped suited men I waited for someone to say something. One of the men said he was the managing director of the company and introduced the other two as directors and the reason for calling me in was to give me a cheque as a reward for preventing the armed robbery on one of their vans before Christmas. The perpetrators had been taken to court and convicted and sent to prison and because they'd been convicted I was entitled to a reward. The security van had a substantial amount of cash in it as it was taking money to three banks, as well as having four factory wages on board and the money had been doubled as it was Christmas so all in all I had prevented a major robbery. They told me that my part in the capture of the villains would remain confidential to avoid any repercussions. The managing director stood up and came over to me to shake my hand then gave me the cheque which I took and looked at the amount. I had to look twice and asked if the amount was right. The managing director said it was and asked if I would keep the amount secret as it was ten per cent of the total amount carried on that particular van. The company didn't want the total amount of money their vans carried made known to the public as it could encourage more attempts in robbing them. I said it would remain a secret and thanked them all and they thanked me for my quick thinking in preventing the robbery. I rode home on the bus in almost a daze, I'd never had so much money before, but the first thing I was going to do was get the cheque paid into my bank. When I got home I got my bank book and went back out to my bank and paid in the cheque and was told it would take five days to clear and was I interested in investing some of the money. I said that I would think about it and left. I went home and had some lunch, packed a small bag and set off to go to my mothers. On the train I sat thinking about the money and thought about buying a car. I had a driving licence and I would ask Stuart about getting one as he knew much more about cars than I did.

When I got home mother was pleased to see me and I was pleased to see that she was walking well and her arm was no longer in a sling. She seemed to be managing very well. She told me that she had to have a check-up in two weeks and she thought that everything would be alright. I rang Stuart to see if he could meet me in the pub that night as I was going to pick his brains about buying a car. My mother cooked my favourite meal - egg, sausage, beans and chips with Angel Delight to follow. I told her that I was meeting Stuart and would be back home just after ten thirty.

I got to the Kings Arms just after seven thirty as arranged with Stuart and as usual he was late. I had a pint waiting for him and was sitting at a table when he walked into the pub. He sat down and asked about me wanting to buy a car. I said that I'd got lucky and won some money and a car would be useful to have. He said that I was in luck because that week they'd just had a funeral and the wife of the deceased had said that she was selling his car and did we know anyone who might be interested in buying it. It was a mini and just two years old. I jumped at the chance and asked if Stuart had the contact details and could we go round next day to see it. He told me that the details were at home but that he would call me in the morning so that I could ring and make arrangements to see the mini that afternoon if it was convenient with the wife. The rest of the evening we chatted and caught up with various bits of news. As we left I reminded him to ring me in the morning with the details and I would call him back if we were going to see the car in the afternoon. When I got home mother was still up watching television and as she looked at me as I walked in she made a comment that I looked happy. I told her about the car and that I was hoping to see it the next day. I also told her the white lie about being lucky and winning some money, which should pay for the car.

The next day, Sunday, Stuart rang me at just gone nine with the details and I rang the lady at eleven o'clock and explained who I was and where I'd got the details about the car from. She was quite happy for me and Stuart to go over and see the mini that afternoon. It was two thirty when we knocked on the door and it was answered by the lady I'd spoken to on the phone that morning. I introduced myself and she recognised Stuart from the Undertakers. She took us to the garage to see a shiny blue mini. She gave me the keys and told me to have a test drive, I said that I didn't have insurance but Stuart did, so the two of us took it for a spin round the block. I was very impressed and Stuart said that if the price were right, he would nod his head when I asked what price she was wanting. Whilst driving round Stuart had said what sort of price it would be but when I was told what price she wanted I thought Stuart was going to nod his head off as it was far below any price he had mentioned. I made arrangements that I would return next Saturday with the money and said that I'd have to arrange motor insurance before then so that I could drive it away. That was all agreed and on the way home Stuart said that I had got a bargain and I told him that I would see him right for his help.

I was so excited the whole week. I went back to my home on the Thursday and rang Emma to take her out for a meal that evening. Throughout the meal she said that I seemed different, a bit on edge in a nice sort of way. I wanted to tell her about the reward money but couldn't and I was keeping the car a secret so that I could pick her up on Saturday evening in it when we were going out for another meal. So I talked about the school trip and that Paul Sharpe and Tony Telford were joining up with my class to go to Flamborough Head, which was going to be a first for me as I hadn't been there before. Emma said that she'd be going with Mrs Cook's class to a farm where there were petting animals and lots to do and see for the six year olds. We spoke about the school summer fete and what was expected from each class and member of staff. The last big event in the school calendar was the school sports day, along with the parents race, which she said always caused controversy amongst them. At the end of a pleasant evening I saw Emma home and said that I would call for her on Saturday evening and would ring with the time as I had something to do before I came to collect her. That was an excuse as I didn't know how long it would take to drive the car back after picking it up.

Friday arrived and I arranged insurance for the car and made a visit to the bank to see if I could withdraw money to pay for the car. I saw the manager and explained the situation that I had put a cheque for a substantial amount into my account on Monday and I needed the cash for the following morning. He looked at my account and said that in my case he would allow the withdrawal and also suggested that I make an appointment with the bank's financial advisor about my account. Saturday morning I was up early and on the train and decided that I would call in to see my mother first than go and collect the car, go back and show mother and have a bite to eat with her then drive home. Everything went well, I saw mother then went round and collected the car and drove round to see Stuart and gave him ten pounds for his help, which he didn't want to take at first but I insisted. Then I went round to my mothers and she was amazed and pleased for me. I couldn't resist and gave her a ride around the block before having something to eat then setting off home.

When I got home I nipped out to the 'phone box and rang Emma to say that I would pick her up at seven o'clock that evening and she said that she'd be ready. I'd booked a table at the Berni Inn and drove round just before seven and parked the car round the corner from Emma's. I knocked on her door and she answered saying that she was ready to leave. She shouted out to her parents that she was going and we walked down the path and round the corner. I'd left the car door unlocked and when I walked past it I stopped and turned to look at it then opened the door and said to Emma, "It's unlocked, let's give it a spin." The look on her face was of pure shock and horror, "What are you doing? You can't be serious!" she said and turned and started to walk quickly away. "Stop!" I said, "I'm only joking, it's my car, look I have the documents here - I can prove it," and I took some papers from the car and waved them at her. She still wasn't sure and it took some time convincing her that the car was mine. Again the white lie was told that I'd been lucky and won some money and managed to buy the car. I explained Stuarts help in the deal. Finally she accepted that I was telling her the truth and got in and we drove to the Berni Inn in almost silence. Halfway through the meal she started to come round and by the end of the evening she had forgiven me, but told me not to play a trick like that on her again. I drove her home and we arranged to have a drive out the next day just to give the car a run out.

    Sunday and the weather was fine and warm, perfect for a day out in the country. I picked Emma up at eleven o'clock and spent the whole day driving round the countryside, stopping here and there for something to eat, ice creams and the cups of tea. For me, the day went past too quickly but I was sure there would be other days to enjoy. After dropping her off at home I decided that I would drive to school in the morning and park the car in the street near the school so that the rest of the staff wouldn't see it. It wouldn't do for a probationary teacher to be driving to school in a car when the deputy head went to school on his bike.

Chapter Twenty Two

The weeks went by and very soon it was time for our school trip to Flamborough Head. We'd checked the tide times and the best time for us to go was on the Wednesday, which also gave us time to get things ready. Each child would have a clip board with some question sheets to fill in whilst we were there. Fastened to the clip board was a pencil and the clip boards were to be kept in numbered cardboard boxes so that the children would know where to find their particular clip board. We had sent letters out to the parents for permission to take the children on the school trip and these were all returned in good time. We'd asked if any parents wanted to come along and help and had a good response for that as well. The parents that had helped me with the nativity play and the pantomime all said they'd come and help. Tony Telford, Paul Sharpe and I had a meeting after school on the Monday of that week to go through all the things that were needed for the trip. Tony had a list and ticked it off as we went through it, insurance cover, first aid kit, buckets and sawdust, maps, work sheets, clip boards, coloured cloth bands to identify which children were in which group, drinking water, paper cups and we also had to give the school kitchen a list of children on free school dinners so that they could make them a packed lunch to take on the trip. We went over the list a couple of times just to make sure that nothing was missed, Tony and Paul were old hands with school trips and they were satisfied that we'd covered everything. The buses had been booked for a nine o'clock start and the children were to be told that they had to be at school for eight thirty. Also the children were asked to bring a towel, a hat and a spare pair of clothes just in case they got wet in the sea, Paul had said that one year on a school trip to the coast a child had fallen headlong into the sea whilst paddling and was soaked and had nothing to change into, so having spare clothing was a good idea. We also made a list of who was going on which coach. My class was on one and Paul's class on the other and Tony's class would be split between the two. Tony made sure that his troublesome pupils would be on the same coach, which was the one I was on, and that he would be with them.

Wednesday came and the weather forecast for the day on the coast was that it was going to be hot and sunny so it was a good job we had asked the children to bring hats. The register was taken in our class rooms and by a quarter to nine, after reading the riot act to the children about how they should behave when out of school, we went to the playground to wait for the coaches. Mr Percy was already there, as were the coaches. I lined the children up and Mr Percy told them they were representing the school whilst on the trip and that they should be on their best behaviour, he also hoped they were going to enjoy the trip and have a good time. Paul Sharpe and Tony Telford and their classes joined us and Mr Percy had the same message for their classes as well. Both coach drivers came over to have a chat with us and told us how long it would take to get to Flamborough Head and what time they would have to set off to get back to school for four o'clock. The journey, they said, would take about one and a half hours, which meant that we would have about four hours at Flamborough Head, enough time to explore and have lunch. Tony, Paul and I, along with some helpers, took the various bits and pieces to the back of the coach to be put in the boot. The other items, the buckets, sawdust and first aid kit would be stored inside the coach just in case they were needed.

All our parent helpers were there so we started getting the children on the coaches. They were told that they could sit next to their friends and a voice from the back sounding very much like Billy Preston shouted out, "If they have any friends," which caused laughter from those around him. Straight away I thought of Matthew Armitage and wondered who he would sit next to on the coach and decided that I would check that out when all the children were on the coach. There was excitement in the air as the children boarded the coaches; the parent helpers were asked to sit at various points around the coach, Tony was going to sit on the back seat and I was to sit at the front and very soon we had all the children sat in their seats with their bags under their seats rather than the overhead shelves. As I was at the front I stood up and looked down the coach and asked if everyone was ready to go. Tony gave me the thumbs up and I told the driver we were all ready, so he started the engine. That must have been a sign for the other coach driver as that coach started up as well and we started moving off. Mr Percy, along with some other children, stood at the school gates and waved us off. Half an hour into the journey Billy Preston called out, "Are we nearly there, sir?" a question he would ask at least six times later on.

Finally we were there and as soon as the children saw the sea there was a cheer from all of them. The coaches parked up in the car park and the driver said that the children could keep their things on the coach and would be able to get them when they wanted to as he would be in the coach all day. We got the children off the coach making sure that they were wearing hats as the sun was shining and it was very warm. The children were wearing their different coloured bands across their chests indicating which group they were in. Tony decided that the first thing to do was to let the children go to the toilet, group by group, which they did. Then they were given a carton of drink each which I thought should have been the other way around, drink first then toilet. The children were then given their clipboards and the first thing they had to do was to put their names on their clipboard. We all walked to big grassy area near the car park and sat down to look at the view. The sea was very calm and we could make out various ships out at sea.

Tony started talking to the children about why the cliffs were white and how they were formed millions of years ago. He then pointed out the lighthouse and how it protected shipping from the dangers of the cliffs and also let captains of ships know where they were at night as each lighthouse had its own way of flashing its light. So as ships passed at night, one light house might have two short flashes and one long flash and another might have three long flashes then a pause before repeating the sequence again. By knowing those sequences of flashes and where the lighthouses where, captains could map their positions on their sea charts. We had timed the tides right as low tide was an hour, then it would start to come in again; when it was high tide we would be back at home. From where we were sitting we could see a lovely cove down a very steep approach. It has a nice beach and I could see quite a few rock pools. Tony suggested that we divide up, with some groups walking to see the lighthouse and the other group to go down to the beach then at twelve o'clock we could all come back to the coaches and have our lunch.

I decided that my group would walk to the lighthouse along with Paul Sharpe's group and some of the parent groups. That meant that half the children would be walking to the lighthouse and the other half would be down on the beach exploring rock pools and caves. The children had been warned that they could only explore the caves if they had an adult with them at all times. With clipboards at the ready we all set off to our various destinations.

We took a nice steady walk to the lighthouse and then the children had to answer some questions on their work sheets and draw a picture of the lighthouse. After that we had a walk to the old lighthouse which is one of the oldest surviving complete lighthouses in England. It was built from chalk and was never lit. The children seemed fascinated by it. We made our way back to the coaches to get our lunches and we all had a picnic on the grassy field near the car park. After lunch it was my groups turn to go down to the beach and explore the various rock pools and nearby caves. The children had taken their bags with them so that they were able to have a paddle and dry themselves off with their towels. There was always one, and it happened to be Matthew Armitage. He'd been paddling and slipped on some rocks and fell headlong into a rock pool and got soaked and he hadn't brought a spare set of clothes with him. It was a case of who could lend him some dry clothes until his dried off. The children were very well behaved and enjoyed themselves searching the rock pools for different life forms. It's amazing how such a small crab can cause so much panic, especially when a boy is holding it in his hands and is trying to get it to bite the girls. Some of the children were sat on the small beach drawing the scenery, others were collecting small pebbles and some just sat there writing. It was all so peaceful; I sat there on the beach watching the children interact with each other. Billy Preston came up to me and asked if he could take some shells that he'd found home in his bag. I told him that I couldn't see any harm in that and yes he could and having the answer he wanted he ran off down the beach.

It was one of those days that you wished could go on forever, but no, Tony came down to the beach to say it was time that we were making tracks. We started rounding up the children and made our way to the coaches. Once there the children got into their groups to be counted. Tony, Paul and I counted all the children ourselves then consulted with each other that our number tallied, which they did.

The children had to sit in the same places they'd been on the way there. I saw Billy Preston and Terry Rogers boarding the coach with their bags, but they seemed to be struggling with them. I was about to go over and have a word with them when one of the parent helpers called me over to say that Matthew had lost his clothes and was crying about it. I said that I would sort it once everyone was on the coach. Tony had a word with Paul on his coach then came over to our coach to say that Paul's coach would set off first and we would follow. Once all the children were sat down I asked them about Matthew's clothes. Nicola put her hand up and said that she had found Matthews bag on the beach and brought it on the coach for him. I collected it from Nicola and the clothes in the bag were still wet, so I told Matthew that he would have to bring the clothes he had borrowed back to school the following morning. Having his bag back stopped the crying and we were ready to set off home.

We'd been going for about half an hour, the children were sat talking to each other and I decided that I would go down the coach and check that everyone was alright. I got halfway down and noticed that there were a couple of bags in the aisle so I went to pick them up. I got hold of the straps of one of the bags to lift it up and was surprised by how heavy it was, so I looked inside. I didn't believe what I was seeing. Tony, who was sitting on the back seat, asked if there was anything the matter. I just nodded and pointed to the bag. He got up and came over and looked into the bag. "Good God," he said, "we'd better tell the driver to stop as soon as possible." I made my way to the front and said, "Excuse me driver but can you pull in and stop. We may have a problem on board." He looked at me as though I was mad but seeing the urgency on my face he saw a lay-by just further up the road. I turn to face the children and asked them all to stay in their seats whilst we sorted something out. The driver stopped the engine and asked me what the matter was. I said that he should see for himself and I led him down the coach to have a look in the bag. "Bloody hell," he said, "Where did they come from?" "Are they dangerous?" I asked. "Too bloody right they are," he said, "They could go off at any minute, who the hell brought them on my coach - and don't move them. We'd better get the kids off the coach as calmly as possible and somebody better ring for the Bomb Squad and police. The other coach won't know that we've stopped and they'll have no idea what's happened."

Tony and I managed to get the children off the coach without any fuss. The driver said that he'd go back to the farm building we had passed five minutes ago and ring the police, the Bomb Squad and then his boss to tell him what has happened. In the meantime we had the children sitting around the lay-by away from the coach. Tony asked me how a bag with munition shells had been brought onto the coach. I told him that Billy Preston had asked if he could take some shells home. Thinking that he meant sea shells I'd said yes to him. Tony said that they must have been swept up onto the beach with that bad weather we'd had the previous week. There's an RAF bombing range further down the coast near a place called Hornsea. It had happened a few times around here previously but the bombs that were found on the beach were left where they were found and the Bomb Squad called to blow them up. "What are you going to tell Mr Yardley?" asked Tony, "As it was you that gave Billy permission to take them home." The colour drained from my face and I felt rather ill and started to imagine what the newspapers would make of it. Tony looked at me and said, "Only joking. He knows what Billy is like and you've done the right thing so, there'll be no blame attached to you. If anything, I'll get the blame as I'm senior teacher on the trip."

About twenty minutes later the driver came back and reported back to Tony and me and told us that the police would be here very soon. The Bomb Squad, however, would take anything up to two hours to get here and in the meantime we were to stay here, away from the coach, and wait. He had also rung his boss to let him know what had happened and as there were no spare coaches to collect us he told the driver that we could only stay there and wait. He also said that he'd inform the school what had happened. Well, that was that. We told the children that we were going to be there for a while, then a police car turned up with a police sergeant and a police constable and they had a word with the driver, then they came over to have a word with Tony and me. They told us to keep well away from the coach just to be on the safe side. They went on to the coach with the driver to see the shells for themselves. When they got off the coach they came over and agreed that we should stay as far away from the coach as possible. So we moved as far away from the coach as possible and had the children sit down and started chanting times tables, quizzing them for the capital cities of different countries, a spelling contest and we even had a sing song with songs from the school pantomime. The police stayed with us just in case they were needed for traffic control once the Bomb Squad arrived.

The Bomb Squad arrived in two military vehicles just short of two hours after they'd been called. The Army major had a word with the police and the driver whilst his men were getting various materials from the vehicles and setting the out on the ground. The Major went on the coach and had a look at the shells and came back to tell the police that they would remove them off the coach, but because of the condition they were in they would be unstable and would have to be detonated in the nearby field. He came over to Tony and me and said that we were lucky that the shells hadn't exploded on the coach. Tony looked at me and said, "Bloody hell. What would Mr Percy have said if we had blown up the coach?" The Major went over to speak to the children and told them what his men were going to do and there would be a big bang but we wouldn't see or hear it because we could get back on the coach and go on our way as soon as his men had removed the shells from the coach. Tony had a word with the driver to find out what time we would get back to school, and then he asked the police sergeant to see if he could let the school know that we should be back there for about half past six. The sergeant said that he would pass the message on and the school would be informed. We got the children on the coach, although there were a few that were a bit apprehensive about getting back on board, and we had to convince them that there were no more shells onboard.

The journey back home was a quiet one, some of the children were disappointed that we weren't allowed to stay and see the explosion. Some of the children started nodding off, after all it had been a busy day and we had all had been doing a lot of walking. We didn't expect the sort of reception waiting for us at the school gates when we got back. Parents and pupils, Mr Yardley and Mr Percy even Paul Sharpe was there, also there was a reporter from the local newspaper who wanted to get a story for the next day's edition.

When some of the children on the coach saw their parents

they started crying as they got off the coach, which lead to the parents crying too. Tony and I were trying to make sure the children had someone to take them home, Mr Percy and Paul Sharpe came over and help us with that. We also had the coach to unload with the clip boards, first aid kits, buckets and sawdust, unused thank goodness, and other bits and pieces we'd taken with us. Once everything had calmed down and the coach had left, Mr Yardley said to the reporter that he could interview us after he'd spoken with us first. We carried the entire luggage to Tony's class room and then went up to Mr Yardley's office, along with Mr Percy.

Mr Yardley told us all to sit down and he poured a cup of coffee for each of us. He then asked what had happened and Tony and I went through the day, how well behaved the children had been and then the misunderstanding of Billy's request of taking some shells home. It was only after we'd been travelling for about half an hour that we discovered the bag with the live shells in. We reported it to the driver who rang the police and the Bomb Squad and the driver was told not to move anything until the Bomb Squad got there, which was two hours later. We said that the children had been well clear of the bus during that time and that we'd kept them occupied until the Bomb Squad came and removed the shells from the coach, it was then that we were allowed to get back onto the coach and come home. Mr Yardley and Mr Percy were satisfied with our story and said that we could speak to the reporter who wanted a scoop and as he was an ex-pupil he would give a good write-up for the school. Tony and I gave the reporter his story and he told us that it would be in the local newspaper the next evening.

Tony looked at his watch and shook his head, I asked what the matter was and he told me that his next bus wouldn't be for another forty minutes. I told him that I would run him home in my car and that it was parked round the corner in the next street. When he saw my car he was stuck for words, so I told him the white lie that I'd been lucky and won some money, I also said that the other members of staff didn't know about my car, except Miss Stark.

After dropping him off at his house I drove home but stopped at the telephone box at the top of my street to ring Emma and let her know what had happened on the school trip. I then went to the chip shop to get my supper.

As I sat in my chair drinking my nightcap, I thought about the years at college training to be a teacher, and in all that time there hadn't been a mention of school trips and how they could go wrong. That was it, my first school trip, almost a baptism of fire, but thinking back, what would have happened if I hadn't seen the bag on the floor of the coach, the Major had said that the shells could be unstable,. What would have happened if Billy had got them all the way home? There was too much to think about, it was over and it was no use thinking about 'what if.'

Things couldn't get any worse than today, could they?

Chapter Twenty Three

A week later Mr Percy reminded the staff about the school summer fete and how each class was expected to have some kind of stall to raise money for the school fund. At lunchtime I asked Emma and Tony what they were doing for the summer fete and Emma said that her mother and some friends had been knitting baby wear, gloves and scarves and knitted toys, something they did each year for Emma. Tony said that he would be having a plant stall as he had an allotment and there were always plenty of plants that other gardeners donated to him for the fete, they also had plenty of fruit and vegetables that they also donated. Tony said that the fruit and vegetables always sold very quickly as did the plants and usually his stall made quite a bit of money. I told them both that I didn't know what to do, so Tony suggested a second hand toy stall with the toys being supplied by the children themselves. If I made a request for quality toys that were no longer used to be brought in to school for my stall it had to be made clear that broken toys were of no use and were not to be brought in. I thought about it and the more I thought the better the idea sounded. I thanked him and said that was what I was going to do. Later in the week Mr Percy wanted to know what each member of staff was doing for the summer fete and he put a list on the staff room wall to be completed by the staff stating what stall they would be running at the fete.

That afternoon I told my class what stall our class would be running at the summer fete and that I needed some of the children to help. Nearly all their hands went up to be picked as helpers. I told them that I would pick those children who were able to behave and do as they were told. Billy Preston put his hand up and said, "I know a way of making money at the school fete, sir." I looked at him and said, "And what would that be?" "I could bring my dancing chicken. People would love to see a dancing chicken and if we charged three pence a time we could make a bit of money. All I would need is one of them square tent things with a door at each end, one door for them to come in and see the dancing chicken and the other door for them to go out after they've had seen it," he explained. I stood there and thought about it, this was Billy Preston after all, the boy with the frogs, the boy who got a live donkey for the nativity play Could he have a dancing chicken I wondered? I told him that I'd think about it and let him know later. I arranged for letters to go to the loyal parent helpers to ask if they'd like to help out at the summer fete. For the next two weeks toys were coming in from all classes in the school for my toy stall. I had to ask Mr Percy if there was a spare store room to keep all of the toys in and he said there was one near Mr Johnson's office which I could use. I was amazed by some of the toys that were brought in, some nearly new and others that had seen better days. There were a few teddy bears and other soft toys that one of the parent helpers said she would have them washed and cleaned so that they would look nearly new. In one of my art lessons I had the children making decorated price tags for the toys, which I thought would make the toys more appealing to the customers.

The Wednesday before the summer fete, Mr Percy put a plan of the layout of the fete on the staff room wall. One or two of the staff objected to where their stalls were placed, but Mr Percy stood his ground. I had a look to see where my stall had been placed and it was between the bottle stall and the tin stall, along the side of the school building. I noticed that the plant stall was near the entrance and I asked Tony why it was there and he said when the parents came into the fete they would only glance at his stall and then they'd seek out the stalls where they might win something which where those at the far end of the yard, the 'hook a duck,' the 'tombola and raffle,' then they'd buy plants on their way out as they didn't want to carry them around the fete. There was an ice-cream van on site and Tony said that the school got a percentage on the number of ice creams sold, so it was a win/win situation for the ice- cream man and the school. At lunch time Mr Percy gave all the staff a copy of the fete layout and asked staff to make a list of things they would need for their stalls, such as how many tables, chairs, litter bins and so on. I remembered Billy Preston's dancing chicken so I thought why not and I put a square tent on the list of things I needed. However I had forgotten to mention the tent and it wasn't on the layout map. We were all told that on Friday afternoon Mr Yardley would have the whole school in the hall to watch a film whilst the staff could get all the things they needed for their stalls ready, which for me meant that all the toys would have to have price tags put on them. Thankfully, Mrs Rogers and Mrs Harris, two of the parent helpers said that they'd come into school on the Friday afternoon and help with that. I had to collect the folded tables that I needed on Friday afternoon and put them in the store room where the toys were being kept. We were all under strict instructions that these tables had to be taken care of as they belonged to the dining hall and would be needed on the Monday dinner time, also after we'd used them they had to be cleaned down.

That afternoon I had a word with Billy Preston about his dancing chicken and that I'd ordered a square tent for it. His eyes lit up and asked if he could make some signs for the tent such as, 'See the dancing chicken, live in front of your eyes only 3 pence a visit' and he also asked if Mark Robinson could help him with the signs and explained that Mark had the wind-up record player and music that the chicken danced to. So, that afternoon as the other children got on with their work, Billy and Mark were making decorated signs for the dancing chicken tent. As they both worked away with enthusiasm on the signs I still wasn't sure about a dancing chicken. That evening I took Emma out for a drink and mentioned Billy's dancing chicken for the summer fete. I think she was in the same mind as I was and didn't really believe a chicken could dance. We talked about school stuff, the summer fete and the school sports day which would be on the Tuesday of the last week of term. If the weather were bad then there were two more days it could possibly be on. The whole school went over to a playing field two streets away from the school to hold the sports day. Emma said that it was a competitive day with the children divided into houses or teams and they competed against each other. There was a parent's race which always caused controversy and some years had almost led to fights amongst the parents. I took a chance and asked Emma if she had any plans for the summer holidays and she said that she had looked at one or two places in Cornwall but her friends were limited when they could take their holidays in the summer. She then asked why I'd mentioned it and I said that maybe we could have a holiday together somewhere, possibly a package holiday to Spain. Emma looked at me and said that she already had a passport but she'd have to think about it. I said that I was thinking of asking Stuart and Pam to go along with us as well. I said that I would have to know soon so that we could get the holiday booked. I said that we could talk it over on Sunday evening when we went out for a meal.

Friday afternoon, whilst the children were in the hall watching a film, I was in the store room with the toys and Mrs Rogers and Mrs Harris and we were putting prices on the toys with the labels the children had made. The prices varied from three pence to five shillings and if one of us wasn't sure of a price of one of the toys we had a discussion between the three of us until we reached a price. I was pleased that we were doing this on the Friday afternoon as it meant that we didn't have to get to school tomorrow until about midday, then it would be a case of getting the tables into place on the playground and filling them up with the toys. I still hadn't mentioned to Mr Percy where the tent for the dancing chicken could go. Once everything had been priced up, Mrs Rogers and Mrs Harris said before they left that they would be back the following day at just after twelve o'clock to help get things ready. I collected the children from the hall after the film had finished and took them back to our class room. I asked if Billy Preston could bring the dancing chicken in at twelve o'clock but he said that he could only bring it fifteen minutes before the fete started as he didn't want to get the chicken tired out. I told him that I would have the tent ready and he gave me the posters to go on the outside of the tent advertising the dancing chicken.

Saturday dinner time and the school playground was being transformed with tables here and there, along with bunting and flags, posters on each table with price lists and produce of all kinds being set out on the tables. I approached Mr Percy and said that I had an extra attraction and where could I put the tent for it. He pointed to a far corner and said to put there. It was quite a distance from my toy stall so I was going to have to move from one to the other as the afternoon wore on. I knew that Mrs Rogers and Mrs Harris along with Susan, Nicola and John from my class could run the toy stall without me whilst I was keeping an eye on Billy and Mark at the dancing chicken tent. I assembled the tent with some help from three year six pupils and waited for Billy and Mark to turn up. At a quarter to two Billy walked into the playground with a big metal cage in which was a chicken and alongside him was Mark with his wind-up record player and some records. I waved and he saw me and came over and I pointed to the tent with the posters pinned around it. Inside there was a table and Billy put the cage on it with the chicken just standing inside the cage. I was asked to step outside while Billy and

Mark got things ready and said that I would be asked in when the show was ready to start. I stood outside the tent looking at all the other stalls around the playground and then at the school gates which had two tables either side of the gates with parent helpers ready to charge admission fee to the waiting queue which, by now, had parents and children queuing up to pay their entrance fee ready to come in at two o'clock. Then I heard music coming from inside the tent and Billy shouted that I could go in and see the dancing chicken. I went in and just stood there looking at a dancing chicken, I couldn't believe it, the chicken was actually dancing to the music, its little feet going up and down to the beat of the music and every now and again it would turn around and go back and forth in its cage. "That's it, sir, you've seen the dancing chicken you'll have to leave," said Billy, "We can't have people spending too long watching the dancing chicken, just a minute or so and that's it."

He pointed to the flap at the other side of the tent which he had put the sign 'way out' so I did as I'd been asked and left, still trying to get over the fact that I had seen a dancing chicken. By now the people had been let in and some were coming this way to find out where the music was coming from, as it was a bit loud. I stood back and watched as Mark stood at the entrance and took the three pence's as people started to be let in one at a time and then as people were leaving round the back Mark let the next customers in. I was satisfied that they were doing a good job so I went back to the toy stall which by now had plenty of customers, both adults and children.

Twenty minutes later an anxious Billy came running to the stall waving for me. I excused myself to the other helpers and took Billy to one side and asked what the matter was. "Have you got any matches?" he asked breathlessly. "Matches!" I said, "What do you want matches for?" "The dancing chicken," he replied. "But what do you want matches for?" I repeated. "The candle's gone out and I haven't got any more matches," said Billy. I was still in the dark and said, "I still don't understand, why do you need a candle?" By now Billy was getting a bit annoyed with me and said, "To go under the chicken's cage, how the hell do you make a chicken dance other than put a lighted candle under its metal cage?" "What!" I spluttered, "Do you mean to say that's how it's made to dance? We'll have to stop it at once; has any of the staff seen it?" Yes, sir, Mr Yardley and Mr Percy have seen it and they both thought it was very good and unusual," said Billy proudly. I got over to the tent with Billy, where there was a queue still waiting to go in. I told the waiting crowd that the show was over as the chicken was unwell and had got a limp which meant that it wouldn't to be able to dance any more today. I went inside the tent and told the boys to take the chicken home straight away. Mark gave me one pound and six pence and I made a quick calculation that eighty two people had seen the dancing chicken. I thanked them both and suggested that it might be a good idea not to let people know how the chicken danced and that it wasn't nice for the chicken and they shouldn't do that act any more as they could get into trouble with the RSPCA. Both boys agreed and they packed up their things and left.

    I went back to the toy stall where by then most of the toys had gone and the crowd was thinning out as people were starting to go home. At half past four Mr Percy came round to tell us all that we could start packing away; some of the stalls had already done that. Mr Yardley came to collect the takings from each stall; the name of the stall was included with the takings. I went over to take the dancing chicken tent down but when I got there it was gone. I looked around but it wasn't there, although the table was, so I folded it up and put it with the rest of the tables against the school entrance. I thanked my toy stall helpers who were just finishing off clearing everything away. Mr Johnson and some of the older children came round with litter bins to collect the rubbish and by five thirty the yard was clear. Emma had already gone so I went over to see Tony and asked if he wanted a lift home, which he did. On the way home he said that his stall had had a good day and that he'd sold almost all of the plants he'd brought in. I thought it better if I didn't mention the dancing chicken. After dropping Tony off I was straight home, had a bite to eat and then a nice hot relaxing bath, and followed by an early night in bed.

    As I lay in my bed I started thinking about Billy Preston and the dancing chicken and wondered what else he would think up.

Chapter Twenty Four

It was Sunday afternoon and I rang Stuart and asked if he and Pam wanted to go on holiday to Spain. I said that I was asking Emma and that I'd told her that he and Pam were already going. I said that I would treat him and pay part of the cost for him. He said that he would have an answer for me before I went out for our meal. I also asked him what dates he was available to go. At six o'clock I rang him back and he said that Pam would love to go on holiday and that the best time would be the second and third week in August. I told him which holiday brochure we would be looking at and could he get the same one on Monday so that if we chose a holiday he could look at it and say if they liked it or not. On Sunday evening I took Emma to the Berni Inn for a meal and to find out if she'd made her mind up about going on holiday to Spain. During the meal I told her that Stuart and Pam were eager to go with us and that they'd be available the second and third week in August. Emma looked at me and said that she would love to go on holiday; she said that the four of us would have a great time. I said that I had some brochures and had seen a lively place called Benidorm and had picked out some hotels but I would get everyone's approval on which hotel to choose then I would get the holiday booked this week. The rest of the meal we talked about holidays and what we might do in Spain, what foods we might try and so on. As I dropped her off at her home I said that I would bring the holiday brochure to her class room before school started.

The next morning at Mr Yardley's briefing we were all congratulated for our efforts at the summer fete and he told us that we had raised more money than last year. He then asked us to sort our classes into team colours for the sports day the next week, then there was the talk of winding down the academic lessons and having more PE this week and we had permission to use the playing field. After he left, Tony Telford came over and asked about the dancing chicken. Mr Johnson had been putting a folded tent into his store room and when he asked him what had been in it he had said a dancing chicken. "So that's where it went, I thought it had been pinched," I said. "Well, what's the news about the dancing chicken?" asked Tony. "If I say it belonged to Billy Preston would that explain things?" I said.

Tony looked at me and said, "So it was a scam." "Not exactly, the chicken did dance in a sort of way, and you would dance about if your feet were being burnt standing on a hot metal floor. After I found out how it danced I stopped it and sent Billy on his way, only after about 90 people had seen it. I'm half expecting to be reported to the RSPCA about it," I explained. "Don't worry about it," he said, "Nothing will come of it." "I thought that the tent had been pinched," I said, "I was going to tell Mr Percy it had gone but thanks for letting me know that Mr Johnson has it." It was time to collect the children from the playground so we all left the staff room. On the way down to the playground Emma saw me and asked if we could meet in her class room at dinner time and go through the holiday brochures and pick out which hotel we could book.

During registration I made a list of the colour teams for the school sports day. All I had to do was go down the list of names in the register, the first name was in the red team, and the second in the blue team and so on until all the children had been allocated a team colour. Children in the other classes would have been given their colour teams as well. All teachers had been given a list of the events and children were to put themselves forward for the three events that they wanted to participate in. I told the children that we would be able to practice for the races through the coming week so they would need their PE kit every day. After assembly I put the list of events on the board, skipping race, egg and spoon race, sack race, three legged race, bean bag race, 50 metre race and the relay, which only required one child from each colour team as the rest of the relay team would be from other classes. The children were excited and keen to put their names forward for different events. I said that we would have trials for the different races and choose the best. Each child would be wearing their team colour and on the sports day the first, second and third places would be awarded points in each event and the total points for each team would be collated and at the end of the sports day the winning colour would be announced. Tony had told me that there was always tremendous rivalry between the teams on the day and the parents got involved as well cheering on the team their child was in.

Dinner time I took my packed lunch to Emma's class room

and we looked through the different hotels in Benidorm. There were quite a few to choose from but eventually we decided that we would go half board then we wouldn't have to go back to the hotel at dinner time for something to eat each day. I said that I would check with Stuart that the hotel we had chosen would be fine and that the flights were on a Saturday which would suit him. That afternoon I had the class practicing the egg and spoon race and the bean bag race on the playground and made a note of who might be best for each race.

After school I rang Stuart at the Undertakers and told him which hotel we had chosen and as he had the same brochure with him he looked at it and thought that we'd made a good choice. He called Pam over and she had a look and agreed with Stuart about it being a good choice. I said that I would book the holiday the next day after school and put a deposit down for all of us but because the holiday was less than six weeks away the whole money would have to be paid by the end of the week. Stuart said that he would have his and Pam's money for me by the weekend. They both said that they were looking forward to the holiday as I was.

For the rest of the week each afternoon was practicing for the school sports day. On the Tuesday after school Emma and I went to book the holiday. There was a bit of a worry at first as the travel agent said the hotel was full but he eventually got us booked and even asked for our rooms to be next to each other. He explained that the balance had to be paid at the weekend and I said I would be in on Saturday to pay it. Emma said that she was so excited about the holiday and was looking forward to it. As I had nothing planned for tea I suggested that we go and get something to eat and ended up at the Berni Inn again. I rang Stuart on the Thursday and said that I'd drive up to mothers on Saturday morning and then he could drop the holiday money off. I also said that I'd bring Emma with me so we could have a bite to eat at dinner time and if he could bring Pam with him we could all get to know each other, then I would have to get back and pay the rest of the holiday money at the travel agents in the afternoon.

I picked Emma up at nine o'clock on Saturday morning and drove up to mothers. The journey took about an hour and a half and on the way we talked about what we might do in Benidorm. When I got home I introduced Emma to my mother, I had rung her during the week to say I was bringing Emma to see her. They both hit it off from the start, chatting away to each other making me the main subject of discussion. Mother had bought some buns to have with our cups of tea and as we were sitting down enjoying them Helen and her family called in. Again, introductions all round and more tea and there seemed to be more buns. I went into the kitchen to help with the tea and asked mother if it was a coincidence that Helen should call to see her. Mother said that she had told Helen that I was calling this morning with my girlfriend. I corrected her and said, "Emma's my friend." "Yes and a girl, so that makes her your girl friend," said mother in a matter of fact tone. When I went back into the living room, Emma was telling Helen and Dave about school and how much the pantomime was enjoyed by all. Helen looked at me and said that I was a dark horse and I wasn't sure if she was referring to Emma or the pantomime. After two hours of chat I said that we would have to be going as we were meeting Stuart and Pam for lunch and then we would have to get back to pay for our holiday. At the mention of holiday Helen looked at me and smiled and I explained that Stuart and I would have one room and Emma and Pam would have the other. Helen just nodded and said yes. I thought to myself that I'd better make that clear with Stuart and Pam that's what was to happen, that's why I'd asked them to come along with us. After leaving my mothers we met up with Stuart and Pam and had a meal together and discussed the holiday. Stuart gave me his and Pam's money for the holiday, a price I agreed with Stuart as I was treating him, and as soon as the meal was over I said that we had to get back to the travel agents and pay for the holiday. After an hour and a half driving back home we managed to get to the travel agents before they closed. We were told that the tickets and luggage tags would be sent to me in the post and the travel agent wished us a happy holiday.

Monday at school we were given the running order of the sports day which was on the next day. I noticed that there was a teacher's race down on the list. I asked Tony about it and he said that it was an egg and spoon race for the teachers and for the past five years Ivan Jenkins had won it, he also said that the staff were expected to enter it. There was also a trophy for the winner, a silver egg cup which was presented to the winner at the end of the events, just before the announcement of which team had won the sports day. It was one of the highlights of the sports day, that and the parent's race. All staff were expected to attend the sports day in track suits and running shoes so that they looked the part. The teachers were also allocated team colours so that the children would cheer on those teachers in their team. The 'Egg and Spoon Race,' I remembered back when I was at school I was never any good at egg and spoon races and now, as a teacher, I was expected to take part in something that I was no good at. That day the children had a final practice at the events they were entered for in the sports day. I had to make some changes to who was going in which race. Mrs Cook had warned me that Matthew Armitage would probably be away for sports day as he didn't like any form of sport at all. He was down for the skipping race and the bean bag race and as he was supposed to be in three events I put him down as a reserve for the relay race so if he were away it wouldn't matter too much as he was only a reserve.

Tuesday and as Mrs Cook had foretold Mathew Armitage was absent. All morning the children were very excited and looking forward to the afternoon sports day. The children in the top class had spent the morning along with their teachers and some parent helpers turning the nearby playing field into a sports field. Mr Johnson had a pick up truck that transported chairs and tables, along with the sport equipment and the sound system that would be needed, over to the playing field. The parent helpers would stay with the equipment over lunchtime so that it wasn't stolen. Areas on the field were roped off for the individual classes; running tracks were measured out and marked with white lines. The children would be one side of the running track and the other side was for the parent supporters. Children were to get changed in the class rooms at lunch time so we would all get to the playing field at the same time as school started for the afternoon lessons.

That lunch time in the staff room was a bit hectic with a lot of banter about the egg and spoon race we were supposed to be in. Mr Percy came in to wish all male staff luck in the egg and spoon race, I didn't realise that it was only the men that would participate in the race. He also reminded staff that the children had to come back to school after the sports had finished and parents hadn't to take them home from the playing fields. Emma came over and wished me luck and hoped that I would beat Ivan Jenkins as everyone was fed up with him boasting of how good he was at the egg and spoon race. No pressure then, I thought. Mr Percy had all the paperwork printed out for the staff giving the order of the races and which pupils were in which race. The information had been given to him by each class teacher and he'd spent a lot of time organising the paperwork so that the sports day would run without any problems or as few as possible. After eating my lunch I went down to my class room and got changed into my track suit. I'd told the children that I would pick them up from the yard at a quarter to one so that they could get changed into their PE kit. At one o'clock, with everyone changed we set off to the playing field, but before we set off I had to tell Billy to get rid of his chewing gum as the afternoon would be like any other afternoon regarding eating or chewing in class. It was only a ten minutes' walk and when we got there other classes were already sitting in their allotted areas. Mr Yardley and Mr Percy were sitting at a table near the finishing line, the sound system had been set up and a microphone was on a stand on the table. I noticed Mr Westbrook-Smith, one of the school Governers, walking round with a portable megaphone in his hand. My class was next to Tony's class and he was already in place with his class. I asked what Mr Westbrook-Smith was doing with the megaphone and Tony said he was the starter. Opposite us were the parents, I was surprised by how many had turned up; some were shouting and waving to their offspring and the children were waving back. Once all the classes were in position Mr Yardley welcomed everyone to the school sports day and hoped that we would all enjoy the afternoon, then he announced the first race. Teachers had to keep an eye on the race order so that we would send children over to the start area three races in advance so that there was little delay in between the races. The afternoon went well, children and parent shouting encouragement to children in every race. Mr Percy would announce the points for each team every five races and the scores were so close, which meant every win was important for each team.

It was time for the teacher's egg and spoon race and each teacher walked over to the start line. As I stood on the start line I looked to the finishing line and something caught my eye to the side of the finishing line. It was a boy in a wheelchair who was looking at the start line and waving. Pupils were giving out the egg and spoons to us as we waited and I was surprised to see Billy Preston coming to me with an egg and spoon and as he handed it over he wished me good luck and winked. I stood there and watched him run to the finish line along with the other children who'd given out the egg and spoons to the staff. Mr Yardley announced the teacher's names to the audience along with which team colour they were running for and each teacher got a cheer from their class, along with children who were in the same colour team. Mr Westbrook-Smith called for us to be on our marks and shouted 'GO!' I held my hand steady and ran, expecting any time for the egg to tumble off the spoon, but somehow it stayed there. I glanced to my side; Ivan was just in the lead and Tony a good second. As we ran past my class the children were shouting and screaming at me which encouraged me to put more effort in the race. I thought if I could get in the lead just for a short time and the egg fell off the spoon there would be no disgrace with that, at least I could say that I was winning in part of the race. I forced myself to run that little bit faster and yes, I was in the lead and the egg was still on the spoon. Ivan seeing this tried a bit too hard to catch me up and disaster, his egg fell from the spoon which resulted in a great cheer from everyone, parents and children alike. Before I knew it I had passed the line in first place and as I slowed down and stopped running Billy came up and took the egg and spoon from me and turned his back to me. I told him to turn around and face me but before he did he put something in his mouth. I looked at him and he was chewing. He smiled and said, "Well done sir, you beat Mr Jenkins," and he gave me the egg and spoon back. Ivan wasn't happy at all; the other staff congratulated me but not him. Tony came over and said, "Take no notice of him, he's a bad loser - and there's someone else who isn't happy with your win as well. Jimmy Moses in your class, you were six to one and both Emma and I bet on you with him." "You were in the race yourself and you bet on me," I said. "I knew that I had no chance against Ivan but you did, so I put a bet on you," explained Tony. "Excuse me, I have someone to see," I said. I went over to the side of the track and there was Alfie in a wheelchair with his grandmother alongside him. "Well done sir," he said slowly, "It's nice to see you." I said that he should go over and see his class mates. As his grandmother pushed his chair she told me that Alfie had suffered some brain damage and couldn't walk well and his speech was slow but improving all the time. Alfie's dad was in prison for the attack but had sent letters to say that he would reform and try to make up for the hurt he had caused. She also said that they'd moved away from the area and had only come back to see the school sports day and me. When we got to the class all the children made a fuss of Alfie and he stayed with them until the end of sports day.

The last race of the day was the parent's race or could it be called the parents dash. Instead of eight competitors there were about twenty on the start line. On the word 'GO!' one parent pulled two others over, this started a fight while the rest went running down the track. Another parent who was in the middle of the race ran diagonal across six others who all crashed into one another, which caused another scuffle. The remaining ten were running flat out when one fell over into the path of two others. The race ended with only six competitors finishing, but those who had been hampered in any way came over and wanted to fight it out with the winner as they said that he'd had the race fixed by knocking out various runners. The only way to stop a massive fight was for Mr Yardley to announce the winning team, but he would only do that when he had order and the race track cleared. The reds, the team I was in, had won the sports day by three points, the three points I had won in the egg and spoon race. The green team, which was Ivan's team, were three points behind in second place, which meant if Ivan had won the egg and spoon race his team would have won the sports day. I wondered if he realised that, if he did then for next three days I'd better keep out of his way. The class said their farewells to Alfie, as did I and I thanked his grandmother for bring him along to see us all. She said that she hadn't seen him so happy in a long time and thanked me for the help I'd given to him whilst he was in my class. We got back to school and the children changed out of their PE kit just as the home time bell rang. I noticed Jimmy Moses leaving the class room holding a notebook in his hand and I knew he would be going round to pay winnings to those who had laid bets on with him.

The next three days passed quickly. On the Friday morning

the children were allowed to play with games from the wet playtime box whilst others helped to take down pictures from the walls, tear unused pages from exercise books so that there would be scrap paper for next year and clear and clean the store room. In the afternoon there was a leaver's assembly with some of the top year girls crying about leaving and some of the boys saying they couldn't wait to leave. There was the presentation of certificates for the sports day and I was presented with the silver egg cup for my win in the egg and spoon race. As my name was called I noticed Billy Preston smiling and he gave me the thumbs up as I walked to the stage to collect my trophy. As it was handed over I saw that Ivan was applauding along with the rest of the staff. The assembly ended five minutes before home time, just enough time for the children to go back to their class rooms and collect their things. As I stood at the front of my class I wished them a happy holiday and hoped they would all keep safe, they all wished to same to me. The bell rang and I dismissed them for the last time.

  As it was Friday and my duty day, I went along to the cloak room and supervised children leaving until there was no one left. I went back to my class room and looked at the empty shell, its bare walls, clean desks with chairs on top of them, then Mr Percy walked in, "There you are John," he said, the first time he had called me John, "Just to say thank you for all you have done over the past year and I can now say that you have passed your probation year and you are a fully-fledged teacher and part of the team, as you always have been. Have a nice break and go on holiday somewhere and come back refreshed in September and don't forget we start a day earlier than the children so we can get things ready for the next day. Have you got a holiday booked?" "Yes," I said, "I'm going on a package holiday to Spain in August." "So is Miss Stark," he said, "It would be funny if you bumped into her while you were there but I supposed not. Spain's a big country. Anyway, have a nice time and take care. Oh, by the way there's a drink and some cakes in the staff room before you leave." I went up to the staff room and there was some wine and cakes and staff sitting talking about what they intended doing during the holidays. After about half an hour people started drifting off. As Emma passed I said that I would ring her later that evening. I asked Tony if he wanted a lift home which he accepted and on the journey he said anytime I felt like going for a drink to ring him. I explained that I would be going to my mothers for a while and then to Spain with Stuart but I might ring him when I got back.

That evening I rang Emma and made arrangements with her that we would spend the weekend at my mothers and that there was a spare bedroom she could have. I said that we would go for a meal with Stuart and Pam on Saturday night and Sunday we could go with mother for Sunday lunch somewhere. She said that would be great and she was looking forward to it. I rang Stuart and let him know the arrangements for the weekend. "Have you seen a ring for Pam?" I asked. "Yes, what about you, did you manage to see Emma's dad and ask his permission?" "Yes, and I told him that I would ask Emma when we were in Spain, are you going to do the same?" "Yes we could ask them both on the same night, maybe book a special meal and ask them both at the end of the meal and celebrate with champagne. I am looking forward to this holiday," he said. "See you tomorrow evening and keep the rings a secret," I said before I rang off.

That night as I lay in my bed I thought about my probationary year as a teacher, the children in my care, the mishaps that had happened to me, the two rewards I had been given from the two robberies, the school colour television and finally Emma.

I thought that my role as the stand-in boyfriend had passed and now was the full-time boyfriend soon to be a full-time fiancé, and did I mind – no, not in the least!

THE END

About the Author

Peter Nicholson

After leaving school and working first in various shipping offices then for the DHSS (Department of Health and Social Security), Peter decided to go into teaching. Since retiring from teaching he has been an exam invigilator in a sixth form college before retiring full time. This is his first book and it was started over twenty years ago and was left unfinished until he was encouraged to return to it during the Covid 19 pandemic.

Born in Kingston upon Hull, East Yorkshire, he spends his time playing bowls in the summer and is a volunteer for Kingstown Radio, the Hospital Radio Service in Kingston-Upon-Hull. Peter hopes that you'll enjoy reading this book as much as he has enjoyed writing it.

Printed in Great Britain
by Amazon